Rumours of Angels

History, Ideas, and Future Directions in Christian-Muslim Relations

Rumours of Angels

History, Ideas, and Future Directions in Christian-Muslim Relations

EDITORS

PACKIAM T. SAMUEL

CHANDRAN PAUL MARTIN

ISPCK

HENRY MARTYN INSTITUTE (HMI)

2019

Rumours of Angels: ***History, Ideas and Future Directions in Christian-Muslim Relations*** —jointly published by the Rev. Dr. Ashish Amos of the Indian Society for Promoting Christian Knowledge (ISPCK), Post Box 1585, Kashmere Gate, Delhi-110006 and Henry Martyn Institute (HMI), Shivarampally, Hyderabad 500052.

Online Order: http://ispck.org.in/book.php

Also available on amazon.in

ISBN: 978-93-88945-10-3

Cover Photo Credit: http://7-themes.Com/6862523-cosmos-wallpaper.Html

Laser typeset by

ISPCK, Post Box 1585, 1654, Madarsa Road, Kashmere Gate, Delhi-110006 • *Tel:* 23866323

e-mail: ashish@ispck.org.in • ella@ispck.org.in
website: www.ispck.org.in

Contents

Preface

The Evangelical Lutheran Church in America's contribution to Henry Martyn Institute is immense—one of them is in the study of religion. This collection of 33 articles since the 1930's was written by members of the ELCA who worked with Henry Martyn Institute in various capacities. These articles appeared in what was then known as *News and Notes*, *The Bulletin of the Henry Martyn School of Islāmic Studies*, *The Bulletin of Christian Institutes of Islāmic Studies*, *Al-Bashīr: The Bulletin of Christian Institute of Islāmic Studies*, *The Bulletin of Christian Institutes of Islāmic Studies*, *The Bulletin of the Henry Martyn Institute of Islāmic Studies* to the present *Journal of the Henry Martyn Institute.*

As a mark of our appreciation and gratitude for the service rendered to HMI—particularly the contributors of these articles towards the study of religion, especially Islāmic studies—we are reproducing their articles in book form. We express our thanks to ISPCK as a joint publisher; Pamhor Thumra for helping in editing and staff members of HMI in making this project a success.

New-Muslim Exegesis and Apologetic

James Windrow Sweetman

To illustrate the way in which an attempt is being made to re-interpret the Qur'ān and to claim for the forces of Islām a civilising influence comparable with the greatest in history the following two passages from the writings of the late Khwāja Kamāl al-dīn, Muslim missionary to England, are worth examining. The article from which these passages are taken is designed to show the relation of the Divine attributes to human life.

a) I refer to the first five verses of Chapter 79. The verses run as follows:

'Consider those who incline (to their business) fully, and those that go forth (to it) briskly (or lively) and those that swim in it swimmingly; then those who are foremost going ahead then those who regulate the affairs.'

Every beginner in a business naturally aspires to reach the height of success in his business. It is not difficult to do so, but we do not go the right way to work about it. The first verse however speaks of what is necessary for us all if we are to achieve efficiency in our work. The words are very eloquent—*an-nāzi'āti gharqa*. I translate *nāzi'āti* as those who incline. The word comes from *naza'* meaning strife or dispute. The other word *gharqa* means to be drawn. The verse says that when we choose anything for our occupation we should incline to it wholly and solely, as if we are drawn into it. The fifth verse in the above quotation refers to that which should be our ideal in such a case. A man should become expert in his affairs that he may be deemed an authority on the subject. We must give our sole attention to our work until we begin to enjoy it. But we must go further. We must attain such an experience in it that our work may become as effortless as a swimming of a fish in a river. The

> verse refers to the agility and facility that we must achieve in business; but this is not the final goal, for we must exert ourselves still more until we become pre-eminent in our work. We must outstrip others so that we may forge ahead of all.

Palmer translates the above passage from the Qur'ān

> By those who tear out violently!
> And by those who gaily release!
> By those who float through the air!
> And the preceders who precede!
> And those who manage the affair!

It will be noticed, therefore, that the interpretation made by Khwāja Kamāl al-dīn is based on what he supplies in his translation in brackets and is not in the Arabic. This forming of a new interpretation by supplying words which are not in the text and then making them the basis of the whole argument is not at all uncommon in modern commentators and the above quotation has been chosen to illustrate this tendency. Anyone who is familiar with Muslim books in Urdu which contain passages quoted from the Qur'ān will be well advised to notice how frequently long phrases are included in brackets. Is the well-known prejudice of some Muslims to the translation of the Qur'ān due in part to a recognition that some of the verse and exclamatory passages of the Qur'ān can only make sense when the reader or translator supplies an explanatory addition which may or may not be based on the traditional interpretation or warranted by the exigencies of translation from one tongue into another? Writing about the style of the Qur'ān, Noldeke says,

> Indispensable links, both in expression and in the sequence of events, are often omitted, so that to understand these histories is sometimes far easier for us than for those who heard them first, because we know most of them from better sources. Anacolutha are of frequent occurrence, and cannot be explained as conscious literary devices. Many sentences begin with a 'when' or 'on the day when' which seems to hover in the air, so that the commentators are driven to supply a 'think of this' or some such ellipsis.

Such passages of the Qur'ān present a great temptation to modern commentators who desire to make the perspicuous book rather more so.

Apparently the real application of the above passage is to celestial beings and particularly the angel of death and his assistants as Palmer says, the phrase "We must outstrip others so that we may forge ahead of all" reduces the whole thing to an absurdity. The exhortation cannot by any stretch of imagination be considered universe. What a spectacle! Everyone outstripping everyone else! This is not ethics but humbug.

In the Muslim press of Palestine, Egypt, India and England a great deal is made of the bounties which have come in the train of Islām. Khwāja Kamāl al-dīn could not resist the temptation to drag this into his exposition of the divine attributes!

> b) *Ar-Raḥmān* and *Ar-Raḥīm*: The former refers to the beneficence of God which has already created everything we need in life—things which have come into existence even before life began. The latter refers to the Divine Beneficence which makes our labours bring forth fruit a hundredfold. The two attributes assure us that everything material that we need to make life happy has already been created, and when we use it rightly our actions will never remain unrequited. The whole creation is full of such material, heaped up and running over and it only awaits our exertion to bring about the desired result. With this assurance Muslims approached nature and unravelled it. They enriched the world and gave its blessings unknown before. It is impossible to praise Muslims too highly for their great contribution to civilization. I may say that the world before Islām was as though it were living from hand to mouth, with very scanty material. The Qur'ān came and informed humankind of the various kinds of riches, beauty and wealth that were stored in nature, and created for human enjoyment. The world was without delicacies of food before Islām, but we find dainty things on Muslim tables in great variety; delicious foods, healthy drinks, tasty pickles and preserves and various kinds of fruit. Human used to clothe themself in coarse cotton materials and rough woollen fabric to protect them from the inclemency of the weather. The skins of animals were used for clothing in colder climates but Islām brought every kind of material, cotton, wool, silk and goat-hide into use and in most beautiful designs. The weavers in the reign of only one Moghul Emperor, Akbar the Great, worked up silk and cotton into thirty designs. I can hardly find anything existing at present in the list of materials worn by well-to-do men in India that does not owe its origin to the Moghul rule. I find similar improvements in architecture and the means of conveyance, with all the advances in traffic, gardening,

> irrigation and navigation, crockery and house hold furniture. *Western culture has inherited the first part of Muslim civilization and is improving it wonderfully, but they are lacking on the moral side.* And when I say that all this was inspired by the Qur'ān it shows that religion from God does not come to supply the human race with a sickly theology and deter us from the enjoyment of life. Rather does it come to enhance our enjoyment, but in a way that may not engender bestial passion in us, at the expense of others.

rising that religion does not come to give us a 'sickly theology' but 'pickles and preserves.' But our surprise may be due to our perverted morality which may also account for the *Encyclopaedia Britannica* and *Chambers Encyclopaedia* giving us quite different accounts of the origin of silk, etc. Huang-ti's wife Si-ling who lived in 2640 B.C.E. was, according to the Chinese, the lady responsible for silk culture, spinning and weaving, and there is a voluminous ancient literature testifying to the antiquity of the silk industry in China. From all accounts silk culture was introduced into Europe by two Nestorian (?) missionaries in 550 C.E. by their bringing some eggs of the silkworm from China to Justinian. With respect to pottery, the Egyptian section of any museum of importance will show that as early as 1600 B.C.E. the Egyptians were most expert potters and were famous for the lustrous red ware for holding 'perfumes, wine, honey and other delicacies.' (vide *Chambers' Encyclopaedia*). The crockery which later became famous as 'Moḥammadan blue' was a lineal descendant of the beautiful blue pottery of the Egyptians. We also read in Arnold's article in the "Legacy of Islām" that the Abbasid rulers imported pottery from China. Expensive works of irrigation existed from remote antiquity in India, China, Mesopotamia and Persia, and the system of canals, etc., in Egypt was a wonderful thing. One would almost imagine from the Khwāja's words that Islām built the dam at Assouan. So we might go on. But when all the credit due has been given to the work of Islāmic civilisations in the world we may ask "What has all this to do with the divine attributes?"

Is it worthwhile drawing attention to these things? Ought we to overlook the misreading of history which is used to bolster up the bad case for Islām? Certainly it all seems very futile and puerile in the extreme. But our readers will remember that this is the sort of thing which is being broadcast to the Muslim youth and however incorrect you may be if you get sufficient publicity for an idea you have every reason to expect that it will assume the guise of truth for millions of uncritical minds.

God is a Spirit

James Windrow Sweetman

In conversation with Muslims about the Godhead, it is inevitable that we should use at some time those words of our lord in John iv: 24: "God is a spirit and they that worship Him must worship Him in spirit and in truth." It is remarkable that when we do so, there is a marked reluctance on the part of the Muslim to accepting this statement. Some will even go so far as to reject statement altogether. It is wise, therefore, that we should try to understand the grounds for their objection to the words. If reference is made to that excellent little book, *The Holy Spirit in Qur'ān and Bible* by Mylrea and 'Abdul Masīḥ, (C.L.S.), much useful information may be gathered on the meaning of the word *rūḥ*, as it is understood in Islam. From this book it will become abundantly plain how bewildered Muslims are when they try to show what is meant by the term.

The vast majority of Muslims with whom we have discussed the matter have interpreted *rūḥ* as referring to Gabriel or Jesus and have excused themselves from further discussion by referring to sūrah xvii: 87. "They will ask thee of the Spirit: Say, 'The spirit is at my Lord's command; but of knowledge only a little is given unto you.'" They are afraid to commit themselves to any definite statement in view of this verse, and try to protect themselves by assuming an agnostic position.

Reference to Lane's Dictionary is very instructive. The main points are summarised below:

a) The general significance of *rūḥ* is similar to that of *nafs*, though in some respects different. It means the vital principle, a subtile vaporous substance, which is the principle of vitality, sensation and voluntary action and is called sometimes *rūḥ-i-ḥaiwāniyyah*. An alternative somewhat similar is that it is a subtile body, the source of which is the hollow of the corporeal heart and which diffuses itself into all the other parts of the body by means of the pulsing veins or arteries. We find a similar idea in the Old Testament cf. Gen. ix: 4; the blood was considered the seat of the vital principle. Al-Faiyūmī in the *Miṣbāḥ* says that the philosophers make *rūḥ* and blood equivalent in meaning because by the exhaustion of it life ceases.

b) The usual view of the Sunnis and the orthodox is that *rūḥ* is the rational soul known as *nafs al-nāṭiqah* or *al-nafs al-insānī*. It is adapted to the faculty of making known ideas by means of speech and of understanding speech. It is peculiarly a human endowment. Hence when the word *rūḥ* is used it is most readily understood as referring to human nature. It does not perish with the body being a substance and not an accident. This fact is referred to, so they say, in sūra. Iii:163. (The popular idea often thinks of it as going into the grave with the dead body).

c) The third classification of meanings is concerned with it as signifying inspiration or the result of inspiration i.e., divine revelation. Sūrahs xvi: 2 and xl:15 are referred to "He throws the spirit upon whom He will of His servants, to give warning of the day of meeting."

   So *rūḥ* becomes synonymous with the Qur'ān in certain passages.

d) The fourth main category is that which applies the word to supramundane creatures. It may be used of Gabriel (Sūrah xxvi: 193). According to Ibn 'Abbās and the *Tāj-al-'Arūs* it means an angel in the seventh heaven whose face is like a man's and whose body is that of an angel. Commenting on Sūrah lxxviii: 38, some would think it refers to certain creatures resembling mankind but not men. Others, going into greater detail would say that the spirits are watchers over the sons of Adam. Their faces are like men's faces and they are unseen by the other angels, even as men do not see the watchers nor the other angels.

From the foregoing it will be at once quite plain that there will be grave doubt in the mind of our Muslims friends as to the propriety of speaking of God as a spirit so long as we do not dissociate ourselves from such a strange psychology and do not explain, as far as that is possible, what significance we attach to the term. What, to us, is the very negation of crude anthropomorphism may be regarded by them as utterly anthropomorphic, especially as the prevalent idea is that spirit is not immaterial but extremely subtle material substance.

How then shall we explain this term? We are not unaware of the difficulty in interpreting it. At the outset it is wise to draw attention to the circumstances in which our Lord made use of the phrase. He was in conversation with the Samaritan woman, who wanted to argue about the worship of God as if His presence were localized either in Mount Gerizim or Jerusalem. Christ teaches in these words that the essential Being of God is not such that it may be confined to a place; and, as Bernard points out in his commentary, the translation would be better if instead of the words, "God is a spirit," we had the words "God is spirit." In this, Bernard follows Westcott, who goes on to say that the reference is to God's nature rather than His personality.

It must, however, be apparent that beyond the merely negative idea of immateriality, we approach most nearly to an understanding of what spirit is when we interpret it in terms of personality. We know through our own consciousness what spirit is.

> Man has a body, but *is* a spirit and is conscious of himself as a spirit,—that is, as a being who thinks and feels and wills. These are the essential powers of a spirit, and it is from our own possession of these powers that we know what it means that God is a spirit.... If the negative meaning is that God is other than matter, the more helpful positive meaning is that God is other than matter in the same way as man, by possessing these

> powers of thought, affection and will. … The composition of spirit we may never understand; but this is the action of spirit, and this is intelligible.[1]

In the article on "Omnipresence" in the *Dictionary of Christ and the Gospels*, the writer warns us against speaking of God as filling all space when we try to give some idea of His omnipresence Martensen[2] and Strong,[3] do, and approves W. N. Clarke's words from his *Outline* which are as follows "By omnipresence, we do not mean a presence of God which fills all space, in the manner we think of matter as filling certain parts of space. It is not universal of the essence of God like diffusion of the atmosphere." The writer of the article goes on to say,

> To introduce the idea of God's filling space is at once inevitably to suggest materialist analogies, as air fills the atmosphere, or the luminiferous ether fills all space, and all such strong analogies are misleading. The saving clause introduced by Dr. Strong and others, that God fills all his universe 'without diffusion and expansion,' does not help us: it merely makes the definition self-contradictory.[4]

Palmer, in his little book on *Oriental Mysticism*, now unfortunately out of print, shows us how Ṣūfī thought verges on a quasi-materialistic view of the nature of God by a most unfortunate use of an illustration to interpret the attribute *al-Laṭīf.* Here, though the intention is to prove God immaterial, the net result is an idea that God is a greatly attenuated and subtle material substance. We quote the passage in full.

> Earth is dense, water compared with earth is subtle, air is more subtle than water, fire is more subtle than air; and the subtle occupies a higher position in the scale of creation than then the dense. Now although each of these four elements occupies a distinct position in nature, they are susceptible of commixture, and are determined one by the other. If for instance, a vessel be completely filled with earth, there will still be space for water, and when it will contain no more water, it will admit of the introduction of air, and when it will contain no more air, it will admit of the introduction of fire; the comprehensive and penetrating capacities of each, being in proportion to their relative densities. It will now be observed that there is no particle of the earth in the vessel but is commingled with the water, and so on of the other three elements, each occupying its distinct and proper position according to its density. It is from the proper gradation and arrangement of these four elements in the world that the phenomena of nature arise; but they are nevertheless

> susceptible of commixture and conjunction... If all this be possible then in the case of material elements, how much more possible is it in the case of the nature of God, which is immaterial and indivisible.[5]

Frequently in a desire to avoid the interpretation of God's nature in terms of personality, God is made less than personal and however much emphasis the Ṣūfī would make on the last few words of the above passage, the danger is very great that God will be conceived by the aid of such illustrations as a greatly attenuated and subtle material substance. What we are conscious of in the operations of thought, whereby man brings the distant near, and in memory, wherein the limitations of time are to some extent transcended, brings us far nearer to the understanding of spiritual omnipresence, So that we should be on safe ground in attempting our explanation of the meaning of 'spirit' if we confined ourselves to the 'personal,' though this in its turn will raise questions in the mind of our Muslim friend, God willing we shall return to this point in our next number.

Endnotes

[1] W. N. Clarke, *Outline of Christian Theology* (n.p.: T.T. Clark, 1901), 66-67.

[2] Hans Martensen, *Christian Dogmatics* (n.p.: T&T Clark, 1874), 93.

[3] Strong, *Manual of Theology*, 132.

[4] Clarke, *Outline of Christian Theology*, 79.

[5] Palmer, *Oriental Mysticism*, 24-26.

Divine Personality

James Windrow Sweetman

Two difficulties arise when the missionary seeks to ascribe personality to God. The first is, that he is in a quandary as to the terms he should use. Nicholson in his *Idea of Personality in Ṣūfism* gives us some valuable information on this point. He says, "I would remark in the first place that the expression 'Divine Personality' cannot be translated adequately into any Moḥammadan language. The dictionaries render 'personality' by *shakhṣiyyat;* but the word *shakhṣ*, meaning 'a person,' is really not applicable to Allāh, though it occurs with reference to Him in the Tradition *lā shakhṣa aghyarn min Allāh.* 'There is no person more jealous than Allāh.'" There can be no doubt that the word *shakhs* is used in common speech with reference to God in Urdu, but that there is also some feeling of impropriety in using it, will at once be admitted by those who have discussed the matter with Muslims. This is partly due to the pious hesitation to go beyond the words used in the Qur'ān, aptly illustrated for us by Macdonald in his *Muslim Theology*, where he tells us of Ibn Ḥazm's reluctance to form any more than the ninety-nine names of God even though these should be full of praise. God "has called Himself *al-Wāhib*, the Giver, and so we may use that term of Him. But He has not called Himself *al-Wahhāb*, the Bountiful Giver, so we may not use that term of Him, though it is one of praise."[1]

This is, of course, more properly applicable to the literalists, but it is interesting to find that reluctance in many who would repudiate Ḥanbalī or Wahhābī affiliation. Now with regard to the word *shakhṣ*, if we turn to a popular dictionary published in Lucknow *Lugat-i-Kishorī*, we find that the meaning of the word is given as "*Jism, badan, khwāh insān kā ho khwāh ḥaiwān ka*," i.e., body, whether of man or of animal. The word *shakhṣiyat* we do not find there. Here we come on the track of a very good reason for the repudiation of such a word as applied to God. With reference to the tradition quoted above by Nicholson, Lane says the *Tāj al-ʿarūs* explains that the word *shakhṣ* is used metaphorically for essence. The Christian use of the term 'personality' with reference to God can hardly be said to be metaphorical. So, at the outset we are compelled by the exigences of language to use a metaphorical term for one which is more than metaphorical and so we find ourselves involved in the second difficulty.

This second difficulty is that we are considered by our Muslim friends to be using a gross anthropomorphism when we speak of God's *shakhṣ iyat*. We are using a term which can be applied to human and animals but to apply it to the Incorporeal is blasphemous. Here we are faced, in a cruder form, with the fundamental objection that our ascription of personality to God is derogatory to the Supreme Being.

In approaching the subject in conversation with Muslims it is therefore necessary, as we found it necessary in the case of the Christian conception of God as Spirit, to clear away misconceptions and misinterpretations of the words we use, and to point out that here we are using a technical term which needs explanation. We are using the term 'personality' *in sensu ementiori*. But we are declaring that God is a self-conscious, thinking, willing and feeling Being.

This will be at once admitted by our Muslim friends. Among the ninety-nine beautiful names are *Al-ʿĀlim*, the Knower and *Al-Ḥayy*, the Living. *Irādah* (Will) is included in the *Haft sifāt*, the Seven Attributes, with the two former, as also *Samʿ*, hearing, and *Baṣar*, seeing, which imply feeling. So while our term may be rejected, it is quite possible that an exposition of what we mean by personality may very readily find acceptance. This has been the writer's experience but with one very important qualification, namely, the obstinate refusal to see anything in these terms analogous to the content of human personality. We have already said that we use the term personality in a special sense, and we would not be disinclined to say that with regard to the mode of God's willing, knowing and feeling we are ignorant. We know that our exercise of the powers of personality is on the whole of a receptive character and that God's is rather active and creative. An illustration of what is meant by this can be found in the words used by Kelvin. "O God we are thinking Thy thoughts after Thee." The movement of God towards His creatures is in manifestation and the response of the creature is in perception. If we regard the will as the executive faculty there is no difficulty in ascribing this to God. So while we would attribute personality to God in a more excellent sense than that in which we would attribute it to human we would claim that there is something analogous in the human and the divine.

Our concern to apply the term 'person' to God is that we may avoid reducing the Divinity to a vague and nebulous force or entity. It is of the essence of our religion that we should have personal relationships with God. With blind force we can have no such relationships. With some entity which is un-regarding in the way suggested by the "I care not" of the Muslim tradition, we cannot have adequate relationship. With one who always stands over and above and legislates as it were from a distance, without that personal relationship which results in the law written in our own hearts, we shall always be at a loss, and meaning will be difficult to see in the world, in human existence, and in moral consciousness. We feel that, there must be something in our thought which answers to Divine Thought, something in our discrimination between right and wrong which answers to a like discrimination in the Divine Nature. Otherwise this universe is chaos and not cosmos.

This is not to imagine that God is such as one as ourselves. We repudiate the charge that this is an anthropomorphic conception of God and claim that it is rather a theomorphic view of human, based on the fact that human being is created in the image of God. God has in perfection what human has in a limited degree by God's gift. The observed limitations in human thought, e.g., that it is discursive; in feeling, that it is response to sense impressions; in will, that it accepts an end external to itself and is bound to seek means, and that all three, and self-consciousness too, are dependent and therefore not to be ascribed to the Infinite, are most probably attributable to human personality *only* and not to all personality *per se.* What is possible of personality is given to creatures subject to their creaturely existence.

To turn once more to the conception of *rūḥ* about which we had something to say last month, there is in the teaching of Al-Ghazālī something which is greatly different from the ordinary views with which we dealt. His view is associated with the words of Gen. i: 27 which have now become a tradition of the Prophet, "God made man in the image of the Merciful," and sūrahs xv: 26, vii: 10, and xxxii: 8 of the Qur'ān. "The *rūḥ* is not a body located in the body as a vessel, nor is it an accident located in the heart and brain as knowledge in one who knows, but it is a substance (*jawhar*) because it knows itself and its Creator and perceives intelligible things." Human is thus spiritual substance (*jawhar-i-rūḥani*). "This is not a case of comparison *(tashbīh)* of man to Allāh, for the specific difference of Allāh is that he is *qaiyyūm,* that is 'Self-subsisting,' and everything besides him subsists by him."[2] This idea was further developed by Ibn 'Arabī and Al-Jīlī with reference to the doctrine of the Perfect Man (*Insān-i Kāmil*). For further information on this subject Macdonald's articles in the above volume of the *Moslem World* and the long chapter in Nicholson's *Studies in Islāmic Mysticism* should be studied. Ṣūfism eagerly seized on what Al-Ghazālī had written because in this doctrine, the possibility of some kinship between the *rūḥ* of Allāh and the *rūḥ* of human was plain to be seen. In Al-Ghazālī's conception surely we have the nearest approach to a Christian doctrine of man ever made in Islām. There are striking similarities between his view and that of the Lotze whose manner of dealing with the question of the personality of God is one that specially appeals to us. Not all theologians were so quick to follow Al-Ghazālī as the Ṣūfis have shown themselves to be. Even a fellow Asharite, Ash-Shahrastānī, passes him over here when in the chapter on the refutation of anthropomorphism in his *Kitāb al-nihāyat al-iqdām fī 'ilmi-l-kalām*, he has occasion to refer to the same tradition about God's creation of Adam, making out that this is the foundation on which the anthropomorphists build. The opinion of the generality, most unfortunately, seems to agree with the latter theologian, and the conception of the utter transcendence of God, which is more suited to the genius of Islām, everywhere asserts itself. It is only among the mystically minded that any emphasis is placed on the alleged tradition and the Qur'ānic texts above cited.

If, therefore, the contention of our former paper on this subject holds good, namely, that spirit can best be interpreted in terms of personality, it is quite possible that we may prevail upon our Muslim friend to admit that, accepting Al-Ghazālī's view, we may say that God is Spirit and hold also that His is the prototype of personality of which human has that which is appropriate to his creaturely condition, a gift of the Divine Grace when He created human being in His own image.

But again we shall find that not all will be ready to concede so much but will prefer to regard spirit as an impersonal emanation from the divine, adopting rather a pantheistic view than a theistic. The Sole Unity is the Universal Spirit of which human spirits are just phases of existence in a world of illusion. Such an idea is more akin to Hinduism than to Islām but we find it in the latter none the less. To us, to whom there is given the revelation of God in Christ, there is neither the temptation to over emphasis of transcendence nor to blur personal distinctions with the corresponding loss of sense of moral responsibility. Von Hugel's words are very important in this connection.

> It is in Christianity, after noble preludings in Judaism, that we get the full deliberate proclamation, in the great Life and Reaching, of the profound fact,—the Self-Manifestation of the Loving God, the Spirit-God moving out to the spirit-man and spirit-man only thus capable of a return movement to the Spirit-God. As Schelling says, 'God can only give Himself to His creatures, as He gives a self to them, and with it, the capacity of participating in His life.' We thus get a relation begun and rendered possible by God's utterly prevenient, pure *ecstatic* love of man, a relation which, in its essence spiritual, personal and libertarian, leaves behind it, as but vain travesties of such ultimate Realities, all Emanational or Parallelistic Pantheism.

There is a mutuality of relationship which is impossible in Pantheism.

> God is here the Source as well as the Object of all love; hence *He Himself Possesses the supreme equivalent for this our noblest emotion* ... 'God is Love'; 'God so loved the world that He gave His only-begotten Son'; 'Let us love God for God hath first loved us'; 'If any man will do the will of God, He shall know of the doctrine if it be from God': God's infinity is here not the negation of the relatively independent life of his creatures, but the very reason and source of their freedom.

Endnotes

[1] Macdonald, *Muslim Theology*, 211.

[2] Macdonald, *Moslem World*, vol. xxii, 154.

Some Additional Notes on Muḥarram

James Windrow Sweetman

It is interesting to note that the tenth day of Muḥarram which is called 'Āshūrah or 'Āshūr is an exact transliteration of the Hebrew name for the day of Atonement (vide Lev. 16:29) especially in view of the fact that the passion of Husain in regarded as having atoning efficacy. Tracts are published from such centres as the Madrasat al-Wā'izīn in Lucknow comparing Calvary and Karbalah.

The *Marthiyah* (lamentation or elegy on the death of Ḥasan and Ḥusain) is frequently great literature. The *Marthiyah* of Mīr Anīs in spite of its extraordinary length, its manifest anachronisms and its hyperbole, is a piece of literature which, when recited during the ten days, stirs the deepest emotions and rouses the strongest feelings. Its descriptive power is great and its appeal moves the strongest to tears. The taunts of the warriors in the battle and the description of the tiny babe, which was slain, so young that it "was not able yet to open its little hands," the depicting of the fierce heat of strife and the equally moving and tender narrative of the calmness and courage and the affection of the family of Husain are such as to affect not merely the Shī'as whose faith inclines them to take these things to heart, but the Sunnīs also, as we know from actual experience. These *marāthī* are stores of information with regard to the ideas which are held by the pious Shī'as.

It would be interesting to have a description of the *'alams* in Lucknow and other Shī'a cities to place alongside the description given us by

Miss Greenfield. In Lucknow a great part of the city is symbolic of the events of Muḥarram. There is the whole of Ḥusainabād, the Shāh Najaf—which is said to be a replica of the shrine of Ali at Najaf, and the extensive 'Karbala' outside the city where the *Tāziyās* are buried. In Ḥusainabād there is in a glass case a stuffed white horse representing Ḥusain's swift steed. And here it should be noted that most frequently the symbols of the horse or horse shoe are associated with Ḥusain rather than with Ali and the lamentation of the passion centres rather in Ḥusain than in his father.

The word *Tāziyah* is in its original significance is applied to any expression of sympathy and secondly to the passion play of the Shī'as. In India it has come to mean the copies of the tombs at Karbala, etc., which are carried in procession. The usual *'alams* are the banner, spear, and bow of Husain. The mourners are given cakes of earth from Karbala scented with musk which they use to place before them as they bow in the ritual prayer and on which they rest the forehead in prostration. These are called *Muhr*. Many strict Shī'a s cultivate the mark on the forehead made by such prostration and make it their boast that the mark of the Passion of Karbala is on their foreheads.

In some case the tears which are shed in lamentation are preserved, sometimes by some authorized person and sometimes by the mourners themselves. They are wiped with cotton wool. These tears are reputed to have power to cure sickness and one common idea is that when the one who has shed them passes away and is subjected to the purgatory or inquisition of the tomb, these tears mitigate the pains from the fires of purgation.

The outspread hand represents the five intercessors including Muḥammad himself. The idea that intercession is efficacious is far more common among the Shī'as than among the Sunnīs who at most accept Muḥammad as intercessor. But in the dying prayer of Husain in the Passion play we find these words:

O Lord, for the merit of me, the dear child of Thy Prophet; O Lord, for the sad groaning of my miserable sister; O Lord, for the sake of young Abbas rolling in his blood, even that young brother of mine who was equal to my soul, I pray Thee, in the Day of Judgement, forgive, O merciful Lord, the sins of my grandfather's people, and grant me, bountifully, the key of the treasure of intercession.[1]

Endnotes

[1] Pelly, *Miracle Play of Hasan and Husain*, Vol. 2, 81ff.

Ṣūfī Thought and Christian Teaching

(Part I & II)

James Windrow Sweetman

Ṣūfī Thought and Christian Teaching

At the Cairo Missionary Conference of 1906, among the suggestions made by Dr. Rouse for the preparation of tracts for Muslims, were the following: to take up the good things in Islam and show how they are perfected in the Gospel, and to explain misconceptions with regard to the Christian religion. With regard to the latter suggestion, we are only too well aware as preachers of the Word to Muslims, that we are not tilling virgin soil. In it weeds have grown in abundance. Our preaching is often met by opposition due to pre-conceptions which are deeply rooted and sometimes from an equally embarrassing acquiescence from uncritical hearers which is no less due to misunderstanding. "Oh yes," they say, "We too believe what you say and no one can excel us in the praise and honour we ascribe to Ḥazrat 'Īsā." How often that praise increases our difficulties and strikes a blow at the truth we wish to expound!

How have these misconceptions arisen? How has the picture of Christ in Islam assumed its definiteness? Are there any elements of that picture of real value to us in proclaiming the message? Many attempts have been made to answer these and similar questions and the misconceptions in the Qur'ān have frequently been dealt with; though even here we have to confess that our knowledge of their origin is very limited. It may be possible, for example, to point to the verse which gives the Sūrah of the Table its name (V. 112), as a confusion of the miracle of the feeding of the multitudes, the discourses of our Lord at the Last Supper and 1 Cor. X. 21; and representing, perhaps, the confused memory of a sermon which brought these together. It may be possible to seek an explanation for the misconception of the Trinity in that passage of the *Gospel of the Hebrews* in which the Holy Spirit is referred to as "Thy mother," but apart from some few such instances it will be admitted that there are many things which remain unexplained, even if we go no further than the Qur'ān.

But outside the Qur'ān there is a vast literature containing references to Christ and Christian teaching, some misleading and the source of still greater misunderstanding and some singularly opposite in application to the exposition of Christian thought. These may be found in collections of stories of the prophets, traditions, Ṣūfī writings and, in great abundance, in the writings of Al-Ghazālī. Here we find the pearl and the rubble, the true alongside the mean and unworthy.

As an illustration of the way in which false ideas have arisen, the following has come to our notice. In the Cairo printed edition of the *Iḥyā 'ulūm al-dīn* of Al-Ghazālī (Vol. 3. p. 117) a story is told of our Lord where the hundredfold reward mentioned in Matthew xix: 29 is interpreted in the Muslim fashion as consisting in the sensual pleasures of Paradise. The application of this in the story is such as to offend our deepest Christian sensibilities, and we wonder how even a Muslim could conceive such incongruities. But when we turn to the comment on this passage in A1-Ghazali contained in Miguel Asin's *Agrapha et Logia Domini Jesu apud Moslemicus Scriptores, asceticos praesertim, usitata*, we find that Jerome in commenting on the passage of this Gospel says, "Ut qui unam (Mulierem) pro Domino dimiserit centum recipiat in futuro." Doubtless the aim of Jerome was to commend celibacy but what a wounding in the house of our friend! What if past errors, perpetuated in Islam are now rising to condemn us! We cannot always be held guiltless of loose speech and careless thinking which have resulted in misunderstanding. But as we become more acquainted with these misconceptions, we shall be more and more inclined to examine ourselves and to weigh carefully the words we use lest we, whose mission it is to guide humankind into the truth, may not lead some poor soul astray. In addition to this we shall have laid the foundation for fulfilling the second of Dr. Rouse's suggestions; namely, that which refers to the removal of misunderstandings. For to do this we must strike as deeply to the root as we can, for these weeds have gone very deep.

Let us turn to the other suggestion. It may be that some will consider that there is nothing in the Muslim literature which can assist us in our preaching. It is true that if our preaching consists of nothing but tags quoted from poets of a Ṣūfī tendency, then we shall not be able to do much more that confirm Muslims in a regard for their own mystics. But those who have tasted the Water of Life and drawn from the Treasury of Grace will not be content with the wine of the Ṣūfī nor the pearls of Rūmī or Ḥāfiz. It is a principle of Logic, however, that the credibility or incredibility of an assertion made to us—apart from the person who makes the assertion is decided by us according to the relation of the alleged fact to our existing knowledge or habit of thought. In other words, if we are to give effective testimony, we must link our message to something which is more or less familiar to our hearer. We must find the common factor. Now we find that these same tags are on the lips of many of our hearers. Sometimes we do not recognise them but practically every one of us has heard reference to the breath of Jesus (*dam-i* ʿĪsā). Even those Muslims who belong to no regular school of Ṣūfīsm have yet a fondness for the *Ghazāl* which may or may not bear a mystical interpretation. It is even regarded as the fitting thing for a male adult to become a *murīd* to some *pīr* and though this is, in many cases, only nominal, in others it means some initiation into Ṣūfī thought. So here we have a means of contact and a vocabulary which is understood by most educated Muslims. Can we shape this to our own use? Let us consider one or two points wherein we may. We wish to bring home the longing of human to be freed from world mess and to encourage the thought that God has set eternity in our heart. The words of Hafiz come to mind:

Muzhda-i-waṣl-i-tū ku kaz sar-i-jān bar khizam
Tāir-i-quds-am, wa az dam-i-jahān bar khizam.

"Where is the good news of union with Thee that I may rise with my whole heart? I am a bird of Paradise and will soar from the snare of the world." We wish to indicate that spiritual things are spiritually discerned. Here Maulānā Rūm says:

Dida-i-bāyad shāh shinās: Ta shināsad Shāh rā dar har libās.
"To know the King in every guise
One needs king-recognising eyes"
Or we may turn to the Urdu *Ghazal* of Atash,
Didā-i-Ya'qūb se dekka jo 'alam ki ṭaraf
Yūsuf is bazār men har sā nazar āyā mujhe.
"When I looked at the world with the eyes of Jacob
Joseph appeared to me in every nook and corner of the bazar"

When we wish to proclaim the truth that to the opened eyes of faith and love the presence of the Beloved is always to be discerned.

But apart from detached instances such as these, in general we may say that *Taṣawwuf* represents practically the sole attempt in Islam to break from the thought of the barren transcendence of God which is characteristic of Orthodox Islam. Provided the Christian missionary can guard against the incipient—or in some cases the complete and manifest pantheism of the Ṣūfīs, here he may find a means of countering that undue transcendence which is driving many Muslims into agnosticism. Christian teaching strikes the happy mean between pantheism and the conception of the utter otherness of God. As Pfleiderer has well said in *Religion und Religionen*

> Christianity sought to combine from the beginning the immanence and the transcendence of God.... On the one hand it says 'Thy Kingdom come,' and on the other hand there was a conviction, present from the beginning, that the Kingdom of God is now here, internally, within us, in the form of righteousness, joy and peace wrought by the Divine Spirit in the heart. (Rom. Xiv: 7 and Luke xvii: 21). Here, God is the super mundane Lord who guides history towards the purpose of His coming Kingdom and who will destroy all His foes on the judgment day: while there Christian faith in salvation holds the union and reconciliation of

> the human and the Divine to be a completed fact in the humanisation of the Son of God and as a permanent presence, existing through the indwelling of the Divine Spirit in the hearts of God's children and in the congregation of the faithful whom he consecrated as the temple of God.

With this in view, compare the words of Massignon on Manṣūr al Hallāj's teaching.

> Before all things, before the creation, before his knowledge of the creation, God in His unity way holding ineffable converse with Himself and contemplating the splendour of His essence in itself. That pure simplicity of His self-admiration is Love. Then God desired to project out of Himself His supreme joy that Love in solitude, that He might behold it and speak to it.

That reminds us of Raymond Lull's defence of the Trinity, and certainly of that great saying of Plato "He was good and so he desired to impart Himself."

But Hallāj is not alone in this. Many a passage from Hafiz could be quoted, did space permit and in the *Masnavī* of Jalāl al-dīn Rūmī (Book V. line 218 ff. of Nicholson's edition), we find words which we could hardly expect to come from the pen of a Muslim with regard to the Love which caused the Universe to be. Strained and warped some of these may be but that is only to be expected from those who have sought without the Light of Lights. Whom they seek, if haply they may find Him, we can declare in the lather whose most wondrous name is Love.

These are but by way of illustration and in introduction to what may be, for those who will carry the study further, a mine of information, revealing errors which need to be rectified and thoughts which need to be amplified by the glorious Gospel of our blessed Redeemer. The Founder of the *M.M.L.*, the Rev. John Takle (now in retirement in New Zealand, and retaining that interest in the work of his prime, the fruits of which are still seen in his gracious pleading to our Muslim brethren, contained in *Ṣirāṭ al-Mustaqīm*) recently wrote to a friend that he thought a study of Christ in the mystics of Islam would be fruitful. We sincerely concur and, from time to lime as opportunity offers, will report the results of our search to the readers of these notes.

There are not a few elements in the teaching of the Ṣūfīs which can be placed alongside similar ideas or practices traceable in the early church or even now current in the Church of Rome. The respect which the *murīd* (disciple) pays to the *murshid* (spiritual preceptor), while it may appear to be distinctly analogous to the similar respect deemed to be due to the Guru or to the Brahmin in Hinduism, is also suggestive of the system of authority which was in force in Christian monasteries. Evidence is not far to seek for the attraction the Christian ascetic or monk had for the Arabs before Islam and for the early Muslims. The monk was very definitely bound to poverty, chastity, humility and obedience and the abbot exercised an almost autocratic authority in enforcing the Rule. 'Direction' has also been a practice in the Christian church and in the absence of an organised priesthood in Islam, the *murshid* seems in many respects to take the place of the spiritual director who is consulted not only by the members of the inner circle of the Ṣūfī 'college' but by those more loosely attached to him who come to ask advice and help in some perplexity.

In our first paper on this subject (News and Notes, November, 1934 and Moslem World, April, 1935) reference was made to the frequency with which the Breath of Jesus is spoken of or used in a figurative manner. The Urdu *ghazal* of Rāsikh is an illustration.

Mushkil tahārat-i-nafs, iḥyā-i-murda sāḥil
Anfās pāk hote to tū bhī Masīḥ thā

"Cleansing of the soul is difficult, resurrection of the dead easy; if thy desires had been holy then thou too wouldst have been a Christ." The word we have translated "desires" is of course plural of *nafs*, with the significance of "the appetitive soul" but in addition there is a play on the word in its use with an allusion to Christ. So the purity of the soul is the purity of the breath which raises the dead, i.e., the Breath of Christ. It is the Breath of Jesus which brings the dead to life and it is the prayer-life of Jesus which gives efficacy to His Breath. What is the origin of this idea? Are we to see in it a common Semitism linked with the ideas contained in Gen. ii: 7, Job xxxiii: 4, Ezek. Xxxvii: 9, etc., that the *rūḥ* (spirit) is the vital principle and is associated with the breath?

Or is the connection more immediately with our Lord's breathing on the disciples when he gave them their commission (John xx: 22.)? It is to be noted that the memory of that act was perpetuated in the practice of insufflation which was the act of breathing on the catechumen before baptism, a custom still practised in the Roman church and common in the Eastern Church in early times. The early Muslims must have been familiar with this point of ritual. The breathing was an act of exorcism to banish the Evil One from the heart of the candidate for baptism. Muslim exorcists in India breathe on their patients and the breath of a pious person is supposed to have power to heal the sick.

Christian teaching emphasizes the importance of the heart in religion. The words of Jeremiah "I will give them a heart to know me" and "I will put my law in their inward parts and in their heart will I write it," are carried to their highest and purest interpretation by our Lord in the Sermon on the Mount, "Blessed are the pure in heart for they shall see God." Paul presents the teaching in other ways, "For with the heart man believeth unto righteousness," and "Seeing it is God, that said, Light shall shine out of darkness, who shined in our hearts, to give the light of the knowledge of the glory of God in the face of Jesus Christ." And again he writes to the Galatians, "Because ye are sons, God sent forth the Spirit of his Son into our hearts, crying Abba, Father." Augustine's words are familiar to all, "Thou hast made us for Thyself, and our heart is restless till it find rest in Thee." Compare with the thought in these words the Ṣūfī's insistence on the place of the heart in religion. Very frequently he appeals to the Ḥadīth Qudsī which says "I could not be contained in my earth nor in my heaven but in the heart of my believing servant." Jālāl al-dīn Rūmī in the *Mathnavī* (Book i, lines 2,653-5 writes:

Gutt Paighambar ki Ḥaqq farmūda ast
Man na ganj-am hech dar bāla o past.
Dar zamīn o āsmān o ʿarash nīz
Man naganj-am. In yaqīn dān Ai Azīz
Dar dil-i-mu min biganjam. Ai ʿajab
Gar mar a jui, daran dilha ṭalab

"I am not contained in High or Low, nor in Earth nor in Heaven, nor even in the Heaven of the Throne; know this for certain, Honourable One. I am treasured in the believer's heart. How wonderful! If thou seekest for me, search in such hearts." And in Book ii, line 165, we find these words:

Ān dile ko matla-i-Māhtabha-st
Baḥri 'ārif fathat-i-abwabha-st

"That heart which is the rising place of moonbeams (i.e., pale reflections of the great Sun of Truth), is for the mystic the opening of the gates (or chapters) of revelation." On this same theme we quoted in our first paper a few lines of Ḥāfiz and here is another poem from the same author:

Sālhā dil ṭalab-i-jām-i-Jam azmā mi kard
Ānchi khud dāsht zi-begāna tamannā mi kard
Gauharī kaz ṣidf-i-kaun o makān berūn būd,
Ṭalab-i-gumshudagān-i-lab-i-daryā mī kard

"For years the heart made enquiry of the Crystal of Jam. What it had itself, it desired of the alien. The Pearl not contained in the shell of the phenomenal world, it sought from benighted people on the sea-shore." Here the picture is of humankind lost on the shore of the boundless ocean of divine knowledge (*ma'ārifat*). Being unaware even of his own identity, how can he possibly apprehend transcendent reality? Even though he should spend long years, making diligent enquiry of the sages (here symbolized by the *Jām-i-Jam*, a fabulous mirror, cup or crystal variously supposed to have belonged to or been the invention of Solomon or Jam, and to have the property of mirroring the whole world), he cannot achieve the knowledge of God. Adam, says the Ṣūfī, left Paradise to live in the world and it was as though he had left that boundless ocean to live on the barren shore. There he lost the knowledge of his real self which was bound up with his mystic apprehension of God. Nevertheless, in the heart of man, which is the vehicle of the Supreme Glory *(Jalīl-i akbar)* and the place of the manifestation of Divine Light, there lingers still some traces of the effulgence of divine knowledge and therefrom some faint moonbeam gleams of mystic apprehension of the Lord Most High.

Ḥāfiz says that the heart longs to be comforted and blessed with the love of the Beloved but it vainly disquiets itself and us, turning hither and thither with its questioning in the urgency of its longing, for it has itself all the secret which is left to us. The treasury of reality and mystic apprehension is in the heart; we seek in vain from others. We may turn to them very wistfully but "Not by these, by these was healed my aching smart." The pearl which is not to be found within the shell which is formed of the overarching heaven and the outspread earth beneath, nor in the great ocean of created existence, we request from the lost on its wide shore when we really have it ourselves. The rays of the eternal beauty are not without but within. Again we are reminded of the words of Augustine, "I was seeking Thee without and lo, Thou wast within." Great is the mystery of the human heart restless till it find rest in God our Father and there is much truth in those other words of his "Our whole work in this life is to heal the eye of the heart by which we see God." All who have had to try to break down the crass legalism and formalism in which Muslims harden themselves must welcome the hungry heart-cry of the Ṣūfī unsatisfied by the stone which is offered him for bread. For when the heart cries out in longing for God have we not the joyous news of the Guest who waits our hearts' hospitality, who will come in and sup with us that we may sup with Him.

But what of the response to the Ṣūfī's longing? Hundreds of instances could be given of the unsupportable loneliness of the human spirit, hands imploringly held out to the silent heaven for one word of love and one crumb of comfort, but with all the language of love found in the pages of Ṣūfī poets and writers, how much is there of the love of God for man? The Beloved remains in cold impassivity. He is the stately and 'free' cypress which has not the trouble of bearing fruit, whose leaves are not subject to the chilling blast of winter and is too dignified to bow from its proud height. It is the human lover who is distracted with passion and longs for the proud Beloved to raise the face-veil which conceals the ineffable Beauty. Hardly ever does the Beloved become the Lover. There is nothing of the Love which loved us while we were sinners, the love which stoops, the love which says "In all their affliction

He was afflicted." The only passages which occur to us wherein some little approach is made to the conception of love as an attribute of God are in the *Mathnavī* Book v. 2, 735-40 and 2,185-7.

Bā Muḥammad bud 'ishq-i-pāk juft.
Baḥr-'ishq u-ra Khudā 'Laulāk' guft.
Gar na-būdī baḥri-'ishq-i-pāk rā,
Kai wujūdī dadami aflāk rā

"The pure love was joined with Muḥammad. For Love's sake, God said to him, 'Except for thee.' If it had not been for pure love how should I have given existence to the heavens?" Here is a sort of *Logos* doctrine associated with the person of Muḥammad. It is the second stanza which is of interest to us, for there a ground for creation is sought not in blind will, but in love. The second passage is not worth quoting *in extenso* but two phrases are of interest. *'Ishq wasf-i-izād ast* "Love is a Divine attribute" and *Pas maḥabbat waṣf-i-Ḥaqq dan 'ishq nīz* "Know that love and even excessive love is an attribute of Creative Truth." Here we find Rumi bursting the bonds of orthodox Islam.

Perhaps one of the greatest difficulties one has to face in the work of evangelism is to bring home the Christian idea of a Moral Law which is authenticated in the moral consciousness, the law written in our hearts. Here we have united the transcendent Law-giver and the imminent Revealer of His own holiness within human's breast. Thus is a true sense of sin born and sin is condemned within and without. No foreign law is arbitrarily imposed but one which, by the indwelling of God's spirit and the conviction he has wrought within, is confessed as holy, just and good. Islam preponderantly accepts the transcendent Law-giver but fears of the doctrine of human made in the image of God which alone can guarantee a moral and ontological concentricity in human and divine, often lead to the rejection of it though it be guaranteed by such a great name as Al-Ghazālī. It is to the votary of *Kashf* (inward illumination) to whom one may look for support for such a Biblical doctrine and Al- Ghazālī's conception of human as spiritual substance (*jawhar-i-rūḥani*) comes into the same category. The classical reference in this connection is to the famous tercet of Manṣūr al-Hallāj: "Praise be to him who manifested His humanity, the secret of the splendour of His glorious Divinity, and then visibly appeared to His creation in the form of one who eats and drinks, so that His creation could perceive Him as in the flicker of an eyelid." In the Urdu *ghazal* of Shāh Ḥātim we have:

Kahīn wuh sūrat-i-insān hokar kalānī kare;
Kahīn wuh ghap men gharībon ke a salām kare

"Here He speaks having the form of Man; there in the guise of the poor He comes and salutes us." We may doubt whether these will bear the interpretation that God is incarnate in humanity, but they certainly are interpreted by Indian Ṣūfīs to mean that an inward revelation of God within human is possible because God made human in His image and after His likeness. The subject of *fanā* (annihilation) and *baqā* (subsistence) and its relation with Christian conceptions is too vast to deal with in our limited space. We shall return to it another time. But, in passing, note the following commentary of the Urdu poet Rāsikh on the saying of our Lord, "whosoever shall lose his life shall preserve it."

Hai azam-i-lark-i-hasti wajh-i-dawām-i-hastī
Jite hi jī fanā ho gar ho baqā kī khwāhish

"The purpose to forsake existence is the cause of the perpetuation of existence. Die while you live if you wish to subsist."

There is the echo of moral conflict in the words of Bedar:

Dil se wahshī ke taīn shikār kiyā:
Ṣaid-i-sher o palang kyā hai ab?

"I have made a prey of such a savage as the heart; what is the hunting of tiger or panther to this?"

Notes on Al-Ghazālī's Psychology

James Windrow Sweetman

There are two meanings of *Qalb* i.e., Heart

a) Physical: In the centre of the heart is the cavity (*khalw*) in which is black blood which is the spring of the spirit. But this is only of interest to physicians and belongs to the physical world.

b) Spiritual: It is a divine and spiritual refinement (*laṭīfah*), which bears some relation to the physical heart. And this refinement is called the Reality of human (*ḥaqīqat al-insān*) and its discerning, knowing, speaking and reproving. It is the heart which is called to account.

The reasons for relating it to the physical heart are often perplexing, for its relation to that is as the relation of accidents to substances, or qualities to things qualified, or the worker to his tool or the dweller to his dwelling. But we are not concerned with this aspect of the matter which belongs to the Sciences of Revelation (*'Ulūm al-mukāshafah*) but only in so far as this affects Sciences of Practice (*'Ulūm al-mu'āmalah*). The solution of the matter depends on the solution of the mystery of Spirit (*rūḥ*) about which the Prophet has given no decision. It therefore behoves no one else to open his lips on the matter. So the object here is to describe only qualities and states of heart and not the nature of the heart in itself. This is not necessary for *'ilm al- mu'āmalah.*

There are two meanings of *rūḥ* i.e., Spirit

a) Spirit is a refinement of which the fount or spring is the *qalb* or the cavity of the heart and which by means of the arteries is diffused into the bodily members. And its diffusion in the body and its imparting life and sense to the organs is as a lamp set in a house and giving light on all sides and illuminating wherever its light lamp passing through a house. This is the meaning in the physician's use, to wit, Spirit is a subtle vapour which receives maturity (?) from the warmth of the heart. We do not use the word in this meaning with which physicians who heal the body are concerned. The Physicians of Religion who cure the heart because they bring it near to the Lord of the Worlds do not use this meaning.

b) Spirit is the intellectual refinement in human which seeks for causal connections. And this is the significance which has already been explained in the second meaning of *qalb*. This is also the meaning in the text *Al-rūḥu min amari rabbī* 'The spirit (comes) at my Lord's command'. And this is such a wonderful divine thing that in the understanding of its essential nature or reality the reason and intelligence are often confounded.

Two meanings of *nafs* i.e., soul, are important for our purpose

a) *Nafs* is that in human which comprises the irascible and concupiscent powers. This meaning is often used by Sufis. They consider the *nafs* to be that in which the guilty qualities of human are gathered. And on this account they say that the *nafs* should be fought and broken in (as a horse is) according to the tradition which says, "Thy greatest enemy is the *nafs* which is between thy sides (in thy breast)." (This is the appetitive soul).

b) It is a divine refinement. And by this should be understood man in himself and the *Nafs al-insān* (Soul of Man) and the *Zāt al-insān* (Essence of Man). It is qualified by different adjectives according to its several states. Thus when its restlessness ceases and it is established in obedience by the constant frustration of lusts, it is called *Nafs al-Muḥamai'nnah*, the tranquillized soul, as we find in Sūrah 89:27

> "O Thou comforted soul! return unto thy Lord, well pleased and pleasing Him." *Nafs* in its first meaning is not considered as returning to God but rather as estranging from Him. It is associated with Satan. When its tranquillity is not perfect but it keeps checking the Carnal Soul (*Nafs-ush-shahwāniyyah*) and taking objection to it, it is called *Nafs al-lawwāmah*, the rebuking soul, because, finding its possessor falling short in the matter of divine service, it reproaches him. This also is found in the Qur'ān (sūra 75:2) "Nor need I swear by the rebuking soul."

When it does not check the Carnal Soul but becomes obedient to the dictates of lust and the promptings of the Devil, it is called *Nafs al-ammārah*, the concupiscent soul, as in the story of Joseph sūra 12: 53. "For I hold not myself excused, because the soul is very urgent to evil." It is also possible that *ammara bilsū*, urging to evil, indicates *nafs* in its first meaning which is very evil. In its second meaning it is very good for in this latter it is the essence and reality of human which apprehends the mystic knowledge of God and other conceptions.[1]

Laṭīfa, translated here refinement, is difficult to translate. It is commonly used to mean a witticism, a subtle point, a rarity. If it were translated 'faculty' some of the original meaning would be lost. It should be noted also that the root of this word is sometimes used in reference to the divine grace and there may be some slight hint of this in Ghazālī's use of it.

For the general psychology of the passages above note the trichotomy of Paul in his use of body, soul and spirit. Of Paul's use of the word 'body' in 1 Cor. vi. 12-18. Johannes Weiss says that it 'almost means personality'. Compare this with what is said of the heart in its second meaning above.[2] It is clear that (the Greek word for) members in Col. iii. 1-8, is used not literally of the members or limbs of the body but metaphorically. As our Lord in the sermon on the Mount said, "If thine eye be evil," referring to the evil disposition which employs the eye as it instrument, so Paul says,

> Slay your member which belongs to the earth, using the word to signify those dispositions or inclinations of the mind or will which use the body

as instruments of the personality .... He is thinking of 'members' and 'body' not so much in their physical connotation as in their function of giving expression to the personality.

Endnotes

1 *Iḥyā al-'ulū al-dīn*, 3-4.

2 Cf. also Scott, *Christianity According to St. Paul*, 208ff.

The Resurrection of Our Lord

James Windrow Sweetman

Again and again we find that Muslim writers are attacking the Christian belief in the resurrection of Jesus Christ. The attacks come from various angles. Christ did not die but someone was crucified in his place. He was crucified but did not die, was revived, and lived to travel to India and die there. Others set forth the varied theories taught them by rationalist critics of Christianity. However, much the materialistic views of the universe have been modified in the West of recent years; there are still those who would extrude what is called, for want of a better word, the supernatural from their theory of existence. Anyone thus minded must of course discount all evidence to the contrary. Such a method is quite unscientific Huxley says, "It is not on *a priori* considerations that objections to miracles can be based. To my mind the fatal objection ... is the inadequacy of the evidence to prove any given case." From this it would appear that the occurrence of miracles must be allowed if the evidence is adequate. Modern science admits that physical nature is not the exclusive criterion of all reality. Any phenomenon of whatever nature is *a priori* possible. At the present stage of our knowledge of natural causes it would be unjustifiable for us to do violence to any scrap of evidence for the supernatural in order that our conventional opinions of what is possible might be satisfied. In this matter we should take heed lest we discount the evidence beforehand, and make it square with our preconceptions.

It must be admitted that between the Christian and the anti-Christian critics there must be a great gulf in regard to the sort of evidence which will be regarded as cogent. The Christian cannot treat the resurrection as a matter of pure history. Apart from the question as to whether there is such a thing as pure history, which we very much doubt, we cannot treat the resurrection of Jesus Christ as such. For us it is inseparably bound up in an appeal to the spiritual nature—the Christian Gospel. Our susceptibility or otherwise to that appeal will influence our view of the resurrection. Again, no mere demonstration of the fact apart from its spiritual significance would be adequate for the Christian. It is not a mere event for the schools to wrangle about. Our interest in it is moral and religious. It belongs in our thought to the series of mighty acts of God significant for our salvation. (Acts v. 31; x. 42). In so far as it is an event it is history but in its character as an act of divine initiative assuring the victory of Christ it transcends history. It is not a metaphysical puzzle and the one who regards the manner of the appearances as the point of interest has the whole situation out of focus. Paul's experience had intellectual content but was definitely more than intellectual. It was personal and religious. "The great conceptions analysed were no mere abstractions, no mere dogmas applicable here and there to persons who might see their beauty and feel their force. They were parts of a religion experimentally verified and these conceptions, these religious experiences were bound up with his faith in the resurrection." Thus in approaching the evidence for the resurrection, it is inevitable that I should ask what value the resurrection has for me, what experience of mine stands related to it and what is the value of these experiences. To emphasise the moral and spiritual phenomena of Christianity in this way is not to adopt a method which violates history. Whatever may be said for the value of the Christian experience, one thing is plain—this experience is historical. The religious and moral phenomena alleged to be the direct result of the resurrection, occurred and do occur. From the first preaching of the disciples which gave evidence of their spiritual transformation, to the present day these phenomena are involved in the development of a large portion of humankind. The Christian church with its influence on two millenniums must be taken account as an historical fact of supreme importance.

As we variously appraise the influence of Christianity so our explanations of it will be coloured. If we hold with Nietzsche that those who hold to the Christian ethic are 'physiologically botched,' if we think the Christian experience a disease, we shall look for its origin in fraud or delusion. If we consider it the holiest, purest, most invigorating, divinest force in the world's life, we shall be disposed to find its origin in some unique and possibly mysterious experience. Is it possible to think that the Christian experience of salvation, of spiritual life through the indwelling Christ, of eternal life in the midst of time, is mere disease and delusion?

The church exists, the New Testament exists, and the Christian experience exists. They demand explanation. How come they to exist? Few would venture to ascribe their origin to fraud but the Aḥmadiyyah cannot be maintained without holding the early disciples guilty of fraud. Most are forced to admit that the Christian ethic is of the highest type. The chief quarrel with it according to these critics is that it is impracticable. It certainly is impracticable without the principle of sacrifice and the dynamic of love which the Aḥmadiyyah tends to dismiss as weakness. But when the Christian rises to the height of that ideal of sacrificial love then the world will learn that the Christian ethic is not impracticable. However, regard the Christian system as the greatest system of moral idealism which the world has ever known, then how can fraud be the origin of it?

Not far from this is the theory that the belief that Jesus *would* rise accounts for the statements that he *did* rise. If the message of Easter was used to bolster up the faith, then the disciples were dishonest. We know that sometimes beliefs have inspired stories, e.g., the story of Psyche and Eros which the Neo-Platonist wrote to embody his belief in the immortality of the soul. But this is vastly different from concocting fictions about an historical person to support a belief. Paul's abhorrence of doing evil that good might come shows what the Christian conscience would be likely to be on this matter.

We have further to consider whether "it is consistent with our belief in the fundamental rationality of the universe to believe that the mightiest force in human history is the result of delusion." Granted the beneficence and moral value of Christianity, is delusion an adequate explanation of its origin? Fraser, in *Psyche's Task*, argues elaborately for superstition as a conservator of human morality, inducing respect for government, human life, private property and the marriage tie. Hence he makes it appear that delusion has been a potent factor for good in the infancy of the race. Can Christianity be brought down to the same level? So far as we can see Fraser's thesis is simply an illustration of the providence of God over-ruling for good what on its merely human side often degenerates into the grossest cruelty and immorality. But Christianity does not show such violent contrasts in its working, for the inquisition is not an illustration of the working of Christianity but of a Satanic perversion of Christianity. If we consider the value of Christianity to the world and its inherent power, beauty and truth, "so much the more inevitable it must seem that what lies behind .... is not an illusion or a morbid experience misunderstood but the highest reality and truth which have ever told with regenerating power on the life of man."

Considering the matter historically, how did this alleged delusion arise? The orthodox Muslim explanation is that Jesus did not die at all on the cross. Another was crucified in his form. Did the disciples know of the substitution? If so then we are back at the theory of *fraud*. The negation of the resurrection is supported by the negation of the death of Christ in the manner in which it is recorded in the Gospel. When we realise the centrality of the cross in Christian teaching, if we accept this theory of what happened, then we can only say that the whole of the story of Christ is untrustworthy. If Christ was not crucified then we can have no confidence that any of the things recorded of him are true. But supposing the disciples were ignorant of the substitution? Then they were deceived. And by whom? We have to accept the horrible idea that Christ himself kept them in ignorance. The Muslim considers that it would be derogatory to the dignity of a prophet that he should die in the manner in which Jesus died. Was it then consonant with that high dignity that he should lend himself to the perpetuation of a lie? The last alternative is that the substitution took place without the knowledge of the disciples and that Jesus himself was unable by the act of God to inform the disciples as to what had actually taken place. Is God then the author of a lie? Such a hideous idea would bring the whole moral structure of the universe toppling about us. Poor Christianity went on in its benighted path for six-hundred years before the matter was put right! Can we really consider for a moment such a scandalous hypothesis which involves the truthfulness either of God, of Christ or of the Disciples of Christ?

Recently the theory of Renan has been advanced by Muslim objectors. He says that the delusion arose from the hysterical imagination of Mary Magdalene, "La gloire de la resurrection appartient done a Marie de Magdala; apres Jesus c'est Marie qui a le plus fait la fondation du christianisme." As an explanation of this statement he says, "Pouvoir divine de L'amour! Moments sacres ou la passion d'une hallucinee donne au monde un Dieu ressuscite!" Renan's poetic imagination has not conceived an explanation of how a weak-minded woman could convince sceptical and despondent men and so influence them that her experiences were reproduced in them. "That so many persons of different temperament and varied intelligence should be deceived by hallucinations of sight and sound is incredible." It should also be noticed that Renan's theory violates the records by putting Mary Magdalene so pre-eminently at the source of Christian tradition of the resurrection. Paul does not include her in his list of witnesses; Luke does not mention any appearances of the risen Lord to her; and though John does so, he does not consider it important enough to count in reckoning the number of appearances to the disciples.

If neither fraud not delusion is considered an adequate explanation, can we explain the belief in the resurrection of Christ by reference only to the life of Christ? Does "the impression made by his life led to the conviction of his immortality," afford an explanation? The whole testimony of the primitive witnesses goes to prove the contrary. They conceived the experiences which came to them as direct consequences of the resurrection and no explanation of the resurrection is adequate which does not take into consideration the significance it had for the early witnesses.

Turning to the record we have a very clear and unambiguous description of the feelings of the early disciples when it seemed that the life of their beloved Master had been cruelly ended. Luke's story of the disciples on the way to Emmaus rings true. It reflects faithfully their thoughts and feelings at the time. They are already speaking of Jesus in the past tense and lamenting what might have been. But it is said: their despair was short lived. The incomparable moral grandeur of Jesus and his winsome grace had so captivated their hearts that his death brought but a momentary extinction of these emotions which after the shock of Calvary burst forth again with greater force. He rose again in their hearts and reasserted his influence and rekindled their love. This of course might be referred to in a metaphorical manner as a rising from the dead, but if such was the experience of the disciples we should hardly have expected a momentary extinction but a gradual adjustment of their thought in face of that altogether unexpected event, the death of the Messiah, a pondering on his teaching, and possibly a return to the Scriptures to find what these things could mean. All this would have taken time. The startling suddenness of the change from despair to joyful assurance seems to demand some other explanation than a pondering on the life of Jesus. Could memory account for all the facts of the Gospel? The memory of the lost usually means regret and the more attached we have been to them, the dearer they have been to us, the more poignant is the regret. Hence normally, the feelings recorded of the disciples before Easter are just what we should expect. It is the transformation which is unexpected and surprising. It is hard to see also how the death of Jesus could have been regarded as anything more than an unmitigated tragedy apart from some extraordinary event which took place afterwards. Memory of the Lord would lead to that poignant regret and despair that his life-work had been cut short, something else is required to account for the change from despair to abounding joy. If it be said that the predictions of Jesus would be sufficient to account this change, we can only reply that the non-fulfilment of the predictions would only increase the despair.

The case of Paul cannot be explained on the lines that the resurrection of Jesus was a deduction from his life. Can an influence be reasserted which has never been felt? What tender memories had Paul to recall? With this in mind we agree with Denney in his confident assertion that "No brooding of his friends on the memory of Jesus would have given to his personality that revival which they asserted when they preached the resurrection."

Nor is this all that may be said in this connection. It must be remembered that the resurrection was a new revelation. The disciples did not grasp the significance of the death of Christ till after the resurrection. Before Paul became convinced that Christ had risen he regarded Jesus of Nazareth as self-convicted of failure, conclusively refuted by the facts of his own experience, cursed and abhorred of God as well as human, demonstrated by his crucifixion to be the opposite of what he claimed; an idea here which has its counterpart in the Muslim idea that a prophet could not have suffered as Jesus did. Paul had held that the death of Jesus was just the divine retribution on an impostor (see Deut. xxi. 23 and Gal. iii. 13). Afterwards he regards that death in quite another way and the resurrection he regards as God's seal on the loving devotion of Christ to death and the act of God which turned a tragedy into a triumph. Note how Sanday and Headlam summarise the significance of the resurrection for Paul. It is the "most conclusive proof of Christ's divinity placed on Christ's death the stamp of God's approval .... is the most decisive proof of the atoning value of Christ's death .... is the strongest guarantee of the resurrection of the Christian." To the person to whom the Christian Gospel is indeed good news, the new and valuable revelation one finds to be an integral part of the New Testament faith and preaching, seems incapable of explanation by anything less than the Easter message of an event commensurate with the transforming and regenerating power which characterises that faith and accompanies that preaching.

Yet again, with reference to the experience of Paul, if it was merely a spiritual and figurative rising in the heart which was the basis of his Christian life, why should he emphasize appearances? Why does he refer to Christ's burial? Surely the rising is relative to the burial. Why does he refer to the third day? What had that got to do with the experience on the road to Damascus? Does it not on the face of it mean that Paul is referring to a datable event? Arnold Meyer tries to explain "buried" with reference to the mystical tendency in Paul, e.g., "Buried with Christ" (Romans vi. 4). This strikes us as nothing more than a ridiculous inversion. Mystical meanings would not have arisen if Paul had been unable to base them on historical occurrences.

Finally there is the strange phenomenon of so-called historical reconstructions of what happened, evolved out of the imagination of the people who invent them, while they ignore or mutilate out of all recognition the only sources of information which we have, Such are that Joseph of Arimathaea stole the body, the fiction of *Toledoth Jesu* which says Judas stole it, the romance of Venturini which relates that Jesus did not die but was nursed by the Essenes ... the probable source of the Aḥmadiyyah romance of the present day. These and many others do far more violence to history and to historical method than could possibly be alleged of the Gospel.

If we find mystery, what more can we expect? With regard to such a transcendent event, who could be adequate to explain what took place? The records do not as a matter of fact explain the mode of being in which Jesus appeared. Lake thinks that Paul's conception

involves the transubstantiation of the body of Jesus into spirit. Then the disciples saw a ghost. But Luke who stands nearest to Paul, strongly asserts the contrary (see xxiv. 37). Which should we prefer, Lake or Luke? We are not in the position to understand the "quasi-physical or fourth dimensional concomitants" of the resurrection appearances but these are not matters of primary consideration. Denney's statement that the spiritual body is not in Paul's thought a body which has been converted into spirit but one in which matter is made wholly subservient to the purpose of spirit, seems to us to be really adequate. When Christ rose, he rose in a manner suitable to the purpose he had in view, which was to convince "his own" of his acceptance by God and to lead them forth to share the victory which God has given to him. We know from the record that condescension was made to the weak in faith. But they are not central to the narrative. What is the manifest triumph of Christ by the power of God which was to lead humankind to faith in the omnipotence of love and sacrifice, and in the abiding presence of the ever-living Christ?

The Echo of A Controversy

James Windrow Sweetman

If our members who keep their old copies of News and Notes will refer to the January number of this bulletin for last year, they will find an article on Christian Literature and the Character of Muḥammad. This article would leave no doubt in the minds of readers, that we regard it as eminently undesirable that, in the course of our missionary propaganda, we should use literature which is calculated to wound the susceptibilities of those whom we address and especially is this to be observed in respect to the character of Muḥammad. If we desire to win a man to our way of thinking, it is, to say the least bad policy to start by knocking him down. If our method is, constructive rather than destructive, and we show what Christ is, and are true witnesses to Christ in our lives, the Muslim himself will draw the comparison which we wish him to draw. There are signs that this is already being done. Let us make a comparison for ourselves between the picture which is given of Muḥammad in the traditions and the articles which are now appearing from the pens of Muslim apologists. What we find is this. There is gradually growing up in Islām a new conception of what a true prophet of God ought to be.

The early Islāmic writers evidently regarded the prophet as a man to whom ordinary rules did not apply. He had a special rank which entitled him to a certain measure of freedom. Within the bounds of the dispensation committed to him he was without blemish. By the order of God he was not as other men and was even exempted from the laws which he was called to enunciate for other men. The ordinary Muslim might have four wives but the prophet might have more. This point of view has not entirely disappeared but there is far more appreciation of the idea that morality, to be really morality, must be of universal application and that no person can be really exempted from what the consensus of opinion regards as the moral law. What we look for is the deepening of this conception. If this conception is deepened it will be fruitful in many directions. One way in which it will work is in establishing the conviction that there cannot be a double standard for men and women and that a code which gives a man the right to have four wives and withholds the right of a woman to have four husbands can never be the expression of a universal law of light. The growing realisation that a prophet has no exemption is bound up in a yet half-conscious admission of the universal moral law. And who has become the type and expositor of moral- perfection? Without doubt our Lord Jesus Christ has, though not yet admittedly. It is the Christian criterion which is at work in the new views of what a prophet of God ought to be. An *a priori* assumption can be observed in modern Islāmic apologetics which has its ground in the Christian ideal. Even the attacks which have been made from some quarters on the character of our Lord and Saviour, and on the behaviour of Christians generally or militarist Christendom in particular are all based ultimately on a moral standard derived from Christ Himself.

In a recent number of these notes we referred to an article by the editor of the *Nigār* of Lucknow in which the modern disgust with the early traditions concerning Mohammed is expressed. Now we have before us the book by Nazīr Aḥmad which gives us food for thought.

Ummahāt al-ummah came to be written in the following way. A challenge was issued by Muslims offering a reward to anyone who could show from the trustworthy traditions that the character of Muḥammad was other than it ought to be. This challenge was taken up by one Akbar Masīḥ, a Unitarian. He published a book using another's name and called *Ummahāt al-muminīn*. This book consisted of quotations from the trustworthy traditions. Nothing was included which could be regarded as of dubious authority and the compiler made little comment. A great stir was made. Indignation meetings were held in many places but nothing could be done. To have had the book proscribed by order of the court would have been to condemn the traditions but this course was ultimately taken. Sir Syed Aḥmad wrote a reply but this was not regarded as acceptable. Then Maulvī Nazīr Aḥmad, who was a superb writer of Urdu prose, took a reply in hand. This reply was the book we now have before us *Ummahāt al-ummah*. But instead of being received with applause, the disapprobation with which this book was received exceeded even that roused by the book to which it was meant as a reply. Pressure was brought to bear upon the author and a fatwa pronounced upon him; his book was burned in public and was forthwith withdrawn from publication. One of the gentlemen who wrote an introduction to the present edition exclaims at this intolerance. He says he had been taught that the charge of burning the library at Alexandria which was brought against the Muslim conquerors of Egypt was a fabrication by Christians, and that in reality Islām had always been tolerant, but this act of burning Nazīr Aḥmad's book had made him think that the former charge might be true.

Now after a quarter of a century the grandson of Nazīr Aḥmad has had the temerity to republish the book which roused such controversy, but its accessibility to the public has again been banned but this time without the furore of the former occasion. The publisher's object has evidently been to clear the name of his grandfather. He has thought that the former banning was due to the temporary sensitiveness of his community due to the attack by Akbar Masīḥ and that perhaps he could, now that the heat of the controversy had cooled, safely leave *Ummahāt al-ummah* to the judgment of his contemporaries.

And at the first glance it was difficult for us to see what it was that had aroused the ire of opponents when the book was first published. Except for a strange phrase, to which however objection does not seem to have been raised, namely, *Ummahāt al-muminīn kī sārī khwāhishen paighambar ṣāhib kī sharf-i hambistarī ke āge maghlūb thīn* and which struck us as being somewhat objectionable, there was nothing much more in the book than a retelling in popular language of the facts already narrated in the traditions and the standard histories.

What was regarded as objectionable was, however, made quite clear in the appendix to the book which consists of a number of objections contained in a book called *Kashf al-ghāmihī* and the replies thereto by the author of *Aḥsan al-Tafāsīr*.

The criticisms which are here expressed are in a very bitter tone and the writer more than once states that Nazīr Aḥmad has cut himself off from Islām. The main objection made is to the colloquial language used by Nazīr Aḥmad.

First the critic draws attention to the fact that the author of *Ummahāt al-ummah* when referring to Muḥammad says simply "Paighambar Sahib" without any other title of respect or the usual invocation of blessings. In reply to this it is said that because the book was a reply to a "Pādrī Ṣāḥib" only such terms were used as would be acceptable to him whereas he might have taken exception to the usual formula. This strikes us as rather a lame excuse, and we are sure that the main tendency in Christian literature is to err on the side of conformity to Muslim usage. We have seen a book in which, whenever the names of Muḥammad or of the persons whom the Muslims esteem as prophets were mentioned, the sign for the reading of an ejaculatory prayer was written above them and in the rest of the text St. Paul was plain Paul, St. John plain John, and even our Lord was simply Jesus. This is carrying things to an extreme and whenever we feel called upon to use any of the conventional expressions after the name of Muḥammad, we should be careful that terms of respect in accord with Christian usage should be given to our Lord and the apostles.

One of the objections still raised to Nazīr Aḥmad's translation of the Qur'ān is that it is too colloquial. Thus it is not surprising that here too the charge is made, and the author has to be defended in his choice of Urdu idioms. An instance is given here. Nazīr Aḥmad says "If Khadija had lived, the constraint of her service would have been such that the occasion for polygamy would never have arisen. And in comparison with her an Ayesha or even a hundred 'Āyeshas would have counted for nothing." The last words of this are *dāl nahīn galtī*, an idiom of which Nazīr Aḥmad was very fond as may be seen from other books of his. This is, says the objector, going out of the way to depreciate one of the holy mothers. The author of *Ummahāt al-ummah* supports his answer to this objection with quotations from the traditions and from Ayesha herself showing in what esteem Muḥammad held Khadija. Another instance of the use of an idiom which was displeasing is *Fāṭimah ser kī thīn aur* 'Āyesha *sawā ser kī* because this is reminiscent of the rivalry of bidding one against the other. Nazīr Aḥmad also ascribes *ghamand* to 'Alī and uses *triya charitr* (woman's wiles) with regard to the conduct of Fatima and Ayesha. This latter, the critic says, is pure abuse and there is no doubt that there is a use of this term which would imply much more than Nazīr Aḥmad meant. We cannot help feeling however that the critic is not so much disturbed by the terms used as by the fact that the intrigues round about the prophet, the quarrel between *Fāṭimah* and Abū Bakr, and the jealousy between Fāṭimah and 'Āyesha are clearly narrated by Nazīr Aḥmad. It is indeed a most unedifying picture. "How" laments the critic, "could it have been possible for those who had come under the influence of the prophet and had the honour of his intimacy, even his wife and his daughter, to behave in the way suggested by the plain blunt speech of Nazīr Aḥmad?" These are not his actual words but this is the substance of his objection. But alas for the objector, assumptions as to what ought to have been have to give place to the stern facts of history, and the author of *Aḥsan al-Tafāsīr* justifies the statements with respect to the schemes of Fatima and Ayesha by appeal to al Bukhārī and Muslim. The jealousy of Ayesha and Ḥafṣah which was aroused by Zainab's (?) company being preferred by the prophet is also confirmed by appeal to the traditions and to the Sūrah 66, though we had always thought that the one whose company was preferred was Mary the Coptic slave.

There is no use in making further references to this sort of thing. The point we wish to emphasise is that again and again in reply to objections it is pointed out that the writer has only repeated the stories found in the traditions. He has not added anything himself and in one place he says that to object to what he has said is to condemn the traditions which are universally accepted in Islām. What Nazīr Aḥmad did not see was that *unless the traditions are scrapped it is absolutely impossible to rehabilitate Muḥammad in the eyes of those whose moral sense has been developed and influenced by Christian truth.* No idealised picture of the home of the prophet and the circle about him is possible with the material which has been regarded as authoritative in Islām until quite recent times. Two possibilities are open to Muslim apologetics: to reject utterly the new system of moral values which is due to the leaven of Christianity, and to forsake the Christ-ideal for the ideal of the Superman, or to jettison the whole bundle of extra-Qur'ānic information about Muḥammad and compose an imaginative picture from the scanty materials in the Qur'ān. The quarrel of Ali and Abu Bakr and the refusal of the latter to let Fatima have her inheritance as narrated in the *Ummahāt al-ummah* does not present to us a picture of a community into which a new moral and spiritual power had come through the teaching of the Prophet Muḥammad, but rather of a community rent by strife and envy and grasping after political prizes, and even in the very hour of the Prophets death-sickness quarrelling over the succession and thwarting him in his desire to leave a written testament. We can imagine Muḥammad echoing David's words "These Sons of Zeruaiah are too hard for me.

Here than in *Ummahāt al-ummah* we have a Muslim document. The work of Akbar Masīḥ which was the occasion of it we have never seen but, as we have stated, that was simply a repetition of what had been found in the traditions. In view of this fact and after a review of all the circumstances in respect to this publication, we come to the conclusion that we can leave the question of the character of Muḥammad and his influence on his immediate circle to critics within the Muslim community. We would at the same time point out that if garbled accounts of what the traditions contain are given, and if they are claimed as a source for our knowledge of the life and character of Muḥammad, there is no equity in forbidding a Christian to refer to, or quote from the traditions.

Good Friday

James Windrow Sweetman

A Muslim criticism that the Christian holds that he has salvation by belief in a fact of history, strikes us at first as a statement of the truth just as we would express it. But the idea behind the objection is that by mere assent to a fact of history the Christian hopes to gain salvation. The belief which the Christian has in the death of Christ is far more than assent to an historic fact. He does assent to the fact but he believes in it *with his whole heart*, for with the heart a person believeth unto salvation.

In the death of Christ on the Cross, the Christian sees the winning of a glorious victory over the powers of evil and in-so-far as faith unites him with Christ in His great atoning act, one shares in that victory and enters into an experience of reconciliation with God.

What happens in us to make the Cross of Christ effective in our lives? When we seek to express the relation of the atoning act to ourselves, we have to confess that there is much here which is utterly ineffable. In this life of ours there are things of which we are so fully aware that they have become part and parcel of our lives but yet we cannot speak of them adequately. Our experience of the atoning work of Christ is one of these. It is also true that Christ deals with different individuals in different ways and so it is quite possible that theories of how the Cross exercises its influence may be very diverse. Thus some Christians would be content to say with Coleridge that there is a great mystery here; we cannot explain it but we know it is a fact and we accept it.

There are one or two preliminary facts to be borne in mind. When asked what the purpose of Creation is, we would say that it is the bringing into existence of a fellowship of moral and spiritual beings. Moral and spiritual personality is, so far as we know, the crown of all the processes of this great universe. At the heart of the Eternal is love which, Fatherlike, would bring sons to birth. The "Worker that hideth Himself" behind the veil of a material universe with its laws, is giving an opportunity to human to develop freely to an ideal of personal and spiritual life, without undue obtrusion or compulsion. Human too feels the attraction of the Divine, and God's purpose is complete when his own self-giving love is met by human's free self-dedication. Thus will the circle be complete and human will be won to spiritual and moral atonement with God.

Muslims would deny the Creative Love in somewhat similar terms to those of Spinoza. In his philosophy we find he would define the essence of love as "seeking union". Similarly in Sir Muḥammad Iqbāl's *Secrets of the Self*, where he says, that love is "assimilation". But the Christian would say that love is self-imparting not a seeking of union or of satisfaction. The form which the reciprocated love of human for God would take would be human's self-dedication; not human's seeking of satisfaction for themselves in union, but their self-giving in response to a love which certainly draws him, but does so by the paradoxical means of separating human into an individual, willing and responsible moral being. It is, as it were, as if God sent out from Himself into a sphere of discipline, those who would thus be bound to Himself by the very act of love which thrust them out.

An illustration is thinkable on the lines of the home where a child may remain in a state of passive acceptance of a love which pervades the whole home, and a will, say of a father or a mother, which is immanent throughout the whole life of the home. So long as the child does not wake to a sense of his own responsibility he may cling to the notion of an utterly unbroken unity and be content, so that his negative calm may not be disturbed, to have his personality merged in the stronger personality which rules the home, without making any truly affirmative response. The wise parent, however, will see the need for the child's development of moral individuality, and the more loving he is and the less selfish, he will encourage this freedom. Thus indeed God acts. He assumes a transcendent relationship in an act of love, giving what is His original inalienable freedom, in some measure, to His creation. In this there is the possibility of a movement of willed return on human's part, to the love which draws while it sends human out to find their moral individuality; and thus a reciprocal relation becomes possible which is not possible under any theory which exaggerates immanence.

God's self-giving in Fatherhood and man's response in perfect sonship, a perfect circle of fellowship, was completed once, when Jesus of Nazareth, in the hallowed deeps of His spirit, with full accord and unclouded assurance, from a heart untainted by sin, communed with His Father.

But when we come to think of the possibility of the response of other human, we are well-aware that sin has raised a barrier, and that it can only be by an experience of forgiveness that we may become at one with God, What came to Christ without mediation can come to us only by His mediation. For what can human do themself to bridge the gulf between themself and God? If they repent, will all be set right then? What can my repentance do? If I have quarrelled with a friend and then, becoming aware of the wrong I have done him, repent even with tears, he may give me his hand and accept my apology but if he does so coldly and unconcernedly, I cannot be sure that he has given me his heart again; indeed I may even feel that he had never really given me his heart. He may have been very magnanimous and I can appreciate that, but I want to know whether he is again my friend. Did my former quarrel touch him to the quick or was he slightly amused that I should take the matter so seriously? Is he even now perhaps saying to himself, "What is this tedious fellow making all this bother about?" I can think of another way in which an injured friend might meet my apology, "My friendship for you was such, and you wounded me so deeply that now I hardly know how I can forgive you." I cannot help feeling that there would be more hope of the ultimate renewal of my friendship with that man, though the way might be hard for him and for me. Out of an estrangement which was a real agony for both of us a new love might be born which would be far stronger than the old.

Are we therefore wrong in thinking that the One who has been offended by our sin must pass through an experience in some sense the equivalent and counterpart of the bitter experience which is ours when we seek a reconciliation? If it is easy for God to forgive, as our Muslim friend would have it, then is sin such a terrible thing and can God be really very troubled that we are sinners? We know it is easy for anyone to say, "I forgive," but forgiveness between those who love is an agonizing thing.

It is true I must repent and my heart must be laden with the pain of the offence *but there must also be a realisation of the hatefulness of the sin which caused the estrangement, on the part of the one who is offended.* We want to know how God looks at sin. If it is with an amused indulgence then sin is not so bad; so our penitence will be correspondingly devoid of pangs. It will be simply confession that we have made a mistake which, if it is not too much trouble, we would like to see rectified.

I can hear an exasperated professor saying to a student for whom he has great hopes and whose work has been disappointing, "Take away this trash, I regard your work as a personal insult." I can also hear the student mutter as he goes away crest-fallen, "I never knew he cared so much." In order that a man should be saved, it is necessary that he should have a true view of sin. It is hard to get a man to realise that his sin is against God. He may be prepared to admit that he has sinned against himself and perhaps that he has sinned against his friends or society, but does God care? When a man looks at the Cross of Christ, he has a new view of sin and he goes away saying "I never knew He cared so much."

What could be more adequate that the Cross of Christ to show the hatefulness of sin? The pride of the Jew, the cruelty of Roman, the self-sufficiency of the priestly guardians of religion and the selfish fear which washed its hands of the crime against the innocent.

White purity is bathed in blood, innocence and kindness the victim of cruelty and pride. That is the end of sin and that sin is what we have cherished. When we condemn the sin that brought the sinless to the Cross we condemn ourselves. What can shake human from their immoral complacency? If the Cross of Christ cannot, then nothing can. Remember how Robert Louis Stevenson prayed for some piercing sin to stab us broad awake. Here is the piercing sin to stab all humankind awake if human will but look with eyes of faith, at Him "Whom God publicly set forth dying a bloody death, as one having reconciling power through men's faith in Him, with a view to conferring a righteousness of His own, through the overlooking of past sins in the forbearance of God, with a view, I say, to conferring his righteousness at this very moment, and to his being righteous and at the same time declaring righteous him who founds on faith in Jesus." (Rom. iii. 25)

When we are asked what was the need of this agony, "Could not God simply declare that a man was forgiven as in Islam?" we ask in reply "Would the sinner turn from his wickedness if he simply thought God was good-natured and easy-going?" The low moral ideal in Islam is in all probability due just to that very notion that if God will, He will forgive and if not, well it cannot be helped and we must just abide it. The message of the Cross is that God's forgiveness is determined by a Heart acutely alive to the evil of sin. Only such forgiveness can save. Sin caused God's heart to break and he showed his broken heart on Calvary, so that he might break these stubborn hearts of ours and fold us into the comfort of His love.

The Aḥmadīs and the Orthodox

James Windrow Sweetman

It is a remarkable thing that though circumcision has been the regular practice among Muslims there is no mention of it in the Qur'ān and very little in the Traditions. It is generally held to be founded on the custom of Muḥammad. Abū Hurairah declares that Muḥammad said it was one of the observances of the *Fiṭrat*, which is natural religion. It is widely held that there is no need for converts to submit to the rite. A writer in the *Light* however voices the opinion of Orthodox Islām that "it plays an important part in the life of a Muslim" and that "it is essential for *Ṭahārat* (purification) which is the basic principle of all religious performances." The line which the Aḥmadiyyah has taken in its approach to the depressed classes is that it is not necessary for these possible converts to Islām. The following taken from the editorial of the *Light* should be of interest.

> In our issue of June 1, while reviewing the conversion field in Malabar, we referred to the general dread of circumcision among the Thiyās who were contemplating joining Islām. They had been given to understand that no non-Muslim could become a Muslim until he had been circumcised. At first we laughed the idea away as idle gossip.
>
> We could hardly believe that any Muslim would insist on circumcision as indispensable for the purposes of acceptance of Islām. Islām is a simple creed, meaning belief in unity of God and prophethood of Muḥammad. We never imagined any one would seriously make to these the addition of a third proposition—viz., circumcision. On the assurance of some Muslim friends as well as Thira leaders, however, that it was no joke and

> the Mullās subjected even grown-up converts to the operation. Mr. K. L. Gauba in consultation with responsible local leaders issued a statement that circumcision though a recognized Islāmic practice and highly advisable on hygienic grounds, was by no means one of the essentials of Islām.

This seems to have become just one more point on which the Aḥmadīs and the Orthodox are parting company. We can be certain that things are not well in the Muslim camp. The most energetic and modernist Aḥmadīs are constantly giving evidence of the fact that they are at loggerheads with the rest.

On another page of the same issue of the *Light* reference is made to a Fatwa pronounced against a professor of the *Ishā'at-i Islām* College, Lahore, (Aḥmad Institution) on the ground that according to this teacher the "question of Jesus' death is a moot point." Although, they say

> the Maulānā belongs to the Ḥanafī School of thought he could not escape the fury of these Mullās. (i.e., among others the President of the *Jama'iyat al-'ulamā* of Delhi, which is the highest court of the learned orthodox). This view of his was adjudged unorthodox. The fatwa declares that Jesus is alive and must bodily descend from heaven someday. This it says is the accepted creed of the *Ahl-i-Sunnat* and whoever does not subscribe to it is a *Mulḥid* (heretic). This should give food for thought to sensible sections of Islām. If this mania for heresy-hunt is allowed to go on without let or hindrance, we are afraid, hardly one sensible Muslim will be able to his laurels for orthodoxy. Maulānā 'Abdul Kalām Azād believes Jesus to be dead. So do Sir Muḥammad Iqbāl, Mr. 'Abdullāh Yūsuf 'Alī and many enlightened Mussalmāns. The famous scholar and thinker of Egypt, Muḥammad 'Abduhū writes in his commentary of the Qur'ān not only that Jesus is dead, but he goes further and opined that the (Aḥmadiyyah) view that he came to India and was buried in Kashmir cannot be called out of the range of probability.
>
> We are strongly of opinion that the Mullās who issue these fatwas are not alone to blame. The enlightened sections who know these absurdities and yet have not the courage to openly condemn them are also guilty of a serious sin of omission in this matter. It is already too late in the day. The solidarity of Islām the most cherished dream of the prophet has been shattered to pieces. Nevertheless if the house of Islām is yet to be saved from further dissensions, well-wishers of Islām must move in the matter and do something to put collars on these fatwa-mongering mullās.

So says the *Light*, but one might very well hear an orthodox Mullā responding that it is not the mass of the orthodox which is responsible for the rending of Islām's unity but the innovators who have brought forward their rationalising theories in order to apologise for Islām.

What is most interesting to us is the prominence which is being given to questions concerning Jesus Christ in all these discussions. May it not be, in the good providence of God that in this manner Christ may be brought more and more to the attention of the world of Islām? As a very well-informed Muslim said to the writer the other day, "The Aḥmadīs have got to count on a good deal of credulity before their reinterpretation of plain texts of the Qur'ān will find acceptance." The reference was, of course, to Muḥammad 'Alī's comments on the passages which refer to Jesus in the Qur'ān. The Aḥmadīs cannot claim that they are the only "sensible section of Islām" and there are many Arabic scholars who would profoundly disagree with Muḥammad 'Alī's "translations."

Trends of Thought in Indian Islām

James Windrow Sweetman

Passing over the communal, political and sectarian problems which are occupying the mind of Indian Islām today let us come to the modernizing and polemical tendencies and activities which represent a missionary religion's urgent need and desire to adjust itself to a new world of thought. The forces of secularism and rationalism have not been without their disruptive influence on the youth of Islām and complaints are frequent that young men are lax in the discharge of religious duties. Indeed we have seen it alleged that the ranks even of the champions of Islām are not free from those who are lax in saying the five daily prayers and in paying the poor-tax. It would seem that there are many who, while accepting the religious character of the community, are yet far more concerned about the community than about religion. The real object of worship of many Muslims is Islām rather than Allāh. Sir Muḥammad Iqbāl's *Six Lectures on the Reconstruction of Religious Thought in Islām* is largely socio-political. Even the new book which has come from the pen of Maulānā Muḥammad 'Alī gives us food for thought when we find in its 760 pages only 33 given to the doctrine of God and 88 to Marriage. It seems surprising to a spectator to see that a religion which has been organized for centuries on social and legal lines, determined in the first instance by a perfect divinely-given code, should in the fourteenth century of its existence still be so concerned with statements and expositions of social matters, while, at the same time, it is at pains to eke out its shallow theology by resorting to lexicons, till one wonders whether Lane is an inspired authority preferable to Baizāwī and Jalālain! Iqbāl's *Six Lectures* is undoubtedly the best book we have seen on its subject but when he comes to the reconstruction of the conception of God, he has to be content with three texts of the Qur'ān, one of which is so obscure that by interpretation in allegorical fashion one might make it mean almost anything, from the Trinity to Persian "Light-philosophy", unless one prefers, as the author does, to read into it modern scientific theories about light.

Iqbāl's great concern, however, is that the door of ijtihād should be open. Explaining modern forces for reform, he says that Sayyad Jamāl ad-dīn Afghānī was the teacher and inspirer of Muftī Muḥammad 'Abduhū and Zaghl al-Pāshā. The Mullās, or orthodox teachers, had grown conservative and would not allow any freedom of ijtihād. The first efforts of the reformers and the Wahhābīs were to secure such freedom. They prepared the ground for Zaghl al-Pāshā in Egypt, Muṣṭafā Kamāl Pāshā in Turkey and Razā Shāh in Persia. These men in Iqbāl's opinion were not influenced in their reconstructive work by alien cultures but were simply exercising their right to reinterpret Islām. Kamāl is not anti-Muslim. He is a true Muslim. The only snag is that he has substituted the Swiss Code with its rules of inheritance. Taking them seriatim, Iqbāl explains away the issue of the Qur'ān in a Turkish dress, prayers in the Turkish tongue, abolition of polygamy and the Caliphate, and he asserts that the Turkish ijtihād on the Caliphate is supported by Ibn Khaldūn.

This reminds us of something which was said in the *Light* on February 24th last. "An interpreter, according to all authorities, is not guilty of heresy, however wrong that interpretation may be." With such a principle to start from, is it any wonder that the mind of Islām should be in chaos? But after all, this expression of opinion is only an extreme assertion of the longing of Islām to break from the iron hand of tradition. Will Islām be able to do it and still remain Islām? The modern school apparently thinks so. The inertia of Islām has been due to a static conception of its character. Hope for the future lies in a new dynamic conception along the lines of Bergson. A principle of movement and change must be admitted along the lines of the philosophy of history contained in Ibn Khaldūn whose conception is of "infinite importance because of the implication that history, as a continuous movement in time, is a genuinely creative movement and not a movement whose path is already determined. This principle of movement in Islām is ijtihād."

This principle of movement must be applied to the law of Islām. Iqbāl quotes from Horten to the effect that the spirit of Islām is boundless. "With the exception of atheistic ideas alone it has assimilated all the attainable ideas of surrounding peoples and given them its own peculiar direction of development." Iqbāl then goes on to say

> I have no doubt that a deeper study of the enormous legal literature of Islām is sure to rid the modern critic of the superficial opinion that the law of Islām is stationary and incapable of development. Unfortunately the conservative Muslim public of this country is not yet quite ready for a critical discussion of 'Fiqh' which, if undertaken, is likely to displease most people and raise sectarian controversies.

And again,

> The 'ulamā' of Islām claim finality for the popular schools of Muḥammedan Law ... But since things have changed and the world of Islām is today confronted and affected by new forces set free by the extraordinary development of human thought in all its directions, I see no reason why this attitude should be maintained any longer. Did the founders of our schools ever claim finality for their reasoning and interpretations? Never.

The fundamental inconsistency here is that it is claimed that Islām of itself has within itself the principle of movement and then it is admitted that the inertia of Islām is giving way under the impact of forces outside Islām. It is also very difficult to reconcile the disclaimer of any influence from alien cultures on events in Turkey, Egypt and Persia with the last quotation we have made.

Now-a-days we have a new way of expressing Islām's view of the sanctity of the *fait accompli*. When the Turks seized the Caliphate the jurists were at a non-plus because their theory was that the Caliphate should be in the family of the Quraish. But Islāmic opportunism and "respect for the logic of facts" led Muslims, as I think Prof. Macdonald puts it, to say "They have it; they are able to keep it; let them keep it." That was the old method; but now that the Turks have abolished the Caliphate, what shall we say? Let us put the old case for compromise in another way, as Sir Muḥammad Iqbāl does.

> The birth of Islām ... *is the birth of the inductive intellect.* In Islām prophecy reaches its perfection in discovering the need of its own abolition. This involves the keen perception that life cannot forever be kept in leading strings; that in order to achieve full self- consciousness, man must finally be thrown back *on his own resources.*

But how can there be such a system as Islām at all, if all that is left to human is to proceed by way of trial and experiment? And how do we reconcile the words which Iqbāl uses towards the end of his *Six Lectures* with human being left to their own resources,

> The Muslim is in possession of .... ultimate ideas on the basis of revelation there can be no further revelation binding on man .... Let the Mussalman of today appreciate his position, reconstruct his social life in the light of ultimate principles, and evolve, out of the hitherto partially revealed purpose of Islām, that spiritual democracy which is the ultimate aim of Islām.

But revelation implies that human is not left to their own resources. To come, however, to Iqbāl's concrete example,

> The Turks argue that in our political thinking we must be guided by our past political experience which points unmistakably to the fact that the universal Imamate (Caliphate) has failed in practice .... Abū Bakr Bāqilānī dropped the condition of *Qurshiyat* (i.e., belonging to the tribe of Quraish) in the Khalīfah in view of the facts of experience .... Ibn Khaldūn who personally believed in the condition .... argued much in the same way. Since the power of the Quraish, he says, is gone there is no alternative but to accept the most powerful man as imam in the country where he happens to be powerful.

It is not our task to write a critique of Sir Muḥammad Iqbāl's interesting lectures but we would point out that if the logic of facts drives a man to compromise with principles, it may end in his discarding religion and, in the case of a Muslim, in his discarding Islām, for the same man who argued that in Islām prophecy came to realize the need for its own abolition. Might at last be constrained to argue that in Islām religion came to realize the need for its abolition.

Another matter which occupies the attention of the re-interpreters of Islām is the relation of Islām to race. In his *Six Lectures*, Sir Mu⊠ammad Iqbāl writes "Liberalism has a tendency to act as a force of disintegration which appears to be working in modern Islām with greater force than ever and may ultimately wipe off the broad human outlook which the Islāmic people have imbibed from their religion." How to reconcile the universalism of Islām with the new nationalism due to the liberals? Bowing again to the logic of facts, Iqbāl, in his pamphlet *Islām and Aḥmadism*, says

> Islām looks askance at Nature's race-building plans and creates by means of its peculiar institutions an outlook which would counteract the race-building forces of nature .... Yet it cannot be said that Islām is totally opposed to race. Its history shows that in social reform it relies mainly on its scheme for gradual deracialization and proceeds on the lines of least resistance .... Considering the mightiness of the problem of race, and the amount of time which the deracialization of mankind must necessarily take, the attitude of Islām towards the problem of race, i.e., stooping to conquer without itself becoming a race-making factor is the only rational and workable attitude .... It is clear that if the Ata Turk is inspired by Pan-Turanianism he is going not so much against the spirit of Islām as against the spirit of the times. And if he is a believer in the absoluteness of races, he is sure to be defeated by the spirit of modern times which is wholly in keeping with the spirit of Islām. Personally, however I do not think that the Ata Turk is inspired by Pan-Turanianism, as I believe his Pan-Turanianism is only a political retort to Pan-Slavonism, or Pan-Germanism or Pan-Anglo-Saxonism. Nationalism comes into conflict with Islām only when it begins to play the role of a political concept and claims to be a principle of human solidarity demanding that Islām should recede into the background and cease to be a living factor in the national life.

The obvious comment on this is that we cannot understand what is meant by Kamal Pasha's opposition being rather to the spirit of the times than to the spirit of Islām, when the spirit of the times "is wholly in keeping with the spirit of Islām."

Advocates of the reinterpretation of Islām are constantly referring to the Muslim's enslavement to the past and in the *Muslim Revival*, a monthly journal in English, dated June 1933, there is an interesting article by Professor Salīm. In this he argues for modern commentaries, on the Qur'ān and compares the sad plight of Muslim exegesis with the wealth of commentaries on the Bible. Under the influence of traditionalism, Muslims "ceased to study the Qur'ān independently. To do so was heresy and heterodoxy." "They ceased to make use of their common sense; they lost their power of discretion, their right of private judgment and finally all trace of an enlightened nation, for no fault of their own, except through the evil influence of the slave-mentality, this refusal to do something, not done previously by the 'ulamā' of the second and third century Hijra."

They also ceased to exercise their critical faculties with regard to the reported sayings of Muḥammad.

> All inquiry regarding the sources and all criticism regarding the contents and the reporters of the traditions came to be looked upon as heresy and irreligion.... Muslims do feel that it is derogatory to the status of a Prophet to tell lies; but neither can they purge Bukhārī (a standard collection of traditions about Muḥammad) of such traditions, nor can they bring out a new collection according to the modern standards of truth and piety. Shī'as, Aryas and Christians draw the well-known contingent of their objections from these very 'authentic traditions' and Muslims in their heart of hearts feel that these traditions are untrustworthy; but they dare not expunge them from the canonical books of traditions.

The writer then proceeds to say that when such opinions are voiced, the critic is asked "Are you wiser than Bukhārī that you dare to differ from him?" "How is it that nobody during the last seven hundred years ever differed from them on any point." The Christian might reply to that last question that it is only now that the impact of Christian teaching as created a new conscience with regard to these matters that Muslims have seen the necessity for expunging from the records certain unacceptable traditions.

We can sympathize with the writer in his desire for a purer faith, but we would point out that the attitude "I don't like it, therefore

I must expunge it," is not a principle of sound exegesis. Historical documents must be accepted for what they are worth and history cannot be expurgated by a subjective test. There can be no tampering with documents however inconvenient they may be unless the study of earlier historical documents warrants the revision. Expurgation may entirely alter the character of a book. An entire break with traditional interpretation would lead to all sorts of reconstructions which would be mutually destructive and end in chaos. In the absence of material to serve for the revision of the Traditions it might be necessary to give them up altogether and then much that throws light on the meaning of the Qur'ān would have to be rejected. Another dilemma is that if the traditions are forfeited, the Sunnat, on which Islāmic practice is founded to a remarkable degree, would also have to go. Although Sir Muḥammad Iqbāl seems even to contemplate the possibility of this, for he says in respect to the Ḥadīth in their relation to Islāmic law, "If modern Liberalism considers it safer not to make any indiscriminate use of them as a source of law, it will only be following one of the greatest exponents of Muḥammadan law in Sunnī Islām," i.e. Abū Ḥanīfah.

In the course of the modern attempts to reinterpret Islām in harmony with modern thought there is a tendency to make a distinction between what is permissible and what is enjoined in the Qur'ān. For instance it is said that polygamy is permitted under certain conditions. Maulānā Muḥammad 'Alī in his commentary on the Qur'ān at sūrah 4 v.3 which he translates "And if you fear that you cannot act equitably towards orphans, then marry such women as seem good to you, two and three and four etc." makes this comment, "This passage permits polygamy under certain circumstances: it does not enjoin it nor even permit it unconditionally." Whether this makes the case better for Islām must be considered very doubtful, especially as the condition expressed in the Qur'ān is one which only the person concerned can judge to be fulfilled and a man who had a desire for a number of wives would not find much difficulty in considering himself qualified for the "permission." But to show how indeterminate the principles of the new interpretation are, we give a quotation from the Light of March 16th this year. This paper is the organ of the Lahore branch of the Aḥmadiyyah of which Maulānā Muḥammad 'Alī is the spiritual head.

> In our comments on Sir Muḥammad Iqbāl's statement in our issue for February 1st we expressed our disagreement with the Allāmah's (i.e., Iqbāl's), view that "the Amīr of a Muslim State has the power to revoke the permissions of the law if he is convinced that they tend to cause social corruption." Attempts have been made to defend this view by drawing a line of distinction between an 'injunction' and a 'permission.' Polygamy, it is contended, is only a 'permission' not an 'injunction' and hence it could be revoked by the head of a Muslim State. We confess we fail to see the nice distinction between a 'permission' and an 'injunction.' To us both are the decrees of God and equally binding on a Muslim and no power on earth can revoke what has been definitely decreed by God. Ḥazrat 'Umar preached that large dowries should not be settled on wives. On this a woman got up and read a verse of the Qur'ān which 'permitted' large dowries. 'Who are you to withhold from us,' she said, 'what God gives us?' 'Umar bowed to the authority of the Qur'ān and even complimented the woman on her knowledge, saying, 'Women of Medina have better knowledge of the law of Islām than Umar.' This clearly shows two things. Firstly that a Qur'ānic 'permission' has as much the force of law as a Qur'ānic 'injunction' and secondly, that the Amir has no authority to overrule the Qur'ān in the matter of such 'permissions.'

Questions relating to the status of women are to the fore in the course of the new interpretation of Islām and there is much conflict of opinion. Deoband, the orthodox centre passes a resolution condemning the United Provinces Legislative Council's decision regarding compulsory education for girls and in the Punjab there is an agitation for degree classes for girls. With regard to the question of polygamy some say that it is not permitted in Islām! Others say it is permitted only in time of war. Others again say it is permitted when there is no issue and others that it is only permitted when there is equality of treatment of the several wives. In this last connection a leader which appeared in the Civil and Military Gazette of Lahore on January 3rd, 1936, is interesting.

> Polygamy may be recognized by the religions or the customs of the East but it does not find recognition in the interpretation which the authorities have decided to put on the electoral rules under the new Indian constitution. Doubts it is understood arose recently about the

> interpretation of the rule which enfranchises a wife on the strength of her husband's property.

Under this rule the wife of a man who was a voter under the old constitution is entitled to vote under the new constitution. The rule enfranchises 376,000 women. "The question then arose, 'What about a man with more than one wife?' The rule is now that only the first wife will be entitled to vote." Because Islām enjoins equivalent rights for each wife, what will be the practical result? Some may say that this revokes the 'permissions' of the Qur'ān because it makes it impossible for the rule of equivalent treatment to obtain when a man has a number of wives, and where a man has already a number of wives then how can the Qur'ānic injunction of equality be observed? It is by such illustrations that we gather how difficult the task of the modernist in Islām must be.

There are two very clear characteristics of all that has come to our notice, namely, propaganda and defence. Even the most conservative seem to justify their opposition to change by their zeal for defence. The Ahl-i-Ḥadīth considers that the slavish following of the four schools of jurisprudence handicaps the defence of Islām in the modern world. The Ahl-i-Qur'ān rejects the Traditions for similar reasons. The Muslim League with its emphasis on Muslim solidarity, the sensitiveness to the rights of the Muslim community behind the communal strife with regard to Shahīdganj, the earnest endeavour of the poet-philosopher Sir Muḥammad Iqbāl to encourage self-respect in young Muslims (a frequent theme in his poetry) his anxiety to bring Islām into line with the spirit of change and development in the West and to prove that Islām has in it the principles which will enable it to adapt itself to a new age, all point in the same direction. The attack he has made on the Aḥmadiyyah, afraid lest it might mean disintegration of Islām, the Aḥmadiyyah movement itself—a purely propagandist movement as we see it—many and various and sometimes even contradictory schools of thought and policy, all are animated by a spirit of loyalty to the community. Men plunge headlong into controversy for the honour of Islām. Often their zeal outruns their knowledge and they hardly see where they are being carried by their enthusiasm. No one will worry much about other things if a defender has zeal for Islām. In the *Light* of December 16th where some remarks are made about a certain propagandist, we have an illustration of this.

> We knew that his … Association was a thing more in the printed notepaper of that association than a genuine over-board [*sic*] affair. Many a friend even accused us of suppressing the truth. Our sole justification was what Ḥazrat 'Āyesha said about Ḥasan. We know he is a good propagandist and an energetic worker. He has been doing propaganda work on behalf of Islām and so we considered it uncharitable to strain at his weaknesses.

In reply to Sir Muḥammad Iqbāl, the leader of the Aḥmadiyyah points to the record of its missionary work. In effect it is said "We are the most active missionary agency in Islām. Why stab us in the back while we are engaged in this work. Let our work speak for us. Our zeal for strengthening this Society should not be a cause of complaint to any Muslim, in view of the fact that we are a vigorous missionary organization." What is not always seen is that in the intensity of zeal, a position may be taken up which cannot be ultimately justified and which may, for a temporary advantage, become at some later time an embarrassment to fundamental Islām, or at least a source of perplexity to the conservative masses.

A correspondent writing to the *Light* voices the opinion of many orthodox when he says that circumcision "plays an important part in the life of a Muslim," and that "it is essential for *Ṭahārat* (purification) which is the basic principle of all religious performances." The Editor considers the matter important enough for an editorial and says: "We could hardly believe that any Muslim would insist on circumcision as indispensable for the purpose of acceptance of Islām."

As a proof of how Islām in India as a whole is taking to heart its missionary task, it may be noted that in the Depressed Classes' Conference at Lucknow in May, no less than seven Muslim missionary organizations were represented: Shī'a, Sunnī, Qādiyānī and Aḥmadī. But here *vis-a-vis* their opponents points of difference did not emerge and an unreal unity remained to be the ground of mutual congratulation. So long as the all-important requirement of loyalty to the community is observed and verbal concord preserved this is all that is asked. The Unity of God may be interpreted as monotheism or as the wildest pantheism and both interpretations will be tolerated. Requirements may be whittled down to such a bare minimum that Islām in its practice may achieve a nominal unity but it will be barren indeed, and even as its *via negativa* banishes the Deity into obscure remoteness, so must its devotees' suppression of their private convictions result in only an apparent harmony within which are all the elements of ultimate disintegration.

People who are fearful for their self-respect are not infrequently betrayed into extravagances which expose their weaknesses. The present-day Muslim propagandist would seek to stimulate self-respect by references to the past glories of Islām. This is quite legitimate and there is much of which Muslims may be rightly proud but when Islām's past greatness is brought into the most inappropriate context and is entirely irrelevant to the theme under discussion one wonders whether the writers have become conscious of the weakness of the case they have set out to prove and are seeking to distract the attention of the reader from this weakness. When exposition fails the golden rule seems to be: Extol the glories of Islām. In a similar manner when keenly sensitive of the decline of Islām, self-respect is sought in referring to the past and conclusions are drawn from the glory of a past age which are not warranted by the present state of Islām. Islām is the patron of learning because there was a University at Cordova and in spite of the terrible illiteracy which characterizes the masses of Islām today. Are people who write like this about Islām the best friends of Islām? Are they not in danger of presenting to the minds of young Islām the materials for a most depressing comparison, which is likely to lead to the conclusion that Islām has failed. When a writer can make an appeal to the depressed classes only on the grounds that Muḥammad brought a golden age to Arabia, might not his hearer reply, "Your golden age is in the past and we look for one in the future. Give us proof that you are capable now of founding the golden age; and meanwhile, we prefer British India to Arabia and so do you?" Perhaps the gravest danger in Islām and the greatest obstacle to any progress within the community is the refusal to face facts and the tendency to go on living in an atmosphere of make-believe. In this atmosphere sober men can bring themselves to believe almost anything. Thus the Editor of the *International Review of Missions* is quoted in the *Light* (February 16th, 1936) "Islām is an extraordinary definite religion and has produced a definite moral type .... one of the fruits of Islām has been that stubborn durable patience which comes of the submission to the absolute will of Allāh." On this the writer of the article comments, "The quotation coming as it does from the pen of a hostile Christian missionary must serve as an eye-opener to the critics of Islām. Only a highly ethical religion like Islām could win such a glowing tribute from one whose Mission it is to misrepresent it in other respects!!" Of the same type but more reprehensible is the following from the *Light* (May 8th, 1936) "The churchman is licensed to indulge in 'unrighteousness, if it commends the righteousness of God' (Rom. 3; 5, 7)." Another instance which is rather amusing is a series of articles in a vernacular paper *Faran* on "Muslim Rule in Switzerland."

Similarly, evidence for the wish being farther to the thought is found in the numerous articles on the status of women in Islām. In last year's August number of the *Islāmic Review* the very learned Maulānā Sulaiman Nadwī has the first of a series of articles on *Heroic deeds of Muslim Women.* Starling with the stirring deeds of Augustina Saragossa and Joan of Arc, he writes, "Our history abounds in scores of such gallant actions on the part of Muslim women, *but of the detail we know little or nothing.*" He then proceeds to ransack literature for the sparse references to Muslim heroines whose names are hardly known to the vast majority of Muslims, apparently unconscious of the extraordinary contrast he presents between them and the women whose names are a household word in Christendom. A far better case could be made for Islām if its defenders fought polygamy, purdah and inequalities between the sexes than by re-writing history. *The history which Islām needs to rewrite is the history of the present-day.* We commend this view to our Muslim friends in all sincerity.

When we consider the propagandist and defensive literature with regard to the Prophet Muḥammad, we have further evidence of extreme sensitiveness. There must be thousands of atheistical books on sale in India in which Almighty God is spoken of in terms which rouse indignation but seldom do we hear a protest about such books, but if an unfortunate sentence occurs with regard to the Prophet, a storm of indignation is roused.

In the Legislative Assembly on March 27th, a question was asked by Sir Muḥammad Yaqūb with regard to a picture of Muḥammad which had appeared in *Every Woman's Magazine* and an offensive article which had appeared in another English journal. He said that he wanted the Secretary of State to be informed of Muslim feeling and of the necessity for stopping such publications and pictures, by bringing pressure to bear on the English press and press associations in England. Sir Henry Craik replied,

> The Secretary of State has already taken action in the matter. On the article being brought to his notice, he wrote to the editor of the paper in question, drawing his attention to the objectionable features in it. He has further issued a circular to all British editors through their professional associations, calling their attention to the offensiveness of such articles to Muslim feeling and warning them of the main points to be avoided when writing any articles on Islām. The Associations have conveyed this warning to their members.

In view of these facts it will perhaps be a matter of surprize to Christians that there are at the present time numerous books attacking the Lord Jesus Christ procurable in India. Let us see what some of them contain. "Mary was dedicated to the Temple so that she might remain forever in the service of the Holy Place and remain unmarried all her days. But when it became plain that she was six or seven months pregnant, the leaders of the nation married her to a man named Joseph, a carpenter and she went to his house and after a month or two her son was born."[1] "We cannot even admit that such an evil-minded, overbearing and enemy of the righteous could be called a gentleman let alone a prophet."[2] "See how extremely pure and chaste his family was. Three of his grandmothers were adulteresses and harlots whose blood came out in his blood."[3] "He had the confirmed habit of using bad language and giving abuse and to some extent had the habit of speaking lies."[4] These are the products of Qādiyān. Orthodox Muslims are at one with Christians in considering them obnoxious. They wonder why the Government has not suppressed them. Might not we also ask, why?

Endnotes

1 *Chashma-i-Masihi* (The Christian Fount), 17 and 18.

2 *Anjam-i-Atham* (The End of Atham), 5.

3 Comment in Appendix to *Anjam i-Atham*, 7.

4 *Anjam i-Atham*, 5.

New Missionary Dimensions

James Windrow Sweetman

Under the above title an article has appeared in *Christendom*, by Dr. Hugh Vernon White, Secretary of the American Board of Commissioners for Foreign Missions, who has recently returned from a tour of the field served by his board. Those who are interested in the evangelization of the Muslim people will find food for thought in what he has written and will probably find themselves in opposition to his findings, though we are glad to see that the question of the relation of the Christian enterprise to the Muslim world has occupied some of his time. We reproduce the passages of greater interest to us as a League.

> A radical departure from proselyting is called for in the relations of Christianity with Muslim peoples. The most impressive and imposing fact that I encountered during a year in the Orient is the fact of Islām. Despite its present moribund condition there is a solidarity in the Muslim world and an imperviousness to missionary propaganda that should cause serious reconsideration of our aim and method. Looked at in the large, the prospects of converting Muslims to Christianity are not at all encouraging. From the days of Raymond Lull, one of the most winsome and devoted of Christian missionaries down to the present time, Christian efforts to evangelise the Muslim have met with signal and consistent failure. The response to such efforts to-day is negligible and there is little likelihood of any marked change in the near future.
>
> There are many reasons for the solidarity of Islām and its resistance to the Christian missionary approach. It is not sufficient to dismiss the matter by characterizing the Muslim as fanatical or conservative. He may be both on occasion, but even to the casual observer certain more positive

and reasonable grounds appear for his attitude to Christianity. The rise of Islām constituted a great reform, religious, social and moral. It created a whole culture and rendered a great service to a part of the world where decadent paganism, Judaism and Christianity made the need for reform desperate. The modern Muslim knows this and takes a just pride in it. Further he is profoundly convinced that Islām is a distinctly better religion than Christianity and most of his historic contacts with Christianity give considerable justification for this conviction. These contacts have caused him to look upon Christianity as barbarous, idolatrous, polytheistic and morally impotent, and the Christianity that he has known has been all that. Beside it has usually been allied with political powers seeking conquest.

In the face of the history and the consequent attitude of the Muslim, the direct attempt to make proselytes to any orthodox form of Christianity, Roman or Protestant is useless and can do positive harm unless it is carried on with rare grace, humility and wisdom. As to the old churches with their emphasis on the trinity and their icons, the Muslim feels towards them about as a modern Protestant would feel toward an attempt to win him to a veneration of relics in a Roman Catholic Church. In matters of ritual and dogma the historic church has little that will ever appeal to the Muslim world and that little is so bound up with elements that are positively repugnant to him that he will never be able to see them without bias.

But fortunately Christianity does not need to come to Islām in such a guise. And the thing in the Christian Gospel that is vital is none of these elements that he so abominates. That vital essence is the moral content of the Gospel and the relation between God and human that it teaches. The old Christian theologies which Islām has heard bear very remote relation to this ethical and spiritual Christianity. They are symbols but symbols which even for modern Christians need much interpretation and explanation before it can be seen that they really did once have relation to the essential interests of the Christian life. But the person of Christ and His teaching and the work of human whose lives truly express His way of love and service—these constitute not alone the really important thing in Christianity but also the universal language of the human spirit. Here is a Gospel that the Muslim ought to have, and for some time to come it will be a distinct gain if we can have it apart from all connection with the religious beliefs and practices that he has abhorred and apart from any attempt to persuade him to renounce Islām and be baptised into some Protestant sect. The Christian Church ought to quit trying to make proselytes of Muḥammadans. It should bring the best works of Christian service to the Moslem world in a spirit of ecclesiastical disinterestedness.

> As to the matter of religious belief there is a great need for open intercourse without propagandist intent between the best interpreters of Christian thought and the leaders of Islām. Especially is there need for this today when at least a few Muslim scholars are using the technique and categories of Western thought and are determined to bring about a thorough reform in Muslim theology. The intellectual and social movements of the modern world are forcing changes in Islām. It is the high responsibility of the Christian Church to present in the most helpful and adequate manner the great conceptions and ideals of the Christian faith.
>
> Such a programme has its own difficulties and obstacles. It may call for more imagination and faith than the modern church has; for that matter most of the church will probably reject this proposal out of hand. But such a mission goes to the heart of the matter. It goes the whole way of disinterestedness in renouncing the intention to create some special form of Christian Church within Islām. The form that is to be taken by any fellowship which seeks to promote and conserve the truth that comes from Christianity would be left to the people of Islām. Whether such fellowship would be called a Christian Church is not important. But it will be unimportant to have the spirit and teaching of Christ truly understood and faithfully lived within Islām.
>
> It is an open question whether the church or any very considerable part of it can maintain enthusiasm for such a disinterested mission. If, as has been repeatedly affirmed, missionary zeal can only be developed with a mission that satisfies the ecclesiastical ambition, the dogmatic temper and the desire to win stars for our crowns by making proselytes then this is a proposal that will have little appeal. But there are many missionaries now actually working in the new spirit and they are amongst the finest representatives of the Western Church. There are growing numbers in the churches to whom the logic and objective of such a mission will come as an expression of their own desire. This may be the new kind of Christian mission which many of us have been seeking, the result both of the wisdom born of experience and of a bolder apprehension of the nature of our Christian responsibility to the world.

Space forbids the adequate discussion of all the points raised in this article. Our general attitude to the whole question is contained in the article in these notes entitled *What are our Plans?* Dr. Bowman of Saharanpur and Dr. Donaldson of Meshed, have both replied to the article in the *Moslem World* of January this year. Dr. Bowman says,

> Dr. White has pointed out what we agree to be a confusion in the use of the words 'to convert' and 'to proselytize.' But there is a more fundamental error than this in the use of these words, and into this error he himself falls. That is, the use of both these words interchangeably for the term 'to evangelize.'... Evangelism is one thing; proselytising is quite something else. The former is the simple proclamation of the Gospel message in the faith that the Word of God, which is sharper than any two-edged sword, will pierce to the roots of personality and work the will of God in renewal and revivification (Heb. iv. 12). The latter is something that depends on the frailty of human method, produces its fruit after the human pattern (Matt. xxiii. 35), and is rightly condemned by the peoples of every race among whom it is tried .... Now if by 'a radical departure from proselyting' Dr. White could bring himself to mean that evangelism in the New Testament sense of detachment should proceed, while the willy-nilly making of proselytes from Islām ought to cease, then I can assure him that the end he seeks is already achieved in numerous mission fields today. I speak out of a wealth of experience of the work that is going forward among the Moslems of North India. .... There is a goodly band of Indian and missionary workers there ... proclaiming the Gospel message in a spirit of detachment such as can only spring from a genuine reverence for personality on the one hand and from a lively sense of the fact that the power is all of God, on the other. Their sole aim is to present Christ and Him crucified in the faith that the Word of God, which alone can change the hearts of men, will eventually grip these lives and turn them from darkness unto the Light.

We are in hearty agreement with Dr. Bowman. Dr. Donaldson puts a criticism in the mouth of a Muslim who is attracted to Christianity but who has never had the courage to make a definite spiritual decision, and who feels the inadequacy of his present position.

From our experience of the Muslim mentality, we can see little to commend the main point of view of Mr. White's article. Inoculation confers immunity. Through its long history Islām has had frequent inoculations of Christianity and its organism has developed a resistance to the contagion of Christianity. Call that resistance 'fanaticism' or 'conservatism' it makes no difference. Until there comes some deep and drastic disturbance of the whole organism by piercing deeply to the heart of the personal units of which it is composed or, to leave our metaphor, until personal conviction is awakened and the dynamic of the Gospel re-energizes the soul of the Muslim we see little hope of any marked change in Islām of the nature of a re-orientation of its thought and ethic towards Christianity.

Dr. Bowman asks, "What sort of 'disinterestedness' is that which seeks to gain the Muslim by permitting that to go unsaid which may prove repugnant to him?" Would not the Christian be accused by the Muslim of hedging? It is also far too lightly assumed that while theological approach to Islām may be fruitless, the exhibition of the ethic of Christianity will be acceptable. Quite apart from the question of differing theological views, the Muslim antagonism is a root a branch antagonism and extends equally to the Christian ethic as found in the teaching of Christ, as to the dogmas of Christianity. Modernist Islām attacks the Sermon on the Mount on the grounds of its impracticability. It accepts its own system of legalistic ethics as an authoritative system. Exemplification of the Christian ethic may in some cases win admiration and this must be an integral part of the Christian witness. Christianity has succeeded in raising vast numbers of the depressed classes in India to a higher moral standard and Muslims have looked on and even blessed what one Muslim friend described to the writer of this article as *making human out of animals*. But this process of uplift is not markedly bringing Muslims to Christ but, as another Muslim said, is rather regarded as bringing the depressed classes into "the half-way house to Islām."

It is our experience that however much we may be able to exhibit the Christian morale, the Muslim will not suffer theological questions to be shelved and it is because they are so frequently shelved by Christians that the Muslim tends to become more and more confirmed in his views of the superiority of Islām. Often the theological enthusiasm of the Muslim is in strange contrast to a certain rationalizing laicism in reluctant advocates of an attenuated Christianity. If the Christian is content to be silent about the Trinity or to relegate it to oblivion, this will not propitiate the Muslim and make him ready to accept Christian truth. He will continue his triumphant way till he has silenced the Christian on the matter of the authenticity of the New Testament and then invite him to accept Islām. In his dealings with Muḥammadans what the Christian needs is not less theology but more and better theology. One of the complaints we have frequently to make is that Christian theology has hardly any time to express itself in relation to the thought world of Islām and some of us are bending our energies to this task. But to impose on ourselves a silence with respect to our theology is not honest and does not do justice to the intellectual travail of Christianity. It will result in our becoming more inarticulate than we already are and place us in an invidious position when confronted with Islām's dogmatic assurance.

Far from adumbrating a new plan to avoid the 'proselyting' of Muslims, Dr. White is only making explicit that defeatist attitude which has for some time cast its shadow over missionary policy. The time has come indeed for new recommendations with regard to our witness to Islām but those can never include the facile adoption of the dogmatic unitarianism of Islām as the basis of a Christian infiltration of that religion. We plead for a deeper and clearer conception of what Islām really is, doctrinally, morally, culturally, a just appreciation of the relations of Islām and Christianity in history and the very substantial interchange of thought between the two, a clearer apprehension of what we have to offer to Islām—the power of God unto salvation. We do not plead for skilled controversialists but for well-informed advocates with clear, positive, unfaltering evangelism. We too, would summon the Christian Church to a discipline and an adventure, calling for more Christ-like behaviour and in addition a travail of thought and spiritual preparation to preach the unsearchable riches of Christ with acceptance.

Qur'ān Taurāt and Injīl

Qāzī Muḥammad Sulaiman
***Translated by** James Windrow Sweetman*

The following is the translation of a reply of Qāzī Muḥammad Sulaimān of Mansurpur to a Christian minister's question as to the mutual relations of the Taurāt, the Prophetic Writings, the Gospel and the Qur'ān.

First Answer: You have written in your letter in one place that the Taurāt is the Law and the Injīl its fulfilment (*kamāl*). So accepting this as correct I have only to say that the Qur'ān is the 'Muhaimin' (protector). The meaning of 'Muhaimin' is 'collector,' the collector of the Law and the fulfilment. This name of the Qur'ān is in the Qur'ān itself but I doubt whether its name 'kamāl' is in the Injīl or not.

Second Answer: In the Taurāt and the Qur'ān there is one characteristic which is not in the Injīl, viz., the words and phrases of the Taurāt and Qur'ān were published in the lifetime of Moses and Muḥammad respectively. But none of the present Gospels had the honour to come to the notice of Christ. From the history of the writing and compilation of the Gospels of Matthew, Mark, Luke and John which you, Sir, will have read in the Mission School, it is known that they were written after the ascension of Christ. And the date of the compilation of some is seventy-five years after Christ. There is thus in comparison with the Taurāt and the Qur'ān this difference in the Injīl, which is self-evident, which Christian scholars admit and which no Christian scholar can deny, for Luke says in the beginning of his Gospel,

> For as much as many have taken in hand to draw up a narrative concerning those matters which have been fulfilled among us, even as they delivered them unto us, which from the beginning were eye-witnesses and ministers of the word, it seemed good to me also, having traced the course of all things accurately from the first, to write, unto thee in order, most excellent Theophilus; That thou mightest know the certainty concerning the things wherein thou wast instructed.

Gospel and Ḥadīth

We should be grateful to Luke, that he has told us that he had first sought correctly the tradition which had reached him and then compiled it. From this account it is established that these Gospels should be ranked with the Ḥadīth among Muslims for these also have been related by great scholars.

The Superiority of the Ḥadīth over the Gospels

How be it, the books of Ḥadīth will remain superior because with the traditions they have related the chain of reporters and the life of each one and have also described the principles which each writer observed at the time of his enquiry. But none of these things is in the Gospels. After Luke's testimony, you will see that the Gospel is devoid of that necessary and most excellent quality which the Qur'ān and the Taurāt had.

The Comparative Test of the Authenticity of the Gospels

You will know that some matters related in Matthew, Mark, John and Luke do not agree with one another. Except for Luke no other writer has said that he has written these traditions after correct enquiry. Shall we therefore think that we should accept only Luke's Gospel as correct? Then what shall we say the writings of those two of whom it is said that they themselves saw the works of Christ. If they are correct then what is the meaning of what Luke writes? As far as I know Luke is the distinguished disciple of Paul, and Paul is the one who Christian scholars believe was arrested from the World of Spirit by Christ's spiritual presence. For this reason Paul in many doctrines rebuked the disciples whom Christ had chosen from before him for His teaching. In short, after thinking of all these different points it becomes difficult for a critic to consider the Gospel in this respect equal to Taurāt and Qur'ān.

The Taurāt and the Qur'ān

There remains the question whether the Taurāt also is equal to the Qur'ān. There is no doubt that those two tablets which Moses brought down from the mountain were equal to the Qur'ān. Then the copies which Moses made of those two tablets were also equal to the Qur'ān, but the question whether the five books which are attributed to Moses in the present Bible can be considered equal to the Qur'ān or not is worth study.

The Opinions of Christian and Jewish Scholars about the Taurāt

In the opinions of Christian and Jewish scholars about these books there are extraordinary differences. There is difference between those who accept the Mosaic origin of the books and they do not regard them as *waḥī* at all. The famous critic Pusey's belief was that the book of Genesis was written by Moses when he stayed with his father-in-law in Midian i.e, before he became a prophet.

From these differences it is certain that that portion of the present Taurāt is equal to the Qur'ān which without any question is inspired. That portion is only the Ten Commandments and at the first glance it is credible that on them there will be no dispute. But the founder of the Protestant religion, Luther's harsh remarks about these commandments and those who practise them make the heart quake.

The Other Writings and Jewish and Christian Scholars

By the writings of the Prophets you will probably mean those writings the collection of which is included in the Bible of the present day, but Jewish and Christian scholars are not agreed about these either. The Jewish sect of the Samaritans does not accept any book but the Pentateuch, Joshua and the Book of Judges. You will know that with regard to the Book of Judges, Dr. Lightfoot says it is written by Phineas,

... (an unknown name) says Eleazar, Watson says Samuel, Henry says Jeremiah. With regard to the authors and the date of writing of the Book of Judges there are thus these differences. This is the case with many books and with regard to some of the books the opinions of Jewish and Christian scholars is very drastic. The Book of Job is called a story of an imaginary person. Watson says the Song of Songs is an erotic song. The author of the Proverbs of Solomon is said to be the guardian of a prince. Some say that of the Psalms only ten chapters are the prayers of David; some say twenty; some say the Book of Psalms is the writing of Adam, Abraham, Moses, Asaph, Jeduthan, Solomon and the sons of Noah.

There are nine books in this collection which the Jews do not accept at all and Christians also have differences concerning them. In these circumstances my friends question "what is their relation to the Qur'ān", is surprising. The reply to this is implied in the historical matters which Christian scholars have gathered for us. If my respected correspondent does not like this, then I have no need to insist further upon it. Prefer my first answer which I gave in your own words. The Taurāt is the law (Sharī'at) the Gospel fulfilment (*kamāl*) and the Qur'ān Preserver (Muhaimin). You will not admit that the Qur'ān is a Preserver though you are ready to admit that it is a law. To prove the fact that the Qur'ān is a Preserver, I have to establish two things: first that it is like the Taurāt, Law, and second, like the Injīl, Grace and Fulfilment. You accept the first premise so now please tell me why the second proposition is denied? Is there any teaching in the Injīl which is not in the Qur'ān?

The Special Teaching of the Injīl

Reading the above words of mine perhaps your mind will turn immediately to Atonement, Trinity, Sonship and Divinity. And it is possible that you may wish to write to me, that these are the special tenets, and mysteries, riddles and abstruse matters which are not found in the Qur'ān. But before you think this and put it in writing it is necessary for you to think that in my opinion and in the opinion of all Muslims the Words of Christ can be pleaded in proof but that the words of any other have not this value. Do not put forward as proof instead of the words of Christ some other person's idea or interpretation or some confirmation of a religious council; and when with this caution you seek for proofs, then you will not find any new thing in the whole of the Gospels which is not in the Qur'ān. Probably with Christians no Gospel is held in greater esteem that the Gospel of John. But it too will be found to fall short in this claim. God forbid that it should be my intention in this place to say anything against the value of any one of the four Gospels for this is not my practice but my meaning is that in fact these tenets and meanings cannot be extracted from the four Gospels.

Unitarians and the Doctrine of Sonship etc

I will put their writings forward in confirmation of this and also the agreed opinions of religious councils. And these will give cumulative proof that if the four Gospels themselves could have been considered sufficient for these doctrines, all this labour and endeavour was useless.

The Qur'ān is the Muhaimin

In short, I hold these doctrines on investigation to be later than Christ. And with the exception of these so far as you can prove from the Injīl other doctrines in reference to human perfection and the knowledge of the Divine, there can be shown to you in the Qur'ān with great perfection and greater light and clarity, with which a critic may well rest content, that the Qur'ān has indeed the status of a Preserver. Here is finished the first reply. In comparison with the importance of the subject the reply is short but it is hoped it will be sufficient to make my meaning clear.

Comparison of the Contents of the Qur'ān with the Bible

When I am writing here of the Qur'ān being a Preserver, I wish to suggest that some Christian scholars investigate the Qur'ān in their own way and it is this. "We will place the subjects of the Qur'ān alongside the Bible and will see what part of it is in accordance with the Bible and what not. That which is in accordance is correct and that which is not, not worthy of acceptance." This method is apparently a good one but it is deceitful. It is good because it is done from God's Word, therefore no one should deny and it is deceitful because with this principle no Christian scholar will care for the New Testament i.e., the Gospels, Acts and Epistles to be compared with the Old Testament. On behalf of the Muslims I am prepared to suggest that we are ready to act on this principle.

It is clear that to put this principle into practice it must first of all be agreed as to what part of the Word is to be accepted, as the basis of comparison with all the other parts.

The Criterion of Comparison

To settle the dispute we agree that the oldest books of the Old Testament be given this status i.e., the books of Moses be accepted as a criterion and then each teaching be set beside these books in the order of the date at which it is found in the world, that is from Joshua to the book of the prophet Malachi, and that everything or every lesson in these books which is not in accord with Moses' teaching be abandoned. After this, this method be applied to Matthew, Mark, Luke, and John. The investigator will then be amazed when he sees how much agreement and unity there is in all the books of the Old Testament and what various ways and numerous phrases they relate one claim.

The New Teaching of the New Testament

But as soon as the New Testament begins a new door opens and the perplexity and confusion of the seeker for concordance keeps on increasing. To escape this confusion the poor investigator sometimes would like to think that the word 'old' is an excuse for the old not being in accordance with the new.

Discrepancies in the Gospels

Therefore it is better that the books of the New Testament should be harmonised. When the unfortunate looks at these books with this intention, the facts in Matthew he does not find in Luke and many things in Luke are not found in Mark. And what shall we say about John. It exceeds the other three in "principles and fundamentals." It can be expected that in this case the Christian investigator will altogether set aside this Gospel which is the most peculiar and teaches new doctrines. But the denouncement is quite unexpected for this Gospel is given the highest rank and is said to be the special Gospel of the Person of Christ. After it the Acts and the Epistles come to his sight.

Paul's Difference with the Disciples

The investigator will quickly see how James, Barnabas and Peter, etc., explaining Christ's teaching but Paul's account does not agree with theirs for there are several doctrines on which Paul is firm in his opinion and does not listen to the word of the disciples whom Christ made His witnesses and chose as his elect above the whole world. This causes the Christian investigator some perplexity and he only understands one way of escape from it and it is this: that he should leave his investigation and apply it to the Qur'ān. We welcome this critic and are frankly ready to join in the investigation and be able to gather together sufficient ideas on the subject. However, to remove our ignorance we first wish to ask whether you, dear Sir, are going to begin first with the task of harmonising the Qur'ān with the Injīl, or with the Taurāt? For our part, you are free to begin your task either way.

If you wish first to harmonise the Qur'ān with the Taurāt and in both books in a majority of places there is harmony and unity but the contents of the Injīl do not square with these, then whose is the victory? And if in some doctrines the Qur'ān and Injīl are at one and there remains a difference with the Taurāt then shall the Taurāt be abandoned? Probably forsaking the Taurāt will be difficult because you first of all reckoned it the criterion. Now will you give up the Qur'ān and the Injīl? If you are ready to do so we will have no complaint that in the case of the Qur'ān and Injīl being in harmony you also leave those doctrines which the Qur'ān alone relates. But if finding most of the doctrines in the Injīl contrary to the Taurāt, you neither doubt the Taurāt nor are the peculiar differences of the Injīl able to shake your assurance and faith, then in that case the Muslims will say with great emphasis that you cannot object to those things which are peculiar to the Qur'ān.

My Dear Sir, I have written the above because your question was about the mutual relations of these three books. I would draw your attention to the many facilities for divorce there are in the Taurāt and how Christ allowed divorce only for adultery although He says that while the earth and heaven remain the Taurāt will not be diminished one jot. I would draw your attention to how the Taurāt insists on circumcision and even that the faithful should not go into the house of the uncircumcised on the Sabbath and, on the contrary, how unnecessary Paul considers circumcision. I would remind you how Christ cursed the Taurāt and what grave differences there were between the disciples of Christ in reference to whether Salvation is by faith or by faith and works. I would remind you that in one place it is said in reference to fasting not being necessary that when the nuptial procession is with the bridegroom he does not die of hunger and in another place the power of working great wonders is made dependent on the observance of prayer and fasting.

In short where scores of similar doctrines are found and a Christian accepts them by faith, he has no right first to invent a principle and then in accord with it to object only to the Qur'ān.

New Development in Indian Islām

James Windrow Sweetman

The Community

It is fitting to begin our enquiry with the Muslim community because the reorganisation, unity and preservation of the community are the chief pre-occupation of Islām today. Sometimes it seems as if Allāh is reduced today to the internal principle of the unification of Islām. When in the latest book written on the Religion of Islām we find in some 700 pages only 33 given to a discussion of the Doctrine of God and 88 pages to marriage alone, this is still further emphasised. Theology is required to take a back seat. Dr. S. N. A. Ja'farī recently gave a lecture before the All-India Philosophical Congress. He roundly declared that Islām was a rule of life rather than a collection of doctrines.

> Nature is God's behaviour. The distinctive feature of Islām is that it takes the empirical view of life and its problems. Its commands and tenets help in keeping an equilibrium between the body and the soul. It teaches us to face facts. The Prophet of Arabia was helped in his mission of creating this empirical attitude by the fact that it is the characteristic of the people of Arabia to hold to the positive, so much so that even in poetry, which is an inspired art, they care more for the concrete than the abstract. The Qur'ān emphasises deed more than idea.... Muḥammad caused an intellectual revolution by stressing the visible more than the invisible. (Note that he first tells us that it was an Arab characteristic and then tells us that Muḥammad wrought a revolution in this respect). There is the crowning principle of *Tawḥīd* in Islām which demands all loyalty to God and this ensures the unity of mankind under one banner ... Islām

> in its attitude towards humanity has even gone so far as to prefer the duty of man towards man to that of man towards God.

In the higher religio-political thinking of Islām there is not lacking the conception of a universal theocracy. In the *Jāmi'a-i milliyah*, the Nationalist Muslim University of Delhi there is a MSS book written by Muḥammad Ali called the *Kingdom of God*. From comments of his on Wells, *God the Invisible King*, I have gathered that his conception is that a simple religious creed without theological, subtleties and an organisation of human society on the lines of Islāmic practices and institutions will bring the golden age.

But the emphasis is always on "under one banner." The brotherhood of humankind is really Islāmic brotherhood. There is a sense in which the brotherhood of the world for which we stand is based on humanity and not on creed. Since our Lord gave the parable of the Good Samaritan, and the breaking down of Jewish prejudices in the early church, Christians have realised their duty to the world outside the Christian community. In Islām however there is always present the tendency to achieve unity by exclusion. Such a unity is really the consolidation of a community and is handicapped at the start in any attempt to universalise itself. An illustration of this can be found in the statesman of June 6th. The Muslim League demands for its better relations with the Congress are such as to proclaim the solidarity of Islām.

> Bande Mataram should be given up.
>
> Muslim majorities in the provinces where such majorities exist at present must not be affected by any territorial re-distribution or adjustments.
>
> Muslims must have freedom to slaughter cows.
>
> The Muslims' right to call *āzān* and perform their religious ceremonies should not be interfered with in any way.
>
> Muslim personal law and culture should be guaranteed by statute.
>
> The share of Muslims in the State services should be definitely fixed in the constitution by statutory enactment.
>
> The Congress should withdraw all opposition to the communal award and should not describe it as the negation of nationalism. Statutory guarantees should be given that the use of Urdu should not be curtailed.
>
> Representation in local bodies should be governed by the principles

underlying the communal award, that is, separate electorates and population strength.

The Congress flag should be changed or, alternatively the flag of the Muslim League should be given equal importance.

Recognition of the Muslim League, as the only authoritative and representative organization of the Muslims.

The formation of coalition Ministries.

The point of all this is that the chief consideration is the united front in Islām and the unity of that community which must not be impaired in any way and that this unity is not to be confined to a unity of spirit but an external and communal unity. Sir Sikandar Ḥayāt Khān said he wanted the Hindus and Muslims to remain as sister communities and remain in peace and good-will. Mr. Fazl al-Ḥaqq the Bengal Premier said that Muslims should unite to protect and defend Islām.

So really the ideal is Pan-Islāmism rather than Divine Theocracy. The God of Islām is useful because he serves the ideal of Islām. In fact one frequently feels that the real object of worship in Islām is Islām itself rather than God.

Islām has always been very strongly community-conscious. In the Arabian Nights in the story of the *Fisherman and the Young King of the Black Isles*, the fish the fisherman caught were of four colours, the white, Muslims; the red, Magians; the blue, Christians; and the yellow, Jews. The custom of the Ottoman Turks was to require the wearing of a special garb by all Christians and the latter suffered all sorts of civil disabilities such as the forfeiting of property as a waqf to the Muslim community. The contention of some enlightened Muslims of the present day that this is peculiarly Turkish and not characteristic of Islām as such, cannot be sustained.

The Light of Lahore asks sadly "Where is the solidarity of Islām? Shall we look for it in the Jami'at al-ulamā, in the Deobandī—Barelvī conflict, in the Sunnī Shī'a feuds, in the struggle of Aḥrār and non- Aḥrār?" Sir Muḥammad Iqbāl attacked the Aḥmadiyyah especially because he considered it a disruptive force in Islām. He even attributed the rise of the sect to intrigues of British Imperialism designed to break up the solidarity of Islām. The Lahori trend to orthodoxy and the infrequency of its advocacy of Mirzā Ghulām Aḥmad may be attributable to the same motive—Let us not destroy the unity of Islām. Muḥammad Ali of Lahore himself deplores the tendency to achieve unity at the expense of liberty of theological thought, and thinks that a middle way can be found whereby there may be freedom of thought and the unity of the community not destroyed. No matter how erroneous an individual's interpretation of Islām may be, let one still be a Muslim. That is his argument. You will notice that this means that no matter how much disunion of spirit there may be, the external unity of Islām must be preserved.

After saying that the direction of prayer is not important the late Sir Muḥammad Iqbāl says,

> Yet we cannot ignore the important consideration that the posture of the body is a real factor in determining the attitude of the mind. The choice of one particular direction in Islāmic worship is meant to secure the unity of feeling in the congregation, and its form in general creates and fosters the sense of social equality as much as it tends to destroy the feeling of rank or race-superiority in the worshippers.

Iqbāl's Lectures in the Reconstruction of Religious Thought in Islām are concerned mainly with the need for the liberation of the community from the "dead hand" of tradition. Hope for the future of Islām lies in a new dynamic conception of Islām along the lines of Bergson's philosophy. Persia and Turkey have made the changes and reforms of recent years in accord with the genius of Islām and not because they have been influenced by non-Islāmic political and social ideals. History must be regarded as a genuinely creative movement and not a movement whose path is already determined. Iqbāl says that this principle of movement in Islām is Ijtihād. The fundamental inconsistency of his thought is that on the one hand he claims that Islām has in itself the power of change and development and yet admits in the same breath that the inertia of Islām is giving way before the impact of forces outside Islām. We would characterise Iqbāl's work in general, in spite of some force and originality, as an undigested mass of Western philosophy and Islāmic terminology.

The Person of Muḥammad

Islām in India and indeed all over the world is attempting to meet the challenge of the person of Christ by presenting an idealised Muḥammad.

The tendency has been on the whole to bring Muḥammad to the Christian standard and then expurgate all that is incompatible with that. Muḥammad's house of women was really a sort of widows' home. Prof. Salīm of Lahore says, "Muslims do feel that it is derogatory to the status of a prophet to tell lies but you cannot purge the pages of Bukhārī nor can they bring out a new collection according to modern standards of truth and piety." We might ask how, if Muḥammad himself is the standard of truth and piety, it turns out that at this late date the records of his sayings and doings have to be expurgated according to a modern standard. We might further ask what is that modern standard? Is it not that which Christ is compelling humankind to judge themselves by? These ideas are characteristic of what one might call the School of Sir Syed Aḥmad. Along with these we find the attempt to prove Islām monogamist in principle etc.

But now there seem to be two other points of view. The first, strange to say, is the intellectuals' avoidance of discussion of the person of Muḥammad. This is especially noticeable in the lecture which I have referred to by Dr. Ja'farī. Some go so far as to say that the test of a Muslim is that one should believe only the first part of the *kalimah*—There is no God but Allāh. Muḥammad Iqbāl in his lectures has nothing to say about the person of the Prophet. In a correspondence he had with Pundit Jawaharlal Nehru he actually says that in Muḥammad prophecy realises the need for its own abolition. Iqbāl's approval of the superman, the man of power and success, is not explicitly applied to the Prophet Muḥammad and may be interpreted to mean that there is no pre-eminence among human but that all are equal and by their very nature are able to absorb into themselves the divine attributes. This at any rate seems to be the teaching of *Isrār-i khudī*—The Secrets of the Self. By this interpretation Muḥammad's dignity is that he came to free human from bondage to any system. Much lip service is given to Iqbāl as the poet-philosopher of Islām but it is highly improbable that all the implications of his philosophy will be allowed to influence Islām in any great degree. However, it must be remembered that the Wahhabis in this country are strongly against what some of them regard as Muḥammad worship. As one such said to me "Muḥammad is nothing but a servant as any other, and it is the glory of Allāh that he needs no particular virtue in the messenger he sends."

On the other hand, the most popular conception of the person of Muḥammad is that he is in himself the supreme ideal. If one could single out any particular new development in Islām which is of outstanding importance in the eyes of the masses it would be the cult of the person of Muḥammad.

Down its long history Islām has shown that it has not been without the hunger for a personal ideal linking the human and the divine. From the very earliest days we find the cult of 'Alī. Later we find the cult of the Ṣūfī saint and this has gained very great hold on the popular imagination. Devotion to a person is very largely the strength of Qādiyān. With these things in the background and, above all, the contact of Islām with Christianity and the realisation that in the Person of Jesus Christ is the strength of Christianity, it is not surprising that now-a-days we see a new and stronger emphasis on the excellencies of the Prophet and the celebration of the birthday of the Prophet on a scale unparalleled in Islāmic history.

It must be remembered that the celebration of the birthday of the Prophet is quite a late development. Khaizūran the mother of Harūn al-Rashīd was responsible in 173 A.H. for special reverence of the birthplace of Muḥammad but it was not till the time of the Fāṭimids about A.H. 500 that we find special birthday celebrations held for the Prophet. These were then confined to a very close circle round the Caliph and were associated with the celebration of the birth of 'Alī, Fāṭimah and the Imām of the time. They had a distinct Shī'a impetus. Later in about 600 A.H. popular celebrations in imitation of the Christian Christmas festivals, with torch-light processions, etc., were held.

This was in the time of Ṣalāḥ al-dīn. Some think that the brother-in-law of Ṣalāḥ al-dīn, who was strongly in favour of the Ṣūfis had a great deal to do with this. The orthodox frowned on the new innovation and called it *bid'at*. Later, because it gradually grew in popularity, it was regarded as *bid'at ḥasanah* i.e., a good innovation. But today in India this celebration is swelling to great proportions. The English newspapers are taking notice of it. Christians and people representing other religions are invited to take part in it. Speeches are made in honour of Muḥammad and reported in the press in a way which we cannot find the praise of Christ at the Christmas festival. It is a salutary experience to read a Christmas newspaper alongside one reporting the *'Īd-i Mīlād*.

The next point of interest is the attempt to expurgate the traditions. Tradition has been unkind to Muḥammad as it has been unkind to Jesus Christ but a wholesale rejection of tradition would leave the biographer of Muḥammad in a most unhappy position. Where is he to get his materials for a life of Muḥammad? The Qur'ān is inadequate in this respect. So we find this silence of some on the question of Muḥammad and on the other hand the creation of a myth which is daily growing.

The Qur'ān

Professor Salīm has complained of the Muslim's enslavement to the past in the matter of the exegesis of the Qur'ān. The commentators of the 2nd and 3rd centuries have fixed everything. There are no modern commentaries on the Qur'ān. (He ignores Muḥammad Ali's). Muslims have ceased to use their common sense and private judgment.

When the first few centuries have fixed the form of commentary, what new material is there by which the Qur'ān can be reinterpreted? Qur'ān of early date are very few. There is nothing like the wealth of MSS. we have for the New Testament and though some people think that textual criticism is an embarrassment, yet we have the important compensation of early translations which are of immense help in the exegesis of the Scripture. Muslims have not.

The attitude of some of the Qur'ān is that all that it contains is a re-emphasis of the fundamentals of religion stripped of the accretions of

Judaism and Christianity. That it contains a protest against unessentials, against trinitarian philosophy and against the ascetic ideal. That it shows the way to the unification of the religious and the secular and substitutes a practical code for a nebulous idealism.

Abrogation in the Qur'ān is felt to be a distinct handicap and tends to destroy the internal unity of the book of Allāh. So there is proposed the doctrine of development. What we have is not abrogation but a careful analysis will show that what have been regarded as abrogated verses are in reality verses which were given in preparation for more complete revelation.

Literature for Muslims

James Windrow Sweetman

The Rev. R.A. Blasdell who has come from Malaya and is working at present in the Henry Martyn School, has completed a most valuable survey of the tracts which were on exhibition at the Tambaram Conference and which represent the bulk of the literature available to Christians for Christian advocacy among Muslims. It is to be hoped that this valuable analysis may be completely available to missionaries. Meanwhile we should like to draw attention to certain conclusions which we have formed from this collection. In presenting these conclusions we are well aware that it may be possible that the collection does not contain some of the books which are used by Christians in the various countries. We have also omitted the English books which were included. The exhibit was divided into various sections as e.g. Bible stories for Muslims, the drama in Muslim evangelism etc. Among these sections we find Apologetics, which is subdivided into General (including commentaries etc.), Scripture, the Cross and the Atonement, the Person of Christ, the Trinity etc. In addition we find a section which deals with the "Literature of First Approach" and another section in which are included lives of our Lord. We have examined these sections with interest to find those which could be described as "theological" or dealing directly with the doctrines which we are supposed to believe and preach, The result is that in all the languages represented viz. Arabic, Algerian, Arabic, Hausa, Bengali, Persian, Pushtu, Ozbek Turki, Urdu, Oriya, Malay, Gujrati, Turki, Osmanli Turki, Gypsy Turki (in Bulgarian script),

Javanese etc. there are 541 exhibits. Of these seventy-six might be classed as theological, though some of them are very slight. This number must be still further reduced by thirteen tracts which are certainly duplicates i.e. the same tract appears in different languages. It is quite possible that a slight change in title disguises the fact that there are other duplicates. But, taking the figure 63 for the apparently theological, we have the following analysis on the basis of theological subjects:

Doctrine of God	3
Trinity	4
The Holy Spirit	3
The Person of Christ	15
Death and Resurrection of Christ	9 (not always theological)
Intercession	3
Atonement	5
Salvation	2
Doctrine of Man	1
Doctrine of Sin	1
Revelation and Scripture	4
Authenticity etc, of Scripture	4
Christian Origins	1
Faith	2
Immortality	1
Worship	1
General	4

It has been noticed that there is not in this entire list any work of any considerable size except Pfänder's book on the *Balance of Truth*. It is noticed that while this is the case a long and difficult book like *Les Miserables* and a so-called religious novel like *Ben Hur* are included in the exhibit. We are in a quandary as to how to express a judgement about these things. Are we to understand that this exhibit was comprehensively representative of Christian literature in Muslim Lands? If not, and there were excluded by those who made the contributions from the different countries, manuals of theology and translations of the books of worship used e.g. the Prayer Book of the Anglican Church, the Offices of the Lutheran Church and the books of Offices of the Methodist Churches, then what can we say to the inclusion of *Les Miserables* and *Ben Hur* and the exclusion of such definitely Christian Literature? Are we to understand, for example, that it is taboo for a Prayer Book to be used to inform a Muslim as to the beliefs and practices of Christians? Perhaps the exclusion is to be explained by a desire not to have any "sectarian" literature. This, however, is not observable in the rest of the literature some of which does not even represent the teaching of a sect but simply the opinions of individuals. Are individuals to be given license and historic churches to be denied any say the matter? We cannot believe that any idea of that description was in the mind of the people who supplied the exhibits. We know that there are these great books of Christian devotion sponsored by the different churches and translated into different languages. What we wonder at is their exclusion, and whether it represents in the general mind of missionaries working among Muslims an idea that a line of demarcation can be drawn between manuals of theology and books of prayers on the one hand and books suitable for Muslims on the other? If this is the case then the sooner we get rid of this idea the better it will be, and the more hope we shall have of being able to give Muslims what they can recognise as statements carrying with them the authority of the great Christian communions.

It we ask a Muslim what Islām is, unless he happens to be a man who has caught the tract habit from Christians and their imitators, the Aḥmadīs; he will almost invariably point to the Qur'ān, explain the ritual prayer and if it is available give us a book explaining the duties and privileges of Islām. Now we are not remiss in giving copies of the Scriptures to Muslims but we would venture to suggest that we are unduly nervous, for some reason or other, in presenting the literature which has the authority of our respective communities. Why? Sometimes we have been asked why we have not books of prayers prepared for the use of Muslim enquirers, as if the prayers for them must, of course, be entirely different from anything else we have ever had.

It may be said that the exhibits was representative only of the interdenominational work of the Central Literature Committee for Muslims and in this case one should not expect to find there the literature sponsored and financed by the various Christian Communities. But Tambaram was from its reports a Conference of an ecumenical character and specially devoted to the idea of the Universal Church. This should have permitted the inclusion of such books as we have mentioned and then the exhibit would have more truly represented the actual position. Moreover it is obvious from the books we have before us that many of them are books sponsored and financed by various Churches.

It is assumed that the Central Literature Committee did the best it could, according to the response which was made to it and we must all be most grateful for the work that committee has done and is doing. If there is any fault to be imputed it is not to any one organisation, much less to one which has rendered such signal service to the missionary enterprise as the Central Literature Committee. The responsibility attaches to us all that we go on publishing old and slight tracts when there is need for better and more substantial books in the various vernaculars on the great matters which are most certainly believed and practised among us.

It is specially worthy of note that while scholarship has been devoted to the editing and translation of books of the East in order that there may be a better understanding of the Eastern systems by the West (and this work dates from the middle ages), except for the outstanding exception of the superlative work which has done in the translation of the Scriptures, there has been nothing on an equal scale to make the great classics of Christian literature (particularly theological) available in the languages of the East. When will the day come that we shall have in important languages of the East something corresponding to the *Encyclopaedia of Islām* or the *Gibb Memorial Series* with the subject not Islām but Christianity and the classics not Muslim but Christian?

A Muslim's View of Christianity

James Windrow Sweetman

S. Khudā Bakhsh was a learned Muslim; his essays on Islām and translations of German works on historical subjects are well known in India. His point of view is not typical but there is much in what he writes which is common to many educated Muslims in India. He may be said to represent a large number of Muslims who have come into contact with Western orientalists and who have modified their views accordingly. Many of his judgments on Christianity are scattered throughout his occasional contributions in the form of essays or in the collections of the same which can be easily procured. It is interesting to find that he had written in *An Outline of Christianity, the Story of Our Civilization* (a symposium written by various writers under the general editorship of A. S. Peake and R. G. Parsons in five volumes) an article entitled *A Mohammedan View of Christendom*. Such an account is bound to excite one's curiosity since it is contained in a book for the consumption of Christian readers in England. It would have been of more interest, of course, if such an article could have been written by 'Abdul Ḥaqq who would have been far more uncompromising and would have represented what is still the preponderating view in Islām, namely, the orthodox.

The article referred to opens with these words, "Closely related as they are, Islām and Christianity should be carefully studied, not to accentuate differences but to emphasize the points on which they agree; for on their mutual good-will in large measure depends the future of

Asia if not of the whole world." It closes with similar words "True Islām and true Christianity are akin; the mission of each is fundamentally identical. Let, then, Islām and Christianity be henceforward faithful allies in the liberation of humanity."

One of the difficulties about a thesis of this sort is that it never clearly emerges what the writer regards as "true Islām" or "true Christianity." Often it is argued that Islām with Christianity and Judaism form a triad of religions whose sole function is to preach "ethical monotheism" and that anything in any of these religions which cannot be fairly described as this as e.g. trinitarianism in Christianity, "Arabism" in Islām, racial exclusiveness in Judaism, are of less account. An exaggerated liberalism might be prepared to accept such a thesis but to the Jew who lustily maintains the exclusive election of their race, or to the Christian who considers that the Incarnation is central and all important to Christianity, there is less inclination to accept the idea that all the world needs is an ethical monotheism.

Khudā Bakhsh considers that the relations of Islām and Christianity were on the whole "happy and harmonious" until about 1000 C.E. that after that time the relations of both deteriorated to a climax in 1829 with the publishing of *Moḥamedanism Unveiled* by Charles Foster. In his opinion there has been an improvement since. "Muḥammad is no longer deemed an impostor, but a reformer of world-wide importance; Islām is no longer regarded merely as a religion propagated at the point of the sword; Islāmic culture is no longer considered a curse, but a stage in human progress for a great portion of the human race." "Indeed when we consider the many similarities subsisting between true Islām and true Christianity, we fail to see (now that 'Arabism' is of the past) why there should be any hostility, or even estrangement between the two cults.

To support such a view Islām is regarded as "a revised edition of Judaism and Christianity." It is asserted that "Mohammed never claimed originality" and that all he fought against was "life-destroying accretions." Muḥammad had no "first-hand" information about either of the two religions and so his accounts are not correctly recorded. This is a tremendous assertion which shows how far Khudā Bakhsh diverges from the orthodox Islāmic view of the Qur'ān as a book sent direct from heaven, inerrant and a miracle which proves the apostolate of Muḥammad. He maintains that the Qur'ān "teems with" stories "drawn from traditions and hearsay." As an example he gives the story of Abraham as the founder of Mecca and the builder of the Ka'bah and he recognizes that there is a mistake in the Qur'ānic view of the Trinity as consisting of the Father, Son and Mary and a great contrast with the Biblical narrative of the Crucifixion. "He denies the crucifixion of the Christ, and teaches that Judas was substituted for Him and nailed to the cross, while the Christ himself ascended direct to heaven." In this statement the writer does not even represent the Qur'ān properly for it nowhere says that Judas was substituted for Christ on the cross. The whole reference is very vague indeed. It is true that some Muslims have added the personality of Judas in their account of the crucifixion but where they got such an idea is difficult to say.

In spite however of these differences, "Islām and Christianity are akin in their veneration for Jesus ... Muslims never mention his name without the formula 'Peace be on Him!'" One might ask here a very pertinent question. Is it true veneration to accept anyone for what he never claimed and to withhold from him the most particular of claims? We often hear such statements from the lips of Muslims. It is hard to describe as reverence the rejection of the unique claims which Christ made for Himself, because at the same time we put Him in a lower order.

That the Qur'ān teaches tolerance is set forth by the quotation of the following verses "Dispute not against those who have received the Scriptures, that is, Jews and Christians, except with gentleness; but say unto them. 'We believe in the revelation which has been sent, down to us, and also in that which hath been sent down to you: and our God and your God is one.'" "Verily the Believers and those who are Jews, those who are Christians and Sabeans, whoever believeth in God, and the last day, and doeth that which is right, they shall have their reward with their Lord, there shall come no fear upon them, neither shall they be grieved." "Unto everyone have we given a law and a way. Now, if God had pleased, He would surely have made you one people; but He hath made you differ, that He might try you in that which He hath given to each; therefore strive to excel each other in good works. Unto God shall ye all return, and He will tell you that concerning which you have disagreed." Reference however is not made to the following verse from the fifth Sūra (verse 85), "Of all men thou wilt certainly find the Jews, and those who join other gods with God, to be the most intense in hatred of those who believe; and thou shalt certainly find those to be nearest in affection to them who say, 'We are Christians.' This is because some of them are priests and monks, and because they are free from pride." Nor is there any recognition of the fact that Muslims have frequently classified Christians with those "who join other gods with God" and so have justified the application of the Verse of the Sword to them also (Sūra ix:5). The truth is that under the fearsome rule of abrogation there are many who hold that the passages which teach tolerance are abrogated by the Verse of the Sword, and this is the solution which is offered for seemingly contradictory passages on the subject.

Khudā Bakhsh has much to say also of the indebtedness of Islām to Hellenism and also to the Persian culture. "Islām freely accepted light from many quarters. It modeled its faith on what had gone before it. We find in Islām precisely the same framework as in Judaism and Christianity: prayer, purification, solemn festivals, scriptures and prophets." The choice of practices is illuminating. Most religions would claim its prayers, its solemn festivals, its rites of purification, its sacred books and its saints and teachers. On such an assumption all religions are the same irrespective of the different conceptions they may have even of these very things.

Of the "borrowing" after the death of Muḥammad he talks of Islām's inheritance of a "Christo-Hellenism" which was "decisive alike for Islām and Hellenism." It is good to see the acknowledgement that the Hellenism which Islām received was already a Hellenism which had been strongly impregnated with Christian thought and belief. To our mind this fact is not sufficiently recognized by Muslims and in it there is certainly the possibility of some approximation in the method of thought and in the doctrinal emphasis in both Christianity and Islām which can at least become an instrument for the better intelligibility of one system to another, but as we have shown elsewhere, when fundamental data are utterly divergent, as is the case between Christianity and Islām, similarity in system may be deceptive and may result in some obscurity in thought. Dressed alike the two religions may present a fictitious likeness to the casual observer. Moreover it is often the fashion of the objector to Christianity to find "accretions" due to the use of a Greek philosophical vocabulary in the creeds, the incursion of Neo-Platonism and the like. Khudā Bakhsh himself hints at the same thing in a passage which we have quoted above.

Now, disregarding this point, the Hellenistic accretions of Christianity are regarded as contributing to the growing Muslim system. It is well-known, and in *Islām and Christian Theology* I have tried to point it out in detail, that much of the Islāmic doctrinal system has been shaped by direct reference to the thought-forms found in Judaistic and Christian Neo-Platonism. Of course, a liberal like Khudā Bakhsh might class the both sets of "accretions" in Islām and Christianity as worthy of rejection or purging, but in the same breath it cannot be claimed that Islām has benefitted from the same. Islām has its emanational trinities, its Aristotelian scholasticism, its Neo-Platonist mysticism and even its two-nature theory of the Word of God combating the so-called "accretions" of Christianity with similar "accretions" in its own dogmatic system. Khudā Bakhsh admits in general what we have particularized.

> By associating with Greek theologians, disciplined in the art of dialectics, the Arabs first learnt philosophical reasoning, which later on they prized so highly. It was from the Greeks again that they received their first lesson in dogmatic subtleties and art in which Byzantine scholarship reveled. Foremost is the enquiry into the essence and attributes of God, which fills the first place in the writings both of the Greek Fathers and of the oldest Arab theologians. The oldest Moslem theologians, just as much as the Fathers of the Greek Church, busy themselves with discussions about fate and free-will.

And this is not disapproved by the writer. "The more we carefully examine this subject, the more we find the pervading influence of Christianity on Islām. Its founder freely made use of Christianity, and the example set by him was followed by his votaries."

The influence of the New Testament on the later Muslims is described by Khudā Bakhsh at some length, particularly the ethical precepts of the Gospel which have been reproduced in Muslim tradition. One instance that is given is the reported version of the Lord's Prayer from the lips of Muḥammad which Abū Dardah vouches for:

> Our Lord God who art in Heaven, hallowed be Thy name, Thy kingdom is in Heaven and on Earth, just as Thy mercy reigns in Heaven, so show Thy mercy on Earth; forgive us our faults and our sins. Thou art the God of the virtuous. Send down (a portion) of Thy mercy and Thy healing power on this pain so that it may be healed.

Other parallels are of Matt. v. 3, 13, vii. 5 and "Render unto Caesar the things which are Caesar's," "The man who does good but keeps it a secret, so that his left hand knows not what his right hand has done," "I stood (said the Prophet) at the gate of Paradise, and observed that the majority of those who found admission there were poor; while the people of wealth were kept away from it."

Of the influence of Islām on Christianity Khudā Bakhsh says that the movement to deny the need of confession to a priest has an Islāmic origin; that the view of the Trinity held by Migetus who denied the divinity of the Word can also be traced to this source; and that Iconoclasm was due to Islām.

Arguing for the enlightened attitude of the Muslims he says

> Moslem jurists and statesmen—always fertile in resources to meet the exigences of the times—put forward the theory that, in certain circumstances *bida'* (innovation or heresy) was permissible. This opened the door for reform; this led to the path of progress. The rigidity of orthodoxy could always be softened or even, as was actually the case, circumvented, by this all-powerful theory, sanctioning innovation in certain circumstances.

One wonders what present-day orthodox teachers would say to such a statement? Or how is it that the works of one of the great band of Islāmic scholars in Spain are hardly procurable here in India let alone known and studied? We refer to Ibn Rushd's *Tahāfut* and his commentaries on Aristotle, which even in his own day were committed to the flames. Ibn Rushd's commentaries are better known in Latin than they are in Arabic.

Reading through this article we are frequently reminded of the saying "The wish is father to the thought." There are many Muslims today who would fain have many things proved with regard to the enlightenment of Islām. It is generally agreed that in its golden age Islām did indeed become a channel for the transmission of learning coordinate with generations of Byzantines who retained the classical Greek learning. The same may be said of other races who have shown no marked religious vigor; and sometimes the cultural advancement was carried on in Islām against the will of the orthodox exponents of Islām. As world powers both Islām and Christianity have had their ups and downs, and their periods of darkness and depression can as little be adduced as proof of the falsity of the respective religions as their periods of culture and enlightenment can be used to prove their truth. Too often we find that opponents of Islām point to the dark periods of Islāmic history and opponents of Christianity to the dark periods in the history of Christian nations. To a historian such points are interesting but a religion stands or falls not by such fortuitous vicissitudes but by the truth or falsity of its fundamentals, which, when true, at one time may be rejected by sinful human to their own destruction and at another time embraced and practiced to their benefit and salvation.

A Brief Introduction to Islāmic Philosophy

James Windrow Sweetman

The common accidents are: movement and rest (*ḥarakah* and *sukūn*), place (*makān*), and time (*zamān*). They are called 'common' because they are to be found in both heavenly and elemental bodies.

Movement and Rest

Matter continually changes from one form to another and the physical power (*quwwat-i ṭaba'iyyah*) is continually changing its state. Not only matter but every single atom in the world of becoming (*'ālam al-kāināt*) is continually in motion whether moving in a straight line (*mustaqīm*) or curved (circular-*mustadayr*), essentially (*zātī*) or accidentally (*'arazī*), because it is agreed that all the bodies on the face of the earth move with the earth round its axis (*miḥwar*), as modern science teaches, or their position changes by the movement of the *primum mobile* (the outermost sphere or sphere of spheres) according to the ancient philosophers. In either case there is no such thing as absolute rest and what is being discussed here is relative (*nasabī*) rest and movement.

When anybody is fixed in reference to another body in any particular position or state, it is said to be at rest (*sākin*) but if its position (*waza'* or state [*ḥāl*]) keeps changing it is said to be moving (*mutaḥarrik*).

Usually 'movement' is applied to change of place (*naql al-makān*) but in the philosophical terminology the meaning is wider. Philosophers call all gradual change or alteration 'movement' whether that is alteration from one place to another or from own quality to another. Thus changes which take place in the fruition of a tree are called 'movement' but any change which is sudden as e.g., a beneficial thing becoming harmful or something dark becoming bright is not called 'movement'.

Movement is connected with six things: that which is moved, that which is the mover or cause of movement, that in which the movement takes place e.g. a journey, the starting place (*mabdā*) of the movement, the end (*muntahā*) of the movement, the extent (*miqdār*) of the movement i.e. the time it takes.

In respect to its cause movement is either essential or accidental. Accidental movement is when the movement of an object is related to some other object. E.g. when, a jug is moved and the liquid contained in it is thereby moved also the liquid is said to be accidentally moved. Essential movement is when the movement of a moved object is set up by itself. This essential movement is of three kinds: natural (*ṭaba'ī*), involuntary or compulsory (*qasrī*) and voluntary (*iradī*). If the moved body's power to move is received from outside itself it is called *qasrī* i.e. involuntary as e.g. the movement of a stone upwards. If the power to move is not from outside and there is volition or purpose behind it then this is voluntary e.g. the movements of animals. But if there is no volition or purpose and the power to move is from within then, this is natural movement e.g. the falling of a stone downwards.

In every movement is involved a line which the moving object describes. When that line is straight the movement is said to be in a straight line and if curved the movement is likewise said to be curved. If the movement throughout from start to finish keeps to one state or mode then it is called orderly or regular movement (*ḥaraka muntazama*) e.g. the movement of light or sound but if the movement does not keep to one condition it is called fluctuating movement (*ḥaraka muta ḥayyara*) e.g. the movement of a stone falling or rising, because a falling stone increases in the speed of its movement and the stone rising goes slower.

It should not be forgotten that a moving object does not immediately pass from its start to its finish but passes through the intervening distance. It therefore follows that until the moving object reaches its terminus it follows a set course from where it was formerly to where it has not yet reached. This is called intermediate movement (*ḥaraka mutawassaṭiyah*). When a moving thing reaches its end without referring to the bounds of its journey, we say that the moving object reached its terminus from the starting point in such and such a time. This is called completed movement (cessation—*ḥaraka qaṭaʿī*). Objectively this has no existence but is only an idea because until the moving object reaches its terminus there is no existence of this movement and as soon as it has reached its terminus the movement has ceased.

Rest is the name applied to what takes place when an object capable of movement does not move.

Place

Ordinary people mean by 'place' (*makān*) that receptacle or vessel (*zarf*) in which some body is present as e.g. water as the place where the fish is or air where birds are flying. According to the Mutakallimūm (scholastics) place is an imaginary thing. The Peripatetics thought that place was the inner surface of a surrounding body which touches the outer surface of the body of which it is the place. In this case the *primum mobile* has no place at all because it is the surrounding sphere and its inward surface circumscribes all parts of the universe, but because there is no sphere encompassing it, it has no place. (This was the theory of Alexander Aphrodisias). Nevertheless the *primum mobile* has situation (*ḥā'iz*). (This is the theory of Ibn Sīnā). Ḥā'iz is that particular position (*wazaʿ*) of a body whereby it is marked out from something else.

The Ishrāqiyyah (Neo-Platonists) consider place to be the name for a separate (or abstract) dimension (*buʿd mujarrad*). Their idea is that there is a physical [*sic*] universe in existence which is devoid of matter and accidents of matter. It also has an earth and a heaven. That incorporeal (separate or abstract) universe surrounds this material universe and so the place of this material universe is the incorporeal universe.

Time

To ordinary people 'time' is the name for the passing of days and nights, months and years. The Peripatetics considered that time was the name for the measure of the movement of the sphere of spheres and just as a line ends at a point which is an indivisible particle and the existence of which is only in the imagination, similarly time also ends as a moment (*an*) and moment is also an indivisible atom and exists only in the mind. It is necessary for there to be time between two moments, just as it is necessary for there to be a line between two points. The majority of the scholastics consider time to be an imaginary thing (*mawhūm*) having no actual (*wāqa'ī*) existence. By the analysis of a period of years it is found that of these years there is a part past and a part to come and so we have present only one year. Looking at this present year several months have passed and several are still to come but only one is present. In this month some days have passed and some are still to come and so only one day is present, and similarly with hours, minutes and seconds and there remains at the last analysis only that ultimate past which is called 'moment'. Who can say that this 'moment' is 'time' or that it exists? Who can say that 'point' which is the name for the end of a line has any existence extrinsically (*fil khārij*)? Thus we cannot say anything more than that time is a mental thing what has no existence extrinsically.

The Spheres (falakiyāt—firmaments)

Ordinary people apply the term 'sphere' or 'heaven' to the blue dome which surrounds the earth from one horizon to another. The philosophers of Greece thought that it was a round body in which generation and corruption, cleavage and adhesion (*kḥaraq* and *ilti'ām*) are impossible and also that it maintains a circular motion. Then they came to think that there must be a cause for the revolution of the spheres, and so they formed the theory that every sphere had a conscious soul (*an nafs ush shā'ira*) by the power of which it revolved. They also considered this movement to be eternal. The earth was in the middle of the sky as the yoke of an egg in the egg. Above the earth is water, but just as sometimes in boiling an egg the yoke comes through the white of it, so some of the earth became displaced from the center and came out through the water to form the habitable world (*rub maskūn*).

Concerning the number of the spheres they thought that there were nine heavens. One of these is devoid of stars and is called the sphere of Atlas, and because it is the highest of all it is also called the "sphere of spheres" (*falak ul aflāk*). Next comes the sphere of the fixed stars (*falak uṭḥ ṭḥawābit*). After this come in the following order: the sphere of Saturn (*Zuhal*), the sphere of Jupiter (*Mushtari*), the sphere of Mars (*Mirrikḥ*), the sphere of the Sun (*Shams*), the sphere of Venus (*Zuhra*), the sphere of Mercury (*'Uṭārid*), and lastly the sphere of the Moon (*Qamar*). Their observations had a great deal to do with this theory, because they saw all of the stars moving daily from East to West and so they thought there must be a heaven surrounding the other spheres and stars and that its movement communicated accidental movement to all the other spheres and stars and that outer sphere was the sphere of spheres or the supreme sphere (*primum mobile—al falak ul a'ẓam*). Then they observed that the stars which are called fixed stars move gradually from the West to East and so they postulated for these stars a second heaven. Similarly they saw that the seven planets vary in their movements and so they assumed the existence of a separate sphere for each.

In modern times, with the aid of instruments, scientists have found that the heaven is nothing at all, but the stars are held together by the force of attraction in space (*fida*) because the power of attraction has an effect on all things existing in the universe. The sun draws the earth, and all the stars move in their orbits (*dā'ira*) round the sun because they cannot exceed these limits on account of the power of attraction exerted upon them. If there had been no such force the whole order of the universe would be upset. In respect to the color of the sky they think that the blue which appears to us and which we call the sky is to be accounted for in the following way. Around the world in which we live is air. Some have estimated it to be 45 miles in depth and others as much more. At any rate, in this surrounding air, the atmosphere, blue rays of the sun are reflected and so the azure vault (*qubba lājawardi*) appears to surround the world. They also say that if it be assumed that the heaven is a spherical body in which the stars are set, as the Greek philosophers thought, it should be said in reply: It is agreed that the moon and other stars receive their light from the sun and so that part of the moon which faces the sun is bright. If the heaven were also a body then it too would reflect the rays of the sun in the same way as the moon, and we should be in moonlike light, although we know that in the dark part of the month this is not so, for the sky is then dark. Those who agree with the Greek philosophers reply that in the Almagest (*Mijasṭī*), the book written by Ptolemy called *Syntaxis Megiste*, it is explained that bodies are of various sorts, some being transparent and some opaque and dark, and some neither quite transparent nor quite opaque. Transparent things do not reflect light and neither have they any natural color. On the other hand opaque things do reflect. Because the moon is half transparent, the rays of the sun which fall upon it are reflected to us and the spheres because they are absolutely transparent do not reflect the rays of the sun which fall upon them.

Elements or Elemental Bodies *(unṣuriyāt)*

According to the ancients, all things in the existing world are composed of the four elements, but modern scientists analyze these four and have found that each element the ancients have postulated is itself composed of many parts and so these parts are the fundamental parts of the elements. The scientist says that fire is not an element at all and it has no special situation (*ḥā'iz*). According to him the greatest power in the world is gravitation (attraction—*kashish*). By it the earth draws all things to itself and when anything is thrown into the air it falls on the ground by virtue of this power. The moon draws the earth and because it can more easily draw water than earth it causes tides in the seas. Because the sun is so far from the earth its influence on the tides is not so great.

The mathematicians of Alexandria claimed that the direction of falling things was to the center of the earth. The philosophers of Islām studied this question and proved that it was necessary because in every body there is a natural inclination to its center. Kepler said that the world drew it and Newton, thinking it out afresh, proved that the direction of the falling body was to the center of the earth because all the parts composing a sphere are drawn (attracted) as if the point of their conjunction were the center of the sphere. And by the power of gravitation (*quwwat-i kashish-i ṭḥiql*) the earth and all the other stars describe an ellipse (*shakl-i baiḍāwī*) round the sun in their revolutions.

Whether water, earth, fire and air are elements or not, the life and progress of all earthly things depends on them. By fire water becomes steam and by the help of steam-engines we travel on sea and land. It was first of all in the Museum of Alexandria that a machine was made which a mathematician invented a century before Christ. This machine worked by steam power (*dukḥāni quwwat*) like the steam reaction turbine engine (*bukhāra-i istirjā'iya* or *radd-i 'amal karnewala*). (This inventor was Hero 130 B.C.E). Similarly four hundred years before Common Era it was discovered that if two pieces of amber (*kahrabā*) were rubbed together electricity could be produced which could attract straws.

The four elements according to the ancients could change their form because their material was one and the same—this is called *inqilāb*. E.g. water sometimes becomes air and sometimes earth. Sometimes air becomes water i.e. takes the form of water. When the heat of fire departs it becomes air; when density takes place in air it becomes water; when earth becomes rarified it becomes water and when water is thinned it becomes air etc. As already said this change of *form* is called *inqilāb* but the change of condition (*kayfiyah*) is called *istiḥālah* and this latter does not involve *inqilāb*. If water is heated, its coldness disappears but it still retains the form of water and in the same way it is very possible that the state of quality of fire might disappear and that it could still continue to be fire (Note that the quality of fire might lose its heat and still remain fire).

The world is round like a ball. Ptolemy thought that the earth was like the yolk of an egg in the middle and the spheres all round it, and when the sun went below the earth by the rotation of the sphere of spheres, it became night. The philosophers of Islām also gave currency to the theory. The sun itself moves and the earth is at rest. By the movement of the sun the seasons are caused.

A new period of philosophy has accepted the Pythagorean system. It is that the earth rotates like a ball or spinning top the motion of which is so quick that it appears to be still. By this motion of the earth night and day are caused. When we remain opposite the sun it is day and when we recede it becomes night. By this movement of the earth two movements are produced: one on its own axis and by this night and day is caused, and another round the sun, by which the four seasons are caused. Those who accept the theory of Ptolemy say that if the earth were really moving then a stone thrown up in the air would not fall down in a straight line to the place whence it was thrown. The reply given to this is that the atmosphere which clings to the earth along with the stone moves with the earth and so the stone falls back in a straight line.

The philosophers proved that in elemental bodies there are heat and cold which are called active qualities (*fiʻl-ī kayfiyāt*), and moisture and dryness, which are called passive qualities (*infiʻalī kayfiyāt*). Of these four there must be one active and one passive in every elemental body, because all the elemental bodies are composed of the four elements and because fire is hot-dry, air hot-moist, water cold-moist and earth cold-dry, then the bodies which are composed of these things must have these four qualities, or rather after acquiring 'disposition' (*mizāj*) only one active and one passive quality remains.

Disposition

Disposition is the middle condition (*kayfiyah*) which is obtained by the elements breaking and being broken (*kasar* and *inkisār*). In determining what breaks and what is broken there is difference of opinion among the philosophers. Some think that the agent is the breaker of the *kayfiyah* and some that the agent is the breaker of the *sūrah* (form) and the patient is matter. Some hold that there is neither act nor passion (potentiality) here but that the concourse (*ijtimāʻ*) of gathered elements is the cause of the loss of the (once) existing condition and the origination of the intermediate (middle) condition. Some consider that the agent is the breaker of the condition the patient broken is the strength and keenness (intensity) of the condition (*kayfiyah*).

The Earth's Formation

There are four strata (*ṭabaqāt*) of the earth: the first age (*'aḥd i awwal*) that of the burning rocks, the second adjacent to the first, the third in which all sorts of minerals and stones are found, the fourth which is the habitable world composed of earth, sand and various stones.

Modern scientists have the idea that this world was formerly a ball of fire. After hundreds of thousands of years, its heat diminished by evaporation (*tabkhīr*) until in its disposition its present equilibrium (*i'tidāl*) was brought about. They call the solid earth on which we dwell the crust of the earth. Even now there is fire in the earth and in those places where the crust is thin volcanoes burst out. Whatever existence fire has it is here and under the sphere of the moon there is no other sphere as the Greek philosophers thought. By the signs of antiquity which appear in the strata of the earth geologists postulate three periods of prehistoric human. The Stone Age (*dawr-i ḥajarī*) when human made weapons and instruments of stone. The Bronze Age when weapons and tools were made of bronze and the Iron Age (*Dawr-i ḥadīdī*) when weapons and tools were made of iron. The ancient remains (lit. traces) by which the conditions of prehistoric human are deduced are of three sorts: bones of animals, bones of human and such things as weapons, household utensils, inscriptions etc.

There are four strata of the air. The first is the Smoky Region which is the region nearest the sphere of fire. In this there are comets, meteors and shooting stars (*niyāzik* and *'umud*). When fumes rise from the earth and reach this region they burn and sometimes remain there and they are called by the forms they assume. The second is the region of clear air and the third the region of intense cold (*zamḥarīrī*), the region of clouds, lightning and dew etc. The reason why it is cold is because it has no connection with the sphere of fire because the air by reason of its rarity does not get hot by the rays of the sun, but when the rays of the sun fall on the earth, the earth being a dense body, gets hot and makes the air hot too.

That which appears to us empty space is not really empty but full of air, but because air is transparent it is not visible, but all the same its effects are felt. Fire and water are also transparent but the earth is dense and so we cannot see through it at all. Various explanations are given of the movement and agitation of the air. One great reason is that vapors and fumes continually rise into the air and sometimes they return to the earth below. For this reason the air is set into motion and this is also the reason for storms of wind. Manifold vapors collide with each other. It is also said that air is essentially moving.

There is also a Region of Water

All four elements are said to have a round shape because the specific forms of the elements are simple (*basīṭ*). And because the round shape is the simplest of all shapes and the other shapes are many-sided the simple elements demand this shape as their specific form.

Weight

Modern scientists think that the weight in things is produced by the attraction of the earth and the weight of anything is in extra proportion to its power of attraction. The ancient philosophers thought that weight was the name for the natural inclination (*mā'il i ṭabaʿī*) or tendency of anything towards the center of the universe (i.e. to the earth). The nearer anything is to the center of the earth the greater is its weight. For this reason earth is most heavy, water less so and airs less in weight than water. Because the sphere of fire adjoins the sphere of the moon fire is most rare (subtle—*khafīf*): for the dense (*thaqīl*) is so called because its inclination is to the center and the light, rare or subtle is so called because its natural tendency is to the circumference and the spheres are the circumference (*muḥīṭ*).

The philosophers have learned the distance of one planet from the others and also their diameter. Thus the diameter of the sun is 866,400 miles and the diameter of the earth is 7,918 miles. The distance of the earth from the sun is 93,000,000 miles. The diameter of the moon is 2,120 miles and its distance from the earth is 239,000 miles. The stars remain in the sky night and day but in the daytime their light is dimmed by the greater light of the sun and so they become invisible.

Sometimes the moon appears new (*hilāl*) and sometime full (*badr*). The reason for this is that the brightness of the moon is not its own but it looks bright because the sun shines on it. So, just as much of its surface as is directed towards the sun is illuminated, and when its entire surface is directed towards the sun then all is bright. Although in *ṭaba'iyāt* there is no discussion of these matters and they really belong to the science of astronomy we have mentioned them by the way.

Things deriving from Water *(kā'ināt i jū)*

The elements, when they are thought of as being the constituent parts in the composition of all composite things, are called *isṭiqsāt* (the Arabic for the Greek word *stoicheion),* and in respect to the fact that after analysis composite things are reduced to certain things, these are called '*anāṣir* (pl. of *unṣur*), while in respect to their being concerned in generation and corruption (*kawn* and *fasād*) they are called *arkān* (pillars).

By the composition and blending (*imtizāj*) of these elements various things are produced in space (the firmament) which are called "productions of water." Rain: Vapors are drawn from the moist earth; seas and rivers by the sun. On reaching the region of intense cold they form again as water and then fall on the earth in the form of rain. Sometimes when this water has formed into drops it becomes so intensely cold that it becomes hail and sometimes before it has formed into drops and while it is still vaporous it becomes cold and falls as snow. There is more snow and rain on mountains and also more cloud. The difference between vapor and smoke is that the former consists of parts of water and parts of air and the latter of parts of fire and parts of earth. Dew is caused by vapors becoming condensed in the cool of the night. (Similarly the rainbow, the red of sunset, hot wind, whirlwind, lightning, thunderbolts, meteors [*shihāb i thāqīb*], comets, earthquakes are spoken of briefly).

Minerals

Vapors and fumes produced within the earth have a special disposition created in them and become various kinds of metals or minerals (*ma'ādin*). Some of these come out of the earth pure and some so mixed with earth that they cannot be recognized at first sight. Muslims knew long ago that there were mineral substances which made small things appear big and by the use of crystal the microscope and telescope have now been invented.

Psychology *(nafsiyāt)*

The Soul (*nafs*—psyche)

Like primal matter, the apotheosis of spirits (*arwāḥ*) was from that universal spirit (*rūḥ-i kul*) which is called in the philosophical terminology Active Intellect (*'aql fā'il*). (Note, The reader should be warned that the statements following are very loosely expressed by the primers which we are seeking to present as typical of the teaching. Terms are interchanged and generalizations made which will not stand any close criticism. The sentence last quoted is full of inaccuracies; detailed criticism of these matters cannot be attempted at this stage though it might be possible sometime later. Nevertheless even the inaccuracies are valuable for our purpose).

Spirit is not a thing we can see with the eye or feel with the hands or perceive by any other of the senses, but just as the sun is known by its rays, and by smoke it is known that there is fire, so we know that there is such a thing as spirit. When we thoughtfully observe anything possessing spirit, its acts, its movements and its rests, we perceive a great difference between them and the movement of the fingers of a watch. In one there is no compulsion (*iztirār*) and in the other there is. In the former there is intention and consciousness and in the latter senselessness and immobility (*jumūd*). Thus in human it is necessary for there to be for the procession of voluntary acts some conscious power. Similarly in human there is growth and increase (*nashw wa numā*). Therefore there is in him/her the power of nourishment and producing heat (*taghzīya wa tanmīya*). Moreover we see that of all material beings in human alone is there the power to think about themselves and the things round about them, and to trace the sequence of causes and effects, and so in a person there must of necessity be the power of thought (*fikr ghawr*). As soon as we observe these facts it is clear that human is the collection of various perfections (*kamālāt*).

The vegetable soul (here *rūḥ* is used and not *nafs* and *rūḥ* is best translated 'spirit'—*rūḥ nabātī* is really 'vegetable spirit') provides for the work of nourishment and production of animal heat, the animal soul (*rūḥ-i ḥaiwānī*) for his movement and sense, and the human soul (*rūḥ insānī*) for the government of the animal soul and for one's discoveries about things round about them. Usually philosophers consider that these three are existing separately in human but probably the meaning of this is simply that there are apparently three. There is however one group of Muslim philosophers which considers that human has but one spirit which they call the *rūḥ insānī* and this does all the work of nourishment, creation of bodily heat, sense, movement and thought and it is by various instruments and powers that the variety of phenomena appears.

The philosophers of Islām of one school also consider that stones (*jamādāt*) possess spirits and this theory is accepted by some modern philosophers also. They find growth in stones and that there is no difference between this and the growth of animals except in the rate of the process, just as the movement of a second-hand of a watch is easily seen but that of the larger hand is not.

Experiments at the present day and modern discoveries confirm this opinion. Nevertheless the human spirit is supreme, which bending its deepest thought upon the wonders of this world finds out the proximate and remote causes of things. In animals there is no power of thought. A bird seeing a gun fears as the result of experience because it knows a ball may issue from the barrel and wound it (?) but it never thinks how this can happen and cannot know how gunpowder works.

The question as to whether the nature and quiddity of all kinds of spirit is one or various is a very vexed one and much debated. One thing is clear and it is that all the powers of the spirits are different manifestations of the Active Intellect. The difference is the nearness or the remoteness from the Source e.g. the shadow of a man falls on the earth and on a mirror. The mirror is bright and reflects the lineaments but the earth does not. In this way in human the perfections of the Active Intellect appear and not in other creatures.

The Vegetable Spirit

Among created things the plants have a middle position. In them is the power of growth, which is called the vegetable spirit. Because the connection of spirits is with the acquiring of perfections, spirits are called forms of perfection (*suwar-i kamāliyāt*). Accepting this we may therefore call the vegetable spirit that form of perfection by which nourishment is accomplished. This spirit is found in all plants in order of importance the spirits may be classified as: the lowest is vegetable spirit; the intermediate is animal spirit, and the highest human spirit (which is the rational soul [*nafs nāṭiqah*]).

The kinds of vegetable spirit according to the physical powers (*quwwah-i ṭabaʿīyah*) are two sorts:

Makhdūma—served

a) Nourishing—*ghāziya* which makes food fit to become part of the body.

b) Growing—*nāmiya*, increasing the body with that which is naturally appropriate to it.

c) Reproducing—*mawlida*, by which another body is produced from a body.

d) Formative—*muṣawwarah*, which is the cause of one body produced from another being of the same shape.

Khādima—serving

a) Assimilating or absorbing—*jāzibah*, which absorbs or assimilates the food.

b) Retaining—*māsikah*, the power by which food is retained.

c) Digesting—*hāzimah*, the power by which food is digested.

d) Excreting—*dāfiʿah* the power which rejects waste.

(Note that the above are put into the Arabic feminine as qualifying *quwwat* e.g. *quwwat-i hāzimah* etc.)

The Animal Spirit *(rūḥ haiwānī)*

This is that perfecting spirit by which animals proceed to act and will consciously. There are two sorts of powers of this spirit.

Perceiving or cognising—*mudrikah*

i) The five external senses: hearing (*sāmi'ah*), seeing (*bāṣirah*), smelling (*shāmiyah*), tasting (*zā'iqah*) and touching (*lāmisah*).

ii) The Internal Senses: common sense (*ḥiss mushtarik*). This is the sensorium, the treasury or storehouse for the external senses. Whatever the animal senses by the external senses goes into the sensorium and then its impressions are gathered into thought (*khayāl*); in dreams or in thinking (*fikr*) these forms appear before us.

Thought (*khayāl*) where impressions mentioned above are gathered. Imagination or phantasy (*wāhimah*) which is the mental power whose work it is to perceive particular significances of the sensible as e.g. love and friendship from the sensed forms of mother and father; enmity from the sensed form of the wolf; sweetness from the sensed form of the bee. Memory (*ḥāfiẓah* and also *zākirah*) and recollection (*mustarja'a*). Here the cognisance of the *quwwat-i wāhimah* is gathered: a sort of store house of the power of fantasy or imagination. (When both the powers *khayāl* and *ḥāfizah* reach the height of their perfection in any person, both past and present impressions is ready to hand. Human thus makes experience their guide and acts by the instruction of reason). Constructive Imagination (*mutakhayyalah* or *mufakkarah*—not to be confused with *khayāl*). This is the power which takes what is stored in the memory and in *khayāl* and forms new combinations by synthesis and analysis. By this all *sorts* of combinations result as e.g. the idea of a man with a horse's head. This is rather imagination in the modern sense but it is not always its work to produce such fanciful things. This is rather the action of the mind "compounding and dividing" but it is not the work of the intellect proper.

b) The second kind of Animal spirit is the Moving Power (*quwwat-i muḥarrikah*). Without this power the senses would be of little use. By the power of movement human moves towards those things which are agreeable to their nature and avoids those things which are disagreeable. *Shawq* is the desire which turns human to agreeable things, *ghazab* is that which repels what is harmful, *tanaffur* or *karāhat* (sometimes also *nafrat*) is distaste or repugnance and *jazbah* is emotion and is the term used when it is intended to assert that a psychical influence has been exerted on the spirit.

The way the power of movement acts is this: There is first of all a feeling or sense-impression or idea (*taṣawwur*) of an act. By feeling, desire or repugnance is produced by which joy or expansion (relief-*inbisāṭ*) on the one hand, or constriction (*inqibāz*) on the other are produced. By the former term (expansion) the relaxing of the nerves (*a'ṣāb*) is meant and by constriction is meant the tensing or contraction of the nerves. Following this there is volition (*irādah*) and the act follows volition.

The Human Spirit *(rūḥ insānī and also nafs nāṭiqah—rational soul)*
The rational soul is a simple substance (*jawhar basīṭ*) which rules all the powers and organs of the body. It is also perceiving (cognizing-*mudrik*) and knowing (*'ālim*) and is of the following kinds:

a) The knowing power (*quwwat-i 'ālimah*) i.e. the Intellect (*'aql*) from which are two: the speculative power (*quwwat-i naḥarī*) at work when we say the world is round; and the practical power *quwwat-i 'amalī* represented in the judgment that injustice is to be eschewed.

b) The acting power (*quwwat-i 'amalī*). This is the power by which the human spirit rules and directs all the powers and members. The real substance within the human body is Spirit. It is the power by which the human spirit rules and direct all the powers and members. The real substance within human body is Spirit. It is this which acts. The senses are its instruments. The real perceiver is the Spirit.

Four Degrees of Human Intellect

a) Material Reason (*'aql-i ḥayūlānī*). In this degree intellect is a clean tablet and speculations (*naẓariyāt*) and self-evident matters have no influence on it.

b) Habitual Reason (*'aql b'il malakah*). In this stage intellect has the perception of self-evident matters (*badīhiyāt*).

c) Acquired Intellect (*'aql mustafād*). In this stage not only the self-evident but theoretical (speculative) knowledge is found.

d) Actual Intellect (*'aql bil fi'l*). This must be differentiated from Active Intellect (*'aql fā'il*). In this stage there is completion of acquaintance with all theoretical knowledge. This is the perfection of the human reason.

The Two Kinds of Knowledge and Perception (*'ilm wa idrāk*)

a) Feeling or Sense (*iḥsās*) which is the perception (cognition) of the five senses.

b) Imagination (*takhayyul*) which is the cognizance of the power of imagination, (*quwwat-i mutakhayyalah*).

c) Phantasy (*tawahhum*) this is the cognizance of the power of phantasy (*quwwat-i wāhimah*).

d) Intellection (*ta'aqqul*) which is the cognizance of the intellect.

As already said, the perceiver is the rational soul, but because its relation to perceived or cognized things is by means of instrument and powers, the names of the different sorts of knowledge are according to those instruments and powers. Here it should be understood what connection the impressions of external things found in mental powers or in the rational soul itself have with the external objects of which they are the impressions.

The Peripatetics thought it was a connection of identity quiddity (or nature) i.e. the quiddity of both is the same. E.g. if it is said that the impression or form of *Zayd* is found in the mind, then the meaning must be that humanity which is the universal quiddity (*māhiya kulliyah*) is found in the mind and whatever particulars (*shakhsīyat*) were externally present, mental particularizations (*tashakkhuṣāt-i zahnīyyah*) of the universal quiddity of *zayd* (i.e. humanity) corresponding to those external particulars were produced in the mind.

The Neo-Platonists held that there are resemblances only (not identity—*ittiḥād*—but *muḥākat*), i.e. by these mental impression there is acquaintance with external things. Therefore only pictures or images of the living and dead, visible facts and appearances are present in the mind and by their means knowledge is obtained in the same way as the pictures of a painter. It appears that the pictures of the artist and the actual things of which they are pictures have only a relation of resemblance or similitude, like the message in the words of a telegram which is put into the telegraph office, has simply a resemblance to the message delivered at the other end. On the same analogy the words of a book and the acts and scenes which are set forth by means of the words in it. Later, in the section on theology, we shall show that it is impossible that the actual quiddity stripped of external existence (abstracted from the concrete existence) should be obtained in the mind from which it would appear that the Neo-Platonist view is near to the truth.

The exemplar (*mithāl*) or image (*shabīh*-similitude) or anything obtained in the mind is called the known (*ma'lūm*) and the perceiving or cognizing mode in the mind is called knowledge (*'ilm*). The likeness of the external thing is called "the-assumed-to-be-known" (*ma'lūm bil faraz*) because sometimes the external thing ceases to be, and the knowledge remains, but for knowledge the existence of the known is necessary and therefore the similitude of the external thing in the mind is accepted as the known.

The Origination (ḥudūth) of the Rational Soul

The rational soul's existence and relation to the body is the same throughout all stages through which a man passes in the course of his life and so it must be assumed that the rational soul is something which has a beginning. If anyone says that the fact that the rational soul is connected with the body is not a proof of its having a beginning the reply is that the aptitude of the body has a great deal to do with the existence of the rational soul. When the bodily capabilities reach perfection then the rational soul is produced. If it had been eternal (unoriginated—*khadīm*) it would have been a substance (*jawhar*) and would not have depended on bodily powers. (Note that it has been previously said that the rational soul is a substance—*jawhar*). But just as a child in the pre-natal state needs the womb but after birth does not, so when the existence of the rational soul is cut off from the body, it becomes powerful and after human's death becomes immortal (*ghayr fānī*).

Physical Death

This physical body is exactly like a boat on a river and the spirit like the wind which moves it. And just as when the boat becomes weak and frail and, being unable to ride the waves, sinks to the bottom, so the connection it has with the wind is no use to it. In the same way when the body loses its balance of disposition (*i'tidāl-i mizāj*) and age overcomes it, the physical powers forsake it. It is then the connection of the spirit with the body ceases and it says farewell to its former companion. This is physical death. And just as a boat may sink for some reason before it becomes weak so sometimes the connection of the spirit with the body may cease on account of some disease and before death.

Philosophers disagree with regard to whether the human spirit's connection is primarily and essentially with some organ. But enquiry results in the conclusion that its connection is with the vaporous body which is produced in the heart and which physicians call vaporous spirit (*rūḥ bukhārī*—vital fluid). Whether spirit is vegetable, animal or human it has a special influence in all parts of the body while its connection with the body continues. This special influence is called life.

True Vision and Dreams (*ruya-i ṣādiqah and khwāb o khayāl*)

Because dreams appear in sleep the nature of sleep should first be considered. Sleep is the name for the turning of the spirit from the outward to the inward. When the vapors of the stomach rise to the brain, the cerebral fluid (*ruḥūbat-i dimāghī*) relaxes the limbs or organs and gradually the external senses cease to function (*mu'aṭṭal*). This is called sleep. In true vision, when the rational soul is relieved from employment in external things and gives its attention to the invisible world (*'ālam i quds*) of which this world is the reflection or shadow, certain cognitions of that heavenly world (lit. heavenlies—*qudsiyat*) cast their reflection on the rational soul. This reflection is called true vision.

The kinds of Vision

a) The Uninterpretable (*ghayr ta'birī*): If impressions of knowledge are preserved in the memory or *khayāl* there is no necessity for them to be interpreted because they are manifest in themselves and not symbolic, i.e. things appear as they really are. Such dreams are called uninterpretable or not requiring interpretation.

b) Interpretable: If the imaginative power (*quwwat-i mutakhayyalah*) occupies itself with the impressions and puts them forward in new shapes then they require interpretation e.g. injustice in the form of a dragon.

c) Vague dreams (*khwāb pareshānī*): Such have no meaning at all. They are only disordered impressions.

Transmigration *(metempsychosis—tanāsukh)*

One school considers that after death the spirit roams round the place of burial, another that the spirit wanders bewildered in the firmament of space or the sky. The idea of the Scholastics is that the spirit remains in the exemplar world (*'ālam-i mithāl*). The philosophers think that the spirit becomes absorbed in the All (*kull*). *Tanāsukh* is conceived by some in the following way: Sufficient time must elapse before the soul reaches Nirvana [*sic*]. Meanwhile in the pursuit of the path of reward and punishment the spirit keeps changing into different moulds and in this change deeds are taken into account. The objection to this is that it can only be believed that the spirit's change from one mould to another is for punishment or reward when each man knows what his former mould was. When this is not known where does punishment or reward come in? The second objection advanced to the theory is expressed in the question "How can any rational intelligence believe that the mother of some man may later become his wife and the son of some woman become her husband? Because the passing of the spirit from one body to another would involve such a possibility"

Evolution *(irtiqā)*

The theory of the Peripatetics is that the source of elements is one and the same and in accordance with this theory there are changes in the matter of the elements according to physical laws. These changes are in this way: gradually vegetable body becomes animal and animal body becomes human body. Of these there is one school which holds that the law of evolution dominates all the things in the universe.

The opinion of Darwin explains this latter theory most fully. He was the first one to relate the theory to anatomy (*'ilm-i tashrīḥ al-a'zā*) physiology (science of the functions of the organs—*'ilm-i waza'if al-a'zā*), archaeology (*'ilm-i athār-i qadīmah*) and zoology (*'ilm al-haiwānāt*) etc. and this doctrine has become famous, throughout the learned world.

Darwin says that every form of body, whether inorganic, vegetable, or animal, has by gradual changes of form reached new shapes. Animal forms have gradually changed from ancient forms to the newest, and human, because they are a most perfect body, has passed through many stages. The struggle for survival (*tanazu' lil baqā*) is operative from inorganic substance to animals i.e. nature causes that individual to survive in which there is most capability of survival (survival of the fittest). And so from the beginning of creation until now countless species have disappeared and more powerful and better beings have regularly advanced until they have reached humanity.

The theory of the philosophers of Islām is that from the most ancient forms to the most recent there has been development in bodies i.e. after inorganic substances plants came to exist; then there came to exist those plants which are nearest to the animal; next animals came to exist until ultimately those animals came to be whose behavior is most similar to human's. Finally human came to exist—the ultimate limit of the perfection of the animal genus.

Divinity (*ilāhiyāt*)

Divinity is divided into two sections: Common Matters (*umūr 'āmmah*) in which those matters are dealt with which are common to material and immaterial substances, and Theology (*'ilm ilāhī*) which deals with the essence and attributes of God and the qualities of separate substances (i. e. incorporeal substances—*jawāhir mujarradah*).

Common Matters

Existence and Non-existence (*wujūd wa 'adam*)

Everything in the world was made by God. There is the same relation between existing things and the Creator that there is between speech and a speaker, or light and a lamp, for word or speech (*kalām*) always requires a speaker (*mutakallim*).

Some people think that the existence of a contingent or possible (*mumkin*) thing is something additional to its quiddity or essence but this is not so because the existence of contingent things is the result of the overflow (*fayz*) of the divine and so their essence and quiddity are both one and the same. Similarly quiddity and existence are the same too. It is therefore unreasonable to suppose that at one time quiddity should exist in the form of the universal and at another in the form of the individual because the very meaning of the existence of any contingent thing is that the universal quiddity (e.g. humanity) is existing (*mawjūd*) in such and such an individual form. This single effluence (*fayz*) is called in the terminology of the philosophers a simple stipulation (*jual basīṭ*).

Here it should be noted that this effluence is not an involuntary overflow. God has the power to do or not to do and He is a free agent (*qādir mukhtār*). For the Peripatetics the stipulation is composite and so they consider that the existence of a contingent thing is additional to its quiddity. The Philosophers of Islām, however, think that the existence of a thing is its very essence. The Peripatetics think that the operation of the creator of the Universe is to bestow existence along with quiddity.

The defect in this opinion is that the bestowal of existence could only be correct if the quiddity was existing before its existence, which is absurd.

Having learned that existence is identical with quiddity, existence is of two kinds, perfect and imperfect—the existence of God being perfect and that of contingent thing imperfect. The difference between these two kinds of existence is referred to as "equivocation" (*tashkīk*). It follows that if existence and quiddity are identical this equivocation must apply to both existence and to quiddity. This is the view of the Ishrāqiyyah but the Peripatetic think there is equivocation in the predication of existence but not in quiddity.

If the meaning of a thing's existence is that a universal quiddity is manifested as something particularised (*mutashakhkhaṣ*), then the existence of the natural universal must be included in individuals (*afrād*), for "individual" (*shakhṣ*) is an expression for whatever of such and such a universal quiddity is existing. Therefore the statement of some philosophers that the natural universal exists solely in the mind is not correct. Further, when existence is identical with quiddity, how can it happen that the quiddity of an external thing should be obtained in the mind denuded of external quiddity? For there is only a formal (logical) difference between existence and quiddity—this is the opinion of the Peripatetics. Nevertheless it is clear that it is impossible to obtain the external existence in the mind, otherwise the external effects should also have to be existing in the mind as e.g. burning with fire. Therefore in the mind the similitude or likeness of the external thing only is obtained (not the thing itself).

The Schoolmen do not accept mental existence (*wujūd zahnī*). In their view the mind comes to have a real, relation with the external things and this relation is the cause of knowledge and discovery. The Philosophers give many arguments for mental existence, e.g the existence of many things is not external (concrete) as, for instance, when an agent does some work he has some purpose or other and so it is quite clear that before the act there is no appearance of the end or purpose externally and so the existence of the purpose must be in the mind.

It only remains to say that the existence of the Necessary Being must be identical with His Essence or something additional. All the philosophers agree that the existence of the Necessary Being is identical with His Essence but usually the Mutakallimūn consider it to be additional.

Quiddity *(māhiyah)*

Quiddity is the name for that common thing which the intellect considers correctly applicable to two or more things when their parts, are not separately taken into account. For in the latter case they would be called "reality" (*ḥaqīqah*). For example, if we look at Zayd, Khālid and Fāṭimah and think about them, it appears that they are all rational animals. So this "animal" and "rational" is the reality of the individual members of humankind but the name for the sum of "animal" and "rational" is "man" or "humanity" and this is called the quiddity (*māhiyah*).

There are two kinds of quiddity: Singular (*mufarrad*) and Composite (*murakkab*). That which is singular or simple is not composed of parts as e.g. the Necessary per se (*wajib bil zāt*). Composite means composed of parts as e.g. "man" who is composed of "animal" and "rational." Again, simple and composite quiddity is of two sorts: real (*ḥaqīqī*) and formal (or logical—*i'tibārī*). Real quiddity is that which does not depend on supposition or logical reference, e.g. man, horse etc. Formal logical quiddity is that the existence of which depends on supposition or logical reference as e.g. a sea of silver or gold, the existence of which is merely suppositional. It is impossible that in real composite quiddity there should not be a relation of dependence between parts, e.g. Primal matter depends in its existence on form and form depends for its individuation on primal matter. So in this case there is dependence on both sides. But sometimes the dependence is one-sided, e.g. genus and species which are both "kinds" (The three terms are *jins*, *faṣl* and *nu* respectively) but species (*faṣl*) has no need of genus although genus has need of species to remove its ambiguity.

Parts (*ajzā*) are of two kinds: extrinsic (*khārījī*) and mental (*zahnī*). Extrinsic or external parts are those which do not exist by one and the same existence but each has a fixed and separate existence as e.g. corporeal form and primal matter which are the parts of a whole. Each of these has a fixed existence of its own (*mustaqil*). Mental parts are those which exist by one and the same existence e.g. "animal" and "rational" which are parts of "man." Here "animal," "rational" and "man" exist by one existence. For this reason each one is predicated of each of the others, for the only reason for predicating one thing of another thing is oneness of existence (predicated-*maḥmūl*).

Of the singular quiddity there are two kinds: the real singular (*mufarrad ḥaqīqī*) which is that the existence of which does not depend or assumption or supposition (farad); and the formal singular (nominal—*mufarrad i'tib*ārī), the existence of which depends on supposition.

Composite quiddity is also of two kinds: the real composite (*murakkab ḥaqīqī*) which is that in the parts of which there is a relation of dependence as e.g. forms and matter (see above); and Formal or Nominal (*murakkab i'tibārī*) in the parts of which there is a formal reference e.g. "man" as universal and "man" as individual. This is called *māhiya makhlūṭ* i.e. mixed or confused quiddity. And if there is "a relation of non-reference" (probably meaning if there is no concrete reference) then it is called abstract quiddity (*māhiya mujarradah*), the existence of which is only in the mind. If quiddity is thought of without reference to either the existence or the nonexistence of a thing then this is called "absolute quiddity" (*māhiya muṭlaqah*). The "absolute quiddity" is also called the "natural universal" (*kullī ṭaba'ī*). There is a difference of opinion as to whether this exists in actual fact (extrinsically or externally—*fil khārij*) See the former discussion. Necessity, Possibility (contingency) and Impossibility. (*wujūb*, *imkān* and *imtinā'*).

The Necessary is that which must be, God. The Impossible is that the non-existence of which is necessary. The Possible is that of which neither the existence nor the non-existence is necessary nor so the Possible always depends on something else for its existence. We know conclusively that there is a connexion between magnetism and iron. If we take a magnet in our hand we learn that iron is attracted to it and when we take the iron in our hand the magnet is not attracted. From this we learn that there is drawing power in the magnet and that in iron there is the capacity to receive this attraction or otherwise the iron would not move to the magnet. So just as the iron depends on the magnet for its movement so all contingent or possible things (*mumkināt*) depend for their existence on the bounty of the creator. Impossibilities have not the capacity to accept the effluence of the creative power. As the possible requires a cause for its existence and origination, so it also depends on a cause for its continued survival.

The word *imkān* may be applied in the following ways: *imkān amm*—common possibility, *imkān khāṣ*—special possibility, *imkān zātī*—essential possibility, *imkān i nafs al-amārī*—possibility of the particular thing itself and *imkān isti'dād*—potential possibility.

a) When we speak of common possibility we simply mean that the non-existence of the thing of which this is predicated cannot be necessary. This is most properly predicated of possibilities (*mumkināt*) but may also be applied to the Necessary because the non-existence of the Necessary cannot be necessary.

b) Special possibility is applied to that thing of which both the existence and the non-existence is not necessary as is the case with all possibilities (*mumkināt*).

c) Essential possibility: If the actual existence (*wujūd bil fi'l*) of the thing of which this is the quality be assumed it should not involve any impossibility. E.g. If there is the possibility of writing in Zayd, then if we assume that he actually writes this does not involve anything contrary to the essence or nature of Zayd.

d) Possibility of the thing itself. When anything has this quality there is nothing impossible per se involved if it is considered actual and also nothing impossible *ab alio*, i.e. when there is nothing contrary to the essence and nothing outside makes a thing impossible then there is *imkān-i nafs-i amārī*.

e) Potential possibility. When anything has this quality there is no assumption or supposition of its existence actually but only in potentiality.

The One and the Many *(wāḥid wa kathīr)*

Sometimes the term "one" is applied in the real sense and sometimes metaphorically. Some things are called "one" only because they are subsumed under the same thing.

Metaphorical Unity (*wāḥid majāzī*) is of the following kinds: One in genus (*wāḥid biljīns*) e g. man and horse are one in being animal, one in kind (*wāḥid bin nu*). Thus Zayd and Khalid are one in being man. One in accident (*wāḥid bil araz*) e.g. teeth and snow are one in being white. One in Subject (*mawzū'*) e.g. a writer and a lawyer are both one in reference to man who is the "subject" of both these. One in relation (*wāḥid bin niṣbah*) e.g. to say that the spirit of man has the same relation to the body as a king has to his kingdom.

Real Unity (*wāḥid ḥaqīqī*) is of three kinds:

a) Particular Unity (*wāḥid juzī*) in which there is no multiplicity either potentially (*bil quwwah*) or actually (*bil fi'l*) used of God's unity.

b) Unity in conjunction or continuity (*wāḥid bil ittiṣāl*) in which there is no multiplicity actually, which by continuity in its parts must be called one, but if we like we can analyse it into parts and so potentially it is not one. (It should be noted that the word *ittiṣāl* conveys the idea of a very close union).

c) Unity in being assembled. This is when a thing is actually multiple but by reason of being gathered or bound up it is called "one" e.g. a chair which is one though it consists of many parts. (Could not this be said of body in 2 above? The really significant difference is in the degree of union between the parts.)

Multiplicity is the opposite of unity and there are as many kinds of multiplicity as of unity.

Opposition *(taqābul)*

Taqābul expresses the relation of two things which cannot be together in the same sense, at the same time, in the same place. Both of two opposites may be existent or one may be non-existent and the other existent. If both are existing and the mode of both is that the understanding of one of them depends on the other then they are called "doubled" (*mutaz'aif*) and the relation "doubling" (*taz'aif*) e.g. fatherhood and sonship.

If the understanding of one does not depend on the other they are called *mutadadd* i.e. contrary and the relation is called *tadadd* i e. contrariety e.g. to be a man and to be a horse.

If one is existent and the other non-existent, then if in the suppositum (*maḥall*) there is something non-existent which it nevertheless has a potentiality to receive then the relation is spoken of as "privation and possession" (*'adam wa malakah*). As an example, movement and rest because that which is said to be at rest is that in which there is a potentiality or capacity to movement, or blind and seeing because one is only called blind when one has the normal capacity to see and yet cannot do so.

If, however there is no potentiality or capacity for the existence of something not found in a suppositum then the relation is simply called "positive and negative" (*ijāb wa salb*) as "man and not-man" i.e. the relation is one of contradiction. (In Logic contradiction is called *tanāqud* and a contradictory is *nāqid*).

Priority ancl Posteriority (taqaddum wa taakhkhur)

There are five kinds of priority:

a) Priority in time (*taqaddum biz zamān*) e.g. the priority of Noah to Moses.

b) Priority in Nature (*taqaddum biṭ ṭaba'*). This expression denotes a relation when the existence of the prior is possible without the posterior but the existence of the posterior is impossible without the prior. As e.g. the priority of one to two is clear for without one two cannot be but one can be found without two.

c) Priority in honour (*taqaddum bish sharaf*).

d) Priority in rank or position (*taqaddum bir rutbah*), e.g. the priority of the one nearest to the *miḥrāb* in the mosque at prayer.

e) Priority in Causality (*taqaddum bi 'illiyah*) when the prior is the cause of the posterior in such a manner that the prior is never found without the posterior nor the posterior without the prior, e.g. The movement of the hand which holds the pen is prior to the movement of the pen.

Cause and Effect *('illah wa ma'lūl)*

That on which there is dependence (*muḥtāj ilaih*) is "cause" and that which depends (*muḥtāj*) is "effect."

There are two kinds of cause: sufficient cause and insufficient cause (*'illah tamīna wa illah-i nāqiṣah*). The former is when no other cause is needed for the thing of which it is the cause. The latter is when this is not the case.

Insufficient cause is of four kinds:

a) Material cause (*'illah-i māddī*) as the wood of which a chair is made.

b) Formal cause (*'illah- sūrī*) which is that from which the effect has its actuality as e.g. the form of a chair. When the form of a chair is present then the material ceases to have the potentiality to be a chair and becomes one actually.

c) Final cause (*'illah- ghā'ī*). That which is the cause of the act of the agent or doer is the final cause. It is the end for which he works as "sitting" for a chair.

d) Agentive or Active cause (*'illah- fā'ilī*) as the one who makes a chair.

It should be noted here that sometimes there is in the essence of the agent (*fā'il*) certain weaknesses or deficiencies which hinder him in acting and sometimes there is a lack of aptitude or intractability in material e.g. if an infant in arms cannot receive the instruction of a teacher, this is not a defect in the teacher but because there is no aptitude in the child. Similarly, if writing of an expert calligraphist does not remain on water no deficiency in the expertness of the writer is implied for there is no aptitude in the water to retain the writing. So often and in the first place any fault is on the part of the material.

Often, because people ignore this point, the agent is blamed for the fault of the material. Often, because people ignore this point, the agent is blamed for the fault of the material e.g. the Lord of the world cannot expel *Iblīs* from his dominions, because nothing possesses the capacity to be expelled from the possession of God. For instance, to say that God cannot make a person stand and sit at the same time, because this is impossible to the person; or again to say that God cannot make anyone like Himself because the matter of the universe has not the capacity for this. The truth is that in such questions there is "composition of opposites." First we postulate something like God and then raise the question whether such a thing can be created. How can a similitude to God be at the same time a created thing? Similarly in the question about sitting and standing which are mutually contrary and to assert in the first place that all things are in the possession of God and then consider the possibility of anything being expelled from God's possession is manifestly contradictory.

The theory of the Peripatetics (*Mushaiyūn*) is that when the agentive or active cause is simple (*basīṭ*) it is impossible for more than one thing (effect) to proceed from it. This, however, is an unfounded claim because the essence of the cause is existing externally (*fil khārij*) and the recognition of its quality of being a cause is by the intellect, i.e. is something intelligible. Similarly the essence of the effect exists externally and its quality of being an effect is a matter of formal or logical reference. Therefore, whenever two things proceed from one cause, multiplicity is not thereby produced in the essence of the cause but two rational references are connected with it i.e. the two things becoming effects. Therefore it is not impossible that many things should proceed from a simple cause, but it is most probable that such will be the case. It is, however, surprising that the Peripatetics should have made this claim when they hold that the Most High is qualified by such attributes as "knowing" "intellecting" "powerful" and similar attributes.

We have accepted the idea that these attributes are identical with God's essence but variety of modes is nevertheless necessary. He is knowing in one mode (*ḥaithiyah*), powerful in another and similarly for all the rest of the attributes.

Potentiality and Act (quwwah wa fi'l)

There are two kinds of potentiality (*quwwah*), viz. power of act (*quwwat al-fi'l*) i.e. potency and power of passion (*quwwat al-infi'āl*) i.e. passivity.

Power of Act is that quality which makes an actor an actor e.g. the heat of fire which is the power by which it burns. Sometimes this power is natural by which *things without volition and* consciousness can produce e.g. the heat of the fire, the *wetness of water etc. Some times* this power is volitional.

Power of passion is that aptitude in anything to receive the influence of something else as e.g. wax by its softness receives various shapes. There is no difference between *quwwat al-infi'āl* and *imkān isti'dādī* (see above). "When there is the potentiality or aptitude to anything that thing is said to be existing in potentiality (*mawjūd bil quwwah*) and when that thing actually is it is said to be existing "in act" (*mawjūd bil fi'l*). Because certain things accept the influence of the Maker after certain conditions have been fulfilled (*sharā'iṭ*) the potentiality of some possibilities is in some other thing and it is not until all the conditions of its existence have been fulfilled and there is nothing left to wait for that these come into existence from non-existence. But with potential contingency or possibility (*imkān isti'dādī*) there must be essential contingency or possibility (*imkān zātī*) i.e. there is no refusal to accept the bounty of existence in the contingent essence.

In some contingent things there is no potential possibility e.g. in spiritualties (*rūḥāniyāt*). These accept the bounty of existence without any condition, being sufficient in themselves. So in such things there is only essential possibility. But the truth is that the origination of both kinds of contingent things is necessary (i.e. it is impossible for them to be un-originated or eternal—*khadīm*) because it is impossible that a voluntary act should proceed from an agent, and that it should not be posterior to the agent.

Origination and Unbeginningness *(ḥudūth wa qadīm)*

These terms are sometimes used in a relative sense and sometimes in a real sense. Relative unbeginningness (*qidm izāfī*) is in the case when the time of the existence of one thing is greater than that of another. Relative origination (*ḥudūth izāfil*) is when the period of the existence of something is less than that of something else.

Of real unbeginningness there are two sorts:

a) Temporal unbeginningness (*qidm zamānī*). This is when there is no period of non-existence before the thing's existence.

b) Essential unbeginningness (*qidm zātī*). This is when something has no need of anything else in its existence.

Similarly there are two kinds of real origination:

a) Temporal origination (*huduth zamānī*) which simply means that the thing of which this is predicated was non-existent before it came to exist.

b) Essential origination (*ḥudūth zātī*). This is said of a thing which depends for its existence on something else.

Substance and Accident *(jawhar wa 'araz)*

Substance is applied to a thing which does not exist in some other subjectum (*mawdū'*) as e.g. man or horse. Accident is that which, on the contrary does reside in a subjectum e.g. blackness and redness.

Some particular (individual) substances also e.g. corporeal form and generic form need a suppositum (*maḥall*) for their existence but nevertheless they are substances. The root of the matter is that the advention of an accident does not change the reality or nature of the suppositum in which it resides, e.g. black is an accident and if it is in some cloth the real nature of the cloth does not change. If it be asked of red cloth whether it is cloth and of black cloth also the answer must be that it is still cloth. But the inherence of a "form" does change the suppositum e.g. there is first of all matter, but when corporeal form is set up in it, it becomes body. So now if the question be asked, what is this?

The answer will be in the first place "matter" and in the second place after the addition of corporeal form "Body." The learned have fixed this terminology to show the difference between "accident" and "form" by calling the suppositum of an accident a "subjectum" (*mawdū'*) and the suppositum of form "matter" (*māddah*). For this reason the definition of accident may be given as "Accident is that thing the existence of which is in a subjectum" and the definition of substance is contrary to this.

There are five kinds' of substance: Primal Matter (*hayūlī*), Form (*sūra*), Body (*jism*), Soul (*nafs*), and Separate Intelligence (*'aql mufarriq*). If the substance be the receptacle or container (*maḥall*) then it is *hayūlī*. If it be the content (state or what constitutes the content—*ḥal*), than it is "form" corporeal or generic. If it is neither *maḥall* nor *ḥal* but is composed of both, then it is "body." If it is not composed of *ḥal* and *maḥall* but has connection with the body then it is "soul." If it has no connection with the body then it is separate intelligence or Separate intellect.

There are nine kinds of accident: quantity (*kam*), quality (*kayf*), relation (*nisbah*), where (place) (*'ain*), when (*zamān*), possession (*milk*) position (*wad*), doing (*fi'l*) and suffering (*infi'āl*). (Note that these are the Aristotelian Categories). Quantity is that which is in essence capable of division. Quality is not in its essence capable of division or relation. Relation is the name of the connexion one thing has to another. "Where" comes about by reference to the place where a thing is as "up" and "down." The disposal of the parts of a thing within itself or in reference to some other thing is "position." Doing is e.g. sitting, walking etc. Suffering is e.g. being broken etc. Possession is of wearing as e.g. shod, armed etc.

The Essence and Attributes of God *(zāt wa ṣifāt)*

Thought will show that the Maker of all things is so mighty that He is beyond the power of our thought but that, nevertheless, He is in every respect perfect and most manifest. The reason is, however, weak and defective in its perception of Him. Ordinary people believe that. God is in Heaven (the sky) above us and His acts distinguish Him from created things. The intellectual say that God is a spiritual form which transcends time and space. The Philosophers' belief is that God is absolutely one and is beyond the limitations of direction, pointing out, up and down. It is He who has created all contingent (possible) things. The causes, natures and properties which human mistakenly consider agents are in reality all created by Him. The Real Agent is that invisible Being who is neither substance (*jawhar*) nor is accident (*araz*). He has created this world a world of causality and in it some things are causes (*sabab*) and others caused (*musabbab*) e.g. the existence of parents is the cause of the existence of children etc. God is the cause of this causality.

Some people think that God is an actor under compulsion (ex-necessitate naturae-my necessity of nature-*fā'il bil ijāb*) i.e. just as the rays of the sun issue from it involuntarily so the universe also issues from God without His volition or free choice (*bilā irādah wa ikhtiyār*) and so the world is eternal—unoriginated or without beginning (*khadīm*) also.

The Proof or Affirmation of the Necessary *(i.e. God)*

Everything made (*masnū'*) points to the existence of its maker (*ṣāni'*). So there must be a Maker of the Universe. Philosophers give the argument for His existence in the following way: Every existence is either possible (*mumkin*) or necessary (*wājib*). If it depends for its existence on something else then it belongs to the first category (the contingent). Otherwise it is necessary. Because generated things (*kaināt*) depend on something else for their existence, that on which they depend (*muhtāj ilaih*) must be necessary of existence (*wājib ul wujūd*).

The Necessity *(wujūb)* of the Existence *(wujūd)* and Attributes of the Creator

The Existence and the Necessity of Existence are the Essence of the Creator Himself. For if this were not so and these were only additional qualities then God would not be existent and necessary in the stage of His Essence and this is impossible. But it should not be understood that the meaning of His existence being identical with His Essence is emanational existence (*wujūd maṣdarī*). Because an emanational entity is a derived thing (*intizā'ī*). In it there is no capacity to be the real nature of a thing (*'ayn*). But the meaning of existence being the real nature of a thing is only that the Essence of the Necessary Being is the source of the derivation of the emanational existence without the addition of anything else. In the same way all the attributes of God are identical with the essence. In us when the quality of knowledge is acquired we are called "knowing," but God's Essence itself is alone the source whence all His perfect attributes are derived and so God is "knowing" *per se* (*bidhatihi*) etc.

Some people think that if the attributes of God are identical with the Essence of God then there is no difference in the significance of one attribute from another. This is a mistake and unfounded. Otherwise the words "knowledge," "power," "will," "life" etc. would all be identical in meaning and from each the same meaning could be inferred. But the meaning of the identity of the attributes with the Essence is that the Essence is the sole source of them all. God's Essence itself is *ḥakīm, ghaffūr*, *khāliq*, *rāziq*, *raḥīm*, *muṣawwir*, etc.

The Unity of the Lord of the Universe

If there had been two then this universe would never have emerged from non-existence into existence, for if it be assumed that two creators made the universe in agreement together, then the question would be whether either of them had any power against the other? If each had not such power then how he be called God? If each had such power, then both would have the attribute of being overcome by the other and so neither of them could be called God. Therefore God is One and Unique and without pair.

The philosophers have set forth the proof of the unity *of* God as follows: if two necessaries be assumed then the question arises: if both are equal in all attributes and all things then they, would not be two but one. If both were different in all things from each other than one would be existent and the other non-existent. If they agreed in some of their attributes and disagreed in other then in the essences of both there would be some things common to both and for both separately something by which they were distinguished. In such a case the essence of both would be composite of something common and something particular. But composition is an act for which an agent is required and so when these two Necessaries in their several existences are in need of an agent (something to act upon them) they are not "necessary" as was supposed. And so the Necessary must be one.

By this argument it is also proved that the Necessary is Simple (*basīṭ*) for if the Essence of God were composed of parts this composition would need an outside agent to accomplish it. And when the Necessary becomes dependent (*muhtāj*) it no longer continues to be necessary. Therefore God is Simple.

The Necessary's Knowledge

Some Greek philosophers believed that God neither knows Himself nor anything outside Him. He cannot have knowledge of Himself (His Essence) because knowledge is the name for that connexion which is between the knower and the known, and thus duality between the knower and the known is involved. And because there is no difference to be found between a thing and its essence then the knowledge of the essence is impossible. There is, moreover, no knowledge of things other than the essence because when He does not know His own Essence, how can he acquire any knowledge of other things? In such a case He would have the knowledge that He knew certain things and in this way he would have knowledge of Himself. But it has been proved that He cannot have knowledge of Himself. (His Essence) therefore He cannot have knowledge of anything.

This argument is met by the question "How is it proved that knowledge is the relation between the knower and the known?" The essence of God is the mirror of cognizance. He has knowledge of His Essence and of all contingent things. Just as He has immediate (i.e. without the medium of a form) knowledge of His Essence, similarly He has immediate knowledge of us contingent things (immediate knowledge—*'ilm huzūrī*).

Therefore God is with us and we are present before His Holy Essence. But we cannot have immediate knowledge of Him. We only know Him by way of proofs and arguments (*adillah wa barāhin*). Thus God is not before our eyes but we are before His and present before Him. It is for this reason that it is said that He is nearer to us than our jugular vein, i.e. His knowledge surrounds us on every side. The Being who created the whole series of possible things by His knowledge and will and Who Himself fixed their laws must know every atom perfectly. Whatever is yet to be created or whatever is yet to happen must also be known to Him.

The knowledge which God has of contingent or possible things is in two ways. Firstly, before its bringing into existence (*ijād*). This is called active knowledge (*'ilm fi'lī*) nd secondly, after it is brought into existence which is called passive knowledge (*'ilm infi'ālī*), Because after they are brought into existence all possible things are in the presence of God. He has immediate knowledge of all possible things, but how He has knowledge of them before they are brought into existence is a debatable matter because the existence of something known is a condition of knowing and it is clear that possible things have not existed eternally but nevertheless the knowledge of God is eternal. Plato's solution is that God's knowledge is those abstract forms, (*ṣuwar mujarradah*) which are existing essentially in the knowing intellect. But about this there is the difficulty as to how He knows those forms. Aristotle and Ibn Sīnā and Abū Naṣr al-Fārābī consider that God's knowledge is those forms which are existing by His Supreme Essence. The objection to this view is that God's Essence itself is not the Knower but in acquiring knowledge He is dependent on the subsistence of forms (in the Platonist view the term "idea" is better than "form"). One school of the philosophers of Islām considers that in reality existence is only in the Essence of God and that all these contingent things are only apparitions of it (*zill*). Therefore before all contingent things exist they are included in His Essence. So when God knows His own Essence he also knows all contingent things. He knows particulars and universals equally. The idea gleaned from the writings of some Greek philosophers that God has no knowledge of particulars is only on account of the fact that we have knowledge of particulars by sensation, thought and phantasy. God does not know particulars in this way.

The Stages of God's Knowledge

These are four: Active knowledge (*'ilm fi'lī*), passive knowledge (*'ilm infi'ālī*) which have already been mentioned, the Decree (*qada*), which is called also Mother of the Book (*Umm al-kitāb*), Preserved Tablet (*al Law¢ al-maḥfūz*), and the Pen (*al-qalam*). This means the separate (incorporeal or abstract) intelligences (*'uqūl mujarradah*). The Tablet and the Pen are not material substances but by *qaza* is meant those cognitive forms (*ṣuwar 'ilmiyyah*) (We might say "intelligibles") which are inscribed (*munaqqash*) on the souls of the separate intelligences i.e. "angels of the near presence" (*malāik-i muqarrabūn*) (c.f. Cherubim). The inscriptions of all past, present and future things are there present. There is no possibility of change in the Divine Decree. The fourth stage is *qadar* or *qadr* by which is meant the cognitive forms in the souls of those angels who have obtained the Tablet and the Pen. This is called the "Book of Annulling and Affirming" (*Kitāb al-maḥw wa ithbāt*). It is possible for there to be change in this because the angels of *qadar* estimate things also by reference to conditions (*ḥālāt*) and events (*wāqi'āt*) e.g. if Zayd does good then the reasonable conclusion is that he will go to Paradise and sometimes the event is to the contrary. Sometimes the souls of the elect (*buzurg*) reach to this in a state of revelation (*mukāshafah*) or meditation (*murāqabah*). So sometimes the event may be contrary to their revelation. Nevertheless their revelation is not conjectural like the knowledge of soothsayers (*kāhin*) and astrologers (*munajjim*), but they have a revelation of a single thing and not the whole.

In reference to *qaza* an objection is raised. When our acts proceed according to the decree of God, then they must necessarily proceed and so all acts of worship, deeds and plans are useless, for, if the things we are trying to achieve and for which we engage in acts of worship are already established and fixed in the Divine Decree, they will remain so whether we try or not or whether we pray or not, and the creature is under absolute compulsion (*majbūr-i maḥaz*). The reply to such an objection is that the Decree here explained is only that the Creator has knowledge of all things and that knowledge is inscribed in the angels also. But the creature is not compelled by such knowledge because knowledge is not the cause of the existence of what is known. If we know that Zayd will get up in ten minutes this knowledge of ours does not compel him to get up. Knowledge must be in accordance with the correct happening but that knowledge is not the cause of the act. Such matters of this kind may be observed in everyday, life, e g. a master gives the key of his house to some servant knowing him to be untrustworthy or honest. Sometimes he is certain that the man will be dishonest and will steal something. Nevertheless he puts him in charge and exhorts him to be honest. Now if the servant steals and the knowledge of the master thus be in accordance with the fact, does it follow that that, knowledge which the master had caused him to steal? Suppose he says in excusing himself that his master knew he was a thief and had no power to resist stealing, will this clear him of the charge of dishonesty and enable him to escape punishment?

God gives human power and if they use it wrongly then they deserve punishment. Human have the power of choice and as they act so will they receive the consequences. The work of the creature is only to use the power, but the existence of the act is from God. The work of the farmer is to prepare the field and sow it, but the one who causes the seed to sprout, the one who causes growth and the one who gives fruit is God. And so the creature is not absolutely compelled and not completely free (*mukhtār-i kull*). One has to use the powers given, use his/her endeavors and after the using of power, it is not within their power to compass the existence of anything. God is the Creator of everything.

The question why God does not always make His servant do right and compel them to serve Him and go in the right way is a vain perplexity, because God did not make human like a stone under absolute compulsion but gave to them the power of proceeding to act (*ṣudūr-i af'āl kī quwwat*). God has given human hands and feet, and it is clear that they can use these for good or for evil. God has also granted human the power of reason so that they may discriminate between good and evil. Moreover, only on account of His grace has He sent prophets to inform human of what is good and evil. More than this, He has given human the power to choose righteousness and guidance. So if God were to compel human to do good, their obedience and worship would be compulsory and that would be profitless. Could a person in authority be happy that one exacted obedience by compulsion and that people did not obey him with their hearts? God does not like the service of hypocrites (dissemblers-*munāfiq*).

From time to time we have explained that God made this world a world of causality. Who knows what is in the Divine knowledge? This can only be known by the event. Human is not guilty because of God's knowledge but because they have not tried to do their duty. When human does their duty they are deserving of praise and if in spite of trying they fail to do their duty they will be excused and worthy to be pardoned, because they had at any rate tried and in truth it was this which was their duty.

Those people who neglect the means to attain their purposes act contrary to the rules and principles ordained by God. They are not obedient to God but disobedient. If a person neglects to eat because one says he/she is dependent on God alone, he/she is not doing honor to God because God has so arranged our life that it is sustained by eating. (N.B.: This is a more or less modernist attack on "fatalism").

The Abstract or Separate Intelligences *('uqūl mujarradah)*

Just as our world moves according to a special arrangement, so too the world of intelligences and angels; and just as in this world one thing is the cause of another, so too there is a causal system to be found in that world.

The opinion of the Peripatetics is that God made a substance which is called the Primal Intellect (*al-'aql al-awwal*). From this Primal Intellect, by the effulgence of the Creator, a second Intellect and the nine spheres came to exist. The Neo-Platonists (Ishrāqiyyah) and the philosophers of Islām hold that for all the spheres and elements in the universe of Intellect (*'ālam al-'aql*) there are directing intelligences by means of which God by His bounty and gift satisfies the universe. In the language of the Scriptures these intelligences are called angels. There are four pre-eminent: Isrāfīl whose work is the bestowal of life; Mikā'īl who provides for food and warmth; Jibra'īl whose special work is in relation to matters of knowledge and cognitions (*'ulūm wa ma'ārif*); and Azrā'īl whose special work it is to take away the souls of human and to deprive of life.

Prophethood and Mission *(nabūwwah wa risālah)*

It is contrary to God's attribute of justice that He should create human and let them go astray. Therefore for the guidance of His creatures He sends His representatives, these are called "prophets" (nabī) or "messengers" (rasūl). When wickedness increases in the world and the order of the universe is threatened with ruin, a messenger is sent down bearing divine instruction. The purpose of the teaching of such a messenger is nothing more than the correction of morals (*akhlāq*). He has no immediate connexion with matters of logic, philosophy or science but only incidentally (*zimnan*) and even then only to draw attention to the manifestation of the divine, because the messenger has a relation with the Almighty in a spiritual way far above our conception and is a mirror to all the attributes of the Creator of the Universe. He has dominion over all created things and so his works contrary to the regular order or custom are called miracles.

Prophets must have the attributes of truth (*ṣidq*), fidelity (*amānat*) power (*quwwā*), preaching or proclamation (*tablīgh*) and intelligence or sagacity (*fatana*). They are also "incarnate innocence" (*ma'sūm mujassam*) i.e. they commit neither great nor small sins. From time to time in the sacred books there is mention of the forgiveness (*maghfirah*) of the prophets but the meaning of this is only that the prophet is hidden within the veil of mercy. For *maghfirah* is of two kinds: to preserve a guilty person from wrath on account of God's mercy; and by his mercy preventing sin and guilt from reaching the good. The forgiveness of the prophets is of the latter sort. The guidance of the prophets is for the purpose of causing souls to live and enlightening hearts. But just as in the stone there is no aptitude to receive the rays of the sun but in the mirror there is, so also those whose hearts are quite black and in whom there is no aptitude left to receive the guidance cannot benefit by this teaching.

The Creation of the World *(ḥudūth al-'ālam)*

All prophets and philosophers have affirmed that the world had a beginning (ḥadīth) and have given proofs and arguments for the same. (Note that this excludes Ibn Rushd and others with whom Muslims show very little if any acquaintance. Similarly, what follows does not properly represent Aristotle's opinion.) A materialist asked Aristotle "Since God is eternal ought not the universe to be eternal? Aristotle gave the reply, "The eternal is that before whose existence there is no non-existence. Since act proceeds from an agent (i.e. the doer of the act) it is impossible that the act should not be later than the actor himself. And when the act is posterior to the essence of the actor then it must have a beginning." The materialist again asked, "Will the world disappear?" "Yes", said Aristotle, "He will destroy this world and make the eternal."

Someone asked Pythagoras (Faithaghuras), "Will this world cease to be?" He answered, "Yes, when this world has reached the end for which it was made it will come to rest and cease to be". Some Peripatetics say that the matter of the universe is unoriginated because the capacity for all material things is in matter. If that matter were to have had a beginning then this capacity of matter would have to be in some other matter and so on *ad infinitum*. The reply given to this is that material things (*māddiyat*) depend for their existence on matter but matter is not a thing and therefore it does not depend on matter. It has simply by its essential potentiality accepted the influence of the divine. Here the further thought arises that one thing comes into existence from another and so how did matter come into existence from non-existence? The reply to this is that it may be illustrated from our word which comes into existence by the speaker and which is a particularized (or individuated) existence of our mental forms.

It is also asked, "What was God doing before the creation of the world?" The answer is that God is a voluntary agent (*fā'il bil irādah*) and every intention or voluntary act must be later than the essence of the actor. The name for this posteriority is origination (*ḥudūth*). Here the question of duration does not arise i.e. that He laid the foundation of the world at such and such a time and was idle or unoccupied before.

It is also said, "Matter was made by or from its quality of essential potentiality and therefore there, must have been some suppositum for this essential potentiality?" The answer to this difficulty is "Not rejecting the acceptance of existence is what is called essential potentiality." So this is a negative thing for which no suppositum is required although potential contingency or potential possibility is a positive (*wujūdī*) quality for which a suppositum is required.

Last Things *(ḥashr wa nashr)*

Just as the assurance of an invisible being enters the nature of human so also human has a natural inclination, to believe in a future life. And just as human's creeds about the invisible are various so also their beliefs about the hereafter. A well-known belief of some philosophers is that the future life will not be in a bodily form but spirits will continue to be their incorporeal state and according as they are nearer or further away from God there will be a manifestation of their ascent or descent.

The Scholastics think that because "man" is the name for a combination of soul and body, it must be that the body must be in some way included in this future life Therefore the original or fundamental parts of all bodies will remain-intact in spite of the changes of time. When it is God's will there will be a second production of this body (from the original parts) and a living form will come to be a second time in order that it may receive the recompense of its deeds. Although the form and shape and appearance will not be the same the original parts will be the same as those existing the first time in this world.

Some philosophers of Islām think that when death separates the human spirit from the body, the power of thought is not separated and because in that power (*quwwa khayāliyyah*) there are retained the impressions of all our habits and morals, our fashions and ways, therefore the kind of thought which has prevailed will determine the form of the future body and so our future life will depend on the impressions which have been dominant in our minds. On this account they deny the "return of bodies" (*iada*) because the parts of the body are continually being dissolved. The bodies we had in youth do not remain in later life.

So the survival of human's personality depends on the rational soul and because the rational soul is not cut off from a body in the future world, there will be a body according to our deeds in this world.

Some people deny such a view because the dissolution of bodies takes place in plants and animals although these do not possess rational souls. In their opinion the personality of bodies does not depend on the human spirit or the animal spirit but on bodily life, which is a hidden substance like sparks latent in a stone and this substance is present in every body. The future bodily life will depend on this physical life but that body will be immaterial. It will have quantity (dimension) but not matter.

In any case there will be a life after the judgment and it will be exactly a perfect manifestation of those deeds which man did in this life.

In *fuṣūṣ al-ḥikm*, Ibn 'Arabī wrote that God is merciful and will therefore not keep any one eternally in punishment. Punishment will only be in order that the capacity for the acquirement of perfection may be achieved as the goldsmith purges gold in the fire. After punishment the forms of the people of Hell will gradually change to those of the people of Paradise. If they were "associators" (*mushrik*), they will remain in the torment the length of time that they lived in this world and afterwards they will enter into Paradise. If they were to be sent to heaven before this their nature would be so warped by their *shirk* that they would not enjoy the pleasures of Paradise because of the inappropriateness of that life.

A Simple Comparison of Muslim and Christian Doctrine

(Part I, II & III)

James Windrow Sweetman

Introduction

Islām, unlike other great religions, developed in more or less conscious contradiction to Christianity and this creates many problems for the Christian in his relations with Muslims.

Scriptures

Muslims believe in sacred books. The Qur'ān is held to be the word of God and the final revelation. It is thought to summarize all previous revelation, which was given by means of a series of prophets. It proves and confirms all previous scriptures and so there is no longer any need for them. Of the Old and New Testaments, Muslims say that they have been interpolated and corrupted, and so the true originals are lost. They complain that the four Gospels were written by Apostles to and not by Jesus and they criticize the epistles as being simply of letters from Paul and others, and so the "Injīl" (Gospel) which descended on Jesus is not now extant. Jesus took it back to Heaven with him.

Our answer is that even if the Qur'ān is the last in time it is not for that reason, therefore, the best. Sikhs have a sacred book dated later than the Qur'ān. Is that the best because it came last? If the Muslims claim their scripture to be best we might ask, "What does the Qur'ān have better than Ps. 139 on the Sermon on the Mount?" If the Psalm and the sermon have been "confirmed" by the Qur'ān, in what passages is this to be found? Muslims do not particularize in this way. This is true also of the way they speak of the prophets. They say they believe in all of them, but when asked even to name them they are unable to do so, much less describe them teaching. We can particularize because we have the prophetic books.

Revelation came through the history of people. E.g. the deliverance from Egypt's bondage, Israel's afflictions; the prophets' expectation of a messiah grew out of their experiences. Then Christ came actually in history, the Holy Spirit was given: the New Testament came into existence in definite relation to these events. Thus we have a record of the acts of God history. How can facts of history be abrogated as Muslims would have us think? In addition, the Bible contains God's promises to humankind. Those promises must be kept if God is true to Himself. He cannot cancel what He has promised without being untrue to Himself. Christian and Jewish Scripture also contains the law of righteousness. External laws of temporary application might be cancelled by laws for the inward life and legal details might be displaced by broad principles, but the eternal law of righteousness cannot be cancelled.

Muslims say Scripture has been corrupted. When? Was it before or after Muḥammad? Muḥammad referred to the Books. Were they intact then? They say that prophecies of Muḥammad were expunged. When? We have documents earlier than Muḥammad.

Among others, people could have two ideas about the sacred books:

a) They contain a great deal of information which God has given to human because human could not get it through their natural intelligence. Sometimes this information is thought to be in the form of mantras and cryptograms. Then these strange documents become the subject of argument and dispute. At last, as time goes on, they become mysterious problems which human have to solve and find difficult to understand.

b) The Bible is not like this. It is not a book of problems, but of solutions. It does not ask us to give an answer about itself. It gives us an answer about our own lives. The Bible is history, the record of human's experiences, but given to us by God through His Holy Spirit, to interpret life, stimulate faith and bring us to God. It is also not simply a revelation of the will of God but of God Himself, and its centre is Jesus Christ by whom we know God.

Revelation

Here is the difference between the Christian and the Muslim view. The latter thinks it is to tell human what to do; the Christian claims that God reveals Himself, shows what He is as He deals with human. The element of the revelation of God's will is not altogether absent, but it is part of the revelation of what God is Himself. Revelation of God's will could be simply in commands, but revelation of God Himself can only be in and through a personality.

God's personality is not the same as humans' but it is possible for God's personality to be revealed in human character. The Muslims often cannot understand how the names of God are to be understood, because they feel that God is altogether different from human. It is true to a certain extent that when I look at my own imperfect life and character, it is out of place for me to think that God is just like that. To think so would not be giving God His rightful due or glorifying Him as we ought. It is necessary therefore that there should be some person in whom could be revealed such attributes of God as human personality is capable of revealing. So instead of looking at our imperfect selves in order to understand what God is, God Himself has provided the perfect manhood of Jesus Christ. So what human lack because of their imperfections, God supplies in our humanity to meet human's obvious need, in their effort to understand what God is. This gift of God is Jesus Christ for Whom Scripture is either a preparation, a presentation or an interpretation.

Islām, to a certain extent, admits this need of revelation in a person but actually makes no provision for it. What is seen in Islām is an accretion. Ṣūfī thought reveals this. Mysticism aims at the direct apprehension of God in the human heart. Human by meditation seeks to have heart-knowledge of God. Most of the great religions have much the same idea. Human go to a teacher who can set them on the way to this new knowledge of God. In Islām the Pīr or spiritual director is often thought of as exemplifying in himself some attribute of God, and Ṣūfīs try to progress to the Perfect Man *(Insān-i kāmil)* who completely embodies the divine attributes. This illustrates the need human has for a revelation of God in personality rather than in a book. God meets this need in Jesus Christ. Muḥammad says (in effect), "He that hath heard me hath hear Allah." Jesus says, "He that hath seen me hath seen the Father."

Is it fit or proper for God to be revealed in human personality? Perhaps the Muslim might agree but he says, "You Christians go further and say that Christ is God and that God became man." Christians do not mean by such words that God was turned into man by a sort of metamorphosis as some primitive people have imagined, when they have said that a man was changed into an ass by magic. When a Christian speaks of God becoming man he does not think that Heaven became empty and something equivalent came into being on earth; that God disappeared from Heaven and Jesus was then born in Bethlehem. God forbid! We will talk about the incarnation later but here we will say that opponents of the Christian doctrine of incarnation are often too much taken with the idea of impassable gulf between human and God.

Doctrine of God

Muslims say, "You believe in God and so do we." They therefore think that we both mean the same thing when we say "God." But do we believe in God in the same way as does the Muslim? The Muslim says that God is one and there is no one beside Him. This oneness one thinks is more important than anything else. But an idolater may think that his idol is the one, only true God. The important thing is: What sort of God do we believe in?

Why do Christians believe in one God? It is important for us that when Muslims ask us whether we believe in one God, we should say "Yes". They may want us to say that we believe in the Trinity and then proceed to attack us on this doctrine. If we say that we believe in the Father, Son and Holy Ghost, they will take it to mean that we do not believe in one God. So our definite reply at this point should be that we *do* believe in one God. Yet we believe this doctrine differently from the Muslim. It is significant for our belief that the declaration of God's unity stands at the head of the Ten Commandments, because there is one command, one fiat running through the whole of the universe. The very word "universe" shows how we think. Belief in one God is in fact partly an inference from the harmony and unity of nature and, as we see so clearly in the Jewish prophets, a conviction that the rule of One should extend over all the earth and His laws should be for all humankind. The Jews had the difficulty that the heathen round them worshipped many gods. If the Jews said "The law of God is this, so obey it," they could reply, "It is not the law of *our* god". If we read Amos we shall see how he speaks to the surrounding nations, and how he fights cruelty and wrongdoing of all sorts among all the nations because he believes that God's laws are the same for the heathen as for the Jew. So the Jew's idea of God's unity is not a matter of arithmetic. It is spiritual and moral. Christians believe in *the unity of the character of God.* God always wills and commands righteously.

So the first reply to the Muslim is that Unity is in the moral character of God. The Muslims seem to prefer the numerical unity and so they attribute to God evil and good, or what would be good and bad if found in human. Thus among His names, He is the Ono who guides and the One who leads astray. In this way the real internal unity and harmony of the divine nature could be destroyed or imperilled and a merely formal unity imposed on things which really cannot form a unity but are in themselves contradictory. It seems shocking to say on the one hand that God is one, and then attribute to Him both good and evil in which there is no unity. If there is division in our own heart and mind we are no longer properly one but have a divided personality.

Both Christians and Muslims believe in a God of power but Muslims exaggerate this. Christians think that there is something which God cannot do. His power is limited by His holy nature, His wisdom and His love. Muslims too often say that God can do anything, even to making the past not to have been. They say that God as power is the author of all the power human have, and this is true, but it does not mean that human have no power. The Christian says that God gave human real power over their actions. Sometimes Muslims say that there is no actor but God. Everything which is done is done by Him. God puts it into my hand to take hold of a book; He creates power in my hand to seize it, creates my hand in very position it assumes in the action of grasping it. The universe consists in atoms of space and time which are continuously linked together by no other power than God's continuous creation. God is working creatively all the time. There is something fine about this idea, but it passes over some very important things. It belittles the power which God has put into things to give them causative action, and it too often weakens the sense of human responsibility and loads to fatalism. We believe, as Christians, that God in a wonderful way has made it possible to do some things by ourselves. Any other belief makes human inclined to think that God is the author of the evil they do. If human being is able to act for themselves then they are responsible for their actions.

Because Muslims believe that God is absolutely different from human they are in difficulty in understanding anything about God. The Qur'ān says that God is forgiving, merciful and holy, but when we ask what "holy" or what "mercy" means, and whether knowing what it is for a human to be merciful can give us a partial idea of what God's mercy is, they say that it is not possible. A Qur'ānic verse says that God is keen on punishment because He is *Raḥmān*, and so God's mercy cannot be like humans'. Once I asked a learned Muslim whether, we could know what mercy and kindness in God was by referring to human experience, and he replied, "God forbid! God is unlike men." When I asked him what *Raḥīm* meant, he said it was unique *(lā thanī)* and he gave the same reply about the other attributes. I asked him how he differentiated between the different attributes and his reply was that they were written and pronounced differently; there was the command of God to use them about Him, and that was why there were ninety-nine beautiful names of God. Further enquiry was useless. God knows what these names mean, and that is sufficient. But for us Christians, revelation results in our knowing something more about God and if the words which are used are used in a way quite different, there does not seem to be much point in revelation at all, so far as our knowing God is concerned.

It is, of course, true that we cannot form a perfect idea of God from what we know from human experience. But it is also true that God can only reveal what He has given us the power to understand. The difficulty is in us and not in God. If God reveals anything to us it must be to us as humans with feelings and reason. Language can only be a means of communication when both the speaker and the hearer are acquainted with it, and if God used Arabic to speak to Muḥammad it was because Muḥammad was acquainted with that language. To understand there must be a connection with our knowing and the knowing of others. Concepts arise from comparison, setting one thing against another, and because of this relation we are able to convey ideas or thoughts one to another. Both "conscience" and "concept" are ultimately related to God. What is moral or intelligent in us is so by the reflection of God's righteousness and wisdom. If there is no likeness between God and us, then what is right for us may not be right for God. Muslims incline to this belief. The law of righteousness which is incumbent on human is not incumbent on God. God is like a master commanding a servant, but it does not matter what He does Himself. The Christians believe that God commands because He is what He is. The law of righteousness is the law of His own nature. God is not like a master commanding a slave but like a father commanding a son and seeking to impart something of Himself to human. By His own act He makes human like Him. He made human in His own image after His likeness.

Not that a child knows all that his father is. A child is not exactly like his father but there is still a kind of likeness of his father in a child and a growth in that likeness. The Christians believe God is a Father in that He wants us to be like Him and "gives us power to become His sons." "Be ye perfect as your Father in heaven is perfect." This is God's gift and it is not something which we steal from Him. He gives this gift in grace and love. He writes His laws in our heart and they become part of our nature. We do not know everything about Him but enough for our human needs.

Moral Attributes of God: Holiness, Truth and Righteousness

Muslims believe that righteousness must be related to law. If a human is righteous it is because one is obedient to commands. Morality is a matter of obedience to law. Can God be obedient to any law? If not, how can God have any moral attributes? The highest attributes include Holiness, Truth and Righteousness in Christian belief, and so all those must be God's. When asked whether he would go to Paradise if he obeyed all the injunctions of the Qur'ān, a Muslim replied "God knows." Pressed by a change in the question, "If you do all God has told you to do, will you go to Paradise?" He gave the same reply. Pressed still further he said, "How can I know? If God wills He can send me to Paradise and if He pleases He can send me to Hell." Thus it would seem that God's promises do not put Him under any obligation. He is not bound by them. This is an exaltation of power at the expense of righteousness and truth. Not believing that God is solely a God of power, Christianity believes that God is supremely loving and that His purposes are loving purposes. This doctrine of the love of god is most inadequately represented in the Qur'ān, where it is really to be thought of as preference or to God's likings. God loves the kind, the patient and so on, those who are not unjust, those who believe. He likes them, but there is no bond between Him and human and no yearning love for sinners. It seems as strange to a Muslim to say "God loves sinners" as for one to say "I prefer bad eggs." It seems wrong to the Muslim that God should love sinners. This is because the idea of love is erroneous.

We here come back to the main thought of Christian teaching—the Fatherhood of God, the sonship of man and the brotherhood of human with human. A man who loves a son who goes wrong is not a foolish man. It is God's very nature to love and thus He loves human, and it is not human's worth which makes God love them. Humankind may wander far from Him, yet He loves and is grieved at human sin. Muslim's opinion considers God to be indifferent. The old story in tradition is that when God made Adam he made to appear before Him all who could be born, and pointing to those on the right He said, "These are for Paradise, and I care not", and then pointing to those on the left He said, "These are for Hell and I care not". The Christian does not believe that God so made humankind. The only reason for creation must be the overflowing love and bounty of God. God *does* care. He cares enough to create humankind and to bestow on them all he has of likeness to his Creator. He cares so much that He gives Himself in the person of His son for the redemption of humankind (John iii. 16). "Herein is love, not that we loved God but that He loved us and sent His Son to be the propitiation for our sin" (i John iv. 10). This love embraces all sinful human everywhere. This is the glory of the Christian Gospel and this is the supreme difference in the Worship of the God Christians worship and the God Muslims worship.

The Lord Jesus Christ

In the Qur'ān there is much written about Jesus, for example, that He came with miracles of healing, cleansed lepers gave the blind sight, raised the dead. The Qur'ān says that God gave Jesus "signs" and aided Him by the Holy Spirit (sūra ii. 31). Jesus is generally spoken of as the Son of Mary. He was born of a virgin (iv. 168-170). "Jesus is only an apostle of God and His Word which He cast into Mary." Jesus is only a creature and a slave (*'abd*) of God (iii. 52). God created Him as Adam was created. This is intended to deny His divinity, but does not necessarily do so. (See Sūra iii. 30-54 where the nativity is described). In the miracle of making birds, Jesus is said to have given life to dead clay and the word used is the same as that for God's creation. Some modern Muslims, the Aḥmadis or Qādiyānīs, deny the virgin birth. Some have said, "Prove the virgin birth" forgetting that orthodox Islām believes it. But how can one prove the virgin birth? Proof of historical facts is by evidence, records or reports and the test is whether such testimony is trustworthy. If we consider the testimony in the Gospel trustworthy, then we accept the fact. Humanly speaking, the only one who knew the facts was Mary. People accepted her testimony and so the record was made and accepted by early Christians. Could there be any other proof? If parthenogenesis is established by science could we prove that it happened in the case of Jesus?

But arising out of this is something very important. The Muslims think that the Holy Trinity is a Father, Mother and a Son. Such a definition is not true and not Christian. It is a pagan idea. Muslims put a carnal meaning on Christ's sonship. Christ is not physically the Son of God as they suggest. How can God have such a son without a wife? How can the unlimited God with no body have a wife? This is the way they argue. This is a complete misunderstanding if not a misrepresentation of Christianity. Because Jesus was born of the Virgin he is the Son of Man. Before He was born of the Virgin He was God the Son. We use the word "Son" a special way, desiring to express the closest relationship there can be. The term may be described as metaphorical, but it is rather more than that because it points to an essential reality and is not merely a figure of speech. When Muslims talk of the "Mother of the Book" (*Umm al-kitāb*) in reference to the Heavenly Prototype of the Qur'ān, no Muslim would consider this to be used in any physical sense.

The Christian believes that God is a Spirit and that partly means that we do not think of God as a body. Moreover, the world "Son" is not a word which Christians have invented for relationship between Jesus and God, but it was used by Jesus Himself and is recorded in Scripture. Asking us to give up using the word would be asking us to disapprove of what Christ said and also to relinquish belief in the Scriptures, it may be that the term "Son" is an offence to the Muslim, but there are other things equally an offence to him, for example, the Cross of Christ.

In the Qur'ān Jesus is spoken of as the Word of God (*Kalimatullāh*) and a Spirit from God (*Rūḥ min Allāh*). Some Muslims even call Jesus the Spirit of God (*Rūḥullāh*). So when the Qur'ān says that Jesus was only a prophet, why does it give Him such high titles?

The Qur'ān says that Jesus did not die on the cross but God raised Him up to Himself (sūra iv. 155-159). If Jesus did not did not die on the Cross, why were records of it kept in the Gospels? Muslims say that the people were mistaken. Why did it take 600 years to the advent of Muḥammad for this mistake to be pointed out? An outline of an argument with a Muslim on this point is as follows. Muslims believe that Jesus came from God and that the dispensation until began with His "prophethood" was a divine dispensation until Muḥammad came. Would such a dispensation based on a mistake? Muslims say that the people were deceived. If Jesus did not die on the cross why did He not tell His disciples? It is a terrible slander against a "prophet" of God that He kept His followers in ignorance of something so important. The Muslim replies to this that Jesus was unable to tell His disciples because He was taken up into Heaven. This would mean that God gave Him no opportunity to tell His disciples this most important thing and so God would be responsible for their error, which would vitiate the truth of that which the Muslim considers a divine dispensation. If we cannot believe that either God or Jesus was responsible, then are we to say that the disciples were? Why should they tell a lie about this? If Jesus had not died at all but had been taken up to heaven alive, this would have been a stupendous fact which could rank alongside the miracle of the resurrection. Was it to the advantage of the disciples that they should assert that Jesus died as others human die, or that he died a death, which other people had died at the hands of the Jews for blasphemy? It was not because they asserted that Jesus had died that the disciples were persecuted, but because they asserted that he had risen from the dead. Why, again, did not the Jews hasten to deny that they had crucified Christ, seeing that for generations they were persecuted for having done so? If they knew the disciples had been guilty of deception they would have said so even if only to save themselves.

Muslims say that Jesus is living and not dead. He is in the fourth heaven and will come again to live on earth, to marry and have children, convert the world to Islām and then die a normal death and be buried in a tomb kept vacant for him by the side of the Prophet Muḥammad. Aḥmadis say that Jesus swooned on the cross, was taken down for dead, put in the grave but revived there after being anointed with a special curative ointment. If we ask them how they know they have no evidence to offer. One might easily start such story about someone else, but it would not necessarily be true because divine authority was claimed for it. A man once told me in sober earnest that Kabīr was born out of his mother's arm! There is no foundation for such stories at all and this Aḥmadis story is a pure invention with no historical evidence. Aḥmadis say that Jesus fled to Kashmir (what unworthy conduct for a "Prophet" of God!) and died there at the age of 120 years, his tomb being at Srinagar. The origin of this tale is an untrue account of a Russian, named Notovitch, who claimed to have travelled in Tibet and to have found ancient Tibetan documents which told of Jesus' stay in a monastery there. Dr Aḥmad Shah of the I.M.S. investigated this and found it to be a fabrication from beginning to end. No historian of repute would accept such a fable. If the Muslims claim that the Qur'ān itself is sufficient evidence for the survival of Jesus without dying, there would be the danger of having to class the Qur'ānic story with that of Notovitch's. Supernatural contradiction of history is a most questionable filing and to support their view the Aḥmadis have to turn from the plain sense of the Qur'ān to a far-fetched explanation, and they are at odds not merely with the Christians but with their own orthodox co-religionists. The Qur'ān distinctly says that the Jews killed the prophets. Why was Jesus exempt?

In the Qur'ān no sin is attributed to Jesus. Later Muslim dogmatics has postulated the sinlessness of all prophets without distinction. Christians are not content with the merely negative statement, but positively say that in Him was every perfection and that He is the pattern of the best life that human can live. But Aḥmadis take the text "Why callest thou me good?" to prove that Christ was not sinless and this would be much against the orthodox Muslim belief as against Christians. The Scripture tells us that Jesus did not give way to temptation that He said, "Which of you convicteth me of sin?" He "knew no sin" and was "without sin." Why then should Aḥmadis try to make the text "Why callest thou me good?" mean something which would contradict those clear statements? The word "good" is used in the LXX almost exclusively for God and

His goodness. So Jesus in this passage reminds the young Jew of the use of this term for God. He said in effect, "Why do you use this word about me when it is used about God?" He wanted to point out to the young Jew the source of all goodness. Goodness is not what human achieves but what God gives.

The Incarnation

It should always be remembered that Christians do not start with a theory of incarnation and then try to fit Jesus Christ into that theory. We can have no *a priori* knowledge of what incarnation is. The fact of the incarnation must come first before we explain what it is. In Christian belief there has only been one incarnation and from that we get all the data available to us to know what it is.

Points to be borne in mind are: (1) the scriptural teaching about the pre-existence of Jesus Christ (2) the incarnation of the Word necessitated an emptying and a relation of faith and obedience on the part of Jesus to His Father. For example, a Muslim might say that Jesus Christ prayed to God, so can he be God. Our reply would be, "How could He be perfect Man and not pray?" The perfect humanity of Jesus is as much a part of the Christian doctrine as His divinity and the Christians maintain that it is necessary for the one who came in the flesh, that there should be this relation of faith and obedience to God the Father. (3) Jesus Christ "in the form of a servant" could not have those attributes which are peculiar to God in His infinity, eternity and immutability. It is true that the finite does not exhibit the infinite in such a manner as to reveal in full what infinity, etc., are.

The Muslim says, "God is eternal, but you say that Christ was born." We admit that since the Son was in the form of a servant He had to submit to the limitations of time (See John i, 1ff. and Phil. ii, 6-8). There are, nevertheless, certain divine attributes which can be fittingly revealed in finite nature without involving any contradiction. The poet may, for example, see the beauty of God in a flower or may speak of the majesty and power of God as seen in the mountains and the starry heavens, or of His wisdom as seen in order of nature. These things in finitude are yet means of expressing that which in God is infinite. Similarly there are some attributes which seem to be fittingly revealed in human nature, remembering again what has already been said about the unlikeness of God. In the very nature of the case, God establishes relations with humankind through Christ not by means of His absolute attributes but by those which it is important for human to know if the relationship is to be established. Thus it is not necessary to understand God's eternity.

We cannot if we try. But it is essential for us to know His mercy and His love. Could a proper revelation of God's love be made in a declaration? Or is a personality needed for this? There can be no revelation of omnipresence, omnipotence, infinity or eternity in their philosophical sense in a human life. These are all negations based on human limitations.

There can, however, be the revelation of such eternity as "Jesus Christ, the same yesterday, today and forever" in its bearing on our salvation. There can be a revelation of "Christ the wisdom and power of God" as the omnipotence of God in the saving of human, and a revelation of omnipresence is to faith of the ever-present Spirit of God and "Lo I am with you always, even unto the end of the world." Whatever the difficulty, it must be true still that the best revelation of personality is through personality and this is what Jesus Christ does.

We are not, therefore, unduly perturbed if the Muslim says that Jesus Christ cannot be the revelation of the eternal God in His eternity, because what we are trying to say to him that the eternal God is revealed by Christ *in time* and hereby takes up our time into His eternity. The perfect life of Jesus Christ, the love of Jesus, shows us something which surpasses anything seen elsewhere. We regard this therefore as divine revelation in Him.

We should also remind ourselves that Jesus forgave sins (Mk. ii, 5) and asserted that his words would outlast heaven and earth (Lk. vii, I4), pointing to an authority transcending human. To thwart evil He showed a mastery over nature (Lk. xxi, 33; Mt. viii, 16, ix, 26). So we would hold that the idea of incarnation only appears credible when based on the life portrayed in the Gospels. We do not find it credible elsewhere. So many things in Christ cannot be attributed to our common humanity. Even the best of prophets would not have dared to say some of the things which Christ said. They spoke of the call of God in a manner befitting human, but He said "I and the Father are one"; "I came from the Father and return to the Father"; "No man knoweth the Father and the Son"; "I am the bread of Heaven, and except a man eat of this bread he will surely die". He places Himself central, saying, "Come unto me and I will give you rest" and claims to be the Way, the Truth and the Life. He claims kingship (Mt. xxv, 31 ff; Lk. xxii, 29, etc.). He warns human that He will judge them (Mt. xix, 28). Thus Christ point to Himself as the object of faith and He thinks that it is important that human kind should recognise Him for what He is. He asks them, "Who do you say that I am" He accepts the title of Messiah, which Islām also admits, and by that He implies that He fulfils an age-long expectation and is specially anointed by God (Mt. xvi, 13ff). He accepts human's worship (John xx, 28). He teaches human to pray in His name (Mt, xviii, 19ff). He promises to be always present with them (Mt. xxviii, 20). We should have no difficulty in the case of ordinary human of putting such things down to delusion, but with Christ it is different and they seem to be appropriate to His character.

What is Incarnation?

Muslims do not bring the historicity of Jesus into question, although sometimes, when forced to attack Christianity they assert that the historical Christ was other than we fine in the New Testament record. But they have no other records of historical value to substitute. The Qur'ān implies that Jesus was unique in some respects; He is Word, Spirit, works miracles and is still living. There is more than a suggestion in the Qur'ān that in the eyes of Muḥammad Christ was more than human and of an angelic nature.

The Muslim's predicament is much like that of the Jew brought up in a pure monotheism. The Jew saw that Jesus thought, spoke and acted with a sense of complete unity with God and claimed to have attributes which are specially the attributes of God. He also did works which were compatible with his claim. They could not deny His power but some said that it was due to the Devil. Under the influence of their severe monotheism they killed Christ for blasphemy. They refused to believe what they saw in Christ because they had preconceived ideas. And in this way Muslim belief is very much like the Jewish. The Muslim, too, has these ideas about monotheism, and though they do not want to deny greatness to Christ, they feel bound to deny His divinity. A similar sort of thing happens when a sort of philosophical theory of Godhead is set up and then it is sought to square the Gospel story with that theory. Muslims will sometimes dare to say that they honour Jesus Christ more than Christians do. They say, for example, that it is impossible to ascribe such an accursed death as crucifixion to Jesus because God would not permit such an indignity to such a person as Jesus. As a result, they are forced to ignore the greater part of the description of Christ found in the Gospels. They reject the facts because they are inconvenient to their theories. Thus, however it is to be explained, it is certain that Christ called God Father and said that He Himself was in a unique sense the Son of God. The Muslim denies the sonship because he has a belief in the remoteness and utter transcendence of God or because he thinks the term 'son' implies birth from human copulation, begetting and birth.

Ṣūfis sometimes think Jesus was right in saying, "I and the Father are one", but that we are wrong in thinking of this as exclusive to Him and not applying to other human. Since Ṣūfis are often pantheistic in their notions they think that anyone who achieves a certain gnosis can say that He is one with God. There is, of course, a sense in which human may be called sons of God. But incarnation, as we understand it, can only happen once. It must fulfil its purpose if it really is incarnation and there ought to be no need to repeat it. If there were more than one incarnation then what prevents God from becoming incarnate in every human? It may be said that all human are not fit. This would imply that it all depends on human attainment whether God was able to adopt the mode of incarnation to reveal Himself to humankind. So God's action would depend on human's. The Christian view is that the incarnation is not human's attainment but God's act. "God came." Christians think not of the deification of a human but the incarnation of God.

We do not look for the attribute of omniscience in Jesus. Philosophical thought has used certain expressions about Deity of which this is one. These begin with a negation of what is human, from the fact that human is limited or finite; and so it is said that God is not finite, not limited in knowledge, or in power, or in time or in space. Accepting such a definition (?) of divinity to start with, how shall we find such attributes in what according to our creed is a human life? If our idea of divinity will not allow us to accept the divinity of Jesus Christ then so much the worse for our idea of divinity. We must get a new idea. The great mystery to human is what God is. He tries in every way to pierce this mystery. The Christian says that Jesus reveals God: "He that hath seen me hath seen the Father". So Christ brings the knowledge of what God is. The Christian is therefore compelled to modify all other ideas of God by the criterion of divinity presented in Christ.

When Muslims want to interpret the attributes of God they often do so in a super-physical sense. God's seeing is described as seeing the black ant on a black stone on the darkest night. Perhaps a cat could do that. Some Muslim illustrations of God's omnipresence are little more than the interpenetration of a dense substance by a rarer one. In explanation of God's name *Laṭīf* (the Subtle or Rare) the example given is of a pot of earth (the grossest element) to which water can be added because it is rarer than earth, air because it is rarer than water, fire because it is rarer than air and which God can penetrate because He is more subtle than fire. Christians do not think of God as an all-pervading substance but as a personal presence. God's presence is to be explained in different terms. For example, my thought is in me. I speak it and it passes to you, but my thought has not left me. I have it and you have it. For a person "to be present" is not simply spatial. A stone in Westminster Abbey was not present when the Queen was crowned; but I was present because I heard it and understood it though I was far away at the time. It is in thought, feeling and will that God's presence is to be interpreted and illustrations from material things are inadequate.

(This should also be said to those people who try to illustrate the Holy Trinity from such things as ice, water, water-vapour, etc.) The revelation of personality can only be by personality.

How Could There Be An Incarnation?

How could a union of the Divine and human take place in the unique way postulated by Christianity? It is best to say that we do not know the mode. Our psychology is inadequate to explain how in us our soul and body are joined. How much more inadequate is it to explain the union of the divine and human in man. We can form a judgment from analogy from our own personality. Even that is a mystery. Here is a man with certain features, shape and colour and he is in this room; yet his thought is not confined to this room. He is twenty years of age and, as such, he cannot be a boy of five. Yet he is the same individual who was a boy of five, by memory being linked to what he was then, and he knows himself to be the same. So we are at one and the same time bodies limited by time and space and yet have something which transcends time and space. When every individual person holds within himself such seeming contradictions, what shall we say about the incarnation?

Muslims use two words derived from the Syrian for the divinity and humanity of Christ: *nāsūt* (humanity) and *lāhūt* (divinity). These two terms are still extensively used by Ṣūfīs. They think of two planes: one is the plane of phenomena, of manifestation (*zāhir*) and the other is the plane of transcendence, that which is hidden and occult *(bāṭin).* It is a useful distinction in thought between what is manifest and what is above that plane. Manṣūr Ḥallāj the famous mystic wrote in his book *Kitāb al-tawasīn*:

> Praise be to Him who manifested His humanity,
> The secret of His glorious Divinity,
> And then appeared visibly to His creation
> In the form of one who eats and drinks,
> So that His creation could perceive Him as in the twinkling of an eye.[1]

The words used here are these two Syrian words, and there can be no doubt that the writer is referring to Jesus and speaking of Him as the manifestation of God.

This word 'Manifestation' is the key word of the Gospel of St. John. This can be for us a starting point when talking to Muslims about this mystery. The only danger in the use of the term is that it is sometimes used for what appears and is not real. So we must say that Christ is not only a manifestation in the sense that He appears or is an appearance (possibly illusory if not expressly repudiated), but present to the beholder with the reality of the God who manifests Himself through Him.

Of the term *mujassam* (embodied) which is the usual term for the incarnation used by Christians, it should be said that it is possible for this term to be misunderstood in the sense that God has become corporeal substance. We are using here a vocabulary which has been used outside the Christian setting, the idea of the Greeks that the gods took bodies. Note that the Scripture says that "The Word became Flesh". Word also means purpose, and in Christ God's purpose is manifested and embodied. But this purpose is not something outside God. God is nothing without His purpose. His purpose is from God as manifested to human, but in God as essential to the integrity of His being. Arabian usage would damn the incarnation by the word which the Arabic language uses for it. This word is *ḥulūl* and it really means indwelling or circumscription. It implies that God is contained in a person which has no warrant in Christian language.

Sin

Law is given for the purpose of teaching humankind but righteousness is not established by Law. For example, the taw of the state is that a person must not murder or steal but that does not make human righteous nor does it do away utterly with murderers and thieves. Muslims always refer righteousness to Law as we have already said. It is obedience to commands and so sin is only the breaking of the Law. A mistake in ritual observances such as neglecting a fast or omitting one of the five prayers is as much a sin in this respect as murder is. It may rank as an act of unbelief which is the worst of evils and worse than the greater sins. The greatest sin is polytheism and non-acceptance of Islām. Sin is also regarded as something external, like pollution. It is spoken of as being "washed off with good works," for example, ablutions, ritual practices, sacrifices, almsgiving and fasting. Particular sins have special punishments attached to them and these can sometimes be remitted if a fine is paid. This casuistical ethical theory and legalism in Islām is the bane of its life. Sin is so seldom thought of as being a matter of the heart. The root of sin as enmity against God and falling short of some perfection in Him is entirely obscured. From sin as an active principle of evil there is an inferior view of sins. Examples are as follows: some say purdah, the veiling of women, is necessary so that men may be saved from sin by not seeing women. It is not said that sin is to have an evil intention or to look with a lustful eye. One man, praising himself to me, boasted that he was so respectable that his wife's voice had not been heard outside the house. He said that this was extreme the degree of purity. This seems a most inadequate and inferior conception.

We can shut humankind in prison and prevent them from wrong-doing but they may still have the intention of doing wrong. If purity and goodness mean being cut off in this way, then people in gaols must be the best people on this earth.

If humankind thinks that they can be good by obeying Laws, they become self-righteous and self-righteousness is sin. Thus a vicious circle is formed. Like a man who said "All these things have I done from my youth up" such person have observed certain rules and avoided certain wrong things. Thus humankind becomes arrogant before God like the Pharisees. Muslims seem to consider the Pharisee the ideal.

Muslims think that all laws express God's will. God says, "Do this and that." This is just an expression of His will. Men cannot see for themselves the goodness or otherwise of certain courses of action, but this does not matter. They may even grumble that they are required to obey certain rules .as, for example, the Fast of Ramadan. There is no sin if they can get a legal exemption from it. They are like the coolie whom the missionary saw going down the line by a train stationary at a station tapping the wheels. The coolie was asked "Why are you doing that?" The reply was "God knows: it is a Government order." Where there is no attempt to engage the intelligence and understanding the morality must be of an inferior order and must be regarded as an imposition from without.

The method of Christ is to win from us an inward assent that the Law is holy, just and good, and by this acceptance of law we come to complete moral autonomy. If we consent to the justice of the law which condemns us we have the hope of righteousness within us. God made human in His own image. His laws are not imposed on us from without but from within and they are the expression of His own holy character, which it is his purpose to create in us. He wants us to be at one with Him in that holy character. Because He desires to impart His holiness, sin is that which interposes between us and God in this purpose.

The Christian also says that sin is lack of love for God and human. Thus it is not only a breach of law but a breach of love and fellowship. It defaces the image of God in us and the image of God in us is the impress of His love. Sin makes us less than God intends us to be. Righteousness is godliness—God-likeness. Muslims cannot use such a term. God is far away from human and there is no link. Human stands by themselves. But the Christian believes that in Christ there is a link which is the perfect manhood of Christ. God is trying to make that link strong and effective in the life of every human by manifesting Jesus Christ through His Spirit as the "very image of His substance". Sin is anything which weakens that link and anything which interferes with the relationship which God would establish by Christ's mediation. So not only gross sins like murder, but other things, sins of the heart and absence of goodness as much as positive wrongdoing, are sinful. "He who knows to do good and doeth it not, to him it is sin". Sin "is falling short of the glory of God." It is missing the mark. We are constantly missing the mark and the realisation of this saves us from self-righteousness. This does not mean that we should fall back into sin, but that it is necessary for us to see more and more as God reveals more and more. Thus to the Christian there is promise of ever new beginnings and everlasting growth.

When the Muslim begins to feel that he has sinned he is apt to say "How can I help it?" "I am weak from creatureliness". Thus he becomes hopeless. The Christian who knows himself a sinner has all the while the impetus to leave sin and reach out to God. Indeed, the more poignantly conscious of sin he becomes the more strenuously he appeals to and inclines to God his Saviour. Even the prodigal in the far country feels that his rightful place is his father's house. The Muslim view would almost imply that the "far country" is the right place for human. It is little thought that human is related to God and so it is sin that seems natural to them. He does not think it an unnatural breach between father and son. For the Christian human nature is seen in Christ and His Sonship to the Father. About sin the Christian thinks before God "I am no longer worthy to be called thy son".

Salvation

The truth about salvation is largely implicit in what has already been said about sin. What is the Muslim idea of salvation? The word only occurs once in the Qur'ān: "O my People! How is it that I bid you to salvation, but that ye bid me to the fire?" (sūrah xl. 44). This statement is significant because it brings before us the two opposites, which are always present in the religious Muslim's mind: Salvation and Hell. Salvation to the Muslim is primarily salvation from Hell. It comes at the end of a good life and as a reward for well-doing. There are some Muslims who hold that Islām has no doctrine of salvation at all and that such a doctrine is an intrusion from Christianity. It should be remarked that in the view of salvation implied, it appears as if any prevenient salvation is unnecessary for a person to live a good life. One reaps salvation as a reward or he/she comes into that to which he/she is predestined, irrespective of what one does oneself.

God's purpose is to forgive some and not others, one thinks. They generally think that they will be saved because they are within the Community of Islām, and so belongs to the saved community. Islām is entered by making certain professions and by certain ritual practices: the Witnessing (*shahādah*) by the declaration of the Unity of God and the apostleship of Muḥammad (kalmia); ritual prayer (*ḥalāt* or *namāz*); the paying of the poor tax (*zakāt*); fasting (*ṣaum* or *rozā*) in *Ramazān* and the pilgrimage (*ḥajj*). More than these is supererogatory. Fulfilling these, adding nothing and taking away nothing one can be saved. This was Muḥammad's reply when he was asked the specific question. Faith is belief in God, His angels, His messengers, His books, the resurrection and predestination of good and evil. This also is Muḥammad's reply according to the traditions (ḥadīth). So the one who does and thinks in this way is a good Muslim and is saved.

There is much in the Qur'ān about guidance and instruction but not about redemption or regeneration. Sometimes the marks of a believer are said to be retaliation for blood shedding, keeping the prescribed fast, hoping for God's mercy if they die fasting, fearing God and the Prophet, not devouring one another's substance in frivolity, not coming to prayer drunk, and avoiding games of chance and the drinking of wine. These are rules which must be observed. Muslims enquiring after Christian belief sometimes ask for a book which contains the same sort of laws for Christians. This shows their emphasis; but this is not the Christian's way, although the Christian may attach a great deal of importance to discipline in its proper place, as we can see in a book like Jeremy Taylor's *Holy Living*.

In Islām salvation is not a change of a moral character in believers. What is required is that a person should know what to do and do it. An outward formalism is the general ride. If we are good then God will love us. To deal with sin only repentance is necessary, that is, we must turn away from it. Of the power to do this, with the exception of what is said about God's power and decree, there seems little to be said. Sorrow for sin is not particularly stressed but rather "turning over a new leaf." That was the advice which the editor of the weekly periodical *Light* in Lahore gave to a girl who said that she could not repent, in the sense of being sorry, because she had liked doing the wrong which she did. The principal question is "How can anyone be saved from wanting to do wrong?" The editor could only say that good deeds cancelled bad deeds. But how begin to do good things after having done bad things?

There is no power to change people in just telling them to do the right. If that were so then it would be best to give all criminals a course in Law while they were in gaol. The essence of sin is to do what we know to be wrong, and what is done in ignorance is not sin although sometimes our ignorance is culpable.

There is a tendency also for people to think that salvation is from certain sins rather than from sin. Even Ṣūfīs have a similar thought. By gaining certain knowledge (gnosis) we may attain a kind of emancipation, but too often this means also being freed from the command of God and being able to do without distinguishing between righteousness and unrighteousness, a freedom from Law. Then a person is said to be *azād* (free) and this is a lapse into license and antinomianism.

The Christian view is irrevocably bound up with the Proper doctrine of the Trinity, which is in its soteriological aspect the redeemer God in His total activity. More will be said of this later. Salvation is not a matter of balances and the weighing of good deeds and appropriate rewards. It is not the reward of a good life. Forgiveness is not something we earn. It is causal and anticipatory. It is the foundation from which the new life springs. From the divine act of forgiveness is born an experience of forgiveness. In our ordinary human relationships we have a good illustration. We wrong someone and we repent. We then do all sorts of things to "put things right". We have saddened someone and now we wish to make them glad and we try acts of kindness to see what they will do. We try to do by good deeds what can only come by a new relationship. The deeds are all right if the relationships have been put right first. When we are really reconciled to our fellow beings then all our acts will be brotherly.

Christian salvation is this reconciliation which must take place at the beginning between the soul and God. Now we are no longer scrupulous about doing this and that and awfully anxious about it, but good acts will spring naturally out of our new relationship. But if we think like Muslims that God is only a Lawgiver and Judge and we must first offer Him our acts, we cannot find the relationship which is Father-son. This reconciliation is something which God Himself initiates. He takes the first step in Christ.

How can we repent? This may be only a desire to escape consequences. It is the goodness of God which moves us to repent. While we were yet sinners God loved us and Christ died for us. This is what wins sinners away from sin. If the Muslims say God loves good people, how it will be when all are sinners. If in our own strength we can do righteousness we have no need of God. Thus we are taught that God is with us when we are sinners and is working in our hearts by His Spirit. So the work of our salvation is His from beginning to end. It is only in Christ and the Christian Gospel that we have this assūrance that God is seeking to win us to Himself.

If we wrong a friend and apologise and our friend accepts our apology in an off-hand way, our first thought is whether he really felt the breach of friendship between us as much as we did. If he shows he was hurt or says, "I valued our friendship so much that I hardly know how to forgive you," we have at least a sign that he did value it. It is not wrong when there is sorrow on both sides, even when one party has been wronged and the other is the offending party. If I am sorry for wrong done on the plane of personal relations, some reflection of my sorrow seems fitting in him who is truly my friend. So God, to complete the work of forgiveness, reveals His love and pain on the Cross and shows that the pain is for love of us. It is here that we are moved to a deeper repentance than a shallow apology. But Islām has no room for the Cross in the heart of God. He thinks we can never know whether God cares and we are left all the poorer and perhaps tremble in doubt as to whether He cares or not.

Here then is the heart of the Christian doctrine of salvation. Seeing God's condemnation of sin in His Son's suffering on the Cross, we see that God hates sin and condemns it and we are led to condemn it too. Before this we were full of excuses for our misconduct. Our chief idea was to justify ourselves and escape punishment, but now this is not the case. Indeed we would even ask God to punish us if He thought fit, because we have entire trust in Him. All we ask is that we should come into His family and we are ready to come on His terms. We know that we are not in a position to stipulate conditions or make any bargain with God. We are not in the Court of a Judge trying to make out the best possible case for ourselves; we are throwing ourselves on what God is, that is, our Father. If we make any appeal it is not on account of extenuating circumstances but to what He is. We are not trying to wriggle out of punishment but are in tears at the feet of our Father. The destiny of our lives is that we should always live with Him and love Him and we cannot enter into that relationship while we leave pain in His heart. It is not even so important, that the pain should be away from our hearts, because that may be salutary but we do want it to be taken away from the heart of our loving Saviour. We want Him to see of the travail of His soul and be satisfied. And when the experience of such gracious forgiveness comes to us our whole life is changed, we are changed. We who were prodigal sons have come home to joyful communion with our Father.

Trinity: Its Holy Redemptive Significance

Already much has been said about the Muslim misunderstandings about the Holy Trinity. It may be that Christians in Muḥammad's days were more concerned with trying to explain the difficulties and subtleties of the doctrine than to discover the redemptive significance of the revelation. The Holy Trinity was a puzzle to solve. It may be a mystery but it was not an enigma set forth for our solution. It was set forth as God's solution of human's perplexities and the answer to human's need of redemption. It is by the Trinity that we learn what God does for man.

Early Theology was much influenced by Greek philosophy, though it is a mistake to say that the early creeds are philosophical, that is, purely metaphysical because they were concerned with the fact of Jesus Christ coming in the flesh. Let us remember what we said earlier about the plane of transcendence and the plane of manifestation. Human tried to explain the transcendent, instead of beginning with what was manifested. They did not begin with what God had given to human in revelation but with what they had tried, with their unaided intellect, to understand in regard to the relations of God the Father, the Son and the

Holy Spirit. Sometimes they tried to explain the mathematical problem how could something be three and at the same time one. Their critics were on much safer ground when they said that one could not be three and three could not be one. Both started with the One Cause of the Universe, so how did three come in? They got into difficulties. If we ask absurd questions we shall always get ridiculous answers.

But if we start with what is revealed of Father, Son and Holy Spirit we are on safe ground. God did not reveal the inner constitution of the Godhead or present Himself for identification with the One whom human had come to think of as the First Cause, or Mover of the Universe. The revelation which God gave was to save the world from sin. However much human are able or unable to understand of the inner constitution of the Godhead, this is not the point. The object of revelation was to show God working for our redemption. And so if we start from what is revealed about Father, Son and Holy Spirit we are on safer ground.

Through the prophets of Israel God showed Himself as Father: (Ps. ciii) "Like as a father pitieth his children so the Lord pitieth them that fear Him." And in Isaiah, "Surely thou art our father." But this was imperfectly understood. The immutable God could not become a Father as human recognised him to be a father. He must have that Fatherhood in His Holy Nature from all eternity. In seeming contradiction to a general idea of beneficence conveyed by the name "Father" human saw in the world diseases, death, earthquakes, and tempests. How could a mere assertion of God's fatherhood mean anything in face of such facts? In addition human beings were conscious of their sin and shortcomings. How dare they claim God to be their Father when it seemed as if it might be truer that they were of their father the Devil? In face of the same difficulty there was much room for doubt. But doubt could never lead to human's redemption. It is also necessary that if a person is to know the redeeming grace of God, mere monotheism will not be sufficient. It might be that of the devils, who accept, according to St. James, the unity of God. The monotheism of the Old Testament, as distinct from mere intellectualist monotheism or belief in a first cause, is based on a spiritual apprehension that there was a distinct relation, between belief in one God and the commandments of moral significance, as we have seen earlier. Then there was the idea that God had made human in His own image and a special insight of Isaiah when he said, "In all their afflictions He was afflicted". But, while these only remained statements or implications from statements, they could suffice. Job might ask "How can it be that in all my afflictions He is afflicted?" How could the sinner, rebuked by the commandments and confronted with his own, unlikeness to God, credit the statement that he was made in the image of God? Islām does well to view the statement with incredulity when it refuses to admit the fact of the incarnation. So the Christian holds and the Scripture teaches that God sent Jesus Christ, His Son, our Lord. Without Sonship there cannot be Fatherhood. How can we know the Father save through the Son? If human dare not, on account of their sin, claim sonship with God, where is sonship to be found, if God Himself does not supply it within our humanity? If human, because of their sin, could not realise their relation to their Father God, it was necessary that there should be someone without sin to demonstrate that sonship. So in a real sense no one knows the Father save the Son and him to whom the Son willeth to reveal Him. The Son came and showed how in our entire affliction the Father was afflicted. In the Son human realised his own sonship, and though human never cease to be plagued with evil it no longer remains the problem that it was because in it is the Divine companionship, sympathy and love.

But if the Sonship we see in Christ were simply a human achievement, it would not be sufficient. This would only lead us to assume that human beings were capable of achieving sonship by their own unaided power, whereby we would be cast into grievous misunderstanding and alienation from God, for whom we would consider ourselves to have no need. After all, the hope of the sinner is not in the relation he bears to God but that which God bears to him. So the Sonship in which the Fatherhood becomes real is from the side of God and not human.

Or we might express it in another way. God created human in love and as gracious Father He wants us to be His true sons. To enable us to know He is our Father He sends us His Only Begotten Son, who shows us in His perfect life what real sonship is, and thus promotes the hope in us that we may love the Father. But we have not seen the face of Christ on earth and so the Spirit is given to us that we may recognise him now. He makes what would have been without Him merely historical contemporaneous. We may imagine three concentric circles. In the outer one are the potential sons of God, with whom the Spirit strives so that they may become real sons by recognition of the Only Son. With this are those who know themselves the sons of God, who crying Abba Father by the Spirit, have recognised the Father by the Spirit through the Only Begotten. This is the Church of the redeemed. In the inmost circle is the only begotten incarnate, conceived by the Holy Ghost, Son of the Father within the circle of eternity. The centre of all is the Godhead whence flows the gracious *agape* of God reaching through His triune revelation and triune activity the outer circle and drawing all to the centre. It is with some such ideas as these that we should approach the doctrine of the Trinity. In a sense the third chapter of St. John is the truly representative text for our doctrine of the Trinity.

Or look at this from another point of view. The revelation of the Son is in a certain time and that revelation could fall back into the same obscurity and ambiguity as statements recorded about God. We could read about our Lord, accept the facts and know no real effect on our lives; its redemptive significance would be lost. Human cannot apprehend this by their own power any more than they can achieve sonship by their own power. We must be born from above. We sometimes find the idea of the Fatherhood of God and the brotherhood of humankind without the power of it.

We might say to someone in trouble, "God is your Father." The answer might be, "How can I believe it? To this one might reply, "I have been told that He is our Father" or I might say, "I have seen one who is His Son." "Well He might be Father to Him but how is He mine?" The only answer to this could be that we have come to saving trust that it is so and that this new knowledge is by His Spirit. The witness of the Spirit is that I am a child of God and this witness is your witness too. It is not only that I knew that the Son lived by the Spirit proceeding from the Father and the Son I know that He lives. When the heart is ready to receive Him the Spirit does this work in it. And the Holy Spirit can be nothing but God, otherwise there is nothing from the Godward side here and now. We are doomed to fall back on our own resources, our own intellect, on which we have already proved there is no reliance in such matters.

A little earlier we said that in the beginning God made human in His own image, but now by the Holy Spirit we find human transformed again into the same image. In this way we come to an experience only possible through the revealed Trinity. In this sense the experience of the Holy Trinity is within our lives. The Holy Trinity is not a creation of our experience but is revealed to our experience. The Holy Spirit within us cries "Abba, Father", which is the Son-taught, name of God.

If the Trinity is in the fullest sense a revelation, if it is real, it is a revelation of what actually is on the transcendent plane. It is not something merely manifestational or phenomenal which might be illusory, but is really what God is. To be a manifestation in the sense that we require, it must be of what really is, a manifestation in the sense of a disclosure of the hidden eternal mystery of divine love. In the very heart of God there is Fatherhood, there is the purpose of redemption (the logos) and the relation of love and the redemptive activity of the Spirit of God. In the communing of the Godhead is the ground of the redemption of humankind. God in His loving Fatherhood purposes Salvation, Christ perfectly expresses that purpose, the Holy Spirit makes that purpose effective within us. In all this there is the personal activity of the Godhead in the redeemed individual. All three are inseparable and all three are essential to the integrity and identity of the Godhead.

Endnotes

[1] That is the veil being lifted for a moment so that they could see the hidden mystery.

Muslim Evangelism and Christian Self-Searching

Henry J. Otten

Although about one-seventh of the people in the world are Muslims, the Christian Church has expended only about one fiftieth of its missionary energy in reaching them with the Gospel of Christ. What is the reason for this small effort in behalf of such a large number of people? Why is that Christians are much more ready to preach the Gospel to people in far-off places than to Muslims who may live very close to them? The answer, which is usually given, is that the results of mission work among Muslims are too meagre. "They will not become Christians anyway," is the usual attitude. Coupled with this there is often a fear that anyone who preaches to Muslims takes his life in his hands and subjects themselves to the threat of bodily violence.

Now if we examine these reasons for the Church's relatively feeble effort at missions to Muslims, we must admit that they are a far cry from the optimism, courage, and love which were characteristic of the New Testament Church. It was more interested in witnessing than in seeing results; those early Christians were more concerned about the welfare of their hearers then about their own physical bodies. If Christ died for all, they believed that the Holy Spirit had the power to make that message meaningful for all. If Christ commissioned them to preach the Gospel to all humankind, they believed that Gospel had blessing for all. So they witnessed even when it meant suffering.

We are inclined to blame the Muslims, their theology and community, for the difficulties of Gospel work among Muslims. There is no doubt that Muslim theology and community pressure create special problems, but in Christ there are resources to meet these problems. The main difficulty is not with the Muslim, but with us Christians. Let us consider one or two problems of Muslim theology and the problem of community pressure and see how they are really Christian problems.

Problems of Muslim Theology

When Christians begin to speak about the treasures of their faith to a Muslim, he/she will very often find that some of the statements of his/her faith which caused him/her no special difficulty are immediately challenged by the Muslim brother. "Jesus is the Son of God," is one such statement. When we first explain the Gospel to Muslims, we may approach them with John 3:16. When we tell them about the riches of that verse, we are thinking about God's love and His desire that we should not perish but have everlasting life. When the Muslims hear that verse, they hear nothing about God's love or everlasting life; they only hear the phrase "only-begotten Son". That is enough for them. When they hear that, their blood becomes hot; they become disgusted with us; and they classify our religion with that of the unbeliever. Our greater treasure becomes an abomination to him/her. It is not that the Muslim is uninterested in God's love or everlasting life; he/she is very interested, but a thought has entered his/her mind, which crowds out all our good intentions. We are thinking about salvation, but they are thinking about blasphemy. When we refer to Jesus as the Son of God a Muslim thinks that we are dishonouring and blaspheming God. The cause for this attitude is not difficult to find as it is rooted in the Qur'ān. Here are some of the pertinent passages:

> They say the Merciful has taken to Himself a son – ye have brought a monstrous thing! The heavens well-nigh burst thereat, and the earth is riven and the mountains fall down broken, that they attribute to the Merciful a son! But it becomes not the Merciful to take to Himself a son. (19:90-92)

> Praise be to God who has not taken to Himself a son and has not had a partner in His Kingdom, nor had a patron against such abasement." (17:112)
>
> God could not take to Himself a son.... When He decrees a matter, He only says to it, "Be", and it is. (19:35-36)
>
> The Jews say Ezra is the son of God: and the Christian say that the Messiah is the son of God; that is what they say with their mouths, imitating the sayings of those who misbelieved before. God fight them! How they lie. (9: 30)
>
> Infidels they are who say, Verily God is the Messiah, the son of Mary. Say: Who has any hold on God if He wished to destroy the Messiah, the son of Mary, and his mother and those who are on the earth together? (5: 19)

When we look at these passages, we see that the idea of divine sonship in the Muslim mind is regarded as an undignified travesty on the majesty of God. With Christians the sonship of Christ is associated with love and self-sacrifice. As L. Bevan Jones has said,

> We maintain that, far from it being derogatory to the Glory of God to seek by such means (Incarnation) to make Himself known to men in a saving way, this is Love's prerogative – for God is essentially Love. The glory of Power might be sullied by an act of condescension. Supreme intelligence might hesitate to appear in lowly guise. Sheer justice might demand some other way. But Love, true Love, does stoop to save, and stooping, is not degraded.[1]

With Muslims divine sonship is associated with dishonour and disrespect to God. What is the reason for this different reaction to the same words? The reason is that Christians understand the phrase "son of God" in a spiritual way. When Muslims see "son of God", they think of marriage and human reproduction. Muḥammad himself understood the phrase this way as is evidenced by the passages from the Qur'ān mentioned above and also from the following passages:

> O ye people of the book (Christians), do not exceed in your religion nor say truth against God save the truth. The messiah, Jesus, the son of Mary, is but the apostle of God and His Word which he cast into Mary and a spirit from him; believe then in God and His Apostles, and say not, Three. Have done! It were better for you. God is only one God, celebrated be His praise from that He should beget a son. (4: 167-171).

> They misbelieve who say, Verily, God is the third of three; for there is no God but one, and if they do not desist from what they say, there shall tough those who disbelieve among them grievous woe.... Will they not turn again toward God and ask pardon of Him?" (5, 73)
>
> And when God said, O Jesus, son of Mary is it thou who didst say to men, take me and may mother for two gods beside God? He said, I celebrate thy praise, what ails me that should say what I have no right to?" (5: 116)

From these passages it is clear that Muḥammad regarded the Trinity as a sort of tri-theism consisting of God, Mary, and Jesus. He had the idea that Christians believe in three gods and the Jesus was the third of these gods produced by marital union between God and Mary. If this is the Trinity, then the Christian godhead is not much different from that of the ancient Greek, Egyptians, and Hindus. For their gods also married and produced offspring. This also explains why Muslims are so horrified when one of their members becomes a Christian. They think he is adopting a lower form of religion. "In their eyes the conversion of a Muslim to Christianity so far from being an advance in religion is a reversion to a lower stage from the bonds of which their fathers with great travail were delivered.[2]

Now who is to blame for this tragic misunderstanding by the Muslims of two of our most precious doctrines, the Trinity and the Incarnation? Someone has suggested that Muḥammad himself was to blame because he had no adequate conception of sin and thus no appreciation for the saving work of God expressed in doctrines of the Trinity and the Incarnation. Now there may be a great deal of truth to this statement, but at the same time Christians cannot free themselves of responsibility for the origin and subsequent misunderstanding of Muḥammad and his followers.

Before the time of Muḥammad, and during his life, the Church was engaged in controversy about the person of a Christ. The Christians did not consider properly how their discussion might sound to an outsider. They used phrases, which easily led to misunderstanding. For example, they referred to Mary as the "mother of God." Now if we understand the Christian theology behind this phrase "mother of God," it may be alright to use the expression. But it does not take a great deal of imagination to consider how such a phrase would sound to a non-Christian, especially to a non-Christian who was interested in combating the polytheism of the Arabs and winning them to a higher conception of God.

As far as we know, Muḥammad never had the opportunity to consult a Bible. He could only gain knowledge of Christianity by word of mouth. When he heard such phrase as "mother of God" in connection with the phrase "son of God" he understood it in the light of his heathen background, the pantheon of the Arabs. His reaction was no doubt the same as that of a certain Muslim who daily witnessed a Christian school bus passing by on the street in Cairo, Egypt, with the words "The School of the Mother of God", written on the side. A Christian friend of this Muslim reported that the mere sight of that bus used to make his friend fighting mad, and one day he said, "God's mother! And who, pray, begot him? Do you expect me in these days of modernity and enlightenment to believe that God Almighty chose some billowy-bosomed Jewess for a mistress and begot Himself!"

If the managers of that school were at all concerned with winning Muslims to Christ, they surely would have changed the name of their bus and school. This points out what we mentioned earlier: the problems of Muslim theology are also Christian problems. Christians are at least partly to blame for Muḥammad's original misunderstanding of the Christian message and for the misunderstanding, which is evident among his followers today.

Christian Problems of Inadequate Interpretation

If the Muslims understand our words in a different way than we do, then we cannot say that we are reaching them with the Gospel when we preach without respect to their background. The evangelist may threaten with damnation and warn of God's judgment for despising the message, but such threats are meaningless if they think that we are tri-theists, or if they think that we ascribe physical reproduction to God. When we explain the Gospel to them, we should either avoid using those phrases, which they misunderstand, or we should explain our phrases. The "Lutheran Hour" Radio Programme was banned from parts of North Africa partly because the broadcasters used phrases which offended Muslims. It is possible to preach the Gospel without using the phrase "son of God." In certain cases this is advisable. If there is no opportunity to explain what we mean, we should not use the phrase at all. But it will not be impossible to avoid the phrase in every case, nor is it desirable to do so. If it is understood properly, it expresses some glorious truths about Christ and God, and it should be our aim to lead our Muslim friends into an understanding of these truths.

Without attempting any complete exposition of the doctrine of the Divine Sonship, let us make clear one thing, which is not implied by it. If we look at the use of the word "son" in the Bible, we see that it is used in both a physical and a figurative sense. We read of Isaac being called the son of Abraham, but we also read of John and James being called the sons of thunder, and Barnabas the son of consolation. Isaac is called as son of Abraham because he was begotten by Abraham in a physical way, but if anyone would try to say that John and James were called the sons of thunder because they were born from thunder, we would call such idea ridiculous and on the same level with ancient Greek and Norse Mythology. John and James were not the sons of thunder by reproduction but because they had the characteristics of thunder. The phrase "son of God" should be understood in the same way. Jesus was not the son of God by reproduction, but because he had the character and attribute of God to a unique degree. Other individual may exhibit some of the qualities of God such as His love and sympathy in a limited way, but Jesus had these qualities and many others completely and "without measure". He had God's wisdom, God's holiness, God's power, and even God's eternity and infinity. That is way he is called the Son of God. Even the Qur'ān uses the word "Son" without reference to reproduction when it calls a traveller a "Son of the road," (2: 177) it is a mark of Semitic language to use the word "son" to describe character and essence. Reproduction was not involved at all when the Bible calls rebels "children of rebellion" (Num. 17: 10) and David a "son of valor", (1 Sam: 18), nor is it involved in Christ the Son of God.

Firstly, we must take time to explain these matters to a Muslim when we are talking to him/her about religion. One will then be much more ready to listen to us and to examine the other doctrines of our faith more sympathetically. If we use theological phrases, which Muslims misunderstand or which require a technical knowledge of Christian doctrines to grasp properly, we should not condemn them if they refuse to consider our message. We must not think that they are resisting the Holy Ghost, but in their own mind they are resisting idolatrous ideas about God. When we speak to them let us be sure that we state our faith clearly and unmistakably.

Secondly, we should be aware of trying to present too much of the Christian teaching at one time. I have heard Christian speakers try to explain the meaning of original sin, the doctrine of the person of Christ, and the doctrine of salvation by grace all in a few short sentences. If it took several centuries for the Christian Church to become clear on the doctrine of the person of Christ, how can we expect a stranger to grasp the full implication of this doctrine in a few moments? In this connection we do well or remind ourselves of Jesus' own method of revealing Himself to His disciples. He did not issue a proclamation concerning His deity right from the beginning. Instead, he performed works and taught spiritual lessons which demonstrated the power, wisdom, and love of God, which was in Him. Gradually the disciples came to their own conclusion about Him, culminating in Peter's confession, "We believe that thou art Christ, the son of the living God."

If we want Muslims to recognize that God was in Christ, we will not succeed in our aim by merely making proclamations that he is true God and true man. Such a proclamation is a true theological statement, but in itself will convince no one. People are convinced when they come in contact with Christ Himself, his works, his words, his life, death, and resurrection. If we wish Muslims to come to the conviction that in Christ dwelleth all the fullness of the Godhead bodily, then let us reveal Him as He revealed Himself to His disciples… in day to day words and works. They reflect the God that was in Him. It is better if our hearers can digest one spiritual truth about Christ than if they hear half of the doctrines of the Christian faith and digest nothing.

More could be said about these matters, but I think we can see from the foregoing that it is not always the Muslim who is to blame for rejecting the Christian message. In the doctrinal Statement of our Lutheran Church we have the phrase "effective confrontation with the Gospel." Has the Muslim been effectively confronted with the Gospel? If we use terms which he does not understand, or if we try to impart too much of our message at one time, it is extremely doubtful if he is being effectively confronted with the Gospel. In that case the problem of non-acceptance is our problem.

Problems of Community

Most of our readers are no doubt acquainted with the fact that it is often very difficult for a Christian convert from Islam to break away from his former religion and community. As soon as one becomes a Christian, one is liable to lose his/her work, wife/husband and children, friends, property, and sometimes even one's life. How many of us are aware that this is only half of the problem. By the grace and power of God numbers of Muslims in various parts of the world have been enabled by the Holy Spirit to make this leap of faith into a world of social ostracism. Then their troubles really began; they were ready to forsake all and follow Christ, but they were not ready to face the next difficulty, and that was a reception into a cold and unsympathetic Church. From their readings in the New Testament they had been led to believe that the Church was a community of love which would more than make up for the community of Islam which they had left. Instead they found out that the Christians held them in suspicion and denied them the fellowship they so sorely needed. As one convert graphically stated, "While an inquirer, I could not be made too much of, but now that I have been baptised my appearance seems to be unwelcome and myself a nuisance." Or in the words of another convert, "The Muslims began an opposition against me which is still going on. But the opposition which had the worst effect on me was that of certain Christians." These statements reflect an experience, which has been repeated in almost every country where Muslim mission work has been carried on.

If we think about the significance of this situation, we realise that a convert from Islam is asked to take a step, which was not even taken by the first Christians. If we think about those first Christians whose experiences are recorded in the Book of Acts we see that they had some similar problems to the Muslim converts. There was the same loss of friends, the same social ostracism and the same threat of death. There was one tremendous difference and that was that the first Christians were immediately received into a fellowship of love where people prayed for each other, encouraged each other in the faith, and shared their worldly goods. There was some doubt about Paul after his conversion, but immediately there arose a Barnabas who befriended him and recommended him into the Christian fellowship. On the same day that Peter so boldly proclaimed the Message of Salvation, the Holy Spirit created a fellowship of love among three thousand strong for those who would leave all to take Christ as their Lord and Saviour. Why should converts from Islam be denied this fellowship of love, which the Holy Spirit intended for all Christians? Is it any wonder that converts from Islam have been known to go insane, or to develop a pathological dependence upon the Christian worker who was instrumental in his conversion or even to revert back to Islam? Surely it is nothing but a miracle of God that a considerable number of converts from Islam have survived not only the social ostracism of Islam, but also the social Ostracism of Christians. They have gone on to lead powerfully radiant Christian lives whose records read like those of the heroes of faith mentioned in Hebrews 11.

When we understand this problem, we can also understand more fully why there have been relatively few converts from Islam. There are not only the theological problems mentioned previously; there is also the problem of social environment. Muslims have a closely knit brotherhood. Until we can demonstrate by deeds that there is a superior fellowship among believers in Christ, the brotherhood of Islam, by threats and personal concern, will continue to discourage those who have understood the theological issues from being baptized into the body of Christ.

What is the cause for the Church's attitude toward the convert from Islam? Why is it that they are made to feel unwanted or suspected? Although this phenomenon of a cold and unsympathetic Church has been observed mainly in the Orient, this is not only a problem of Oriental Church. The Western Church has not been faced with the problem because there are hardly any Muslims in that area. But I do not think that the reception of converts in the West would be much different than in the East because the basic attitude of Christians towards Muslims is much the same all over the world.

What is this basic attitude? It is one of enmity rather than love. From the time of the Crusades until the present Muslims have been regarded by many Christians as enemies to be defeated or feared, rather than as fellow human beings who are to be helped and loved. I have heard such statements in India and seen them in magazines of the West. That early sin of the Church in resorting to the sword instead of the Gospel, at the time of the Crusades, has borne its bitter fruit far beyond the third and fourth generation. And when a convert comes into the Church, this same spirit of enmity manifests itself. It may not even be recognized, but it shows itself in suspicion and fear. The Christians suspect the convert of being immoral. They suspect them of trying of get some earthly or material advantage. They fear that he/she will create trouble for them. They dislike their independent spirit and accuse them of being proud and arrogant. They think that they are really a copy. They will not give their daughters in marriage to him and they think that he will revert back to Islam in the end anyhow. These are the attitudes which people have toward enemies. These suspicions and fears dog the steps of the converts as they try to integrate themself into the Church.

At the very time when one needs sympathy and prayer to overcome temptations and meet the higher standards of the Christian life, one is made to fight the battles alone. It is the very time when he/she is intensely lonely because he/she may have lost his/her wife/husband and children and all their Muslim friends, more causes for loneliness are heaped upon them. At the very time when he may not know where his next piece of bread is coming from, he is denied the love and warmth of Christian hospitality. These are all difficulties, which the first Christians did not face. They left one area of security, but were immediately received into a deeper security; a security provided by God Himself on that first Pentecost Day when he brought into being a community of Christians. The extension of this community exists today and its divine purpose is still the same. The convert from Islam is denied the benefits of that community. If he/she fears to leave the community of Islam, whose fault is it? Clearly it is a Christian problem.

The Christian Problem of Lovelessness

What is the remedy for this regretful situation? The remedy is prayer that, firstly, God will remove the spirit of enmity and instill a spirit of love and helpfulness among all Christians in the relationships to Muslims. Secondly, we should pray that this spirit of love and helpfulness will manifest itself in a desire to share with Muslims the riches of the Gospel. It is not enough if only a handful of persons here and there become interested in Muslim evangelism. That is the case now, and we have the picture of converts being won and then turned over to a Church, which has no interest in them. It is only a Church, which is interested in winning others which will provide the suitable atmosphere for their spiritual growth. Therefore Muslim Missions must become the interest of the whole Church, not just a few individuals. Finally, we should pray that every congregation will become a potential home for converts, a place associated with all the warmth, sympathy, and helpfulness which we associate with our own homes. Canon Temple Gairdner said that the church or congregation, which desires to be, sets out to be, and succeeds in being, a home for those converted from Islam is in itself a gospel. It is a gospel that will be easily understood and easily loved by those without, and which will powerfully attract them to come in. If the Church as a whole is characterized by a spirit of love and helpfulness toward Muslims, if the Church takes up the call of evangelism among Muslims, and if the Church aims to be a home for those who leave all to follow Christ, the social pressure exerted by the Muslim community will lose most of its force. Instead of regarding Muslim social pressure as an insurmountable barrier to work among Muslims, let us recognize it as a Christian problem, which can be solved with the resources, which God has put at our disposal.

Conclusion

We have seen that two of the difficulties connected with Muslim work are misunderstanding of our message and social pressure exerted upon converts by the Muslim community. We have also seen that these are problems, which are not outside of our control. In fact, we Christians are at least partly responsible for them, and accordingly can also do much to eliminate them. With repentant hearts let us ask God to fill us with those graces of sympathy and love, which are required to alleviate the difficulties of misunderstanding and community pressure. If such is our prayer, we can look forward joyfully to the day when many of the followers of Muḥammad today will rejoice in the pardon and power of Christ.

Endnotes

[1] L. Bevan Jones, *The People of the Mosque* (New Delhi: ISPCK, 1980), 273.

[2] Orientalist, "The Muslim Point of View," *The Muslim World* (Jan. 1936).

The Muslim Doctrine of Salvation (Part I & II)

Roland E. Miller

To begin with you might be interested in the reasons I had for preparing a study such as this. There were two reasons. In the first place, I had previously had some interest in the Muslim doctrine of sin, and I had thought it would be natural to follow that study with an examination of the Muslim doctrine of salvation. Now, as a matter of fact, this is a Christian "naturalness," a Christian logic. For Christians discussion of sin and salvation is quite inseparable. In the Muslim situation this is not the case. The two doctrines are not integrally related as in Christian theology. It is possible to discuss them in a disconnected way. There are, of course, tangent points in the two doctrines, but for the Muslim neither sin nor salvation have the same connotation as they hold for the Christian. My second reason for making this particular study was a perplexity of mine that you may have shared. What is salvation for a Muslim, and how does he attain it? In my practical experience the pattern of answers did not seem to be a consistent one and I was left bewildered. So I thought it might be well to explore the matter mere systematically than I had previously done.

The primary sources for this study are particularly the Qur'ān and the Ḥadīth. My quotations from the Qur'ān are from J. M. Rodwell's translation. For the Ḥadīth I have quoted from the well-known compilations of William Goldsack (*Selections from Muḥammadan Traditions*), and Alfred Guillaume (*The Traditions of Islām*). The standard handbooks on Islām provide a limited amount of help for this subject, as a whole, although they usually touch upon some segment of it. On the Qur'ānic doctrine H. U. Weitbrecht Stanton's book, *The Teaching of the Qur'ān* provides a very useful summary. W. R. W. Gardner's *The Qur'ānic Doctrine of Salvation*, is very helpful, though at one or two critical points I cannot agree with his interpretation. On the theological development of the doctrine of salvation J. W. Sweetman's *Islām and Christian Theology* (Part one, Vol. II) is particularly illuminating. *A Commentary on the Creed of Islām*, as translated by E. E. Elder is a valuable primary source. And A. S. Tritten's *Muslim Theology* has much helpful material. An older book by W. St. Clair Tisdall, namely, *The Religion of the Crescent* and the more recent *Gospel of God* by Harold Spencer present Christian comparisons. In Dr. Kenneth Cragg's writings we enter most deeply into the strivings of the contemporary Muslim and we are shown in a most penetrating way what should be the response of Christian love towards these strivings. These are but some of the sources to which I am deeply indebted for materials used in the following discussion.

Because this study, strictly speaking, is not intended as a comparative one, I have not at length entered into the matter of the Christian response. The purpose is to set forth the Muslim doctrine. Yet all of us in passing will note the similarities and differences between the Christian and Muslim doctrines of salvation. We see that in their theology the Muslims faced many of the same questions that Christians had to meet. And we are confirmed once again in our faith that it is only in Jesus Christ that we possess the critical plus-factor, the hub where all theological strands meet and find a unity which faith can grasp.

Our opening question in this discussion will be, "What is the actual meaning of the word 'salvation' as used by Muslims?" This will lead into the main area of the discussion, namely, the means of salvation, which we shall discuss as God's will; God's mercy; Faith plus Works; Intercession and (briefly) The Mystical Way.

Throughout it should be borne in mind that salvation and Paradise are identical in the Muslim mind.[1] To bring clarity to a "fuzzy" subject we have categorized the means of salvation, as stated above. As a methodology this might be suspect on the ground that we are setting up artificial boundaries and violating the wholeness of thought. Nevertheless, that the subject matter does break down into something approaching these categories will appear evident from the discussion. And at no time do we intend to minimize the fact that there is a very close inter-play of thought and expression. This indeed is the heart of the problem in determining what the Muslim doctrine of salvation is.

I. The Word "Salvation" in the Qur'ān

We hear occasionally the statement that the Qur'ān is not concerned with the doctrine of salvation. We may accept this as a correct statement only if we are thinking exclusively in terms of the Christian concept of salvation, or if we are thinking of the use of the word "salvation" itself. Though it may be true that the basic factors of the Christian concept of salvation are not reflected in the Islāmic doctrine, this does not necessarily mean that the Qur'ān does not have its own theories of salvation, whatever they may be. Nor does the infrequency of the word "salvation" in the Qur'ān indicate the absence of a doctrine or theory of salvation any more than the absence of a word for "thank you" in Malayalam proves the lack of a concept of gratitude among Malayalis. The Qur'ān does have certain theories of salvation, though confused, and though not apparent under that terminology. At any rate, no matter what the situation may be in the Qur'ān itself, in this essay we are concerned with the Islāmic view of the doctrine. And it must be admitted by all that Islām, using as its authority both the Qur'ān and the Traditions, has dealt extensively with this problem of salvation.

The usage of the word "salvation" in the Qur'ān, even though it is rare, does give us an essential clue to what Muslims mean by that word. As used, in the Qur'ān this word has the connotation of "rescue." Both the word *najāt* and its synonym *khalāṣ* strictly mean "escape, deliverance." The important thing concerning this escape is that it is the "rescue" from the circumstances of hell to the better circumstances of heaven. The escape is from the punishment of sin, not from the bondage of sin. It therefore does not involve a change of nature, but the bestowal of the privilege to enjoy sensual pleasures in Paradise. Sūra 39: 62 says "Allāh shall rescue (*najā*) those who fear him into their place of safety." Sūra 3:182 states: "Whoso shall escape the Fire and be brought into Paradise shall be happy." In the only single reference to salvation in the Qur'ān by the term which has become common in later Islām, *najāt*, Muḥammad cries (40, 44): "O my people, how is it that I bid you to salvation, but that ye bid me to the Fire?" Here again salvation is contrasted with hell and is primarily concerned with the escape from hell.

At this point a comparison may help to make clear this basic thought. In the Christian faith salvation, conceived negatively, refers to deliverance from sin and therefore also from sin's curse, death and hell. In Islām salvation conceived negatively, refers to the escape from hell. In Christianity salvation conceived positively, refers to eternal life beginning now and devoted eternally to the service and praise of God. In Islām salvation, positively conceived, refers to the enjoyment of physical desires in a pleasure-laden heaven. This salvation does not begin now for the Muslim, but rather can only be accomplished at some future date when God's judgment is finally declared.

II. The Means of Salvation

The thought that salvation is an escape from hell's torment to heaven's delight leads us to the main section of our discussion, namely to the question, "How does a person escape?" In dealing with this problem we are considering a question to which no single answer can be given. "How shall I get to heaven?" is a question to which Islām itself has given a variety of answers. It is a question which perturbed Islām and which gave rise to numerous controversies in the course of Islām's theological development. The problem has its roots in the Qur'ān. Muḥammad was a preacher, not a philosopher or systematician. As D. B. MacDonald says: "In theology as in law Muḥammad was an opportunist. On the one hand Allāh is the absolute Semitic despot who guides aright and leads astray ... On the other hand men are exhorted to repentance, and punishment is threatened against them if they remain hardened in unbelief."[2] Despite its production by one mind the Qur'ān, because of its inner variations and contradictions, can be used to support a variety of positions. It was so used. Some put salvation under predestination, or under mercy, or under faith, or under works, or under mediation, or others associate it with the mystical way. It is indeed not easy to unravel these various approaches which fade into one another. A man may hold to one of several positions, or to some combination of theories, and still remain a good Muslim. The implication is obvious. In dealing with individual Muslims one cannot operate with any single premise, but rather he must first discover to which of the several Muslim doctrines the man before him gives credence or precedence.

a) Salvation by the Will of Allāh

Some Muslims put the salvation of human completely in the realm of God's sole activity. Of these some will attribute human's salvation to God's predestining will, others to God's mercy. Let us first consider the theory that a person is saved by the eternal and immutable decree of God's will. This is a well-known emphasis. But because it is an essential factor in the Muslim doctrine of salvation we must first of all take up this aspect of the problem. In investigating this theory we may consider the point of view of the Qur'ān, of the Ḥadīth, and of later Muslim theology.

Consider these passages from the Qur'ān which speak to this point:

> 7:177: He whom God guideth is the guided, and they whom He misleadeth shall be the lost.
>
> 14:4: But God misleadeth whom He wills and whom He will He guideth; and He is the Mighty, the Wise.
>
> 6:125: And whom God shall please to guide, that man's breast will be open to Islām; but whom he shall please to mislead, strait and narrow will He make His breast.
>
> 7:173: Many moreover of the jin and men have we created for hell. Hearts have they with which they understand not, ... They are like the brutes. Yea, and they go more astray.

> 11:120: Had thy Lord pleased He would have made mankind of one religion; but those only to whom thy Lord hath granted his mercy will cease to differ. And unto this hath he created them, for the word of the Lord shall be fulfilled, 'I will wholly fill hell with jin and men'.
>
> 13:33: Who is it then who is standing over every soul to mark its actions? Yet have they set up associates with God... But prepared of old for the infidels was this fraud of theirs, and they are turned aside from their path; and whom God causeth to err, no guide shall there be for him.
>
> 36:6-9: Just now is out sentence against most of them. Therefore they shall not believe. On their necks have we placed chains which reach the chin and forced up are their heads. Before them have we set a barrier, and we have shrouded them in a veil, so that they will not see. Alike is it to them if thou warn them or warn them not; they will not believe. And everything have we set down in the clear book of our decrees.
>
> 54:49: All things have we created under a fixed decree. It is He who causeth you to laugh and to weep, to die and make alive.

These passages, not exhaustive, indicate a major trend in the Qur'ān to place both salvation and damnation solely in the prerogative of Allāh himself.

In fairness it should be noted that there are modern Muslim commentators such as Muḥammad Iqbāl, and also Christian commentators such as W. R. W. Gardner, who try to explain away the absolute determinism indicated in these passages. They treat Allāh's eternal decree to hell as something subsequent to human's action; a punishment in view of human's infidelity. The decrees to eternal felicity are also given an *intuiti fidei* nature. To these commentators God's guiding whom he pleases means, as Gardner holds, that the conditions on which the direction and guidance of God become available are God's own choice. As regards times and seasons, means and methods, none can will to accept the guidance of God except as God wills, but the faith itself is not the direct result of God's action.[3] This interpretation seems to be begging the question, for the God who is responsible for the conditions, circumstances and means of believing is in effect responsible for the believing. A more serious objection is that such interpretation does not represent an accurate exegesis of the Qur'ān. It is as wrong to say that the Qur'ān does not teach an absolute determinism as it is wrong to say that the Qur'ān does not proclaim human's responsibility.

Furthermore, the main stream of orthodox Islām itself, as evidenced in the Traditions and later theological writings, has understood the Qur'ān to proclaim God's sole responsibility in salvation and damnation. Consider these representative traditions:

> 'Umar said, "I heard the apostle of Allāh questioned concerning this...and he replied, 'Verily Allāh created Adam and then stroked his back with his right hand and brought forth Adam's descendants from it. And he said, I have created thee for Paradise, and they will perform the acts of the people of Paradise. Then Allāh stroked Adam's back and brought forth other descendants from it. And he said, I have created these for the Fire, and they will perform the deeds of the people of the Fire.' Then a man said, 'Of what use, O apostle of Allāh, will deeds of any kind be?' Then the apostle of Allāh replied, 'When Allāh creates a servant for Paradise, He bids him perform the actions of the people of Paradise and thereby causes him to enter Paradise. And when Allāh creates a slave for the Fire, he bids him perform the actions of the people of the Fire and thereby causes him to enter the Fire.'"

> It is reported from Ibn 'Abbās that he said, "Know thou that if all the people were gathered together with the purpose of doing thee a benefit in any matter, they would not benefit thee except in that matter which God has already written down for thee. And if they come together with the purpose of doing thee an injury in some matter, they would not do thee any injury except in that matter which God has already written down. The pens have been lifted up, and the pages are dry." (Aḥmad, 294)

Traditions such as these may easily be multiplied, and they indicate strong support in the Ḥadīth for the idea of God's total sovereignty in salvation and damnation. The fact that the prophet Muḥammad, both in the Qur'ān and in the Ḥadīth, seemed at times to emphasize this control of an absolute Deity, but at other times addressed human as a free agent, meant that this doctrine of predestination would not be accepted in Islām without a challenge. It was challenged, but nevertheless it eventually won out as the orthodox doctrine of Islām. In Islāmic theological development a group called the Mu'tazilites upheld the doctrine of human's responsibilities, and their thought held away for almost a hundred years (850-950 C.E.). But the day eventually came for the end of the sway of these Mu'tazilites who had given reason almost more authority than the Qur'ān, and also who had dogmatically persecuted those who held differing views with respect to predestination. Al-Ash'ari, who lived in the tenth century, ushered in the system of thought that has become accepted as the orthodox understanding of the doctrine to this very time.

Al-Ash'ari held that in the last analysis God, who acts as He pleases, is totally responsible for both salvation and damnation. Since God alone is Creator, all acts must ultimately be attributed to Him. He is always saying "be" to what He wills to create. And since He is the Lord, He can do what He likes with His creation. He is not bound by reason, or anything else. Should He send all human to hell, it is not an injustice. Should He send all human to heaven, it is not wrong. His activity has no cause outside of Himself, not even the repentance of the penitent, for that would make Him dependent on something outside of Himself. "His activity is the cause of everything, and His activity has no cause." Even His own command cannot be identified with His own will, for He can command what He does not will, and will what He does not command. He is above everything, and the same time He is the Cause of everything, including man's salvation or damnation.

Of course, al-Ash'ari ran hard up against the problem of how human can participate at all in any action if one is thus under the sway of God's creative impulse. He tried, to escape the problem by his unconvincing doctrine of acquisition (*iktisāb*). According to this theory human "acquires" the act which God creates. God does not will absolutely, He wills something to be the act or acquisition of the human being. Human is connected with his/her acts in the sense that he/she gives them the character by which they merit recompense. Thus, while God creates the acts of bowing and prostrating, in some way human makes them prayer. Acquisition, said al-Ash'ari, is the "connection of the human power with the deed without causation. This sort of specious reasoning brought into being a truthful proverb "more subtle than the acquisition of al-Ash'ari."[4] Al-Ash'ari had followed the Qur'ānic emphasis on God's absolute power to its logical conclusion and had come up against a dead end. Human was only an automaton played with by God's wilful fingers. He didn't like this conclusion, and he tried to evade it by the doctrine of acquisition.

Because al-Ash'ari's thoughts held close to a strong theme in the Qur'ān they were accepted and reflected in the orthodox creeds of Islām. This is true for example in the Creed of al-Nasafī (ca. 1050), as well as in the commentary on this creed written by al-Taftāzānī (ca. 1400). In the Creed of al- Nasafī we have these words:

> Allāh is the Creator of all the actions of his creatures, whether of Unbelief or of Belief, of obedience or of disobedience. And they are all of them by His will and desire, by His judgment, by His ruling, and by His decreeing. His creatures have actions of choice for which they are rewarded or punished. And the good in these is by the good pleasure of Allāh, and the vile is not by His good pleasure.

To these words the commentator al-Taftāzānī, gives the comment:

> Decreeing is the limiting of each creature to the limit within which he exists, whether of goodness or vileness, of use or harm, and to what he occupies of time and place, and to what results thereby of reward and punishment.

We can see how al-Taftāzānī was caught on the horns of the dilemma where al-Ash'ari and al-Nasafī had left him. But he sees no way of escape. He illustrates the problem by quoting a discussion in which 'Amr b. Ubayd, an early Mu'tazilite, said to a Magian:

> Why dost thou not become a Muslim? He said, 'Because Allāh has not willed my becoming a Muslim; if He wills it, I shall become a Muslim.' So I said to the Magian. 'Allāh wills your becoming a Muslim, but the Shaytāns do not let you alone.' So the Magian replied, 'In that case I shall stay with the more victorious partner.'[5]

But al-Taftāzānī, as well as al-Nasafī, finally must admit the absoluteness of God's decree. Though this may seem to conflict with human's sense of justice no other solution to them seems possible. Therefore al-Nasafī states:

> Everyone receives in full his Appointed Sustenance whether from things permitted or forbidden; and it is inconceivable thata man will not eat his own Appointed Sustenance or that another than he will eat his Appointed

> Sustenance. Allāh leads astray whom he wills and guides when he wills, and it is not incumbent upon Allāh to do that which is best for the creature.

In his comment on these words al-Taftāzānī spells out even more clearly the implications of this doctrine. He says:

> So if the creature purposes a good action, Allāh creates the power to do good, and if he purposes an evil action, Allāh creates the power to do evil, and he thus loses the power to do good and deserves blame and punishment 'Allāh leads astray whom he wills and guides aright whom he wills' (means) that he does so by creating the actions of going astray and being guided Guidance is figuratively related to the Prophet by way of assigning causation, just as it is ascribed to the Qur'ān, and leading astray may be ascribed to Satan just as it is to idols, yet it is Allāh who leads astray and guides aright 'and it is not incumbent on Allāh to do that which is best for the creature' otherwise he would not have created the poor unbeliever who is tormented in this world and the next; … nor would the power of Allāh continue to bear any relation to the welfare of his creatures, since He would have performed that which is incumbent on him...If there is any denial of good to the creature by the one who has the right to deny, this is absolute justice and wisdom.[6]

Does this exaggeration of God's all-powerful will represent the orthodox faith today? It seems to me that the majority of orthodox theologians, if pressed, would still admit to this view. It has been said that "most modern Muslim theologians are Mu'tazila."[7] For example, the famed Muḥammad 'Abdūh of Egypt held that religion requires independence of mind and thought. Right and wrong are not created by God's will, for reason can distinguish good and evil without waiting for revelation. And God does act for the advantage of his creatures. This is no doubt the view of many educated and enlightened Muslim teachers. But it is probably correct to say that most orthodox mullahs, if questioned, would generally agree with the interpretations of al-Ash'ari and al-Nasafī , and in that agreement they would be holding true to a leading motif in the Qur'ān. But not only that. This doctrine is the dark background that lies behind the thinking of many an ordinary Muslim as he considers salvation. It is true that some Muslims, their views modified by other influences, have specifically denied this determinism. Others have banished it from their every-day thinking. Others seem not to be well aware of its total implications. But for many it is the reason why they are driven to say: "I cannot say, 'I am saved'. I can only say, 'I am saved, if God wills.'"

Is there anyone who has studied the history of Christian doctrine and has faced in that study the great tensions that developed in the effort to reconcile God's sovereignty and human's freedom who will fail to sympathize with the problems that the Muslims encounter at this level of their thought. Christians too have had difficulty in reconciling the conception of God's matchless sovereignty with His moral government of free human. Nevertheless, there must be a clear Christian response to this one overwhelming facet of Muslim theology, which Tor Andrae so aptly terms "the lost equilibrium."[8] Since it is the function of this paper to set forth the Muslim doctrine of salvation, we cannot enter at length into the nature of that response. Yet in passing, one or two aspects of the Christian witness at this level become very clear.

In the first place, the Christian must be ready to say unequivocally to the Muslim that God is totally apart from evil, evil as it is understood by human's conscience. He is holy, that is, altogether separate from evil, and not its creator. God is limited by this fact of His own nature. Does this mean that He therefore becomes something less than God? Is He not more truly God in that His nature is a beautiful harmony, rather than if he were the slave of one run-away attribute, namely Power? Secondly, has not God by His act of creation brought forth natural laws of cause and effect, apart from His immediate action? Has not God by creating human with the power of reason along with it willed for human an area of freedom in which that freedom may operate according to its created capacities?[9] Within that God-willed area of freedom human being is responsible even though he/she barters his/her freedom and sells himself away to the slavery of sin. Does not being alive unto God (once again, through Jesus Christ cur Lord) mean this that we are freely able to say nowhere Adam and Eve said Yes? Thirdly, we will maintain that in the area of salvation God's power is not the power of compulsion, but the power of attraction. Through the uplifted Jesus God the Father will draw all human kind to Himself. God will not unleash His power to rape His own creation, but rather with the power of His love He will woo human into the marriage of faith. That wooing, freely accepted, implies a relationship far more beautiful than any bond of compulsion.

b) Salvation by the Mercy of Allāh

It might be thought that, from the extreme point of view we have considered, there would be little purpose in speaking of the love, mercy and grace of God. But, however logical this deduction may be Islām must speak of the mercy of Allāh because of the fact that in the Qur'ān it is frequently mentioned. Accordingly, we are brought to the second stand-point from which a Muslim may view the doctrine of salvation, that of the mercy of God.

The Qur'ān and Islām speak of the love of God very seldom (except for the mystics). Love in Allāh does not seem to represent a personal relationship. It is not a drawing near to human on His part, but rather the willing from all eternity to give power to the creature to draw near to God.[10] At the same time, in the Qur'ān it is usually represented as following the love which human shows God. Sūrah 3:29 says: "If ye would love God, then follow me and God will love you." Rather than a love for sinful human, the love of God in the Qur'ān is a preference, or liking, seemingly directed as much to human's good qualities as to human being themselves. So Allāh loves the kind, the patient, those who trust, who do good, the pious and the clean. He does not love the unjust (3:134), the arrogant (16:25), the unbelieving traitor (22:39), those who exult (28:76), the evil-doers (28:77), the unbelievers (30:44), the miserly (4:41), the corrupt (5:69), the transgressors (5:89), the extravagant (7:29) and the treacherous (8:60). Thus the love of Allāh seems to be an affection for a loyal servant.

In considering the question of God's goodness toward human the Qur'ān and Islām usually use the term "mercy" or "grace", rather than "love." There does not appear to be a clear distinction in meaning between these two, words which are used interchangeably in the Qur'ān. The two common cognates of "mercy", *raḥmān* and *raḥīm*, stand prominently in the invocation which appears at the head of every sūra but one in the Qur'ān. The former signifies the One of tender heart, inclination to show favour. The latter, applied to Allāh, seems to refer mere to merciful action than to the quality of mercy. Often *raḥmān* is used, without direct reference to its meaning, as a proper name for Allāh, for example in 25: 28 "The true kingdom on that day will belong to the Merciful, and it will be a hard day for unbelievers."

The "grace" of Allāh (*fazl* and *ni'mat*) really means "superabundance;" it refers most often to the abundance of created blessings which are bestowed in this life and in Paradise through the divine goodness. The "favour" of God is usually used in connection with the joy that awaits believers in heaven, and so represents fulfilled mercy. The "guidance" of the Lord refers to the way God's purpose of mercy is proffered to human, namely, the Qur'ān. Yet none of these distinctions is clear-cut. Exactly the same implications are often given to God's mercy, favour, grace and guidance. They all refer to God's "good" will toward human.

God's purpose of mercy towards human is indicated in the Qur'ān in such passages as 57:9: "He it is who hath sent down clear tokens unto his servants, that He may lead you cut of darkness into light; for God is merciful and compassionate toward you." To this end God purposes to instruct human kind concerning Himself and the way in which human may please Him. This premise of guidance, given already at human's fall, represents the mercy of God which will lead them to Paradise (7:47) and save them from hell (6:16). On the one hand this mercy seems to be prevenient. "Were it not for God's grace upon thee and His mercy, ye had followed Satan, save a few" (4:85). From this point of view it is a sort of awakening grace whose operation is not clearly defined. "But God hath endeared the faith to you and hath given it favour in your hearts, and hath made unbelief and wickedness and disobedience hateful to you" (49:7). On the other hand God's mercy at times is spoken of as being dependent on human's response to His proffered guidance. "And believers, men and women ... bid what is reasonable and forbid what is wrong and are steadfast in prayer and give alms and obey God and His messenger. On these will God have mercy" (9:72).

God's mercy at times resembles a sustaining mercy and grace: "Were it not for God's grace upon thee and His mercy, a party of them would have tried to lead thee astray, but they only lead themselves astray. They shall not hurt thee in anything, for God hath sent down on thee the book and the wisdom and taught thee that thou dost know, for God's grace was mighty on thee" (4:113). We see in this verse the strong connection of grace with the giving and possession of the Qur'ān. Allied to this sustaining grace is a sanctifying grace: "We also made them (Isaac and Jacob) models who should guide by our command; and we inspired them with good deeds and constancy in prayer and alms-giving, and they worshipped us" (21:73). This grace increases: "God will increase the guidance of the already guided" (19:78). The greater the endeavour, the greater the grace: "And whoso maketh efforts for us, in our ways will we guide them; for God is with the righteous" (19:69). God's proffered grace has a two-fold effect, leading some but hardening ethers: "Whenever a sūra is sent down ... it will increase the faith or these who believe, and they shall rejoice; but as for those in whose hearts is a disease, it will add to their doubt, and they shall die infidels" (9:125). But if a man, simply because of the weakness of his nature, falls away from divine grace, there is for him a restoring mercy: "Go to Pharaoh, for he hath burst all his bounds, and say—wouldst thou become just? Then I will guide thee to the Lord that thou mayest fear him." (79:17).

In considering the mercy of Allāh in the Qur'ān what appears as the glaring weakness is that it does not represent the expression of God's inner nature, which can never be fathomed. Allāh's mercy is rather an arbitrary attitude which He may take or discard at will. God wills and acts and among the things he purposes and does are those which may be described as compassionate and merciful. Grace is not an inner compulsion of Allāh's nature, but rather it is something which he has prescribed for himself, much as he causes his decrees to be written. This is well indicated by sūra 6:12: "Say: unto whom belongeth whatsoever is in the heavens and the earth? Say: unto Allāh. He hath prescribed for Himself mercy, that He may bring you all together to a Day whereof there is no doubt ..." Thus the mercy of Allāh may be regarded "as a policy rather than a disposition, a policy which by an act of his will he has laid down for himself."[11]

Secondly, it is clear that the mercy of God is exclusive rather than comprehensive. Despite the occasional universal emphasis we see that the mercy of God in the Qur'ān is directed mainly to believers: "And whosoever shall obey God and the Apostle these shall be those to whom God hath been gracious" (4:71). But this mercy is not for sinners, for "verily, He loves not the misbelievers" (30:44). "God loves not there deceitful sinners" (4:108). His mercy, as Spencer puts it, "is conditioned by his determination to fill Hell with men and jin."[12]

Thirdly, there is no doctrine of the means of grace, or anything corresponding to the work of the Holy Spirit. Most often the means of God's grace is identified with the Qur'ān, sometimes with his general guidance of human, and sometimes also with the five pillars or the general good works of human.

The mercy of Allāh becomes evident through forgiveness. That which makes the mercy of Allāh an object of human's hopes, despite its limitations, is the fact that it is the source of God's forgiveness. Forgiveness (*maghfir*, *ghufrān*) in the Qur'ān is essentially a negative concept and consists in not punishing, especially on the Day of Judgment. As salvation in Islām is essentially an escape from Hell to Paradise, as a hope, so also the mercy and forgiveness of Allāh concern especially the remission of punishment that allows for this escape. Sūra 6:15-16 says: "Say: I fear ... the retribution of an Awful Day. He from whom (such retribution) is averted on that day (Allāh) hath in truth had mercy upon him ..." It is from this point of view of the preservation of human from the touch of punishment that we must consider the repeated Qur'ānic proclamation that God forgives the sins of human. "But thy Lord is forgiving endowed with mercy; were he to punish them for what they have earned, he would have hastened for them the torment." (18:57).

It is obvious that forgiveness in the Qur'ān is not only conditioned by the nature of Allāh's mercy, but also involves the Qur'ānic view of sin. As to the former, justice and mercy in God do not require reconciliation with respect to human, for both are subordinate to His almighty will; therefore God does not have to suffer to forgive. As to the latter, God can easily forgive sin, for human's sin is God's own doing. He created human weak, and human's acts continue to reflect God's own amoral, creative will. God can forgive sin as easily as he can create sin. This is no contradiction of His inner nature, but rather a confirmation of it. Accordingly, Muslims are bidden to pray: "O Lord, perfect us for our light and forgive us; verily thou art mighty over all" (46:8). Such Muslims are assured: "Say: O my servants who have been extravagant against own souls, be not in despair of the mercy of God; verily God forgives sins, all of them, verily He is Forgiving, Merciful." (39:54)

With this understanding of sin we see how forgiveness in the Qur'ān often appears merely as an indulgent concession or relaxation of the law. Thus God himself is called *al-Ḥalīm*, the Clement One, who is calm, not easily put out. That is, He is one whom the disobedience of the disobedient does not flurry, but who has appointed to everything its own conclusion. This concessional aspect of forgiveness is indicated by 2:168 where God says he will overlook a technical breach of requirements relating to forbidden food. And 2:226 states: "God will not punish you for a mistake in your oaths." Other passages indicate that an important aspect of God's forgiveness is God's making things easier for human in condescension to their weakness. 2:286 declares: "God will not burden any soul beyond its power ... O our Lord, punish us not if we forget or fall into sin. O our Lord, lay not on us that for which we have not strength; but blot out our sins and forgive us and have pity on us."

That forgiveness should take this turn is not surprising when we remember that Allāh's mercy, and the forgiveness which flows from it, are basically subservient to His will. "He pardons whom he pleases and torments whom he pleases, for God is forgiving, merciful" (48:14). By His predestination will God divides human to "mercy" or to "wrath": "Your Lord knows best; if He please He will have mercy on you, or if He please He will torment you" (17:56). This forgiving "grace" is completely arbitrary and irresistible: "Should Allāh touch thee with his harm there is none to remove it save he; and if He wish thee well, there is none to repel his grace. He makes it fall on whom He will of his servants, for He is Pardoning, Merciful." (10:107)

That mercy essentially becomes a "policy" of Allāh's will is also well illustrated by many traditions. For example,

> It is reported from Abū Hurairah that the Apostle of God said "Verily there were two men of the children of Israel who were friends together. One of them was intent on worship but the other used to proclaim himself a sinner. And the first began to say, 'Give up that in which thou art entangled.' His companion said, 'Leave me and my Lord.' Until one day he found him engaged in grievous sin. Then he said, 'Forsake it.' He replied, 'Leave me and my Lord. Hast thou been sent a guardian over me?' He said, 'By God. God will never forgive thee nor enter thee into Paradise.' Then God sent an angel to them both, who took their souls, and they were brought together near to God. He said to the sinner, 'Enter Paradise, by my Mercy!' And He said to the other, 'Art thou able to forbid my servant my Mercy?' He replied, 'No. O God.' God said (to the angels), 'Take him away to the fire!'" (Aḥmad, 11)

Traditions such as this one may readily be multiplied.

The doctrine of Allāh's mercy as outlined above may produce a variety of reactions in Muslims. Many orthodox Muslims, if pressed, will concede that trusting in the mercy of God is equivalent to submitting to His almighty power and will. By some, such as Ḥasan al-Baṣrī, it is accepted as a mystery with submissive wonder. He said: "The mystery of the divine mercy is great; wonder not at those who perish but at those who escape."[13] In others it may produce a sense of freedom from responsibility leading to licentiousness. The punishment for sin has no fear for one who recognizes that Allāh's mercy is completely arbitrary and is not qualified by a moral nature within Himself. The story is told of a Muslim who took a glass of wine and said:

> Now if I say that it is right to drink this wine. I deny God's command to men and he would punish me for blasphemy. But to take this glass, admitting that God has commanded me not to drink it and that I sin in drinking it. Then I drink it off, so casting myself on the Mercy of God. For our religion lets me know that God is too merciful to punish me for doing a thing which I wish to do when I humbly admit that to do it is to break his commandment.[14]

But in some other Muslims, probably relatively few indeed, the many Qur'ānic statements about the mercy, grace, favour, guidance and forgiveness of God produce a different reaction. These are they who do not follow the virtual identification of mercy and will to its logical conclusion. These are they who close their eyes to the fact that God's effortless forgiveness seems unrelated to justice and morality. They in hope cling to the conception of Allāh as *Al-Tawwāb*, the Easily Turned, the Relenting One. They cling to such a promise as: "He repented over them that they might also repent, verily God is easily turned and merciful." (9:19) It is claimed by Muslims that the Traditions reproduce accurately the words of Muḥammad. Though the accuracy of this claim may be doubted, at the least we must admit that we see in the Traditions what Islām hoped that Muḥammad might say. Surely it was Muslims who yearned to trust in the mercy of God who are at least in part responsible for the production of such traditions as these:

> It is reported from Abū Hurairah that the Apostle of God said, "When God completed the work of creation He wrote a book which is with Him above His throne ... 'Verily mercy outruns His anger.'" (Muslim, 118)
>
> God is more merciful towards his servants than the mother of the young birds to her young. (Abū Dāwūd, 110)
>
> It is reported from Ibn 'Abbās that the Apostle of God used to say, "O God, for thee have I become a Muslim, and in thee I trust, and upon thee I lean, and to thee I return." (Muslim, 125)
>
> It is reported from 'Āyesha that she said, "I heard the Apostle of God saying in certain of his prayers, 'O God, take from me an easy account.' I said, 'O Prophet of God, what is an easy account?' He replied, 'That He looks into His book and passes over it. Verily Ayesha, he from whom an exact account will be taken on that day will perish.'" (Aḥmad, 272)
>
> It is related from Ibn 'Abbās that the Apostle of God said, "70,000 of my followers will enter Paradise without account. They are those who do not use spells or draw bad omens, and in their Lord put their trust." (Muslim, 253)

The hope of some Muslims who "in their Lord put their trust", how many is hard to say, is that God will have mercy upon them and will save them. This is the second level from which salvation may be viewed in Islām.

When a Christian meets a Muslim at the level of salvation which we have been discussing, the problem of what must be said is certainly easier than the question of how to say it. All these beautiful words in the Qur'ān—grace, mercy, favour, guidance—how much more beautiful and meaningful do they become when we add "in Christ"! In the first place, in Christ we find that these words convey an assuring eternal validity, stemming from the heart of God Himself. To the Muslims we say that because of Christ it is clear that the mercy of God is more than a policy which he adopts and changes as He pleases. Because He creates and keeps His covenant of love, even though it means suffering for Himself, it must be that God is more than "merciful." It must be that He is Mercy itself. He is "gracious" to human because of the unchangeable compulsion of His own nature to love. He wills "favour" toward human because His will is the will of love. He works out the salvation of human because His power serves the desires of love. In Christ we see not that God is loving, but that He is love.

Secondly, in Christ we see that God really intends His mercy to reach humankind. He therefore goes beyond the sending of a gracious word in the form of a written book. His love stops at nothing in its effort to reach humankind. Therefore He sends His Word personally in Jesus Christ who confronts human as the Way of God.

Thirdly, we say to the Muslim that God's love is not dependent on human. It is spontaneous and unearned. It comes to human, despite human's unworthiness. Therefore it comes to sinners, to those who are sick and lost. Because there is within the heart of God the fearful incumbency of love, it is incumbent upon Him to do that which is best for His creatures, even though they have no claims of worth or merit. God's love commends itself towards us in that while we were yet sinners Christ died for us.

And finally we agree with the Muslim that God's mercy truly becomes known in forgiveness. But even as sin is not a light thing for the holy God, so also is not the forgiveness of that sin. Therefore when mercy goes out it does not go cut to man in simply overlooking the punishment due to sin. Rather mercy demonstrates itself most truly in bearing that punishment, annulling the guilt of man, and destroying forever the power of sin and death. To those Muslims who would take refuge in the mercy of God let us show the Cross of Christ where the mercy of God reveals its eternal depths and where it becomes known to sinful man as a sure and unassailable refuge.

c) Salvation by Faith Alone

The third strand in Islām's doctrine of salvation is salvation by faith. Here once again we experience difficulty in delineating the teaching, for in the Qur'ān faith and works are often closely connected. The possibility of being saved by works alone without faith is never admitted in the Qur'ān. For example, if the Jews and Christians were to have a chance for salvation it was because of the amount of faith which they possessed and which would prepare them for the ultimate acceptance of Islām in the last days; it was not because of the works they might have done (5:73). Faith is always the prerequisite. But does the Qur'ān teach that a person is saved by faith alone, or are certain works required to make faith saving faith? This is the question which did disturb Islām. To this question many in Islām gave the answer—yes, salvation is by faith alone, and the absence or presence of works cannot finally affect the faith which saves.

When Islām speaks of faith, what does it mean? In considering this question it is essential to remember that what is implied is belief rather than trust, intellectual acceptance rather than loving confidence. Abraham typifies true faith, but his faith is regarded as an act of judgment by which something is held to be true, not a grasping hold of Allāh. To be sure the word for faith, *'īmān*, really means "trust." But actually faith was taken to mean *taṣdīq*, the intellectual assent to certain propositions. For example, in his creed al-Nasafī said that belief is assent, assent "to that which the prophet brought from Allāh, and the confession of it." To this al-Taftāzānī commented that belief is assent, the acknowledging the judgment of a narrator, accepting it and considering it to be veracious."[15] While no one will deny the emotional content of Islāmic faith, the factor of assent remains the critical one.

The great Muslim theologian, Al-Ghazālī, made the action of faith the equivalent of surrender and submission. In effect since his day there is no real difference between "faith" and "Islām." While faith emphasizes the belief, Islām may include the practice as well as the dogma. Thus a *mu'min* may be one who has faith in dogmas, while a Muslim may be one who performs the actions that confirm the faith. But generally the words are used interchangeably. Thus, for example, al-Taftāzānī said that belief and Islām are one, for Islām means resignation and submission, the acceptance and acknowledging of judgments, which is the real essence of assent.

To what is it that the believer is to assent? Both the Qur'ān and tradition give as the content of saving faith the message of the prophet Muḥammad, including especially his doctrine of God. The elements of faith which are included in the usual listing are found in Sūra 2:177 "Righteous is he who believeth in Allāh and the last day and the angels and the scripture and the prophets ..." According to this the Muslim is to accept the truth of Allāh, the last day, angels, books, and the prophets, as it is presented by Muḥammad. Of this message it is said: "O our people, respond to God's crier and believe in him." But though these five elements are present in the Qur'ānic faith its essential terms of reference are to the truth of Allāh and the validity of Muḥammad's presentation of that truth. This is reflected in the most common Muslim creed, or testimony of faith: "There is no God but Allāh, and Muḥammad is the apostle of Allāh." A Tradition states: "It is related from 'Abbās bin 'Abdul Muṭṭalib that the Apostle of God said, 'He has tasted the food of faith who is pleased with Allāh as his Lord and with Islām as his religion and Muḥammad as his Apostle.'" (Muslim, 2)

To the five-fold Qur'ānic listing of the content of faith orthodox theologians later added the article of predestination. As the basis for this development a tradition was quoted:

> Gabriel was said to have appeared to Muḥammad and asked him, "Teach me about faith." The prophet replied, "It is that thou believe in God and his angels and his books and his apostle and in the last day and that thou believe in predestination both of good and evil." He said, "Thou hast spoken truly." (Muslim, 2)

Despite this apparent clarity there was dispute about the essential content of faith. For example, the Mu'tazilites said that faith is the knowledge of God and everyone by first principles can have this. Al-Ash'ari himself admitted varieties of faith, saying that faith may be belief in God, his prophets and his revelation; or it is belief in the prophet's message, partly in outline, partly in detail; or it is the knowledge of the Creator. But generally speaking the consensus was that saving faith is assent to the truth of the prophet and his message and his God; Allāh is the true God, and Muḥammad is his true representative. Therefore al-Bājūrī said: "Faith is the inner assent given to the Prophet of Islām, to that which he has brought and to that which he has taught concerning religion. It involves obedience and submission to the message of the Prophet, he who is the true witness to Allāh's revelation."[16]

Many Muslims agree that this sort of faith brings as its reward salvation no matter what else a person may say or do. They point to the promises of such a passage as: "O ye who believe, fear Allāh and believe his messenger; He will give you two portions of his mercy and will make light for you to walk in and will forgive you." It is claimed by these that various passages with a phrase such as "those who believe and do the things that are right" (2:23) separate faith and works and make faith the condition of works. Various traditions are quoted in support of this understanding of saving faith. For example,

> It is related from Tawban that the Apostle of God said, "There is no Muslim servant who says three times, when evening comes and when morning comes, 'I am satisfied with Allāh as Lord and with Islām as religion and with Muḥammad as prophet,' but it becomes incumbent on God to be satisfied with him on the day of resurrection." (Aḥmad, 121)

> It is reported from Abū Zar that he said, "I came to the Prophet and ... he said, 'There is no servant who shall say, There is no God but Allāh, and shall die relying on that, but will enter heaven.' I said, 'Although he commits adultery and theft?' He replied, 'Although he commits adultery and theft'" (Muslim, 3)

But dare a Muslim ever say merely "I believe. Therefore I am saved"? The Qur'ān says "God hath endeared the faith to you and hath given it favour in your hearts, and hath made unbelief and wickedness and disobedience hateful to you." (49:7). The Qur'ānic emphasis on the sole sovereignty of Allāh, which we considered as the first level of salvation in Islām, meant that the theologians had to play around with the question: "Can a man say, 'I am a believer'? Or must he say, 'I am a believer, if God wills'?" Many did uphold the latter view, thus forsaking this level of salvation which we are considering. Al-Ghazālī quotes approvingly the statement of one Fuzayl: "If you are asked, do you love Allāh, be silent; for, if you say 'no', you become an unbeliever; if you say 'yes', your saying so is not the description of those who love."[17] Some learned Muslims said that there is no higher blessedness in the Garden than that of the people of the knowledge and love of Allāh, and no more serious punishment in the Fire than that of the one who claims to have them. Nevertheless, a representative orthodox thinker like al-Taftāzānī does not support this extreme view. Rather he maintained that it is permissible to say, "I am a believer, if God wills", if one says it because of good breeding, or in order to refer matters to the will of Allāh, or through doubt about the final consequence and outcome of life, or because of an expected blessing from mentioning the name of Allāh, or to clear oneself from self-righteousness, but not with reference to the state of present belief; for that would be doubt, which equals, unbelief. And many present day Muslims find it just as easy to omit the "if God wills" from the statement "I am a *mu'min*", as they find it simple to omit the "if God wills" from the declaration "I am a Muslim."

Another question which arose in connection with this understanding of faith was this—Is not at least confession necessary to make faith saving faith? We have seen that the element of confession was not absent in the traditions quoted above. A man who spoke the creed on his death-bed was a recognized believer and saved. Nevertheless, some theologians used such a passage as 58:22 "On the hearts ... hath God graven faith" to prove that belief is essentially a matter of the inner spirit. Thus they said, while it is not permissible at all for one to fall short in the matter of assent, it is permissible for one not to confess, for example, in a time of persecution. So to these thinkers confession is not of the essence of saving faith. But commonly it is held that one who utters the witnessing formula, "There is no God but Allāh, and Muḥammad is the apostle of Allāh," is a believer. Therefore, unless there are exceptional circumstances, some sort of public declaration is regarded as inseparable from saving faith. It is an integral part of salvation "by faith alone."

That a person is saved by faith, by faith alone, is a phrase that rings familiarly in Christian ears. We agree with the Muslim that only through "faith alone" is God permitted to assert his true sovereignty in the realm of salvation. But "by faith alone" means something quite different to the Christian than to the Muslim who stands on this level of salvation. To the Muslim we say that faith is more than an intellectual assent to the verity of a proposition concerning the unity of God or the validity of a prophet. Faith is rather the whole inner soul of man turning in an intensely intimate trust. But trust in what?—a proposition, a book, a command, or even the oneness of God? No, there must be something more to make of faith a personal relationship of trust.

We must say to the Muslim that while belief in God is possible to any human, faith becomes saving faith only when it lays hold of the saving God. Trust in God is possible only to those who know that God is trustworthy. Faith looks up, not simply to the God who is, but to the God who is reaching down to save. Who is the saving God who inspires such trust? He is the God who sends the Saviour. In Jesus Christ God has reached down to save. For He was in Christ reconciling the world and me to Himself. In this saving God faith will become trust. And because the trust is in the saving God such trust will save. The true point of comparison is that, for the Christian, salvation by faith means justification by faith, God justifying humankind in Christ, and human receiving that work of grace in humble trust.

So, secondly, the Christian will say to the Muslim—salvation must be by faith alone, for it is through faith alone that reality is served in the realm of salvation. Sinful human can really do nothing towards their salvation. They are in the bondage of sin, and sin's curse, blindness and death is upon them. Only God can really save. He only can justify. He only is the loving Creator who can re-create that which we have lost. Faith is the link that connects our inability and rebelliousness with

God's ability and mercy. For by grace are ye saved, through faith, and that not of yourselves, it is the gift of God.

Finally the Christian will not say, "I believe in God, if God wills." In Jesus Christ one knows that God wills all humankind to be saved and to come to the knowledge of the truth. Faith trusts firmly that to any human who grasps the hem of His garment power will go cut from the Lord. Rather, therefore, the Christian's prayer is: "Lord, I believe, help Thou mine unbelief."

d) Salvation by Faith and Works

The fourth position from which a Muslim may view the doctrine of salvation is the way of faith authenticated by works. According to this view, to be saved a Muslim must not only believe but he must also perform the works of God according to the principles and rules mediated by His prophet Muḥammad.

Those who hold to this belief find ample support in the Qur'ān where the necessity of works to salvation is commonly emphasized. In the very passage, previously quoted, which outlines the content of faith, in the same breath the obligation of deeds is brought out.

> Righteous is one who believes in God, and the last day and the angels and the book and the prophets, and who gives wealth for love of Him to kindred and orphans and the poor and the son of the road and beggars and those in captivity, and who is steadfast in prayer and gives alms, and those who trust in their covenant when they make a covenant, and the patient in poverty and distress and in time of salvation (2:172).

Again it is said: "Those who misbelieve, for them is keen torment. But those who believe and do right, for them is forgiveness and a great hire" (35: 7). Such a passage as this seems to strike strongly at faith which is mere lip-service. For those who believe and do good works Muḥammad is to announce the glad tidings of "gardens beneath which rivers flow" in Paradise (2:23).

The good works which are especially commended to the Muslim are, of course, the "five pillars"—confession, prayer, fasting, alms-giving, and the pilgrimage. Also included are the various ceremonial rites.

These are given the same status as moral virtues. For example, the ablutions before prayer must be done correctly to make of the prayer a valid work. In addition to those commands such virtues as these are recommended—honesty, kindness, gentleness, slowness to anger, a forgiving-spirit, perseverance, and patience (e.g. 90:12-18).

What is the motive for good works? One motive stated in the Qur'ān is the fear of God: "We feed you for the sake of God only; we seek from you neither recompense nor thanks; a stern and calamitous day dread we from our Lord" (76: 9-10). Because Allāh is Lord his commands must be obeyed. But even in this passage we see that the reason why the "needy wretch, the orphan, and the prisoner" is to be fed is not because that action reflected Allāh's nature, but because Allāh will judge on the basis of obedience to His commands. "Whatsoever is in the heavens and the earth is God's that he may reward those who do evil according to their works; and those who do good will he reward with good things" (53: 32). This emphasis has meant that in the minds of ordinary Muslims the motive for good works is to avoid the impending judgment and to gain the righteousness that will avail for a favourable decision on judgment day. In other words, they will make him eligible for salvation—Paradise.

We see this idea represented in such a passage as 21:94, "Whoso shall do the things that are right and be a true believer, his efforts shall not be disowned; and surely will we write it down for him." A passage commonly quoted by devout Muslims is 99:6. "On that day whosoever shall have wrought an atom's weight of good shall behold it. And whosoever shall have wrought an atom's weight of evil shall behold it." The glad tidings of Allāh are that a good action will have a good result on the judgment day.

> Verily the unjust—for them is a grievous woe. Thou shalt see the unjust shrink in terror from what they have gained as it falls upon them; and those who believe and do right, in meads of Paradise they shall have what they please with their Lord—that is great grace. That is what God gives glad tidings of to his servants who believe and do righteous deeds. Say ... And he who gains a good action we will increase good for him thereby; verily God is forgiving, grateful" (42: 20-22).

It is not surprising therefore that this thought combined with the lack of an adequate doctrine of sin-expiation meant that inevitably a commercial approach to good works would develop. This is illustrated particularly by passages relating to alms-giving. "Give ye alms openly? It is well. Do ye conceal them, and give them to the poor? This too will be of advantage to you and will do away your sins" (2:273). And Muḥammad declares: "O ye who believe, shall I lead you to a merchandise that shall save you from grievous woe?—to believe in God and His messenger, and to fight hard in God's cause with your property and your persons" (61:10).

The thought that good works are merits and expiations that bring absolution from sin's punishment is related to the Islāmic idea that a person is God's slave. As a slave he piles up debts or credits. Sins are the debts and good works are the credits. The latter must outweigh the former on the scale which determines the Muslim's fate. "Then as for him whose scales are heavy (with good works) he will live a pleasant life. But as for him whose scales are light, the Bereft and Hungry one will be his mother raging Fire" (101,7f.). In another analogy the good deeds are represented as being heavy and evil deeds light. The greater the number of good deeds the heavier the worth of a person. The Qur'ān says: "The weighing on that day is true. As for those whose scale is heavy they are the successful. And as for those whose scale is light: those are they who lose their souls because they disbelieved our revelations" (7: 7ff). Thus, while faith is the necessary basis, according to this view a man's relative happiness or woe after this life depends on the amount of good works he has accumulated. And when once the scale has been measured and he is found condemned, his condemnation and punishment will be in direct proportion to the sum total of evil deeds insofar as they outweigh the good. The converse will also be true, except that the reward will surpass that which was merited.

Traditions amply support the view that a Muslim may be justified by works:

> It is reported from Abū Hurairah that the Apostle of God said. "Whoever says, 'There is no God but Allāh alone ... He is powerful over all' one hundred times in a day, there will be for him a reward equal to the freeing

> of ten slaves; and one hundred good actions will be written for him, and one hundred evil actions will be erased for him ... And no one will come with anything better than what he brings except the man who has done more than he" (Muslim, 114).
>
> It is reported from Abū Said al-Khudrī that the Apostle of God said, "He who fasts one day in the road of God, removes his face seventy years from the fire" (Muslim, 95).
>
> It is reported from Abū Hurairah that the Apostle of God said, "Shall I not point you to that by which God blots out sins and raises your rank?" They replied, "Yes, O Apostle of God." He said, "The completion of ablutions in a time of difficulty, and thegoing a long distance to the mosques, and the waiting for another prayer after the completion of one. This is protection for you" (Muslim, 95).

These are but a few of the many Traditions that promote the idea that it is through good works that Allāh "has made the fire prohibited" for the Muslim.

At this point it may be proper to note the one work that automatically qualifies a Muslim for immediate entry into Paradise. That work is martyrdom, fighting and dying for Islām. After urging on his followers to fight for God Muḥammad promised: "And repute not those slain on God's path to be dead. Nay, alive are they with their Lord richly sustained" (3: 169). Al-Tirmīzī and Ibn Mājah report that the martyr has six privileges with God: his sins are pardoned when the first drop of blood falls; he is shown his seat in Paradise; he is safe from the punishment of the grave and secure from the great terror; a crown of dignity is placed on his head; he is married to seventy dark-eyed virgins; and he makes intercession for seventy of his relatives (Kitāb-i qadar). In addition to the martyrs, prophets are apparently exceptions who will go to heaven directly. The companions of the prophets also seem to merit special treatment. For example, of those who fought at Badr God said, "Do what you like; I will forgive you."[18]

From the various passages from the Qur'ān and the Traditions in regard to works we can gain an impression of how this doctrine seems to work. Through the performance of good deeds there accrues to the benefit of the believing Muslim a large number of merits. He may also at the same time acquire a certain disposition of heart and mind which is pleasing to Allāh. This combination of faith, works and submission to Allāh is righteousness. But this righteousness never is, nor is expected to be, perfect. Human who is weak because God created them so cannot be expected to fulfil God's commands perfectly. But all shortcomings and lapses are forgiven if a man sets before himself God's rules as portrayed in the Qur'ān and tries his best to keep them. If he tries, he can do more good works than he does sins, and thus he can atone for those sins and weigh the balances in his favour. Not only that, insofar as he does attempt to advance upward to that degree he will find Allāh merciful and ready to overlook his miner failings and lapses.[19] Thus by doing good works a Muslim can outweigh and some for his sins, and can make himself eligible for the mercy of God and His Paradise.

In our discussion of "salvation by faith" we have already seen that the majority of orthodox theologians had decided that works, though good and desirable, were not absolutely essential to salvation. Their general theory was that God remains perfectly free and is under no obligation to reward the virtue of any creature. So also sinful actions were not regarded as sufficient to alienate man from the Muslim brotherhood. To these the one sin that damns, that is unforgiveable, is *shirk,* associating another being with God. This is the sin that makes a man a *kāfir,* an unbeliever, and bars him from Paradise. Often closely associated with this sin was the denial or the non-acceptance of the authority of Muḥammad. According to this view a Muslim could not become a *kāfir* simply by wickedness or the absence of good works. As al-Nasafī explained it in his creed, great sin does not remove from belief the creature who believes, because assent, which is the real essence of faith, continues. Sins therefore do not make the Muslim an infidel, but only a sinner. For great sins the Muslim sinner may have to spend a period of purgative punishment in the Fire, but the fact that he had faith means that he will eventually enter Paradise.

A great dispute, however, arose within Islām when the Mu'tazilites, who supported the close tie of faith and works, and the Khārijites—an Essene-like group, took up the cudgels for the necessity of good works.

They pointed to the many Qur'ānic passages and Ḥadīth that give faith and works equal importance. They pointed to the many occasions when Muḥammad castigated and condemned evil-doers. For them the doing of great sins was the equivalent of unbelief, and there were various listings made of the sins which would make of a Muslim a *kāfir*. Though eventually this point of view lost out and became a minority opinion among the theologians, nevertheless in popular Islām today both the Mu'tazilites and the Khārijites have many spiritual descendants. The neo-Mu'tazilites are those modern Muslims who, influenced by their education and other contacts, argue on rational principles that the moral life of goodness and virtue is the only one that can commend itself to a reasonable man and the only one by which the world can be governed. The modern Khārijite is the orthodox Muslim who takes at face value the Qur'ānic admonitions to various virtues and attempts to observe them. Many ordinary Muslims, affected by these admonitions and certainly influenced by the unwritten laws of human's conscience, have come to accept the theory that good works are necessary to salvation, and that these must be done with some degree of devotion and regularity.

But though it might be expected that all those who operate on this level of salvation would widely practise good works in the Islāmic sense, nevertheless in practice we observe that a good deal of lip-service is paid to the principle of good works even by those who maintain their necessity for salvation. In the first place this is due to the emphasis on the commercial value of the works. Each man interprets for himself what is sufficient, and a calculating and self-righteous attitude easily results. Secondly, concentration on the ritual and ceremonial commands of the Qur'ān has led to a formalistic approach to good works, and the demands of mere formalism are not compelling ones. Thirdly, a Muslim can see from the Qur'ān that Allāh Himself is indulgent and grants concessions. The law is to be obeyed, but often that is achieved by the slackening of the obligation to meet human's capabilities. This stress on indulgence means that the individual does not greatly fear the result of their sinfulness or lack of good works. There is no doubt that all Muslims on this level will support the necessity of good works for salvation. But the lack of a moral God, the possession of an indulgent

God, the arbitrary nature of the commands, the commercial importance of works, the emphasis on externals—all these have combined to make the doctrine of good works a mechanical and unspiritual thing for the majority. In practice it has meant that the average Muslim on this level regards minimal prayer, fasting and alms-giving to be sufficient to obtain the desired result of good works, namely, salvation. Though this Muslim may not have thought through the implications of this position, yet according to our observations, this in many cases is what is actually happening.

For the Muslim who operates on this level faith without works is dead. So also for the Christian, faith without works is dead. But when the Christian asserts that neither circumcision nor un-circumcision (that is, no mechanical connection with a religion) means anything, but rather faith which works by love, one maintains an integral relation between faith and works that is not observable in the Muslim doctrine. For the Muslim, faith is submissive assent to the sovereignty of Allāh and works should be done because all the commands of Allāh are sovereign. Thus the works depend on a relationship of willing submission. For the Christian, faith is a relationship of love, and works are the inevitable outflow of that relationship of love. Faith lays hold of God who is both holy and loving and makes us the children of a holy and loving God. As children reflect the nature of their parents so the children of God will reflect His nature through their works of holiness and love. Therefore, for the Christian, faith in God through Christ involves not just submission, but a change in nature—the old self is dead and the new self, the mind of Christ, rules in them. As God's works flow out of what He is, and inevitably demonstrate what He is, so the Christian's works flow out of what he through faith in Christ has become, and inevitably demonstrate what he now is.

Secondly, though the judgment on the basis of works is common to both the Muslim and the Christian faith, the distinction between the Muslim and the Christian doctrine of works in relation to salvation is quite clear. For the Christian the loving work of God in Christ on the Cross is the all-sufficient work of redemption. No right can unmake a wrong. No good works of a person can cancel one's sins: The works that the Christian can do and does are the result of the great expiation-work of Christ our Lord. Perhaps it is true to say that the Christian ethic of love is the most widely recognized distinction of the Christian faith. But has the Muslim understood that the Christian is not saved by good works, but rather does good works because he has been saved?

Thirdly, therefore, in the Christian context works can never rightly become formalistic, calculating or infrequent—though the Christian must constantly confess his failures in this respect; not formalistic—for the motivation of life is not an arbitrarily given set of rules, but the principle of love which ever calls to new obedience and action; not calculating—for the Christian is to serve as Christ served, selflessly and sacrificially responding to need; not infrequently—for in Christ we are possessed and led by His Spirit to daily victories over the flesh and an ever deeper devotion to Christ's way.

e) Salvation by Intercession

The fifth aspect of thought which may be present when the Muslim thinks of salvation is the idea that salvation may be granted because of the intercession of the prophets, particularly Muḥammad or Ḥusain.

The doctrine that the prophets are mediators before God on behalf of their followers was developed very early after the death of Muḥammad. Muḥammad himself more or less denied that there would be any intercession by himself or anyone else. He said: "And fear ye the day when soul shall not satisfy for soul at all, nor shall any intercession be accepted from them, nor shall any ransom be taken, neither shall they be helped" (2: 45). Again he says: "No soul shall labour but for itself; and no burdened one shall bear another's burden" (6:164). The individual is responsible for oneself and one cannot be helped by anyone else but God, for "intercession is wholly with God; His the kingdom of the heavens and the earth" (39: 45). The Last Day is "a day when one soul shall be powerless for another soul; all sovereignty on that day shall be with God" (82: 19).

These passages seem quite explicit, and they coincide with Muḥammad's personal view that though he was a prophet he was a sinful man like everyone else. But once again Islām was confronted by the fact that the Qur'ān is self-contradictory. Other passages, though not quite as definite as the ones quoted above, seem to leave place for a future intercession. "God! There is no God but He; Who is he that can intercede with Him but by His own permission?" (2:256). So also in 19:90 he indicates the possibility of intercession. "None shall have the power to intercede, save he who hath received permission at the hands of the God of Mercy. The general possibility becomes more explicit when Muḥammad says the angels may intercede: "They who bear the throne and they who encircle it, celebrate the praise of their Lord and believe in Him and implore forgiveness for the believers:—'O our Lord! Thou embracest all things in mercy and knowledge'" (40:7). Those who truly witnessed to Allāh may intercede: "The gods whom they call upon beside Him shall not be able to intercede for others; they only shall who bore witness to the truth and knew it" (43:86). Traditions also supported the possibility of intercession.

But probably the real reason why this doctrine developed was not the fact that some Qur'ānic and Traditional support could be found for it. Rather it developed to offset the particularly depressing effect of the doctrine of *qadar*—God's eternal decree. As Samuel Zwemer says, this alien doctrine of a saviour came in through the pressure of human need, "as a last hope for uneasy minds."[20] The believer does not know for certain whether the worth of his actions will modify the fate that predestination has fixed for him. Therefore to ensure salvation a doctrine of mediation was found necessary. A secondary influence in the development of the doctrine is the fact that Allāh, in contrast to the gods of other peoples, was very remote from human, so the mediators by the warmth of their nearness in a sense took the place of the ancient gods. Because of these factors intercession soon became for many Muslims an article of faith. The theologians had their usual struggle over the matter, but the orthodox soon accepted intercession, supporting it with the Qur'ānic passages listed above. They also argued that if pardon and forgiveness are possible without intercession, how much more permissible are they with it. The fact of the matter was that they were practically "forced" to accept the doctrine under the compulsion of human emotion.

Once the possibility of intercession was admitted it was almost inevitable that Muḥammad would become the mediator. Had not Allāh premised: "It may be that thy Lord will raise thee (Muḥammad) to a laudable position" (17:81)? Therefore, though it was admitted that others might intercede also, the act of intercession became identified with Muḥammad particularly. Traditions illustrate the development, particularly applying Muḥammad's intercession to the great sins which, some said, could not be wiped out by good actions alone. "It is reported from Anas that the Prophet said, 'My intercession is for those of my followers who commit mortal sins'" (Al-Tirmīzī, 277). According to a tradition related by Anas, in which we can see how this intercession is supposed to work out, the Prophet said, "In the day of resurrection Muslims will not be able to move; they will be greatly distressed and say, 'Would to God that we had asked him to create someone to intercede for us.'" The tradition goes on to say how they sought the help of Adam and the prophets of the old dispensation and how one and all excused themselves on account of their own sinfulness, Jesus because people worshipped him as God. After that the Prophet said:

> They will come to me and I will ask permission of my Lord to enter His house; and permission will be given me for that. And when I shall see Him I will fall down in prostration. And God will leave me as long as He wishes to leave me and will then say, 'Raise (thy head), O Muḥammad and speak and thou wilt be heard; intercede and thy intercession will be accepted; ask and it shall be given thee.' Then I will raise my head and will praise the Lord with praises and adorations which He will tell me. After that I will intercede, and a limit will be fixed for me and I will go forth. And I will bring them out of the fire and take them into Paradise ... until there remain in the fire none except him whom the Qur'ān has restrained, that is he for whom eternal punishment is proper. (Muslim, 274)

Naturally there was much discussion as to the nature of Muḥammad's intercession. It is usually compared to advocacy in court. The advocate possesses an essential attribute, a kind of sacred emanation called *barakah*, with the help of which he carries on the intercession.[21] The intercession itself will be of several kinds:

i) The great intercession in which all people, greatly fearing, will come to a place where they will praise the prophet. After Muḥammad has said, "O my people, I am appointed for intercession," their fear will pass away.

ii) Intercession for the purpose of entering Paradise without rendering account. Concerning this authorities differ.

iii) Intercession on behalf of a Muslim who ought to go to hell.

iv) Intercession for those already in hell.

v) Intercession for an increase in rank for those already in Paradise.

Though, in accordance with the above, orthodoxy generally interprets Muḥammad's intercession to be the equivalent of the work of an advocate, this advocacy has developed so far in the minds of some that Muḥammad practically becomes a type of saviour from sin. This is very far from the mind of Muḥammad, who omitted from his teaching the possibility that propitiation or atonement might be made for the sins of human. Yet, if we are to believe Samuel Zwemer, who possessed an unexcelled knowledge of popular Islām, "One has only to question the Muslim masses, whether in Morocco or Java, to understand that in the minds of many Muḥammad has become a saviour from sin."[22] Such traditions as these indicate this development:

> It is recorded that when Adam was punished and sent into the world on account of his sins, he repented of his sins with weeping and sorrow, but his repentance was not accepted, until at length he took Muḥammad, the Apostle of God, for his mediator, saying, "O God, forgive my sins for Muḥammad's sake!" God asked him, "Whence knowest thou Muḥammad?" Adam replied, "At the time when thou didst create me, the foot of the Throne was straight opposite my sight, and I beheld written on it: 'There is no God but Allāh; Muḥammad is the Apostle of Allāh.' Then I knew that the nearest and noblest of beings in thy sight is Muḥammad, whose name thou hast joined close to thine own name... [23]

> In the days of the children of Israel there was a sinful man who, for the space of 200 years, wearied everyone by the enormity of his offences. When he died they threw his corpse on the dunghill, but no sooner had this been done than Gabriel, coming to Moses, said: 'Thus saith the Almighty God … Let that corpse be dressed and prepared for burial without delay; and ye shall speak to the children of Israel that they forthwith recite the burial service over his bier, if they desire pardon.' Then Moses marvelled exceedingly and inquired why forgiveness was required. And God answered, 'The Lord knoweth well all the sins which that sinner hath during these 200 years committed; and verily he would never have been pardoned. But one day this wicked man was reading the Torah and seeing there the name of the blessed Muḥammad he wept and pressed the page to his eyes. This honour and reverence shown to my beloved one was pleasing to me, and from the blessed effects of this single act, I have blotted out the sins of the whole 200 years. Lovers of the blessed Muḥammad! Rejoice in your hearts and be assured that the love for the holy prophet, the Lord of creation, is in every possible condition the means of salvation!'[24]

At this point let us call to mind that the idea of mediation or intercession has been carried much farther by that group of Muslims known as the Shi'ite s than by the orthodox Sunnī Muslims. Shi'ite s believe that when Husain, the grandson of Muḥammad, died in the battle of Karbala, whose causes were as much political as religious, he died for the sins of Islām. Since that time "unable to believe that their Imam (leader) was conquered and killed against his will the Shia have made the whole tragedy a predestined case of vicarious sacrifice,"[25] So on the tenth day of the month of Muḥarram, in memory of Husain's "vicarious" death at Karbala, it is customary for men and boys to endure voluntary suffering from self-inflicted wounds. They believe that at the resurrection Husain will rise with the intercessory power he has purchased with his blood. According to a tradition Husain says: "All rational creatures, men [*sic*] and jinn, who inhabit the present and the future world, are sunk in sin and have but one Husain to save them."[26] So the Shi'ites have Muḥammad as the special mediator for the community of Islām and Ḥusain as the "self-renouncing redeemer." But not only that, according to the Shi'ite s their Imams, the eleven leaders who followed Husain, have the same power of mediation, and without their intercession it is impossible for them to avoid the punishment of God.

We see, therefore that in the Shi'ite community the doctrine of intercession reached its most extreme form of development. The development went from Muḥammad to Husain, from Husain to the Imams, and then, as we go into the matter further, we see that the development went from the Imams to the saints generally. This ended in the saint worship so common among Shi'ite Muslims. But the orthodox Sunnī Muslims were net far behind the Shi'ite s in this development. They started with, and first accepted only, the intercession of Muḥammad, who continues to hold the rank of first and most powerful mediator. But they could not stop there. The minds of simple believers reflected and came to the conclusion that if the man Muḥammad could save them, why should not also the saints be able to intercede, albeit less powerfully? Accordingly there infiltrated into orthodox Islām the veneration of the saints that contrasts so vividly with the austere preaching of Muḥammad, and that can be well compared to certain phenomena existing in the Roman Catholic Church. Practically every local Muslim place found its own saint who, it was hoped, would intercede for the local inhabitants on the Day of Judgment. In the 18th century, the Wahhabis, the "Protestant" reform movement in Islām, swept through Arabia, but in most other Islāmic nations they have not been successful in tearing from the grasp of the people the intercessors without whose mediation they believe it to be impossible to stand before the unfathomable Allāh and gain his salvation.

To complete the picture we should note that even ordinary living Muslims can in a sense become intercessors for their fellow believers. This is done by prayers for the dead. Prayer is to be said for every deceased Muslim, good or bad, and this prayer is held to be efficacious. Many traditions illustrate this point, most of them having reference to the funeral prayer and the reading of the Qur'ān over the bier of the dead, but some including also the giving of alms on behalf of the dead. A1-Taftāzānī approvingly quotes the tradition: "The prophet said, 'No group of Muslims amounting to a hundred in number performs worship over a dead person, all of them interceding for him, without their intercession for him being welcome.'"[27] Another tradition states: "It is reported from 'Abdullāh bin 'Abbās that the Apostle of God said,

"Verily God most certainly causes to enter the tombs, on account of the prayers of the people of the earth (rewards) like mountains. Verily, the gifts of the living for the dead are asking forgiveness for them'" (Al-Bayhaquī, 117).

In the Muslim theory of salvation by intercession we see the acknowledgement of that which makes us all brothers and sisters—a common sense of need. We need intercession with God because we dare not appear before the Judge in the garments of sin. Though the Muslim fears God the uncertain One rather than God the holy One is there not in this sense of need, this seeking for another's help, a rare opportunity for the message that God in Christ has provided our Intercessor? But first of all we need to point out that we do not need an intercessor just to make up for a few things that we have failed to do. Our need is radical. We require the intercessor because we are completely under the wrath of the holy God.

Secondly, we may say that the Qur'ān speaks truly when it says that "intercession is wholly with God, His the kingdom of the heavens and the earth." Intercession must come from God, not from human. There is no human worthy to intercede with God. God Himself must provide the worthy Intercessor. This God does when He sends from Himself Jesus, His Word. Jesus Christ is not a pleader come from human to God. He is God the Father's own Advocate, sent from above to seek our release. By His coming we see that God is a God at hand and not afar off. We need not seek human mediators, for there is no one closer to us and our needs than the God of love.

Thirdly, we declare that the Qur'ān speaks truly when it says: "No soul shall labour for itself, and no burdened one shall bear another another's burden." But now One who is not burdened with the load of his own sin has come to bear our burdens. He is the sinless Lamb of God "who bare the sins of many and made intercession for transgressors." He is an intercessor who not only pleads, but He Himself provided the adequate ground for His intercession. That ground is His Cross whereby He has put away the sin and guilt of the world. Looking at our sin crucified in Christ God says, "Peace be unto you." Thus Jesus is the true Mediator between God and human, the Mediator of a new and better covenant, redemption through His blood and the forgiveness of our sins, according to the richness of His grace. This is the God-planned and God-provided mediation that avails for sinful human now and in the Day of Judgment.

e) Salvation by the Mystical Way

The last level from which a Muslim may view the doctrine of salvation is salvation by the mystical way that leads to union with God. In this connection we are not only dealing with another means to gain salvation, but the salvation itself differs from our original definition.

In the beginning we pointed out that Islāmic salvation is escape from hell to Paradise. But from the point of view of the Muslim mystic salvation is the achievement of an ultimate mystical union with God. Many volumes have been written on Islāmic mysticism which is known as Ṣūfīsm. Both because it is somewhat removed from the main trend of our discussion, and because it is in itself too large a subject to treat here, we will not enter into the study of the Ṣūfī way of salvation. It shares many of the characteristics which are common to mysticism in religions the world over; indeed, some of the developments in Islāmic mysticism may be traced to non-Islāmic sources. Briefly, through a series of stages and states, both ascetic and emotional, mental and physical, the Muslim mystic arrives at a state of ecstatic illumination, an immediate experiential knowledge of God, called *tawḥīd*,—unity. This loving interpenetration of God and the soul is the mystical union, by which a person passes away from self and abides in an essential oneness with God that transcends all individuality. This is the salvation of the Ṣūfī.

In the course of history Ṣūfīsm swept through Islām, while the orthodox theologians fought against it. The orthodox leaders had first led the movement, initiating asceticism as a reaction against the prevailing corruption. But when Ṣūfīsm became a popular people's movement marked by various esoteric practises and a theosophical structure, the orthodox opposed it. They recognized that there was a basic contradiction. For the Ṣūfī doctrine of a direct and personal experience with God passed by the claim of the orthodox theologians that they were the guardians of the truth, in exclusive possession of the science of theology and law. But they could not stem the tide of Ṣūfism that seemed to fill a great need in the soul of many Muslims. Finally the great Muslim theologian, Al-Ghazālī (d.1111), managed to combine orthodoxy and Ṣūfism into one system of thought, in which he retained all the tenets of orthodoxy and at the same time made Ṣūfī thought respectable.[28] Despite his brilliant effort at reconciling the two streams of thought, this continues to be at the best an uneasy union within Islām. But, because of his effort, ever since his day salvation by mysticism is a possibility within orthodox Islām. In the ordinary course of events we find very few Muslims today who actually view salvation from this level. Yet, it cannot be denied that there are some. And because of the additional influence of Shiʿism and Hinduism it is among the Indian and Persian Muslims particularly that we may find the protagonists of this view of salvation.

III. The Most Commonly Accepted Means to Salvation

As the various means to salvation in Islām we have considered predestination, the mercy of God, faith, faith and works, intercession and the mystical way. The question will be asked, which of these various emphases represents the one ordinarily present in the mind of the average Muslim? The answer to that question is not easy. It is a difficult to define what an average Muslim is as it would be to define what an average Christian is. But the majority of Muslims probably accept that faith is the essential means to salvation, for faith alone makes a person a Muslim. When a person accepts that Allāh is God and Muḥammad is His prophet one becomes a Muslim. The doing of certain works, such as the five pillars, will distinguish a person as a good Muslim, but their absence, in everyday opinion, does not mean that he has ceased to be a Muslim. If he believes, he is a Muslim; and if he is a Muslim, he is a member of that community which, if God wills, shall receive the promised reward of Paradise. It is true that the uncertain decree of Allāh is the forbidding background to this commonly felt assurance, yet, perhaps out of emotional necessity, that background has been shrouded by the proud belief that because a person bears the name "Muslim" one is more or less automatically going to be saved.

One of my first and most instructive experiences with Muslims, in this connection, was with a man to whom we had pointed out the seeming uncertainty of salvation in view of God's unfathomable decree. The Muslim admitted the uncertainty. Then we inquired, "Does this not put you in despair?" He replied, "Yes, I am in despair." But the disconcerting thing was that he said it with a smile. To a Muslim, theoretically, salvation must be uncertain. But his actual attitude over against this problem seems to be most truly reflected in such a proud claim as this: "Am I not a Muslim! My face is towards God wherever I am."[29]

But individually becoming a Muslim by faith passes over quickly into the idea of thereby becoming a member of the blessed and sacred community of Islām. Salvation by faith is inseparable from the idea of safety within the embrace of the Islāmic community. For to have faith means to be a Muslim, and to be a Muslim means being a member of God's chosen community—Islām. Dr. J. W. Sweetman in a very fine way sums up this merging idea of faith and identification with the Community. He points out that Muslims regard Islām as the interim state of the theocracy from which human may remain separate at their peril. This theocracy is the means to salvation, for through it human takes upon themself the way of life which is consonant with the expectation of God's mercy. In it they can avail themself of the facilities Allāh offers to humankind, such as the prophet, books, angels, ordinances, etc., which are a mercy from Allāh. Though they may not know what to think of the uncertain decree in this particular case, they share with all Muslims the hope that a peculiar efficacy attaches itself to their life of faith in this community. Dr. Sweetman concludes by saying:

> Thus in Islām salvation is by identification with a community ... In the answer to the question how to escape from Hell, the answer might be "faith and works" ... but the whole answer was "Islām" ... the tangible and concrete community in the common agreement of ... the practice of the Prophet, and the authoritative Book ... He might be a heretic, i.e., guilty of *bida'* or innovation, but had not the prophet said that Islām would

> be divided into 73 sects ...? but to forsake polytheism and to conform to the community in all externals of religion was clear and simple, and afforded him at least a chance of belonging to the saved sect ... Thus primarily, the institution of the community of Islām, enshrining within it the practice of the Prophet, possessed of the authoritative code of God in the Qur'ān, presenting a concrete and external unity, composed of members rejoicing in a special divine election, the interim stage of the theocracy, never to be superseded, endowed with inerrancy despite apparent differences, is the first means of salvation and all that follows must be within this framework.[30]

To this concise summary we can only add that it is *faith* which is the door to this saved community. It is the confession that he/she is a Muslim that gives a man/woman all that is described above.

The idea that salvation by faith, by bearing the name Muslim, by being a member of the community of Islām, is the popular belief is borne out by a phenomenon well known to us in Kerala. A man may be a doctrinaire Communist, but despite all the implications involved he is not cast out of the community, for he still bears the name "Muslim." He may be anything but a true Muslim, yet if he does not take a name with other definite and generally recognized religious implications, in other words, if he does not destroy the unity of the Community, he is still tolerated within the circle of Islām. And perhaps the essential reason why converts to Christianity sometimes get killed is not so much because they have become polytheists, but because they have broken the unity of God's own community. If a man is either by the simple accident of his birth or through conversion a member of the community of Islām, if he voluntarily bears the name "Muslim", he is eligible for the salvation offered to all within that community. "Am I not a Muslim! My face is towards God wherever I am."

Conclusion

Let us briefly sum up the foregoing discussion. We see that salvation is essentially construed as the escape from hell and the entry into Paradise, and as such it is a future event. There are various points of view in Islām as to what finally brings an individual to that salvation. According to the individual opinion one may look at salvation from the level of predestination, the mercy of God, faith, faith and works, intercession, or the mystical wall. In establishing these categories we have tried to indicate all the various ways in which a Muslim may consider the problem of how to reach Paradise. These various categories will not be distinct in the minds of ordinary Muslims. The common view gives emphasis to faith, the bearing of the name "Muslim" and the accompanying membership in the Islāmic community, as the means of salvation. But other Muslims may base their view of salvation on one or several of the other above-mentioned categories. He may, for example, look at salvation from the levels of both predestination and faith, from the standpoint of both works and intercession, or from the view of the mercy of God and the mystic way. In fact, several of these aspects of thought may go into the formation of an individual Muslim's view of salvation. Yet through these categories perhaps we have made clearer the various influences that may altogether or only in part be working on the individual Muslim as he/she thinks of salvation.

The implications for our Christian witness to the Muslim should be clear. Theoretically a wide range of thought is possible to the individual Muslim on this question. It is therefore the Christian's task in confronting the individual Muslim to try to discover which particular means of salvation that he or she has taken as one's trust. Though this is not always an easy process, it is a necessary one. For only then can he in an understanding and relevant way bring to bear on the Muslim before him the beautiful and unchanging truth that it is the Lord Jesus Christ who is the Way and the Author of eternal salvation.

Finally, this study of the Muslim doctrine of salvation will also remind us of, and confirm for us, the unique and compelling force of the Christian Gospel of salvation. In comparison with the various theories we have examined God's grace in Christ shines like a beacon light, attracting us and enlightening our hearts. Amidst the many ways of salvation in Islām we do not see the Way. Muḥammad had promised to his followers: "Allāh calleth to the abode of peace" (10:26). But thoughtful Muslims have not found in the possibilities offered them a clear way to that abode and their inner unrest has not been stilled.

They have understood that there is in Islām no satisfying way to God's house and no certainty that they will ultimately be saved. Therefore a few peaceless hearts have been compelled to regard this call to an "abode of peace" as a hollow mockery or an unattainable goal. We see this despair in the funeral dirge of Islām, but also in the writings of tormented Muslims.

Al-Ḥallāj was one who therefore cried out: "Would that God ... when he put us in this world had made us independent of the next and delivered us from anxiety about what will save us from punishment!" An ascetic said: "The thought of death leaves the believer no joy, his knowledge of God's laws leaves him neither silver nor gold, his obedience to God's command leaves him no friend." When another lay dying and his friends visited him, he said to them, "I have no hope though I have fasted 80 Ramadāns."[31] Abū Bakr is said to have cried in despair: "O would that I were like a bird and had not been created as a man."[32] Ḥasan of Basra said: "The man who reads the Qur'ān and believes in it is generally filled with trembling in this world, and much sorrow."[33] Abū 'Imrān, a companion of Muḥammad, said at the point of his death: "What peril can be greater than mine? I must expect a messenger from my Lord, sent to announce to me either Paradise or Hell. I declare solemnly, I would rather remain as I am now with my soul struggling in my throat till the Day of Resurrection, than to undergo such a hazard." 'Ammār Ibn 'Abdullāh, who spent days and nights in prayer, cried out in the stillness of the night hours: "O my God, the fire of hell robs me of sleep. O pardon my sins! The lot of man in this world is care and sorrow, and in the next, judgment and fire. O, where shall the soul find rest and happiness?"[34] Where, indeed, but in Him who says to tortured souls, "Come unto me, all ye that labour and are heavy-laden, and I will give you rest."

Note: In a few cases the Qur'ānic quotations are from M. M. Pickthall, *The Meaning of the Glorious Koran* or from *The Koran* translated by E. H. Palmer, but otherwise from J. M. Rodwell's translation.

Endnotes

[1] In the original of this presentation I concluded the discussion by returning to the original question in terms of its eschatological implications—judgment, heaven and hell. For the sake of brevity, and because this is a well-known emphasis, it has been omitted from the present article.

[2] D. B. MacDonald, *The Religious Attitude and Life in Islām*, 135.

[3] W. R.W. Gardner, *The Qur'ānic Doctrine of Salvation*, 4ff.

[4] A. S. Tritton, *Muslim Theology*, 175.

[5] E.E. Elder, *A Commentary on the Creed of Islām*, 80 ff.

[6] Elder, *A Commentary on the Creed of Islām*, 88-89, 96-98.

[7] Tritton, *Muslim Theology*, 203.

[8] Tor Andrae, *Muḥammad the Man and His Faith*, 91, quoted in J. W. Sweetman, *Islām and Christian Theology*, Part 1, Vol. III, 180.

[9] I have found many valuable thoughts on this subject in my notes of lectures given by Dr. Kenneth Cragg at Hartford. Perhaps it will be someone like Dr. Cragg who will lead us to a deeper understanding of the doctrine of God's will and human's freedom in the light of the Muslim thesis. Surely there is no area of theological comparison in greater need of clarification than this. The problem is complicated by a great lack of Christian unanimity at this point.

[10] D. B. MacDonald, "Blessedness," in *Encyclopaedia of Religion and Ethics*, Vol. II, 678, quoted in Sweetman, *Islām and Christian Theology*, 60.

[11] H. Spencer, *Islām and the Gospel of God*, 961. Mr. Spencer has thoroughly examined the relationship of Allāh's will and mercy.

[12] Spencer, *Islām and the Gospel of God*, 961.

[13] Tritton, *Muslim Theology*, 57.

[14] Quoted in W. St. Clair Tisdall, *The Religion of the Crescent*, 60.

[15] Elder, *A Commentary on the Creed of Islām*, 116.

[16] Spencer, *Islām and the Gospel of God*, 78.

[17] Elder, *A Commentary on the Creed of Islām*, 125.

[18] Ibn Taymiyya, quoted in Tritton, *Muslim Theology*, 203.

[19] Gardner, *The Qur'ānic Doctrine of Salvation*, 39.

[20] S.M. Zwemer, *Islām: A Challenge of Faith*, 47.

[21] Cf. B. Guadefroye-DeMombynes, *Mulsim Institutions*, 54ff.

[22] Zwemer, *Islām: A Challenge of Faith*, 47.

[23] S.W. Koelle, *Mohammed and Mohammedanism*, 335.

[24] Zwemer, *Islām: A Challenge of Faith*, 48.

[25] J. Hugronje, *Lectures on Mohammedanism*, 56.

[26] Hugronje, *Lectures on Mohammedanism*, 56.

[27] Elder, *A Commentary on the Creed of Islām*, 163.

[28] H.A.R. Gibb, *Mohammedanism*, 141. For a brief but masterful summary the reader may refer to Gibb's chapter on "būfīsm" in this volume. A.J. Arberry's volume, *būfīsm*, presents a fuller picture of the būfī approach to salvation.

[29] Quoted from b' Sad 5, 105 in Tritton, *Muslim Theology*, 14.

[30] Sweetman, *Islām and Christian Theology*, 210-211.

[31] Tritton, *Muslim Theology*, 10-12.

[32] A. von Kremer, *Geschichte dur heerschenden Ideen des Islām*, 24.

[33] Quoted from Dozy, *Essai sur l'Histoire de l'Islāmisme*, in J. Hauri, *Der Islām*, 67.

[34] Tisdall, *The Religion of the Crescent*, 93.

The Son of God in the Early Church Fathers before Nicaea

Roland E. Miller

The Council of Nicaea in 325 C.E. represents a turning point in the history of the doctrine of the Christian Church. Though the struggles over church dogma had only begun, yet now a council as such had made some definitions. Not only that, the definitions were given legal authority insofar as it was considered the duty of the emperor to enforce the decrees of the council, demanding obedience and punishing disobedience. Thereafter people tended to speak of church doctrines in terms of these fixed definitions.

The period within the purview of this article, that is, from the time of the apostles until Nicaea, is of a different nature. This is not a period of fixed definition, but of growing realization. While it is therefore more difficult to get hold of its thought, it is in a sense more exciting to make the attempt. We travail with the birth of great men's thoughts as under the guidance of the Holy Spirit they strive for the fuller understanding of the teachings of Jesus Christ. We suffer and learn with them as they learn of Christ, often in suffering. We who are involved in the witness to Islām feel a fellowship with many of the conditions and thoughts encountered.

This is not to say that we can gain help for every theological need from these early church fathers. If, for example, we are searching for aid in understanding the doctrine of justification by faith, we find that the majority of these men have not concerned themselves with the problem. Many do not seem to be aware that there is a problem in the sense of what we learn from the Letter to the Romans.

Possibly one reason for this strange neglect is that these early church fathers were preoccupied with another question ... the question of the doctrine of God. When we look to them for help with this problem, we are gratified. We obtain help specifically in that area where witnesses to Muslims need it so much—that is, with regard to the significance of the teaching, Son of God. This help does not come through the deliverance of a body of credal affirmations (this help came later). The help comes through our participation in the sometimes slow and fitful, sometimes obscure, sometimes painful, but Spirit-guided and revealing evolvement of the Christian doctrine of God in the minds and hearts of its early leaders and thinkers.

That the thought of the apostolic fathers but especially that of the apologists[1] was very much concerned with the doctrine of God is quickly evident from their writings. This is not unexpectedly so. These men were in a sense still participating in the transition from the revelation of the Old Testament, to its fulfilment and expansion in the revelation of the New Testament. It was the Christian understanding of God in its fullness that had now to be worked out for the strengthening of the faith of the church. But additionally, the doctrine of God was so powerfully in their thought because it was the doctrine that had to be fought out in the face of opposing religious views. These were men committed to preaching the Gospel of God. Their preaching was not in a vacuum. It was a preaching in a god-obsessed milieu of Greek and Roman philosophy, mystic and esoteric practise. Their doctrine of God was not, therefore, just a part of their growth in personal faith and understanding; it was also truth hammered out on the anvil of communication.

That is why so many of the thoughts of these early Christians are clearly pertinent to the subject of this issue. In particular they aid us in pursuing the actual meaning of the specific word "Son" in the specific phrase "Son of God." In the first place, these men lived at a time when this phrase was still relatively new. It was not yet the automatic verbalizing of the believer, practised in expression, but unnoticed as to meaning. They were still at the point where the phrase had to be looked into for its positive meaning. But secondly, also, in their work of witness these men stood over against the non-Christian world in the same way as we stand over against the Muslim. Even as we have to explain the meaning of the word "Son of God," so did they have to communicate it? Hoping, therefore, that by our study we may be helped to rediscover the positive meaning of the truth of the "Son of God" and thereby to make more meaningful the proclamation of the Gospel among Muslims, let us see some of the thoughts that these men expressed in, their communication.

1) The Apostolic Fathers

This group of earliest fathers, who closely follow the apostles in time, inherit their circle of thought from the apostles. The various questions concerning Christ's persons have not yet developed so insistently and diversely as in later years. Christ is identified with God. How this is to be explained or defined has not yet become a pressing problem, though there are hints of it. Of the various writings Clement of Rome, Epistle of Diognetus, and Ignatius are of the most help in showing the earliest development.

a) Clement of Rome (Quotations from Epistle to Corinthians)

The relative simplicity of the early expressions is seen in Clement. He calls Jesus "Lord" against the background of the Old Testament idea of Jehovah (Lord). "Have we not all one God and one Christ?" who is the "Sceptre and Majesty of God." In company with the majority of the early fathers the passages Ps. 2:7 "Thou art my Son, today have I begotten thee," and Ps. 110:1 "Sit thou at my right hand ..." are consistently applied to Jesus. The relationship with the Father is expressed only in the words "This Christ was sent forth from God."

b) Ignatius (Quotations from Ephesians, Magnesians, Trallians, Smyrnaeans, Polycarp)

We see that this was not a day for discussing and defining Christ, but for laying hold of Him personally and fighting the good fight. Like others of his day (such as St. John) he had to emphasize the *manhood* of Christ against those who said He had not come in the flesh. In referring to His deity he speaks of him more often as "God" than "Son of God," often using the phrase "Jesus Christ our God". He even speaks of the "blood of God." In hinting of Origen's later view he writes of the Son of God: "He was truly of the seed of David according to the flesh and the Son of God *according to the will and power* of God." There is a suggestion that Sonship of Christ is due to the activity of the Father. "Jesus Christ came forth from one Father and is with and has gone to one." But how in the simplicity of faith lie unconsciously passed over difficulties is indicated by his conclusion to Polycarp: "I pray for your happiness forever in our God, Jesus Christ, by whom continue in the unity and under the protection of God."

c) *Epistle of Diognetus*

This writer speaks from a deep faith so that his passages concerning Christ are devotional as well as didactic. Jesus Christ is God's Son. The use of the word "Son" indicates that He is distinct from the Father, while yet in union with Him. The union, the relationship of oneness, is expressed by mutual deliberation.

> For God the Lord and Fashioner of all things formed in His mind a great and unspeakable conception, which He communicated to His Son alone … He was aware then of all things, along with His Son, according to the relationship subsisting between them.

This hint that the relationship between the Father and the Son can best be understood in terms of knowledge and revelation portended a major theme of the early fathers. A second major theme, namely, that the eternal Son ship of Christ is best understood through meeting Him in His incarnate form, is also indicated. For the identity and distinction between the Father and Son is made evident in the work of redemption. "As a King sends His Son, who is also a King, so sent He Him; as God He sent Him; as to man He sent Him." Meeting Him as He was sent one is brought to the conviction that "this is He who was from the beginning, who appeared as if new and was found old, and yet who is ever born afresh in the hearts of men. This is He who being from everlasting is today called the Son."

Perhaps the one leading thought that these earliest heroes of faith make clear for us is that "Son of God" cannot mean less than that Christ is God. The Gospel depends on this—that God Himself is with us in Christ. No definition of Son of God dare weaken or confuse this clear message. Apart from it there is no Gospel. This is what is to be proclaimed to Jew and Gentile—and to the Muslim. But will the offence be intolerable? … Perhaps the reader has shared the experience that it seems less offensive to the thought pattern of Muslims to declare that God became man rather than to say that Jesus is the Son of God.

But can we be satisfied with this? After all, Jesus *is* the Son of God. For further help let us turn in our quest to the Apologists.

2) The Apologists

This larger group of men produced writings which were definitely apologetic rather than hortatory or pastoral, as the apostolic fathers. They attempted to set forth Christianity "in forms intelligible to the cultured classes of their age, while at the same time repealing all unjust accusations.[2] Hence we can expect from them closer attention to the problem of the meaning of "Son of God."

a) Justin Martyr: (Quotations from First and Second Apology, Dialogue with Trypho)

This well-versed thinker dealt with Gentiles against the background of broad personal knowledge of Greek philosophy and a deep acquaintance with the Christian Scriptures. (It was well indeed if we knew Islām and the Scriptural replies with corresponding thoroughness). He brought to the fore the concept of Jesus Christ as the Word of God and combined with it the idea of Sonship, a combination so fruitful for the understanding of Jesus the Son of God.

In his second Apology Justin indicates what we are to understand from the names of God. They cannot encompass God, or define Him. He is too great for that. They are rather pointers describing some activity or attribute of God. This consideration applies especially to such names as God, Father and Son of God. To understand what the name "Son of God" points to, we must move to the concept of the Word of God. "The first power of God the Father and Lord of all is the Word, who is also the Son." The progression of the Son from the Father is, therefore, associated with God's desire to reveal Himself. For the Word—Son is sent forth from the power of the Father "to declare whatever is revealed."

By a process of spiritual generation the Word becomes the firstborn of God. " … We say also that the Word who is the first-born of God, was produced without sexual union …" Here we have the same statement of what the Son of God *is not* that we must repeatedly make to Muslims. The difference, however, is that Justin is here talking about the *Word.* In terms of being we are to talk about the Word's generation prior to the Son's generation. "Jesus Christ is the only proper Son, who has been begotten by God, being His Word and first-begotten and power, and becoming man according to His will."

To make clear the generation and nature of the Word. Justin in his "Dialogue" gives an example:- though we speak a word, the word (as thought) remains in us, where indeed it had been before being spoken. So also "this power was begotten from the Father, by His power and will, but not by abscession, as if the essence of the Father was divided … (but) that which is begotten is numerically distinct …" This example we find constantly repeated in the early fathers in their discussion of the Sonship of Jesus.

This generation of the Word is by will of the Father.

> God begot before all creatures a beginning, a certain rational power proceeding from Himself, who is called by the Holy Spirit now the glory of God, now the Son, again Wisdom, again an angel, then God, and then Lord and Logos (Word) … He can be called all these names since he ministers to the Father's will and since He was begotten by the Father by an act of will.

This emphasis is very useful with Muslims. God can express Himself. It is in the prerogative of His will to send forth the Word. He can do this if He wishes. Who of His creatures can say to Him, "you cannot" or "you should not"?

Because Jesus Christ is the first-born of the Father he is rightly to be worshipped as God. "... The Father of the universe has a Son, who also being the first-begotten Word of God, is even God." A special characteristic of Justin is his constant reference to the Old Testament in proof of the divinity of Jesus. He cites a bewildering array of passages to prove that the Messiah was and had to be God, and therefore Jesus, the Lord of the Old Testament, is to be worshipped as God. "If you had understood what was written by the prophets you would not have denied that He was God, Son of the only unbegotten, unutterable God." But he also depends on Christ's testimony to Himself in the New Testament. He points out that Christ re-named one of His disciples "Rock" because

> he recognized him to be the Christ, the Son of God by the revelation of the Father. And since we find it recorded in the memoirs of His apostles that He is the Son of God, and since we call Him Son, we have understood that He proceeds before all creatures from the Father by His power and will.

b) Tatian (Quotations from Address to the Greeks)

In Tatian we begin to think more carefully of the implications of the "generation" implied in the name "Son." He states that by God's simple will the Logos (Word) "springs forth", "emanates" from the Father who begot Him." In this way the Logos (Word) from the Logos-Power (God the Father) becomes the "first-begotten work of the Father." This act of begetting does not lessen in any way Him who begets.

So the Logos coming forth from the Logos-Power of the Father has not divested of the Logos-Power Him who begot Him. I myself, for instance, talk and you hear. Yet, certainly I who converse, do not become destitute of speech by the transmission of speech.

c) Theophilus (Quotations from Theophilus to Autolycus)

Theophilus was the first man to explicitly distinguish between the Logos "uttered" and the Logos "internal". Christ is the Word whom God had "internal, within His bowels," "the Word that always exists, residing within the heart of God." Before anything came into being "He had him as a Counsellor being His own word and thought."

But God determined to make the world. So He "emitted (belched forth) Him along with His wisdom before all the world." This then is the explanation of the fact that the Word of God "is also His Son." This Sonship is not like that of the poets and writers of myths who talk of sons of gods begotten by intercourse [*sic!*]. Rather when God wished to make all as He determined, "He begot this Word, uttered the first-born of all creation."

At this stage we see that the generation of the Son in the minds of men like Theophilus is associated with the act of creation, God's first "public act," rather than referring to an eternal going forth. He is always internally the Word. He becomes the Son externally at a specific moment in time.

d) Athenagoras (Quotations from A Plea for the Christians)

This Christian philosopher from Athens speaks vehemently for the unity of God. But this one God is also a Trinity, and it is by the knowledge of this that "we are conducted to eternal life." "We acknowledge a God and a Son, His Logos, and a Holy Spirit, united in essence—the Father, the Son and the Spirit, because the Son is the Intelligence, Reason, Wisdom of the Father, and the Spirit an effluence, a light from Fire."

We should not think it ridiculous that God should have a Son. The relationship is not to be confused with the physical relationships of the gods in the poets. Rather, "The Son of God is the Logos of the Father, in idea and in operation … the Father and the Son being one—the Son being in the Father and the Father in the Son—in oneness and power of spirit. The mind (nous) and the word (logos) of the Father is the Son of God." But if the Word and the Son are one and the same, what need of the word "Son"? To this Athenagoras replies that He is called the Son because

> He is the first product of the Father, not as having been brought into existence (for from the beginning God who is eternal Mind had the Word

> in Himself, being from eternity instinct with Word), but inasmuch as He came forth to the idea and energizing power of material things.

This is then similar to the idea expressed by Theophilus.

e) Irenaeus (Quotations from Against the Heresies)

With prodigious research, painstaking refutation and an intimate knowledge of Scripture this "grandson" of St. John fought especially the Gnostic heresies. In so doing he presented many thoughts useful for our understanding of "Son of God."

The phrase "Son of God" has now become common usage. It has not replaced the term "Word", but it takes its place beside it, and it seems to have become the technical mode of reference for the second Person, Jesus Christ.

Irenaeus begins with the assumption of the earlier fathers that the Son of God is truly God. "He is Himself in His own right beyond all men who have ever lived God and Lord and King eternal and Incarnate Word." Jesus' own words: "I shall openly appear to them who seek me not" is a fulfilment of Ps. 50:3: "God shall come openly; our God shall not keep silence." In the last days "the Son of God shall come, who is God ..." Jesus as God before Jesus as Son of God is the priority in the witness of Irenaeus.

The Son of God is not thereby "another" God. Jesus Christ himself "knows no other God" than the one God. Neither did the apostles in their witness "bring in another God." Faith in the Son is not to take away from faith in the Father. As we direct our faith towards the Son, so also we should possess a firm and unmoveable love to the Father.

Jesus Christ, the Son of God, is the Word of God, and the latter to Irenaeus seems logically prior to the former. So also Paul taught the Gentiles that "His Son was His Word." How is this Word relationship with the Father to be explained? Irenaeus says: "But God being all Mind and all Logos both speaks exactly what He thinks and thinks exactly what He speaks. For His thought is Logos, Logos is Mind, and Mind comprehending all things is the Father Himself."

It is in the light of this Word-Mind relationship in God that we must understand the phrases: "The Father begot the Son," "the first-begotten of all Creation," "the only-begotten of the Father." Jesus is "His offspring, the First-begotten Word." Irenaeus recognizes the mystery involved:

> If anyone therefore says to us, how then was the Son produced by the Father? we reply to him that no man understands that production or generation or calling or revelation —by whatever name we may describe his greatness—which is in fact altogether indescribable.

But "that a word is uttered at the bidding of thought and mind, all men indeed well understand." On this basis, seeing the analogy but acknowledging the-mystery, we must confess: "He is Himself the Word of God, Himself the only-begotten of the Father, Christ Jesus our Lord."

For Irenaeus it is in the Lordship of Jesus Christ over our lives that we truly discern His divine Sonship. He consistently puts his discussion of the Sonship of Jesus in the light of the saving purpose of God and His Incarnation. That the revelation of Jesus the Son of God is not a truth arbitrarily dropped from heaven and to be parroted in reply, and that it is also not a discovery of human's philosophic wisdom to be raised on the flag-pole of pride, but that it is *part of the Gospel* of the incarnate Jesus is as significant today as in Irenaeus's day. Because the Word became flesh, palpable and visible, "The Father shown forth", and He is also the Son, it may be said that "all saw the Father in the Son, for the Father is the invisible of the Son, and the Son is the visible of the Father." So also Muslims will come to know Jesus as the Son of God only by first meeting him as he walks in the flesh through the fields and streets of human's lives in search of the sheep that is lost.

The intimate relationship of fellowship and union in the being of the Father and the Son is reflected especially in the witness of one to the other, that is, in revelation: "God has been declared through the Son who is in the Father, and has the Father in Himself—He who is the Father bearing witness to the Son, and the Son announcing the Father." Because the Son reveals the Father knowledge of salvation is therefore "the knowledge of the Son of God who is both called and actually is Salvation, Saviour and Salutary."

f) Tertullian (Quotations from Ad Praxeas)

Tertullian, the North African father, plays an important role in fixing the Christian understanding of the Holy Trinity and its terminology. In his discussion of the Son of God he shows great clarity of expression. He, for example, introduces the term "person" for the Son of God; a term which is both meaningful in itself, but which also is a symbol of that which is beyond understanding.

Before all things, Tertullian says: God was alone, alone in the sense that there was nothing *beside* him. Yet not even then was he alone, for he had Reason which was in Himself. Although God had not yet uttered His Word, He always had it within Himself along with His Reason. This was the condition of His existence while He silently thought out and ordained within Himself the things which He was shortly to say by the agency of the Word. While doing this He converted Reason into Word. Unspoken thought and spoken Word, both essentially the same.

To explain this Tertullian cited the analogy of self. When one argues with oneself, every thought is the consciousness of reason, and at the same time every thought is in a sense already a word. So the word in a way is a different thing from yourself within yourself. It is a "second person" within you. Through it in thinking you utter speech. And through it also (by reciprocity of process) in uttering speech you generate thought.

In what sense, however, is the Word also the Son? The Word receives its outward manifestation and equipment as sound and voice, when God utters it, e.g. when God says, "Let there be light." This is the complete nativity of the Word when it comes forth from God. For the Logos "became the Son of God when by proceeding from Him, He was begotten." This, however, is a process taking place before time, for He is begotten before all things. And he is the only begotten because the Word alone is begotten out of God in a true sense *from the womb of his heart*, even as the Father testifies.

In interpreting the passage "I ascend to my Father and your Father, and to my God and your God", Tertullian says: In thinking of Himself as *Son* He will ascend to One whom He calls Father. In thinking of Himself as *Word* He ascends to One whom He calls God. The two things are on a par. But the Son truth derives logically from the Word truth.

This description of the being and relationship of the Word-Son does not in any way diminish the objectiveness of His reality as a separate Person. The Word is not just God's moving of the air in order to create sound. He is substantial and objective, so that there are two—God and His Word, Father and Son. "That cannot lack substance which proceeds from so great a substance." Not only that, "How can that be empty and void by which all substances were made?" Therefore, "the substance of the Word was that I call a 'Person', and for it I claim the name 'Son', and while I acknowledge Him as Son, I maintain that He is another beside the Father."

But neither does this mean that the Son is separate from the Father. Rather God brought forth the Word as a root brings forth the ground shoot, as a spring brings forth the river, as the sun brings forth its beam. These are "projections of those substances from which they proceed." The Son of God is like that. You would not hesitate to say that the shoot is the son of the root, and the river the son of the spring, and the beam the son of the sun. *For every source is a parent, and everything brought forth from the source is the offspring.* So you may say that the Word which proceeds from God is the Son, and God is His Father." This does not separate the two, just as the shoot is not cut off from the root, nor the river from the spring, nor the beam from the sun. The idea of "two gods" we "never let issue from our mouth." For "although the Son is called God when he is named by Himself, yet this does not for that reason make a duality of gods, but one God by this very fact that he has to be called God as a result of His unity with the Father."

It is through the God-Word and Father-Son relationship that revelation of truth and spiritual knowledge become available for human. For it is the Son who reveals the invisible Father to us for our salvation. He does this especially through His Incarnation in which He has assumed "immortality and approachability." By means of Him

> the Father was both seen in acts and heard in words, known in the Son, who was ministering the Father's acts and words. We may not look at the sun in respect to the totality of its substance in the sky, but we can look at the beam because of "the moderation of the assignment" which reaches out from thence to earth.

In this way Tertullian shows how the Son reveals the inner heart of God and, more than that, graciously "makes the Father present *for us*." It is when one ignores the Father's desire to reveal Himself personally that "the devil makes a heresy out of unity."

g) Origen (Quotations from First Principles)

Origen, called by some a heretic, by others "the greatest teacher of the church after the apostles," and "the Augustine of the Greeks," turned his superior mental abilities to the problem of working out the doctrine of the Son of God.

Origen first explicitly pronounced the doctrine of the *eternal* generation of the Son hinted at in Irenaeus. The Son of God is God not by mere emanation from a super-cosmic being, nor by participation in the divine essence, but because He is Himself the eternally begotten essence of the transcendental God. With Origen, however, there also arises in an explicit way the question of sub-ordinationism. Can Jesus be the eternal Son and "less than the Father" at the same time? In his discussion the problem was not reconciled, and this compelled the church to take up the formal definition of the nature of the Son in the creeds. Origen himself did not feel that every problem had to be answered in this life; for God in truth "is incomprehensible and immeasurable ... We must of necessity believe that He is far and away better than our thoughts about Him." With Muslims too we must maintain that we do not discover God, but God reveals Himself. That revelation of His own self, profound as it is, we His creatures are bound to accept.

Origen also maintained the unity of God by thinking of Him in terms of mind and intellect. He is not a kind of body but "a single, intellectual existence, admitting in Himself of no addition whatever, so that He cannot be believed to have in Himself a more or less, but is Unity ..." Because the unity of His Being is characterized by intellectual existence, He can be known. Not being a body, He cannot be seen. But to know and to be known is an attribute of intellectual existence. Against this background we are to understand Jesus' words: "No man knows the Father but the Son." With this starting point Origen deals with the doctrine of Jesus' person to a large extent under the heading of "the Wisdom of God," using extensively, as all the early fathers did, the passage Prov. 8:22-25 in support.

In stating that "the Wisdom of God has here substance nowhere else but in Him who is the beginning of all things," he puts forward two main emphases: that God the Father is the primary source of all existence and that Jesus is eternally born of His essence. Since the Wisdom of God has its source in God, it may be said that it took its birth from Him and is begotten by Him. This begetting is not a physical act.

> There must be some exceptional process, worthy of God, to which we can find no comparison whatever, not merely in things, but even in thought and imagination, such that by its aid human thought could apprehend how the un-begotten God becomes the Father of the only-begotten Son.

Origen finds this "exceptional process" in the act of God's will. As an act of will proceeds from the mind without cutting off any part of the mind or being separate from it, "in some similar fashion the Father has begotten the Son, who is indeed His image." Jesus is the "son of His will" like "the son of His love."

This only-begotten Son of God has an eternal existence. "Can anyone … suppose or believe that God the Father ever existed, even for a single moment, without begetting His Wisdom? … Wherefore we recognize that God was always the Father of His only-begotten Son, who was born indeed of Him and draws His being from Him, but is yet without any beginning…" If Jesus is the "image of the invisible God" there is no time when He did not exist. For when did God have no effulgence of His own glory? "Let the man who dares to say, 'There was a time when the Son was not,' understand that this is what he will be saying: 'Once Wisdom did not exist, and word did not exist and life did not exist.'" In fact, let him beware that he not utter impiety against the unbegotten

Father Himself "in denying that He was always the Father, and that He begot the Word and possessed Wisdom in all previous times or ages."

In looking inwardly the term "Son" refers to the fact that God is the eternal Source. But in looking outwardly it refers to the fact that Jesus is the Revealer of the Father. Origen brings out this thought in his commentary on the phrase "image of the invisible God." In human language image may be understood in the sense of a replica, painting or carving. It may also, however, be understood in the sense that a child is the image of its parent, when the likeness of its parent's features are faithfully reproduced in the child. In the case of Jesus we must understand the latter meaning. The Son is the faithful image: and likeness of God in his nature, and He patterns God for human. "Son" therefore has a double significance … offspring and revealer.

The way in which Jesus carries out His work of imaging God to human is primarily through His self-giving Incarnation. For "when God emptied Himself, His desire was by this very emptying to display to us the fullness of the Godhead." In humbling himself and suffering for our salvation Jesus revealed with filial faithfulness the depth of the Father's love for us and all humankind. "We are lost in amazement that such a Being, towering high and above all, should have emptied Himself of His majestic condition and become man and dwelt among us …"

Conclusion

It may be presumptuous to try to summarize in a few words the many suggestive thoughts and rewarding explanations of "Son of God" that we find in our examination of the early church fathers. However, let us try to briefly bring together the leading ideas we have discovered, so that we may have them available in our minds and on our tongues as we approach our Muslim friends,

a) The phrase "Son of God" reveals truth about the Being of God:

   i) The idea "Son of God" depends on the idea "Word of God" for its understanding.

ii) The Word of God is eternally in God. Unspoken it is thought-reason. Uttered it becomes the heard or visible Word.

iii) Being eternally in God it is eternally God.

iv) But the relation of the Word to God is that of "generation". The Word is generated by God in the same sense as mind generates thoughts and words.

v) What is generated may rightly be said to be begotten. And something begotten is truly termed "Son". What issued from a source is truly an off-spring. Jesus is the begotten Son because He is the generated Word.

vi) Jesus is the only-begotten Son because there is only one Word proceeding from the heart of the one God.

vii) The unspoken Word becomes the uttered Word by the power and will of God in order to express His love. The Word may then also be called the Son of His will and the Son of His love. And that is how we meet the Son of God.

viii) Perhaps therefore, the most all-inclusive paraphrase of "Son of God" would be "the Utterance of God's heart." That is what we also learn from John 1:14 and John 3:16.

b) The phrase "Son of God" reveals truth about the Character of God:

i) "Son of God" is an eminently suitable description, not only because it truly states the relation of the Word to God, but also because it expresses divine truth concerning the character of God.

ii) The term "Word" implies creation, communication, revelation.

iii) But to designate Jesus as "the generated Word" reflects a certain coldness of thought not true to the Jesus we know. The warmth implied in the final designation "Son" is needed to express to humankind the kind of person Jesus is.

iv) For Son implies love, knowledge, and obedience.

v) At the same time, the term "Son" is subject to physical misinterpretations. The expression "Word" is needed to take us back into the realm of Spirit in which God truly exists.

vi) Both the terms "Word" and "Son" are therefore complementary. They need each other to express the fullness of Jesus' relation with the Father. And they need each other to defend the greatness of God against the misunderstanding of human.

vii) Both terms symbolize God's desire to share his fellowship through self-revelation. They do indeed tell us what God is like in His being. But far more important, they tell us that God wants to share His being. For what the second Person, Word-Son, clearly is, is God communicating Himself.

viii) The God who so communicates Himself, communicates Himself as the God of love. He shows Himself to be Father in the sense of One who is Compassionate as well as in the sense of One who originates all things. That, in essence, is why "Son of God" is the revelation that saves.

Are the fathers of the church of help to us in reaching a clearer understanding of who it is to whom we witness among Muslims as "the Son of God"? I believe that they are. But if they are so, it is only another tribute to the Spirit of God who enriches His Church with a cloud of witnesses to bear and to bare His truth. That same Spirit is ours, and He will not cease to speak this same truth through us with power, if we but open our lips to show forth God's praise.

Endnotes

[1] The early Church fathers are usually divided into the *apostolic fathers*, a small group of authors from within the year 150, and the *apologists*, a larger group of men within the period 150-250.

[2] Reinhold Seeberg, *History of Doctrines*, 110.

The Sonship of Jesus: Some Muslim Observations and Some Christian Responses

Ernest Hahn

Introduction: The Sonship of Jesus and Islām

Who do human say that the Son of Man is? The various responses of several members of a Muslim family in a nearby town are sufficiently interesting to record. Says father: "Your religion and our religion are the same except that you say that Jesus is the Son of God." But God has no son. For father, this qualification virtually renders any sameness between the two religions into an infinite difference. In any case, his opposition to any Christian ministrations to other members of his family so indicate. Say some female members of the household: "Jesus is Allāh and this we believe. But do not say that Jesus is Allāh's son!" How extensive and how sincere this confession is, only God can ultimately know. In any event, the confession is a veto imposed upon the Islāmic veto that the Messiah cannot be Allāh. Nevertheless, even if the confession is "Christian," it still manifests the deep-rooted antipathy in many a Muslim heart to the idea of Sonship. God can have no son. But says one of the sons in this family: "I believe that Jesus is the Son of God." The power of the Spirit has begun to make an impression upon his heart regarding Christ and his relationship to God.

Father would conclude that he alone of all those mentioned continues to confess a true Islām. Are not the women folk trespassing into dangerous territory, though still attached to Islāmic moorings? Concerning his son? Could he pray that God would guide his son or would he conclude as Al-Ghazālī, the Muslim theologian par excellence, quoting the Qur'ān: "Whom God has led astray, for him there is no guidance."

Nor would father find difficulty in substantiating his position. Allāh is greatest, because He only is God. He has no partners or associates and thus He has no sons or daughters, equals with or subordinates to Him, who merit worship and praise. If Christians insist that God has but one Son, be they People of the Book (as the Qur'ān calls Jews and Christians) or not, they become as pagan Arab, as ancient Greek or Roman, as Hindu or any other that attributes a partner to God. Evidence there is plenty: "Your God is One God; there is no God save Him, the Beneficent, the Merciful" (2:163);[1] "Lo thy Word is surely One" (37:4).[2]

Qur'ānic Observations

If the father were to systematize the doctrine of Allāh's Oneness in contrast with "polytheism", he would find no shortage of passages from the Qur'ān to substantiate his argument. The chapter called "The Unity" offers him the perfect thesis which he can buttress with a host of passages to act as commentary:

> In the name of Allāh, the Beneficent, the Merciful.
> Say, He is Allāh, the One;
> Allāh, the eternally besought of all;
> He begetteth not nor was begotten.
> And there is none comparable unto Him (112:1-4)

There are few passages in the Qur'ān that father like many another Muslim knows better.

If Allāh does not beget, it follows that He has no sons or daughters, nor wife through whom He begets sons and daughters:

> Yet they ascribe as partners unto Him the jinn, although He did create them, and impute falsely, without knowledge, sons and daughters unto

> Him. Glorified be He and high exalted above (all) that they ascribe (unto Him).
>
> The Originator of the heavens and the earth! How can He have a child, when there is for Him no consort, when He created all things and is Aware of all things? (6:101,102).
>
> Or chooseth He daughters of all that He hath created, and honoureth He you with sons? And if one of them hath tidings of that which He likeneth to the Beneficent One, his countenance becometh black and he is full of inward rage (43:16, 17).

Hence also Allāh begets no sons:

> And (we believe) that He exalted be the glory of our Lord hath taken nether wife nor son
>
> And that the foolish one among us used to speak concerning Allāh an atrocious 'lie' (72:3, 4)
>
> And they say: Allāh hath taken unto Himself a Son. Be He glorified! Nay, but whatsoever is in the heaven and the earth is His. All are subservient unto Him (2:116).
>
> They say: Allāh hath taken (unto Him) a Son—Glorified be He! He hath no needs! His is all that is in the heavens and all that is in the earth. Ye have no warrant for this. Tell ye concerning Allāh that which ye know not? (10:69).
>
> And say: Praise be to Allāh, who hath not taken unto Himself a son, and Who hath no partner in the Sovereignty, nor hath He any protecting friend through dependence. And magnify Him with all magnificence (17:111).
>
> He unto whom belongeth the sovereignty of the heavens and the earth, He hath chosen no son nor hath He any partner in the Sovereignty. He hath created everything and hath meted out for it a measure (25:2).
>
> Say (O Muḥammad): The Beneficent One hath no son. I am first among the worshippers (43:81).
>
> And they say: The Beneficent hath taken unto Himself a son. Assuredly ye utter a disastrous thing whereby almost the heavens are torn, and the earth is split asunder and the mountains fall in ruins that ye ascribe unto the Beneficent a son when it is not meet for (the Majesty of) the Beneficent that He should choose a son. There is none in the heavens and the earth but cometh unto the Beneficent as a slave (19:88-93).

> Thus no son or sons of Allāh can be a god or gods besides Allāh; Allāh hath not chosen any son, nor is there any God along with Him; else would each God have assuredly championed that which he created, and some of them would assuredly have overcome others. Glorified be Allāh above all that they allege (23:91).
>
> Or have they chosen Gods from the earth who raise the dead? If there were therein Gods beside Allāh, then verily both (the heavens and the earth) had been disordered. Glorified be Allāh, the Lord of the Throne, from all that they ascribe (unto Him). He will not be questioned as to that which He doeth, but they will be questioned.
>
> Or have they chosen other gods beside Him? Say: Bring your proof (of their godhead). This is the Reminder of those with me and those before me, but most of them know not the Truth and so they are averse.
>
> And we sent no messenger before thee but We inspired him (saying): There is no God save Me (Allāh), so worship Me.
>
> And they say: The Beneficent hath taken unto Himself a son. Be He glorified! Nay, but (those whom they call sons) are honoured slaves;
>
> They speak not until He hath spoken, and they act by His command. He knoweth what is before them and what is behind them, and they cannot intercede except for him whom He accepteth, and they quake for awe of Him.
>
> And one of them who should say: Lo! I am a God beside Him, that one we should repay wiith hell. Thus we repay wrong-doers (21:21-29).

As Allāh is not begotten, thus Allāh cannot be the Messiah, nor can the Messiah be Allāh:

> They indeed have disbelieved who say: Lo! Allāh is the Messiah, son of Mary. Say: Who then can do aught against Allāh if He had willed to destroy the Messiah son of Mary, and his mother and everyone on earth? Allāh's is the Sovereignty of the heavens and the earth and all that is between them. He createth what He will. And Allāh is Able to do all things (5:17).
>
> "They surely disbelieve who say: Lo! Allāh is the Messiah, son of Mary. The Messiah (himself) said: O Children of Israel worship Allāh, my Lord and your Lord. Lo! whoso ascribeth partners unto Allāh, for Him Allāh hath forbidden Paradise. His abode is the Fire. For evil-doers there will be no helpers" (5:72).

Hence the impossibility of the Trinity (as the Muslim may see it), establishing Jesus and Mary (or any other) as gods alongside Allāh:

> And when Allāh saith: O Jesus, son of Mary! Didst thou say unite mankind: Take me and my mother for two gods beside Allāh? He saith: Be glorified! It was not mine to utter that to which I had no right. If I used to say it, then Thou knewest it. Thou knowest what is in my mind, and I know not what is in Thy mind. Lo! Thou, only Thou art the Knower of Things Hidden. I spake unto them only that which Thou commandedst me, (saying): Worship Allāh, my Lord and your Lord. I was a witness of them while I dwelt among them, and when Thou tookest me Thou wast the Watcher over them. Thou art Witness over all things (5:116, 117).
>
> They surely disbelieve who say: Lo! Allāh is the third of three; when there is no God save the One God. If they desist not from so saying a painful doom will fall on those of them who disbelieve. Will they not rather turn unto Allāh and seek forgiveness of Him? For Allāh is Forgiving, Merciful.
>
> The Messiah, son of Mary, was no other than a messenger, messengers (the like of whom) had passed away before him. And his mother was a saintly woman. And they both used to eat (earthly) food. See how we make the revelations clear for them, and see how they are turned away! (5:72-95).
>
> O People of the Scripture! Do not exaggerate in your religion nor utter aught concerning Allāh save the truth. The Messiah, Jesus son of Mary, was only a messenger of Allāh, and his word which He conveyed unto Mary, and a spirit from Him. So believe in Allāh and His messengers, and say not 'Three'—Cease! (it is) better for you!—Allāh is only one God. Far is it removed from His transcendent majesty that He should have a son. His is all that is in the heavens and all that is in the earth. And Allāh is sufficient as Defender.
>
> The Messiah will never scorn to be a slave unto Allāh, nor will the favoured angels. Whoso scorneth His service and is proud, all such will He assemble, unto Him" (4:171,172).

In fact father may conclude that it can be wrong to attribute sons or a son to Allāh in any sense of the word:

> The Jews and Christians say: We are sons of Allāh and His loved ones. Say: Why then doth He chastise you for your sins? Nay, ye are but mortals of His creating. He forgiveth whom He will, and chastiseth whom He will. Allāh's is the Sovereignty of the heavens and the earth and all that is between them and unto Him is the journeying (5:18).

In sum, Allāh alone is creator, sovereign, independent, possessor of all. To speak of various gods or sons of gods is to speak of various sovereigns, to suggest strife between the gods and a resultant chaos. He is neither a son nor has sons for as He is free from all needs, so He is free from a consort, and therefore from children. All else is created mortal and subservient to Him. No one can intercede unless He grants permission.

What applies in general applies specifically to the Messiah. He is neither a god nor son of God, for Allāh can easily destroy him. Even though the Messiah is His word, a spirit from Him, yet the Messiah is only a messenger like other messengers, a slave like other slaves, eating food as they eat, worshipping Allāh as they worship Him, proclaiming that he is not a god besides Allāh.

Curious yet certainly consistent with the Qur'ān is the bracketed interpolation of our translator: "When it is not meet for (the Majesty of) the Beneficent that He should choose a son" (19:92). Allāh's majesty cannot be shared and thus He can have no son. Merely uttering the idea almost splits the heavens. He who speaks such a lie is an evil doer and his reward is hell.

Some Early Muslim Observations

As Islām spread and Muslims came into closer contact with Christians, it is not surprising that the Muslim apologist, Qur'ān in hand, readily defended the Qur'ānic thesis regarding the Sonship of Christ. In a letter stated to be written by a convert to Islām, al-Hāshimī, to the Christian, al-Kindī (9th cent. C.E.), the former assured al-Kindī of his close association with Christian dignitaries and his thorough knowledge of the Bible.

> So now … I invite you to accept the religion that God has chosen for me … And it is this,—You shall worship the one God, the Eternal, He begetteth not, neither is He begotten, who hath no consort and no son …
>
> Then give up your unbelief and error … and speak no more of Father, Son and Holy Ghost, these words that you yourself admit to be so confusing …[3]

Ibn Ḥazm (d. 1064 C.E.) asserting that the true writings of the Bible no longer exist (though through a miracle of God references to Muḥammad in the Bible are preserved!) pours ridicule upon the significance of Christ for Christians:

> Sometimes they say of Christ that He is the Son of God, and sometimes Son of Joseph, Son of David, Son of Man; sometimes He is God the Preserver and Creator, sometimes Lamb of God ...; They say that He was God, although they assert that there is no other God but Allāh ... [4]

Al-Ghazālī (d. 1111 C.E.) taking the Bible more seriously accepts the term of "Father" applied to God, yet applies sonship to all prophets as to Christ:

> Furthermore, the reverence of the people toward Allāh ... their submission to His prohibitions ... far exceeds the conduct of sons towards their father. So He is to them the most merciful Father and they to Him are pious sons. This then is the secret of the metaphor in applying this comparison.
>
> Thus when Jesus adopted the metaphor in applying "Father" to Allāh ....[5]

Some Contemporary Muslim Observations

Contemporary Muslim verbal or written apologetic against Christianity generally deviates little from the patterns of the ancient apologists. Few, however, resemble. Al-Ghazālī who on the evidence of Scriptures accepts a "liberal" interpretation of the Fatherhood of God and the Sonship of Christ as others can also be sons of God the Father. A more recent expositor, Amīr 'Ālam, contends that Jesus can be called the Son of God in a moral and spiritual sense, yet in this same sense all are in some measure sons of God.[6] Others in personal conversation may express a similar view. Yet the majority versed in Islāmics and labouring under the assumption that our Scriptures are corrupted consider Christianity to be a form of polytheism, the Sonship of Christ perhaps to be derived from paganism, the Trinity a metaphysical puzzle and contrary to reason.

In order to ascertain more fully present responsible opinion on the Sonship of Jesus, I recently circulated a letter to about a dozen Muslim leaders. Following is the main body of the letter:

> "... In order to represent Muslim opinion correctly as it has existed in the past or present, I would appreciate your opinion regarding the matter. Perhaps you could centre your response around such questions:

1. Why is the term "Son of God" when applied to Jesus normally unacceptable to the Muslim? Is this your view also?

2. Could you document your response from Islāmic sources, especially the Qur'ān and Ḥadīth? Perhaps you could also make some references to well received Muslim commentaries.

3. Is the phrase "Son of God" in itself unacceptable in any situation? Or are there any exceptions when the phrase could be validly used, i.e., in a non-physical sense, in relation to Jesus also? Do you consider it possible that the term "Son of God" as applied it to the Messiah Jesus in the Bible could have a revelatory significance, and as such find its equation (partially if not fully) in the term "Kalimatullāh" (The Word of Allāh)?

4. Since the phrase "Son of God" is so often used in the New Testament to describe Jesus, how do you account for its presence? When applied to Jesus, is it just interpolation, an addition to the "original" Injīl? If so, at what point in history? If not, why its presence and what is its significance?

Perhaps there are other points which the above questions do not cover. If so, please consider them also ..."

Perhaps it is significant that only four replies came. For them we may be grateful. Though they by no means represent all phases of Muslim opinion, they are worth quoting in part or full. The editor of "Ṭolū-e-Islām" in Lahore writes:

> ... The clear text of the noble Qur'ān declares this belief of the Christians that Ḥazrat Masīḥ (upon him be peace) is the son of God to be *kufr* (unbelief) and Allāh Most High reveals His displeasure concerning this (term). Therefore how can Muslims apply this name to Ḥazrat Masīḥ?
>
> The present Injīl is surely not the Injīl which descended upon Ḥazrat 'Īsā. Even the Christians themselves do not make this claim that it is the same Injīl; therefore on the basis of the Injīl Muslims can never acknowledge that God Most High called Ḥazrat Masīḥ by this name or that Ḥazrat Masīḥ chose it for himself. This is a later invention of Christians and it can be shown by investigation when and why this term was coined. But for us such investigation is not necessary because we have the noble Qur'ān and the judgement of the noble Qur'ān in this matter is absolutely clear.[7]

Here are a few extracts from a letter written by a Muslim in Vaniyambadi who is constantly engaged in apologetics:

From the contents of the writings themselves in your possession which are called Anājīl (plural of Injīl), the four Gospels), it is evident that after Ḥazrat Isa disappeared from the people these writings were written as biographies of Ḥazrat Isa in the name of his disciples. In them there is present a mixture of truth and lie. So much I can say concerning this that any person in whose heart there is a love and a reverence for Ḥazrat Isa can never be content to see the picture of Ḥazrat 'Īsā (drawn) from these Anājīl. If anyone is desirous of seeing the greatness and stature of Ḥazrat Isa he can see the greatness and nobility of the son of Mary in the noble Qur'ān.

The saying of some undiscerning commentators of the Qur'ān that Ḥazrat Isa is the word of Allāh (Kalimatullāh) and His Spirit cannot make Ḥazrat Isa the word of Allāh and His Spirit because the Word of Allāh is eternal, uncreated and immortal but Ḥazrat Isa without doubt is a creature, temporal and moral ...

... The matter is thus as clear as the light of day that the Creator and Originator ... is worshipped by the whole creation and the relationship of the one worshipped with his servants cannot be that of father. If Ḥazrat Isa would be the Son of Allāh then he could not be his servant, but that he is servant is especially shown in this way: 'The Messiah will never scorn to be a slave unto Allāh ...' (4:172).[8]

Abul 'Ālā Maudūdī, the leader of the Jamā'at-i-Islāmī movement which also wields an extensive influence in India, writes:

... In a clear and unmistakable manner, the Qur'ān makes plain that in no sense whatsoever does Allāh have a son. He has given birth to no one nor has He made anyone His son. To attribute children to Him is surely *shirk* (associating someone with Allāh, the great sin). The Messiah (upon him be peace) is the servant and apostle of Allāh, not His son, and apart from the fact that Allāh by his special command created him from the womb of the Virgin Mary without a father, there is nothing special about him. In this peculiarity Adam also shares with him and is like him because he was created without a father directly from clay.

Regarding this kindly note the following verses of the glorious Qur'ān: (there follows a list of passages ...)

These explanations of the Qur'ān are so clear and definite that there is no further need to cite any tradition or commentary. You know that in Islām any matter that is clearly proved in the Qur'ān needs no other proof.

How the belief that the Messiah is the Son of Allāh came into the Injīl: regarding this it is not expedient for me to say anything. Better that you yourself would investigate the following three points and arrive at an opinion:

1. From among the writings which are found in the "New Testament" of the Bible is there any which contains the original words of God Most High and is not mixed with human speech?

2. Has the Messiah himself anywhere used the expression "Son of God" for himself? Is not the fact of the matter thus that he used the expression "Son of Man" regarding himself rather than the expression "Son of God"? And if the idea of being the Son of God derives from calling, God "Father", did he exclusively call God his Father only?

3. Can any matter which has not been fixed by Christ's own teaching be established as firm confession by an interpretation of another especially when it clashes with the belief of the Oneness of God as taught by the Messiah and because of which men along with the worship of God may fall into the worship of the Messiah also?[9]

Raḥīm Aḥmed Fārūqī, Head of the Arabic and Persian Department, Government Arts College, Madras, writes:

1. The Muslim conception of God is based on a verse of the Qur'ān which, rendered into English, reads: "There is nothing like unto Him". This idea has been expanded by a famous Persian poet in an invocatory verse the English rendering of which is: "O You, who are beyond imagination, guess, conjecture or surmise and beyond everything which we have seen, heard or read about." There is no cause for wonder, then, if the Muslim people, believing as they do in a God that transcends man's experience, both individual and racial, should be allergic of such a phrase as "The Son of God". I admit that a certain amount of anthropomorphism is inevitable in our human situation, but that does not mean that man should create God after his own image. The situation is further aggravated by the special kind of arithmetic involved in the "Doctrine of the Trinity" which to a Muslim mind does not appear to belong to the spatiotemporal order in which man has been living and moving even since his first birthday.

2. The verses of the Qur'ān and the Traditions of the Prophet disapproving of any idea hovering round generation as determining the relationship between the Creator and the created are too numerous to be mentioned here. I shall, however, con tent myself with giving below the English translation of three relevant verses of the Qur'ān: (there follow three quotations)

3. I am not able to think of any situation in which the phrase "Son of God" can shed its anthropomorphic character and become acceptable to a Muslim. To suggest that the phrase may be used in a non-physical sense is mere sophistry which renders the metaphor pointless. The Qur'ānic term "Kalimatullāh" cannot be equated with the Biblical phrase "Son of God", even partially, as the former refers to "Kun" or "Be" which ushered the entire work of God into being, Jesus not excepted.

4. I strongly suspect that the word "Son" in the phrase "Son of God" has crept into the New Testament through the carelessness of the first Greek translator of the original Hebrew which, as we all know, is now lost for ever. I am of opinion that a Hebrew word bearing two meanings: i) A messenger or a creature or a servant or a slave, and ii) A son, or, in case there is no such single word in the Hebrew language, two words, resembling each other in sound and form, one bearing the meaning of No. i and the other bearing the meaning of No. ii are responsible for the mistaken rendering.

Arabic language has numerous examples of such types of words. I am not prepared to believe that Hebrew, belonging as it does to the same family, can be entirely free from the characteristics of its stock.[10]

Some Christian Responses to These Muslim Observations

To the Muslim: "What then shall we say to this? If God is for us …" It is this context of God's being for us which we must preserve in attempting to show the Muslim what the Injīl means when it speaks about Jesus as the Son of God. God is for us: God who created us for fellowship with Him and who redeemed us from the slavery of sin and death into his fellowship of holiness and life once more. It is the Injīl (Arabic for Evangel), the Good News of God's *tanzīl* (descent) to be with us and for us in Jesus which we must proclaim so that the Muslim may espouse the contents of the Book he considers holy but only normally knows in name. This context lost, our witness is no longer Christian witness but at best academic and philosophical speculation, hardly God's wholesome cure for the malady of human's rebellious nature.

To Qur'ānic Observations

The man who is our immediate concern is a Muslim. To understand him as a man whose thoughts and way of life are moulded by the Qur'ān, for him God's final revelation to man, will help us to make, our witness to him the more effective. To what then does the Qur'ān address itself and what is its address which concerns us here?

We may initially note that the Qur'ān does not address itself to an atheistic situation. Hence it is not interested in establishing the existence of Allāh. The Arab in Mu¢ammad's day believed in Allāh. Yet along with Allāh, he worshipped other deities. The Qur'ānic declaration that God is *One* who has no *associate* serves as an anti-thesis to:

i) Arab paganism which recognized a series of deities or intercessors, be they jinn, angels, sons or daughters of Allāh, alongside of or even subordinate to the supreme God, Allāh. To Allāh were at least attributed daughters, according to the Qur'ān. Where the mention of a son of Allāh occurs, it is not necessarily always in connection with Christian belief concerning the Sonship of Jesus. It can be inferred that such sons and daughters became as such through consort or consorts though it may be that they are understood as sons or daughter metaphorically (non-physically). From this aspect little distinguished Arab paganism from that of ancient Greece or Rome or any religion which professes that God has a wife and child.

ii) The Christian belief as the Qur'ān understands it. Though *several* Qur'ānic passages speak highly of Christians, it is difficult for the Christian to grasp the Qur'ānic interpretation of Christianity as belief in a plurality of Gods. The Qur'ān appears to consider the Christian doctrine of the Trinity (Tri-unity) as really a doctrine of tri-theism; a belief in three gods: in Allāh, Mary and a son—Jesus. Or it appears to represent Christians as making the Messiah, the man, into a god to be worshipped along with Allāh, or in making the Messiah Allāh Himself, so that the worship of the Messiah who is called Allāh actually displaces the worship of Allāh. Readily to be understood then is the conclusion of many Muslims who know the Qur'ān and do not know the Injīl that Christianity is similar to or only a variation of polytheism.[11]

With these Qur'ānic vetoes the Injīl can only agree. Stated thus there is no conflict between *Qur'ānic* and Biblical witness. For the Injīl does not state that there are three gods, nor that Allāh takes a wife, and through this wife a son, all three to be worshipped. Sex does not characterize the Creator. Nor does that Injīl support the belief that man can become God, that divinity can be imposed on one who is only a creature. The Injīl does not assert that the man, Jesus, the Messiah, became the son of God or Allāh and that worship of Him displaces worship of the God who created the man.

There are perhaps only two points at which a clash of Biblical and Qur'ānic evidence can occur regarding these matters:

i) An interpretation of the Qur'ān which states that in no way or under no circumstances can God have a son or can a son be attributed to God. In other words, God can only not have a son physically, he cannot have a son spiritually, morally, metaphorically or in any other way. With this most Muslim interpretations seem to agree. With such an interpretation the Injīl frankly clashes, for the Injīl states in unambiguous terms that Jesus is the Son of God.

ii) The conclusion of some Muslims that Christianity as represented by the Qur'ān represents the common tradition of Christian belief. If the Muslim considers the term Son of God as applied in the Injīl to Jesus as an unfortunate misnomer, a name really not applied to Jesus in the "original" Injīl (whatever that may be the Muslim cannot tell) and a further confirmation that the present Injīl is corrupt, just as unfortunate is the representation of Christianity as portrayed by the Qur'ān and as the average Muslim understands Christianity from his knowledge of the Qur'ān, and for that matter the average Christian who sees the Qur'ānic understanding of Christianity as such. There may be reasons for such a representation in the Qur'ān; representations of perversions of Christianity which speak of Christianity as a religion of three gods—father, mother and Jesus (such a historical aberration of Christianity is in fact hard to trace); as a religion which has elevated Jesus to a god besides Allāh or in place of Allāh etc. *But such "Christian" doctrines cannot claim to be rooted in the Injīl,* regardless of whether or not one talks of the present Injīl differing from the "original" Injīl. Thus either the Qur'ān is representing false interpretations of the Injīl (a rather uninviting prospect, as Muslims would rightly ask that any non-Muslim would represent Islām not upon a strange Muslim heresy which gains no support from the Qur'ān, but upon the Qur'ān itself); or else the Qur'ān is not representing the Injīl at all (but then why these portrayals?). Regarding the basic Christian beliefs in relation to the Trinity (which is not a doctrine of three gods, or a doctrine of father, mother and Jesus) and to the Incarnation (not a man becoming a god or a son of God) as expressed in the ancient universal creeds and liturgies of Christendom, the Qur'ān is *silent.* On the other hand all this does not imply that the Qur'ān supports such Christian teachings.

Relevant to the above observations is the traditional Muslim understanding that the witness of the Qur'ān is the same that of the Injīl and other holy books. Since the Muslim knows Christian doctrine to differ from Islāmic doctrine, he concludes that the discrepancy is rooted in the Injīl. Therefore his next conclusion: the Injīl the Christians have is corrupt and not the original Injīl. If asked why, he will normally say that the Qur'ān so testifies (which in fact the Qur'ān does not). If asked how he knows this, he will normally reply he has thus heard, probably from a religious leader. The tragedy, and so it is—and so extensive—is two-fold: a) If the Muslims reads the Injīl, he thinks that what is in the Injīl regarding the above doctrines is rejected by the Qur'ān. Yet, as we have attempted to show, the Qur'ān really does not deal with the Incarnation or the Trinity.

b) If he reads only the Qur'ān, he will assume from his Quaranic study that Christians believe in a plurality of gods, make the man Jesus into a god etc. It is amazing how even educated Muslims are astonished at the Christian contention that the Injīl gives no witness to a confession of three gods, nor does the Injīl testify that God has a wife and through the wife a son, nor does the Injīl state disciples of Christ make the Messiah into a son of God or God etc. Deny the witness of the Injīl regarding the Christian doctrines he may. *But not very effectively on Qur'ānic grounds.* If only then a little brush is cleared, that he would read the Injīl you give him without such bias … And this is the point.[12]

To Muslim Non-Qur'ānic Observations

a) *The Doctrine of Sonship is against Reason*: Muslims sometimes also consider the witness of the Injīl to the Sonship of Christ (hence to the Trinity also) as unreasonable and therefore invalid. Linked with this consideration is the Muslim contention that the Qur'ān and its doctrine of the Unity of God are reasonable, but what, may we ask, is this criterion of reason whereby God as Unity and not God as Trinity conforms or should conform to it? If the doctrine of the Unity of God is exclusively reasonable, in just what form does the Unity assume this reasonable nature; as a unity aloof from the world or encompassing the world; a deistic, theistic or pantheistic unity; a unity which is exclusive or inclusive of divisions? And if exclusive of divisions, what of the relation of the essence and attributes of God within this Unity?[13] The application of reason has caused humankind to spill as much ink over the "metaphysical puzzle" of the doctrine of the Unity in Islām as over the "metaphysical puzzle" of the doctrine of the Trinity in Christianity. And these are only a few of the elementary questions that have been raised. Such questions scarcely touch upon the yet more philosophical speculations.

Muslims continue to point to the Qur'ān as revelation for their doctrine of the Unity of Allāh as do Christians to the Bible as revelation for their doctrine of the Trinity. Both are scarcely considered revelation on the basis that they conform to the criterion of reason. Reasonable people, both Muslims and Christians, continue to accept the doctrine of the Unity of God according to the Qur'ān or the doctrine of the Trinity according to the Bible as reasonable, better perhaps as beyond reason, certainly not against reason. Similarly reasonable people deem it not against reason that the Son of God dwells within the Godhead as God of God and Light of Light ... being of one substance (or essence, *zāt)* with the Father (thus the Nicene Creed) and that Jesus reveals God to human as God's eternal Word to human at a particular place and time in world history. Again we may recall that though the Qur'ān may not support the Christian doctrines of the Incarnation and Trinity, it hardly explicitly rejects them. Moreover the Unity of God as expressed in the Qur'ān scarcely intends to be a full-blow theological analysis and exposition of the Being of God which in traditional Islām remains *ghā'ib* (hidden), hence scarcely to be measure by reason; rather the Qur'ān proclaims that there is no divinity but Allāh. He alone is God. But this the Bible also says: Better to dismiss any attempt to establish either the Unity or Trinity (hence also the doctrine of Jesus' Sonship) on the grounds of reason, or conversely to reject ether because it appears unreasonable.[14]

b) *The Doctrine of Sonship is Anthropomorphic*: Similar educated Muslims sometimes suggest that the doctrine of *Jesus'* Sonship is anthropomorphic; that such Sonship indicates that human in making God after his own image, and that therefore the doctrine is unacceptable to the Muslim since "there is nothing like unto Allāh." Again we note the witness of the Bible which testifies that:

i) Human does not make God after human's image, but God did create human in God's image.[15]

ii) That a man was not elevated to the position of God but the Eternal Word of God became flesh and dwelt among us.

Once more the question arises regarding the criterion of anthropomorphism. For both Qur'ān and Bible, both coming to human through human who hardly show interest in philosophy, are frankly anthropomorphic in language. Muslims are quite familiar with the *mutashābih* (ambiguous; thus *tashbīh*, anthropomorphism) verses of the Qur'ān where it appears that human acts and attributes are ascribed to Allāh. Thus the Qur'ān speaks of Allāh sitting on his throne, coming (from one place to another), the face, the eyes, the hand of Allāh, etc. As there are trends among Christian theologians to "demythologize", so there are Muslim theologians attempting to divest these verses of anthropomorphic elements through *tatil* (interpretation). Others who accept the verses literally (because the Qur'ān is held to be the exact transcription of the Book inscribed on the preserved tablet in heaven) and as being consistent with the divine, add that they neither know the nature nor manner of the attributes and actions of Allāh. Such is the Muslim dilemna in brief: *tatīl* (the divesting from Allāh of all attributes) versus *tashbīh* (anthropomorphism). If then it be legitimate to speak of Allāh sitting upon his throne, the believer enjoying a vision of Allāh, etc., in a metaphorical manner, why should it be sophistry to speak of Jesus as Son of God in a spiritual manner (i.e., non-physical manner), especially in view of the common Biblical phraseology which describes God's relation with his people in terms of covenant depicted by family relationships.[16]

Metaphorical usage of such terminology is probably common to most or all languages: the father of the nation, sons and daughters of light etc. Arabic speaks of *Bint al-Shafah* (daughter of the lip, a word)[17] the Qur'ān of *Ibn al-Sabīl* (son of the path, a traveller), and *Umm al-Kitāb* (mother of the book).[18] Crude yet illuminating is the common expression "son of Satan". In general such metaphorical language is also very common in the Bible. Even the Jews while firmly upholding their doctrine of the Unity saw no contradiction to this doctrine in referring to the Torah (Taurāt), the revelation of God, as the daughter of God. Nor, as we have seen, is the expression "God the Father" and prophets as "sons of God" rejected outright by all Muslims as the writings of Al-Ghazālī testify. May we only remind ourselves again that the Sonship of Jesus, though obviously exclusive in the New Testament, does not involve the sex act. Jesus does not become the Son of God because of Mary. On the contrary it is through the power of God Most High that the Son of God, God's Word, God's revelation of himself to humankind, becomes flesh through Mary. His Name: Jesus, the Son of Man.

c) *The Finite cannot contain the Infinite:* Yet the Muslim may say, granted that the above objections concerning the possibility of Jesus being the Son of God are invalid. Still, he continues, the fact remains that it is impossible for God to enter this limited world of time and space. For God is unlimited and is not bound by such worldly limitations. He cannot be or exist as other than himself. Why then the Christian claim that God (or the Son of God) came into this world?

This observation also labours under an old philosophical premise that the finite cannot contain the infinite. But is this a legitimate premise and one which is really applicable to both Christian and Islāmic theology?

Does not the premise that the unlimited or infinite God cannot enter the limited and finite world fall into the danger of imposing limitation and finitude upon the unlimited and infinite God? And granted that the premise be valid: if applicable to Biblical theology, should it not also be applicable to Qur'ānic theology?

Islāmically speaking, such a premise would appear defective on two scores: i) for does not the eternal omniscience of Allāh extend to every word, thought and deed of His creation? And is He himself not present in His infinite omniscience? Is He not involved in the creation of every act of His creation, yet especially close to human? "Lo! He is the Hearer, Nigh" (Qur'ān 34:50). "We verily created a man … and we are nearer to him than his jugular vein" (50:16).

ii) The normal Islāmic teaching regarding the descent (*tanzīl)* of the eternal Word of God which finds itself "historicised", "enbooked" in a particular time and place. Yet should it also be noted, that Allāh dwells in heaven (67:16), which He created, which passes away and will be recreated? So also traditional Islām informs us that finite human will enjoy the vision of Allāh, the infinite.

If it then be possible to talk of the omnipresence of Allāh in this world and the presence of the eternal Word of Allāh enbooked under the spatio-temporal accidents of cover, paper, ink, words, etc., surely the testimony of the Bible that God is omnipresent and that the Son of God, God's Word enfleshed at a particular time and place in history remains a possibility. Rather than upholding the premise that *finitum non capax infiniti,* is not the promise of both Bible and Qur'ān that God, neither inwardly (pantheism) nor outwardly (deism?) is super worldly? Though in both religions God remains distinct from his creation (in Christianity the separation of God and human is essentially the result of sin), yet is there not a belonging togetherness in both? So both pose the possibility of the infinite and eternal entering into the sphere of the finite and temporal.

So often, indeed, philosophy is like a fire: a great blessing to human, yet often a source of injury to themselves. Do not Muslims and

Christians in burning each other with the flame of philosophy also burn themselves? How salutary a balance the old adage of the old Church father Tertullian: "What has Athens in common with Jerusalem?" Is it not correct to say, if we are to maintain our historical bearings at all, that Mecca at the time of Muḥammad hardly had a more intimate connection with Athens?

d) *The Textual Problems of the Injīl*: But does there not yet remain one knife sharp enough to cut the Gordian knot, a knife forged in the fires of Biblical scholarship itself? Do not the findings of the textual critics of the Bible indicate the imperfection of the present Injīl? "If textual criticism of the Injīl indicates so many variant readings, how can we trust its text; specially how can we know that the term "Son of God" really belongs to the text and is not a mere fabrication of later Christians?" The Muslim may ask.

To be sure any student familiar with New Testament textual Studies is aware of problems concerning the text. Yet if such a text which exhibits variant readings is a cause for doubt, just what type of text can one trusts: a text which is historically indisputable in every word and letter? Such ancient texts do not exist. In any event, many a Muslim knows that the Qur'ān is no exception to the rule. So often the ancient Muslim historians and commentators testify to the contrary: textual omissions, variants, problems of vowels and diacritical pointing. To avoid this problem by merely dismissing these difficulties regarding the text of the Qur'ān is questionable scholarship if not intellectual dishonesty. Bearing these, difficulties, in mind, would it not be analogous logic, for example, for the Christian, to say: the text of the Qur'ān shows variant readings. Therefore the text is doubtful. Therefore especially all references to Muḥammad as prophet and apostle are doubtful. Similarly, references to the Sonship of Jesus in the Qur'ān may have been removed from the "original" Qur'ān etc. rather poor logic by which to dismiss or uphold either the apostleship of Muḥammad or the Sonship of Jesus!

If then the textual problem is a problem for the Injīl, it is also a problem for the Qur'ān. But one wonders whether in either case it is a real problem. Better perhaps an indication from God in his mercy that our faith does not depend merely upon a text, nor upon an infallible theory of inspiration used as a "firm foundation" to safeguard or establish the validity and infallibility of a text. Our faith depends upon God and is in God. For the validity and value of a text, its inspiration if one wills, lies in and is to be derived from the content of the text. Yet in the case of either the Qur'ān or the Bible there need be no grave doubt concerning reliable transmission, or basic integrity. It is well recognized that such variants as exist in the Bible do not affect the basic doctrines of the Bible. That Jesus is Son of God, Son of Man, Messiah and Servant of God is clearly attested in the Injīl. Neither higher or lower criticism effectively demonstrates otherwise. The frequency and usage of the former term will be dealt with elsewhere in this issue.

But why this objection at all from the Muslim? May we not ask him if in raising the question he speaks as a Muslim? And in suggesting his doubt about the Injīl, is he not perhaps unwittingly casting doubts on the Qur'ān? As previously noted, the Qur'ān does not suggest the Injīl *qua* text has been corrupted, abrogated or that the original Injīl has disappeared or is lost. On the contrary, Qur'ānic evidence presupposes and even clearly indicates the presence of the Injīl *qua* text until at least the time of the coming of the Qur'ān.[19] And if so, which one? Obviously the one available with Christians in Mu¢ammad's time. It would seem that this fact deals a blow also to some of the other contentions regarding the Injīl in the letters from our correspondents. Else does the Qur'ān contradict itself?

Christian Communication of the Sonship of Jesus

In the face of opposition to and general misunderstanding of the term "Son of God" some Christians have wondered if it would be advisable to avoid the term in witness to the Muslim and substitute for it an equivalent or an approximate equivalent.[20] In our initial verbal witness it may be normally advisable to avoid the term, though in some circumstances such avoidance may be impossible. At least to recognize such Muslim misgivings regarding the term and to explain the term accordingly are imperatives. Perhaps also to speak of Jesus as the Word of God may serve as a useful transition in explaining the meaning of Jesus' Sonship.

For though the term "the Word of God" for Jesus in the Injīl may not bear the significance to Muslims that it does to Christians, yet from the Qur'ān the Muslim knows Ḥazrat Masīḥ as His (Allāh's) Word[21] and he also knows the Word of Allāh as eternal and as the revelation of Allāh. A point of contact for communicating the meaning of the Injīl there *may* be. For does not Allāh in speaking his eternal Word "give birth" to his Word among humankind? And in this sense cannot this eternal Word which proceeds from Him to humankind be called His son? Allāh only says: Be and it is (36:81; 16:40). Through his Word, He creates and brings all things into being. Can we then begin to show the Muslim that the Word which was in the beginning, through whom all things were made, became flesh and dwelt among us as God's revelation of himself? Certainly such language can be understood by Muslims and can serve to remove offences. Perhaps it is then also useful to include a simple explanation of this Sonship in a glossary or as a separate tract enclosed in the Injīl we distribute to our Muslim friends.

Yet the Sonship of Jesus cannot be avoided indefinitely. Indeed would not such avoidance give reason to the Muslim assertion that Christians corrupt the Injīl? The term is inscribed too deeply and too frequently within the text itself. Nor can there be an adequate substitute for it. For it is Jesus as Son who knows the Father and who reveals Him to humankind that they may also inherit the blessed promise of God to be sons and daughters of the living God—as our Christology so our Theology (Matt. 11:25-27; John 14:1-11).

Conclusion: The Injīl and the Son of God

It is Jesus as the Son who is the Injīl: for the Injīl is no mere repetition, variation or relaxation of a previous law (Sharī'at). For the Injīl is the Gospel, god spell, good news, the Word of covenant and promise which according to the Injīl God gave before He gave the Sharī'at and which no Sharī'at can annul. Such a distinction is vital to the Injīl and to our understanding of Jesus as the Son of God. To confuse the Injīl with Sharī'at is to change the very character of the Injīl, to negate its purpose, to make it into something it is not, nor states itself to be.

So many years before, the prophet prayed to God: "O that thou would rend the heavens and come down" (Is. 64:1). In Jesus the Son we see the fulfilment of this hope, the mercy and compassion of God *fait accompli.* God's heavenly Word and promise of salvation precipitated into deed, mystery of his love revealed on earth. For in Jesus the Son, God is pleased to dwell with humankind in a way that humankind can understand that He alone is Sovereign, Most High. Such was the gracious will of God.

Endnotes

1 Qur'ānic references are taken from M.M. Pickthall, *The Meaning of the Glorious Koran* (New York: 1954), since the translator is a Muslim.

2 Though Al-Ghazālī insists that the doctrine of *Tawḥīd* (oneness) in primitive Islām is essentially a matter of the heart and a confession from the heart he states that for the people "this precious stone" is primarily an apologetic weapon against *Tathlīth* (the Trinity). Al-Ghazālī, *Ihya Ouloum ed-Din*, Analyse et Index par G. H. Bousquet, Paris 1955, 28, 29.

3 T.V. Arnold, *The Preaching of Islām* (Appendix 1) (London: n.p., 1935), 428-435—from which these observations and quotation derive.

4 J. Windrow Sweetman, *Islām and Christian Theology*, Part Two, Volume One (London: n.p., n.d.), 247 as taken from *Al-Fisal*, vol.2, 69.

5 Sweetman, *Islām and Christian Theology*, 291.

6 A. Jeffery "New Trends in Moslem Apologetic," in *The Moslem World Today*, edited by J.R. Mott (London: n.p., 1925), 313.

7 S. Saleemi, in an Urdu letter.

8 V. Abdul Subhan, in an Urdu letter.

9 Abul 'Ālā Maudūdī, in an Urdu Letter.

10 Ra%īm A%med Fārūqī, in an English Letter.

11 It is essential to show the Muslim that the Bible testifies to the worship of one God; cf. Ex. 20:3,4; Deut. 4:35; Ps. 96:5; Is. 43:10, 11; 45:22; Matt. 4:10; Mk. 8:33; 12:29, 30; Lk. 10: 25-28; Acts 17: 16-31 etc., the witness of the Tuarāt of Mūsā, the Zabūr of Dāwūd, the writings of the prophets, and the Injīl of 'Isā. In the same way the Bible teaches the folly of idolatry; cf. Is. 41: 24; 44:9-20; Rom. 1:23; 1 Thess. 1:9; 1 Cor. 10: 6-14 etc. So God is incomparable: cf. Nu. 24:19; Ez. 28:2; Hos. 11:9; Is. 31:3, 40:12-31. Thus the Nicene Creed, a universal creed of *Christendom* "I believe in one God ..." and christendom's universal hymn of praise: "They only do we worship ... Thee alone do we acknowledge."

12 Certainly not the reasonable proof of mathematics, for god is not a mathematical formula. As ridiculous to disprove the Trinity by the formula 1+1+1=3 (or 1+1+1=1

as the Muslims infer that the Christians contend) as to prove the Trinity by the formula 1+1+1=1. Strange as it may sound to the Muslim ear, the fact remains that from one aspect, Trinitarian theology formulated itself as it did in the early Church in order to maintain the Unity of God. It serves as a fuller expression of the Being of the One God as He has revealed Himself to humankind as testified to in the Injīl.

[13] The Muslim can speak of Allāh as the "Union of Attributes" (*Majmū ʿ al bifāt*) an indication that perfect unity is not exclusive of plurality for the Muslim.

[14] Considered rightly, a healthy reminder to all is the old Muslim saying: "Deputation about the nature of God is blasphemy."

[15] Though the idea that human was created in the image of God may not be common idea among Muslims, it is not foreign to their thought. On the Biblical idea that there is nothing like unto God (cf. footnote 11).

[16] The study of the use of "father" in the Old Testament in reference to God is an illuminating one.

[17] For this and some other examples, cf. W. Montgomery Watt, *Mu%ammad at Mecca* (Oxford: n.p., 1953), 106.

[18] Translated by Pickthall as "the source of Ordinance."

[19] "Conforming that which is in You," *The Bulletin of the Henry Martyn Institute of Islāmic Studies* (January 1961). Note especially Qur'ān 2:113, 121; 5:41-49; 4:44-47; 10:95; 6:15, all of which indicates the Scriptures are with Christians and Jews.

[20] For example, L.E. Browne, *The Quickening Word* (Cambridge: n.p., 1955), 67.

[21] Grammatically in Arabic, His Word equals *the* word of Allāh, not a word.

Dangerous Business[1]

Ian H. Douglas

There can be no hiding the fact that the call to sympathetic involvement in the thought life of Buddhism, or Islām, or any other faith is, from the Christian point of view, a call to danger. To say this, is not to argue against such involvement. It is merely to draw attention to what, in any case, loyalty to Jesus Christ means in this world. The old hymn puts it graphically,

> Must I be carried to the skies?
> On flowery beds to ease,
> Whilst others fight to win the prize
> Or sail through bloody seas?

Unfortunately all such militarist metaphors, though perfectly biblical, and very appropriate when correctly understood, encourage the equation of the Christian Church with the side of the right, and non-Christian people with the enemy, or the side of wrong. In fact it is not as simple as that. The great enemy, unquestionably at work within non-Christian systems, is also very much at work within the Christian Church—indeed within me as a Christian individual and would-be evangelist. By this call to danger, then, we do not mean a rallying cry to sally forth against the ranks of the enemy in public debates, condemnatory open-air preaching, or mass distribution of undisguised hostile Christian propaganda. If such activities were still permissible in Asian countries they would indeed represent danger and we must give all due honour to the heroes of the faith who displayed such courage in this type of activity in the past. What must be made clear is that the sympathetic involvement called for today is just as fraught with danger, in fact danger of a far more subtle and spiritual kind. It is in fact a danger so great that those weak in the faith will be well advised to stay clear of it. To state the situation positively, the Christian who would, in loyalty to Jesus Christ, seek such involvement in another faith must be assured in his/her own personal experience of the saving power of God in Jesus Christ. One must be daily growing in grace through the Scriptures, prayer and the life of the Church.

Preoccupation with Accessions

Let us then face honestly some of these specific dangers. Firstly there is the danger of an excessive concern for individual conversions. This is a very difficult subject to talk about because the presentation of the Gospel emphatically does involve the call to personal response. There is no hiding this. "Make disciples" is written into the terms of the Great Commission. Everybody knows that Christianity is a missionary religion. Let us not forget the paradox, which is involved here. While the Christians have the responsibility to present the claims of Jesus Christ they must remember that ultimately conversion is a divine activity. They can therefore honestly and correctly disclaim the purpose of "making converts" since this is ultimately God's business. We spoke then of the danger of excessive concern with individual conversions. There are certainly cases where individual Muslim conversions have served to cut off the possibility of further Christian influence on the community from which they came. Now, of course, we cannot ultimately deny baptism to the person who seeks it, the life-giving evidence of the work of the Holy Spirit. We should recognize the delicacy of this situation and be careful of the danger of excessive preoccupation with statistics. Dr. Kenneth Cragg has very well made this point in a chapter in *The Call of the Minaret*. But his "Call to Patience" has not been sufficiently heeded. We need to be much more concerned with the faithfulness of our presentation of the message of the Gospel, striving for adequate translation and praying that it be understood. We can then afford to leave the question of conversions to God, knowing that He may wait a generation or even a century or more, before there is the widespread response that we might like to see now.

Subversion of Christians

Secondly there is a completely opposite danger of the other faith exerting such influence that the Christian is converted to it! There certainly are cases on record of such conversions of former missionaries. The Christian may well wish to question the nature of the presumed Christian experience in the first place, in such cases. But if there is to be a genuine openness to other faiths, this possibility of conversion must be granted. I would not be a convinced Christian if I believe that such conversion would actually have happened to one whose Christian experience was genuine. Neither, presumably, would the convinced Buddhist—as I know to be true of the convinced Muslim—believe true conversion to be possible out of a genuine experience of that faith. If there is to be a complete exposure of one faith to the other, and a free exchange of ideas, both sides must concede to this possibility, at least in theory. And there is certainly the danger of influence, short of actual conversion, which would be contrary to the Christian faith. The point is that such openness to the attraction of the other faith is a fact, an invaluable qualification for the evangelist. It has even been said that no Christian can be an effective evangelist to the convinced Buddhist or Muslim or adherent of another faith, without experiencing something of the pull of that faith on one's own soul. It is no use for the Christian to say, "I cannot see what anyone can find in that religion." If one has not hitherto understood what anyone can experience in that religion it is his/her business to find out! In fact many people do see much in their religion to satisfy. The saintly Henry Martyn, pioneer Protestant missionary to Muslims, recorded in his diary on one occasion.

> I have been ... occasionally troubled with infidel thoughts which originated perhaps from the cavilling of the Muslims ... but these never have been suffered to be more than momentary.

I would like to suggest that, rather than regretting this experience of all failure in faith, he might well have rejoiced in it as preparing him better to get close to the Muslims.

False Pride

The third danger is of an inadequate exposure to the non-Christian faith, which results in a false superiority on the part of the Christianity. Too often I hear Christians say things about Islām which I know is just not fair to Islām. This is the old trick of comparing the best of empirical Christianity with the worst in the expressions of the other religions! How anxious Christians are to score debating points off their opponents. If we are secure in our own faith we have no need to fear acknowledgement of what is worthy in others. Of course it is perfectly right and proper that the Christians should gain a new appreciation for their own faith by contrast with what one had studied of the other faith. This must never be at the cost of unfairness. Any evidence which the Christian gives of not having properly understood the other person's belief will only hinder one's witness.

Concern for Self

A fourth danger is one to which Christians are particularly prone when they represent a minority in a state experiencing a resurgence of national sentiment expressed in the area of religion. This is the danger of making the object of our study of Buddhism simply that we, as Christians, should be well thought of by the majority community. This certainly happens to the Christian community in Muslim lands. The idea appears to be to persuade the Muslim that the Christian is worthy of respect as a fellow citizen. Ultimately this means that the encounter is made to serve the interests of Christian self-esteem, or at least of Christian self-preservation.

Academic Detachment

But the last danger is perhaps the subtlest of all. The Christian who gets into the business of encounter with another faith, out of Christ like concern for those who profess it, may find himself more and more enthralled by the merely academic study. The lifetime study of many western orientalists, who are only nominally Christian or Jews or perhaps profess no faith at all, is proof enough of the attraction of such an academic pursuit. Not, of course, that it is wrong for the Christian to enjoy his/her study of Buddhism! The danger lies in allowing such pleasure to submerge the primary motivation of love for people for Christ's sake. This appropriately brings us back to the point with which we started. The presentation of the Christian Gospel does involve an invitation to personal response. The first danger was of excessive pre-occupation with conversion, whereas the right interest in conversion is that which arises out of genuine Christ-like love for the other person. An impersonal interest in a system is no substitute for this.

This danger is amusingly, but pointedly, illustrated by the story told in America of the Catholic girl who found herself becoming friendly with a Jewish boy. The boy found his interest growing likewise and because of his love for the girl decided to study her religion. Knowing that there could be no question of her parents' agreement to marriage unless the boy became Catholic. The girl naturally took great interest in the evidence of her boyfriend's increased interest in the Catholic faith. His continued weekly sessions of instruction with the priest, when the last session of the course came, in which the girl and her family knew the priest would make a definite invitation to the inquirer. Hopes ran high. When the Catholic girl returned home after seeing the boy, following that final session, she was obviously crest-fallen. Anxiously the parents asked, "What's the matter? Did he not decide to become a Catholic after all?" Back came the pathetic answer "Oh yes he decided to become a Catholic all right. In fact he was so enamoured with Catholicism this he announced his decision to enter the priesthood and remain celibate!" His interest in the system had become so great that the original interest for the person was forgotten!

These then, are some of the dangers, of which we should be aware when we talk about entering into appreciation of another faith. Unless there were Christians prepared to expose themselves to these dangers, the sad comment will again be appropriate, "they all forsook Him and fled," and the love of Christ will not be made known to men and women in our society. Let us then, counting the cost, go forth into the danger area in full assurance that He is with us always, ever to the end.

Endnotes

1 Talk given to a week-long Institute of Buddhist Studies in St. Luke's Anglican Church, Colombo, Ceylon, October 17, 1964.

Thoughts from the Early Church Fathers for the Christian Approach to the Muslims

Henry J. Otten

Introduction

The world of Islām constitutes the largest neglected field of today. Although the followers of Muḥammad, the founder of Islām, number approximately one-seventh of the world's population, they have been the objects of only one-fiftieth of the mission efforts of all combined. Churches and mission societies have often bypassed Islāmic community on their way to other lands. The Roman Catholic Church has a definite policy of refraining from all-out mission efforts for Muslims at this time in world history (Pre-Vatican II).

The reasons for this paucity of effort lie primarily in the difficulty of the task. Islām has been peculiarly resistant to the claims of the Gospel. Christ's witnesses in Muslim-lands find that the most precious facts of the Christian faith are challenged not only by the educated priests of Islām, but also by farmers and women at the stove. The reliability of the Christian Scriptures, the historicity of the Crucifixion and Resurrection of Christ, and the event of Incarnation are denied and disputed. These denials are complicated by misunderstandings and misrepresentations of the Christian position.

This negative reaction of the Muslims has often caused discouragement to missionaries and churches. They tend to look for greener pastures or to think that the Muslims have hardened their heart to the Gospel and are such as those from whom Jesus advised His disciples to "shake the dust from their feet."

A closer study, however, will indicate that such thoughts are oversimplifications. Before the Christian dismisses the Muslims as being outside the pale of mission concern, one has the responsibility to ask themselves if they personally or the Church in its empirical aspects may not be serving as dams rather than as sluices to the Water of Life. It is my personal conviction that most Muslim opposition to the message of the Gospel can be traced to failures of either Christian life or doctrine. There is no scope in this paper to consider the failure of Christian life which contributes to the problem, but it should suffice to say that the Crusades did not represent the methods of the Master. And if one considers that average Muslim does not distinguish between Western government and Western religion, it can be safely seen that the Crusades, in some sense, are still being carried today.

But let us go on to the other stumbling-block, namely Christian doctrine. If the Muslims were rejecting the Christian faith in its truth, we might feel justified, thinking that they have had their chance and go our way. But closer investigation reveals that this is not usually the case. The Muslim rejects their understanding of the Christian doctrine, not the doctrine itself. For example, a certain missionary wished to proclaim the Gospel to Muslims in the Near East even before he had learned Arabic language. So he memorized John 3: 16 in the language and recited it in the bazaar. Aside from the suitability of such a method, the missionary did realize that his audience was not prepared to digest the meaning of that verse. He was thinking about God's eternal life; they were hearing the phrase "Only Begotten Son." In their minds such phrases degrade God to the level of the old Greek and Roman gods, who married and produced children. Since they understand the phrase in a physical way, they rejected the message in honour for the character of God. Similarly, a school bus in Egypt was the cause of offense because it painted the name of the school: "The School of the Mother of God." A Muslim who saw this bus daily said, "Every time I see that bus, it makes my blood boil. Did God have some billowy bosomed Jewess for wife and produce a son?" From these two examples it will be seen that glib phrases falling from the mouths of unthinking Christians may be the cause of much needless offense on the part of Muslims. Radio broadcasters to Muslim lands would do well to keep these factors in mind also. It is better not to use such phrases unless there is an opportunity to explain the meaning.

Muslims are very jealous of the majesty of God. Indeed, it may be said that their vivid conception of the majesty of God is the most determining single concept of their religion. It was the awareness of this concept which separated Muḥammad from the other religionists of Arabia at his time and inspired him and his followers to disseminate their faith to large portions of the globe. It is in the blinding light of God's majesty that they accept their own position and judge that of others, including Christians. One of the most loved verses in the Qur'ān is called the Throne Verse:

> God—there is no god but He, the Living, the Everlasting.
> Slumber seizes Him not, neither sleep; to him belong all that is in the heavens and the earth.
> Who is there that shall intercede with Him save by His leave?
> He knows what lies before them and what is after them,
> and they comprehend not anything of His knowledge Save such as He wills.
> His throne comprises the heavens and earth;
> the preserving of them oppresses Him not;
> He is the All-high, the All-glorious (2: 255).

From the foregoing discussion and the verse just quoted it will be seen that the Muslims cannot be approached as if they were a crass idolater or animist. In fact, it may be necessary to show the Muslims that the Christian is not an idolater. The witness to Muslims, therefore, demands theology proper—that is the doctrine of God. For such orientation the early Church Fathers are refreshing sources of aid. Dialogue with Gnostics, heathen philosophers and critics, Jews, Arians, and Pelagians forced the Early Fathers to plumb depths of theology, which anticipated many of the questions raised later by Muslims. A Christian in dialogue with Muslims can well profit by the experiences of the Fathers.

The Unity of God

It has been mentioned that Muslims may regard Christians as idolaters. The opinion rests upon a misunderstanding of the doctrine of the Trinity. The misunderstanding can be felt by listening to two verses from the Qur'ān:

> Infidels are those who say that God is the third of three. There is no God but one God, and if they refrain not from what they say, a severe punishment will befall the unbelievers among them.
>
> O' Isa (Jesus), son of Maryam, hast thou said to mankind, 'Take me and my mother as two Gods beside God?'
>
> He said, 'Glory be unto thee. It is not to me to say what I know is not the truth' (5:116).

The worst sin for a Muslim is the sin of *shirk*, associating partners with God. From the two verses just quoted, it can be seen that Muḥammad considered Christians guilty of the sin of *shirk*. He had the idea that Christians worship three Gods—Father, Mother, and Son. One could wish that some of the Christian controversy-lovers could see some of the fruit of their discussions and aberrations. Be that as it may, the Christian certainly has a responsibility to expose this misunderstanding and to show the Muslim that the Christian faith is firmly rooted in the doctrine of the Unity of God. Such a witness will help remove some of the stigma, which the Christian faith has for the Muslim, and put the witness in a position where the Muslim is willing to listen to me. A very useful portion of thought in this connection is Cyril of Jerusalem's section on the Unity of God in *Catechetical Lectures*.

> Now though the mind is most rapid in its thoughts, yet the tongue needs words, and a long recital of intermediary speech. For the eye embraces at once a multitude of the starry quire, but when anyone wishes to describe them one by one which is the Morning-Star, and which, the Evening-Star, and which each one of them, he has need of many words. In like manner again the mind in the briefest moment compasses earth and sea and all the bounds of the universe; but what it conceives in an instant, it uses

> many words to describe. Yet forcible as is the example I have mentioned, still it is after all weak and inadequate. For of God we speak not all we ought (for that is known to Him only), but so much as the capacity of human nature has received, and so much as our weakness can bear. (6: 2).
>
> A great and honourable man was Abraham, but only great in comparison with men, and when he came before God, then speaking the truth candidly he said, 'I am earth and ashes'... and when in thought thou hast surveyed all the heavens, not yet will even the heavens be able to praise God as He is, nay, not if they should resound with a voice louder than thunder. But if these great vaults of the heavens cannot worthily sing God's praise, when shall 'earth and ashes,' the smallest and least of things existing, be able to send up a worthy hymn of praise to God, or worthily to speak of God, 'that sitteth upon the circle of the earth, and beholdeth the inhabitants thereof as grasshoppers.' (6: 3)
>
> God then being thus great, and yet greater, (for even were I to change my whole substance into tongue, I could not speak His excellence: nay more not even if all Angels should assemble, could they ever speak His worth), God being therefore so great in goodness and majesty, man hath yet dared to say to a stone that he hath graven, 'Thou art my God!' O monstrous blindness, that from majesty so great came down so low! The tree which was planted by God, and nourished by the rain, and afterwards burnt and turned into ashes by the fire,-this is addressed as God, and the true God is despised. But the wickedness of idolatry grew yet more prodigal, and cat, and dog, and world were worshipped instead of God: the man-eating lion also was worshipped instead of God, the most loving friends of man (6:10).

These verses portray some of the majesty and Unity of God in which Muḥammad and Muslims are interested. A beginning can be made in building the bridge over the wide chasm, which separates Islām and Christianity, a thought well expressed by Erich Bethmann in his book, *Bridge to Islām.*

> In building a bridge over a deep gorge or a wide swift-flowing river, the engineers have to do a vast amount of planning before the first digging can be done. They have to survey the terrain with the greatest care in order to be able to select the most suitable spot where the future structure is to be erected. They have to plumb the depth of river, measure the swiftness and volume of the current, and observe the high and low watermarks before they decide what kind of bridge they are going to build. They have to make most exact calculations in order to choose the kind of material

> best suited to the amount of stress and strain, which the structure must bear. Only after having laid these plans most carefully and after having estimated the costs closely is work begun on the great enterprise.[1]

Many Muslims have the idea that Muḥammad was the first man who preached the doctrine of the Unity of God. Although the Qur'ān itself bears witness otherwise, many Muslims have no knowledge of history and disregarded religious insights of former generations. The Christians cannot, of course, introduce involved courses in history into their witness, but they can defend their faith when it is misunderstood. A Muslim friend should not be allowed to continue in the belief that Christians worship three Gods. The Early Fathers are witness that Christians have believed in one God from the beginning.

The Incarnation

Muslims are liable to have more difficulty with the doctrine of the Incarnation than of the Trinity. They know that Christians refer to Jesus as the Son of God. Their conception is based on the idea that Christians have exalted a man to the station of God rather than God becoming man. This thought is expressed in the Qur'ān:

> People of the Book (Christians), go not beyond the bounds in your religion, and say not as to God but the truth. The Messiah, Jesus son of Mary, was only the Messenger of God, and His Word that He committed to Mary, and a Spirit from Him. So believe in God and His Messengers, and say not 'Three.' Refrain; better is it for you. God is only One God. Glory be to Him—that He should have a son! To him belongs all that is in the heavens and in the earth; God suffices for a guardian. The Messiah will not disdain to be a servant of God, neither the angels who are near stationed to Him (4: 171-172). It is not for God to take a son unto Him. Glory be to Him. When He decrees a thing, He but says to it "Be," and it is. (1: 9, 36)

In these verses Muḥammad refers to Jesus as the Messiah, son of Mary, Messenger of God, His Word, and a spirit from Him. His Sonship is rejected as detracting from the Unity of God and as being unworthy of God's majesty. It will do no good for the Christian to assert the Sonship and to have the Muslim deny it *ad infinitum.* Rather the Christians will do well to define their meaning of Sonship and to show how the

Incarnation, far from detracting from the majesty of God, adds to it new depth and richness. The Early Fathers are especially helpful in this regard because some of the Gnostic critics raised the very same objections repeated by Muslims today.

First of all, the Christian should make clear that the term "son" in no way implies physical sexual relationship when used in the phrase "Son of God." Example of the metaphoric use of "son" is even found in the Qur'ān, as when a traveler is called a "son of the road." Biblical sources include phrases such as "son of valour," "sons of thunder," etc. Marriage and reproduction is not involved in these examples. The word, "son" used in the metaphoric sense conveys the ideal similarity in character, not in physical form.

> And whenever thou hear of God begetting, sink not down in thought to bodily things, nor think of a corruptible generation, lest thou be guilty of impiety.[2] The divine generation must not be compared to the nature of men, nor the Son considered to be a part of God. [...] Scripture speaks of 'Son' in order to herald the natural and true offspring of His essence; and on the other hand, that none may think of the Offspring humanly, while signifying His essence, it also calls Him Word, Wisdom, and Radiance; to teach us that the generation was impassible, and eternal, and worthy of God.[3]

The latter statement of Athanasius is especially helpful in work among Muslims. It is possible to preach the Gospel without using the phrase Son of God. It is a phrase, which expresses a truth about God and His relation to Jesus, but there are other expressions, which can also be used. At any rate, the Early Fathers concur in the idea that physical connotation is to be avoided and was never intended. Muslims will welcome this thought.

Secondly, it is the task of the Christian witness to show the Muslim that the idea of the Incarnation does not threaten the majesty of God, but rather magnifies it. The feeling of the Muslims on this point can be appreciated by listening to a modern Muslim apologist, Muḥammad Zafrullāh Khān, in his book *Islām: Its Meaning for Modern Man*

> The central pivot around which the whole doctrine and teaching of Islām revolves is the Unity of the Godhead....
>
> The Qur'ān is insistent upon the Unity of God and emphatically condemns any doctrine, idea, or concept which might directly or indirectly tend to associate any other thing or being with God as a partner or equal. "Say; 'He is Allāh, the One; Allāh the Independent, and Besought of all. He begets not, nor is He begotten; and there is none like unto Him.'"[4]
>
> The Qur'ān not only excludes all idea of any equal or partner with Allāh, it specifically excludes all idea of His having a son except in the purely metaphorical sense in which all mankind are His children, and in which the peacemakers are spoken of in the Bible, as "the children of God" (Matt 5.9). God is Ever-Living-All-Knowing, All-Hearing, and the Creator of all whose authority extends over every- thing. To attribute a son, in any but the purely metaphorical sense, to God, would amount to a denial of His unity and in effect to a denial of His Godhead. "Verily, Allāh is only one God. Far is it from His attributes of Holiness and Perfection that He should have a son.... Sufficient is Allāh as a Creator."[5]

In this connection it should perhaps be mentioned that the Muslim concept of the Holiness of God differs from the Biblical concept. The Muslims define God's holiness as His separateness from creation. The idea of moral perfection of separateness from evil is not emphasized. Thus Khān's statements indicate that God's coming to earth in human form would militate against His unity and majesty.

It is interesting to note that the Early Fathers viewed God from other aspects than bare majesty. In this they were merely reflecting the Biblical revelation in its menness. Not only God's majesty was at stake in human's fall into sin and the subsequent destruction of creature and creation caused by sin, but also His goodness. Athanasius therefore does not only speak from the view-points of God's majesty, but also His goodness.

The truthfulness or faithfulness of God to His Word is also a vital factor in the theology of the Fathers. God does not go back on His Word. This thought is not always evident in the Muslim faith. The Qur'ān itself contains verses, which were later abrogated by new verses. God is not limited by any moral standard according to the Muslim conception. He does what He pleases, and what ever He pleases becomes right.

His will is the dominant feature of His actions. His many attributes are not bound together by the thread of morality. The Christian can rightly ask: Which king is more majestic, the one who sits exalted and alone on His throne, or the one who mingles with His people for the sake of helping them?

In the Muslim conception God exhibits no personal concern for the lost. Indeed, He may well be the cause for their predicament. For in at least three places the Qur'ān says, "He leadeth astray whom He will, and guideth aright whom He wills." (13: 27; 16: 93; 74: 31). Muslim therefore has no real conviction about God's interest in His salvation. He has only a wistful hope that things might turn out all right. "Each one can but hope that Allāh will guide him aright, submit himself to Allāh in absolute fear, and trust that Allāh will not cause him to forget and be of the losers in the Fire."[6]

In contrast to this rather passive and unconcern attitude toward human's sin-dilemma we hear the fervent thoughts of Athanasius:

> The human race was in process of destruction. The thing what was happening was in truth both monstrous and unfitting. It would, of course, have been unthinkable that God should go back upon His Word and that man having transgressed, should not die; but it was equally monstrous that the being which once had shared the nature of the Word should perish and turn back again into non-existence, through corruption. It was unworthy of the goodness of God that creatures made by Him should be brought to nothing through the deceit wrought upon man by the devil; and it was supremely unfitting that the work of God in mankind should disappear... As, then, the creatures whom He had created reasonable, like the Word, were in fact perishing, and such noble works were on the road to ruin, what then was God being Good, to do? ...Surely it would have been better never to have been created at all than, having been created, to be neglected and perish; and, besides that, such indifference to the ruin of His own work before His very eyes would argue not goodness in God but limitation.... It was impossible, therefore, that God should leave man to be carried off by corruption, because it would be unfitting and unworthy of Himself.[7]

It was unthinkable that God, the Father of Truth should go back upon His Word regarding death in order to ensure our continued existence. He could not falsify self.

It is difficult for the Muslim to feel this tension within the character of God. The Muslim recognizes the reality of sin, but it is not a matter requiring drastic action. One gets over the problem by doing damage to the character of God. In some cases one resort to a fatalism which comforts in the idea that God is somehow responsible for his/her sin. In other cases they rely upon a type of cheap grace, which rests on a Qur'ānic passage in which it is said that it is easy for God to forgive. Thus we see the majesty of God actually being soiled by evil. The Fathers do not fall into this danger. Rather, by upholding the character of God in all its goodness and faithfulness they exalt His majesty far above the exaltation found in creation. God is exalted not only through creation, as Muslims also affirm, but He is exalted also in redemption.

This redemption was achieved through the Incarnation. At this juncture the Muslim is likely to say together with the Greek critics of Athanasius, "If God wanted, instruct and save mankind, He might have done so, not by His Word's assumption of a body, but, even as He at first created them, by the mere signification of His will." The Muslim feels that God could have solved the problem with a decree, because He only needs to say: "Be," "and it is". But Athanasius is ready for help at this time also. He points out that fiats and decrees do not change character. A mere pronouncement of absolution would not remove the corruption, which was under the surface.

> If God had but spoken, because it was in His power, and so the curse been undone, the power had been shown of Him who gave the Word, but man had become such as Adam was before the transgression, having received grace from without, and not having it united to the body; nay, perhaps has become worse, because he had learned the transgress .... Had he been seduced by the serpent there had been fresh need for God to give command and undo the curse; and thus the need had become interminable, and men had remained under guilt not less than before, as being enslaved

> to sin; and ever sinning, would have ever needed one to pardon them, and had never become free.[8]

Irenaeus treats this question from a different viewpoint. He feels that salvation by decree would violence both the character of God and the personality of humankind.

> And since the apostasy tyrannized over us unjustly, and though we were by nature the Prophet Mohammad of the omnipotent God, alienated, us contrary to nature, rendering us its own disciples, the Word of God, powerful in all things, and not defective with regard to His own: justice, did righteously turn against that apostasy, and redeem from it His property, not by violent means, as the apostasy had obtained dominion over us at the beginning when it insatiably snatched away what was not its own, but by means of persuasion, as became a God of counsel, who does not use violent means to obtain what He desires; so that neither should r justice be infringed upon, nor the ancient handy-work of God go to destruction.[9]

The God of counsel, who seeks to win by persuasion, who foregoes the use of violence, is a God worthy of honour on the part of all. Far from detracting from the majesty of God, both Athanasius and Irenaeus have magnified it by giving it great depth and deeper concern.

But still there are objections. The body of human is not a fit vehicle for the revelation of God, say the critics. It is also too limiting to the activity of God. The Fathers treat both of these difficulties.

First of all, there are those who regard God's entrance into a body as degrading. Athanasius meets this doubt with confidence when he writes:

> Nor was He defiled by being in the body. Rather, he sanctified the body by being in it. Just as the sun is not defiled by the contact of its rays with earthly objects, but rather enlightens and purifies them, so He who made the sun is not defiled by being made known in a body, but rather the body is cleansed and quickened by His indwelling, 'Who did not sin, neither was guile found in His mouth.'[10]

This view presents the picture of a God of action, one in which the Muslims themselves show interest. They often portray Christ as being too passive to deal with the problems of today's world. Muḥammad, they say, took much more interest in the affairs of humankind and participated directly. For that reason they regard his message as more meaningful to today's world than Christ's. Athanasius in the foregoing verse presents not only a, prophet in action, but God in action—a God who is not afraid to tarnish His dignity by mixing in the affairs human's pain, suffering, anguish, blood, and death. Rather than being pulled down to the level of humankind, He lifts them to the level of Himself.

For those with a philosophic inclination, Athanasius has other thoughts. Since Islām also had its brush with Greek philosophy, many Islāmic doctrines have been framed within the reference of philosophy. Thus, when a Christian can speak on the basis of philosophy and reason, he can expect a sympathetic response in at least some quarters of Islām. Muslims pride themselves in being rational and possessing a religion which appeals reason. To such as these Athanasius says the following:

> If the Word of God is in the universe (something admitted by Muslims), which is a body, and has entered into it in its every part, what is there surprising or unfitting in our saying that He has entered also into human nature? If it were unfitting for Him to have embodied Himself at all, then it would be unfitting for Him to have embodied Himself at all, then it would be unfitting for Him to have entered into the universe, and to be giving light and movement by His providence, to all things in it, because the universe, as we have seen itself a body. But if it is right and fitting for Him to enter into the universe and to reveal Himself through it, then, because humanity is part of' the universe along with the rest, it is no less fitting for Him to appear in a human body, and to enlighten and to work through that.[11]

> Does not the mind of man pervade his entire being, and yet find expression through one part only, namely, the tongue? Does anybody say on that account that Mind has degraded itself?[12]

Athanasius can deal with philosophers, but he goes beyond them. He is not interested in mere dialectics; brings the question down to the level of the needs of man; he leaves the ivory tower and shows how the Incarnation is vital for both the character of God and the predicament of human.

> Some then may ask, why did He not manifest Himself by means of other and nobler parts of creation, and use some nobler instrument, such as sun, or moon or stars or fire or air, instead of mere man? The answer is this. The Lord did not come to make a display. He came to heal and to

> teach suffering men. For one who wanted to make a display the thing would have been just to appear and dazzle the beholders. But for Him who came to heal and to teach the way was not merely to dwell here, but to put Himself at the disposal of those who needed him, and to be manifested according as they could bear it, not vitiating the value of the Divine appearing by exceeding their capacity to receive it.[13]

Irenaeus expressed a similar thought:

> Our Lord, in these last times, when He had summed up all things into Himself, came to us, not as He might have come, but as we were capable of beholding Him. He might easily have come to us in His immortal glory, but in that case we could never have endured the greatness of the glory; and therefore it was that He, who was the perfect bread of the Father, offered Himself to us as milk because we were as infants.[14]

Muslims tend to regard the concept of Incarnation as degrading to the majesty of God. They also raise another objection. "If God became man," they say, "how could the world continue to exist while the Creator and Sustainer was localized to one body and one place?" It will be seen that they are again thinking of God in physical concepts. The body becomes more real to them than the character in the body. But love does not become less because it gives of itself. Mercy does not shrink when it is exercised. Truth does not diminish with the speaking of a true word. Athanasius anticipated this difficulty of the Muslims and had an answer:

> He became visible through His works and revealed Himself as the Word of the Father, the Ruler a King of the whole creation.
>
> There is a paradox in this last statement, which we must now examine. The Word was not hedged in by His body, nor did His presence in the body prevent His being present elsewhere as well. When He moved His body He did not cease to direct universe by His Mind and might. No. The marvelous truth is, that being the Word, so far from being Himself contained by anything, He actually contained all things Himself.... Existing in a human body, to which He Himself gives life, He is still Source of life to all the universe.... His body was not for Him a limitation, but an instrument, so that He was both in it and in all things, and outside all things, resting in the Father alone. At one and the same time – this is the wonder – as Man He was living a human life, and as Word He was sustaining the life of the universe, and as Son He was in constant union with the Father.[15]

The Crucifixion and Resurrection

One of the most frustrating discoveries to the Christian who wishes to speak the Word of the Gospel to Muslims is to find out that they deny the crucifixion of Christ, one of the cornerstones of Christian faith. Some Muslims deny that Jesus was crucified in any sense; others say that He was nailed to the cross, but did not die on the cross. At the last moment it is held that God rescued Christ from the cross by replacing Him with Judas. One of the more modern Muslim sects, the Aḥmadiyyas, advocates the swoon theory, holding that Jesus did not truly die on the cross, but only fainted. Later he is said to have revived and gone to preach to the Lost Ten Tribes in Kashmir, India, where he finally died and was buried. A tomb at Srinagar is pointed out as the tomb of Jesus. Orthodox Muslims, however, regard this theory as mere fancy; they believe that God took Jesus directly to heaven from where He will again come to this earth, help the whole world to become Muslims, and finally die and be buried next to Muḥammad in Arabia. The Qur'ān is plain in denying the death of Jesus on the cross:

> And for their (the enemies of Jesus) unbelief, and, their uttering against Maryam mighty calumny, and for their saying, 'We slew the Messiah, Jesus son of Mary, the Messenger of God'—yet they did not slay him, neither crucified him;
>
> Only a likeness of that was shown to them. Those who are at variance concerning him surely are in doubt regarding him; they have no knowledge of him, except the following of surmise; and they slew him not of a certainty—no indeed; God raised him up to Him; God is All-mighty, All-wise. (4: 156)

Since Muslims see no death for Christ on the cross, message of the Resurrection is also lost. They know no resurrection of Christ except the final one at the Last Day.

What can the Christians say? Should they enter upon the Battle of the Books, pitting the accuracy of the Bible against the accuracy of the Qur'ān? Such battles more then not end up in rancour and bitterness which deny the very Cross which the Christian wishes to present. Furthermore, the promise of the Spirit is closely connected with the Gospel, not with argument about historical accuracy. Before the Christian speaks in controversy, it is better for him to think. Why does the Muslim deny the death of Christ on the cross? The key can be discovered in the last line of the Qur'ānic reference mentioned above "God is All-mighty, All-wise." The Muslim again judges Christian history from the touchstone of God's majesty. If Jesus, the Messenger of God, died on the Cross, is it not a dishonour to God? Does it not mean that God's enemies had the last word? Does it not imply that God was not strong enough to vindicate Himself? Such thoughts are at the bottom of the Muslim objection to the death of Christ. When one, considers this tragic misunderstanding one wonders if Muḥammad ever heard the news of the Resurrection. Had Christians in Arabia lost the joy of Christian faith, which we find in Irenaeus and Athanasius? Were the hermits whom Muḥammad met in his travels perhaps obsessed so much with the passion of Christ that they failed to communicate His victory and power? If some of the pictures that decorate the homes of Eastern Orthodox Christians in India today are any indication, it is not difficult to understand why a virile Arab from the desert might react negatively against morbid and insipid concentration upon the physical sufferings of Christ. One could wish that some pictures had never been painted.

Which direction should witness take? Is it not in the same direction, which the witness takes when faced with denials of the Incarnation? Help the Muslim to see that the death on the cross does not diminish the majesty of God, but assuredly deepens and magnifies His glory. Kenneth Cragg in his, book *Call of the Minaret* has stated the problem well:

> The God of the Muslim cross—of a substituted sufferer and an abstracted Prophet—is the Deus ex *machina*, God of the old Latin phrase; a God who turns the tables, opens the trapdoor, and confounds His foes; a God who deals not in the sure, if slow, processes of a moral order where love wins by suffering, but in the arbitrary assertion of the inscrutable. Yet it must be remembered that the Muslim rewriting of the crucifixion story is in the interests of God's glory. God, it is held, cannot be honoured in the victory of a prophet's foes. He cannot be thought not to rescue His servant such a people as the Jews. So the question moves into the realm of what is most appropriately Divine, what is most truly consonant with the Divine glory. Indeed, we may say, what makes God God and glory

> glory? How is God characterized as God? So deep do the issues go which are raised by the Muslim attitude to the Cross.[16]

The Early Fathers met the issue of Christ's death with confident assurance. They pointed out clearly that the mission of Jesus aimed at nothing less than to destroy death itself. Surely this gives a much more glorious portrait of God than one would run away from it. Athanasius exuberantly declares:

> He, the life of all, our Lord and Saviour, did not arrange the manner of His own death lest He should seem to be afraid of some other kind. No. He accepted and bore upon the cross a death inflicted by others, and those others his special enemies, a death which to them was supremely terrible and by no means to be faced; and He did this in order that, by destroying even this death, He might Himself be believed to be the Life, and the power of death be recognized as finally annulled. A marvelous and mighty paradox has thus occurred, for the death, which they thought to inflict on Him as dishonour and disgrace has become the glorious monument to death's defeat.[17]

> The supreme object of His coming was to bring about the resurrection of the body. This was to be the monument to His victory over death, the assurance to all that He had Himself conquered corruption and that their own bodies also would eventually be incorrupt.[18]

> This action showed no limitation or weakness in the Word; for He both waited for death in order to make an end of it, and hastened to accomplish it as an offering on behalf of all.[19]

When 'Umar, the leader of Muḥammad's armies and one of his successors to the headship of the Muslim community, was upon his deathbed, he faced death with foreboding, fear, and trembling, not knowing if he would go to the Garden or to the Fire. Though fatalism has somewhat muffled the anguish that 'Umar experienced in the Muslims of today, they still have no certainty of salvation. It is a matter of the capricious will of God.

The attitude of Athanasius and his fellow believers stands in sharp contrast:

> A very strong proof of this destruction of death and its conquest by the cross is supplied by a present fact, namely this. All the disciples of Christ despise death... They take the offensive against it and, instead of

> fearing it, by the sign of the cross and by faith in Christ trample on it as on something dead.[20]

The intuition of Athanasius was to demonstrate the truth of the Christian faith by life, not by argument. In his *Incarnation of the Word* he does not devote long paragraphs to rationally prove the Resurrection of Christ. He immediately points to the lives of the Christians. Christians of today would do well to heed this method of witness. But ere it can be effective, it must be evident that Christian lives are demonstrations of the living Christ. By aggressive physical action against Muslims and by words that suggest the mentality of warfare rather than the Spirit of Christ Christians have often been truer witnesses to the God of Muḥammad than to the God revealed in Christ. The God of Islām is a winner in the worldly sense, but He wins by ignoring His own moral standards. The Cross with its implications of suffering wrong even unto death, and its trust in the ultimate vindication of God, contrary to all human machinations, illumines the heart of God. He would rather suffer wrong than to do wrong. Here we see a majesty, which draws men to willing service rather than to servile fear, a majesty that creates the voluntary pursuit of that which is Good. Dr. Kenneth Cragg has captured the spirit of the Cross when he writes:

> The final and inclusive encounter Jesus faced, in full loyalty to His own doctrines, not rendering evil, nor countering hatred with guile. Out of it only the Cross could emerge, if Jesus was not to unleash violence, appeal to force, or make Himself a King....
>
> How did he behave confronted with the worst that men could do? In fidelity to the course He had freely chosen, He endured the Cross and suffered the contradiction of sinners against Himself with forgiveness on His lips and in His heart. And from that forgiveness forgiveness flows. Had Jesus died in resentment or in blasphemy, in imprecation or sullen silence, there would have been no redemption. Only by bearing, does the Redeemer bear away the sin of the world. The words from the Cross-words which never could have been uttered had Jesus allowed Himself to be mercifully stupefied by the gall and the reed—illuminate the inner nature of His passion and proclaim the Cross as a supreme deed of redemptive sacrifice. Truly 'with His stripes we are healed.' Here we find a quality of love, which makes an end of evil because it freely takes all

> its consequences upon itself. In revenge and hatred evil is perpetuated. In pardon and long-suffering it finds its term.[21]

Many of the Fathers and early believers were so filled with the Spirit of Christ that they were enabled to suffer for their faith with the same disregard for purely human values, which they found in the Saviour. Perhaps the adamancy of Islām exists to call the Christians of today to such deeper explorations of their faith. Muslims must see the reality of the Cross and the Resurrection in Christ's followers if they would also become His disciples. "The question, 'How does Christ save?' must be answered out of the experience that He does."[22]

The Question of the Scriptures

It will have been seen from the foregoing that there are definite contradictions between the Qur'ān and the Bible. Muḥammad accused the Jews of tampering with the text of their Scriptures; the followers of Muḥammad accuse Christians of the same activity. Although the Torah and Gospel are regarded as the Word of God in the Qur'ān any appeal to these books is met with the statement that the Scriptures in the hands of Jews and Christians today are corrupted and unworthy of belief. A Muslim accept no proof which is based on the Bible as an authority. They believe that anything which was of value in the original Torah and Gospel has been incorporated into the Qur'ān, and that there is therefore no need for them to investigate the older revelations, especially because the text of the present versions is said to have been altered. Fortunately, many Muslims have enough curiosity to want to read the Scriptures of the Jews and Christians and often alter their viewpoint. A Muslim priest has been known to confess, "Any Muslim read [*sic*] the Gospel of Luke can never erase it [*sic*] mind."

Yet, it is still generally true that the Christian witness cannot rely upon the Bible as an authority for Muslims. This dilemma has caused some Christians to elaborate proofs for the inspiration of the present text and also to call attention to deficiencies in the Qur'ān. Though there is a place for such studies, they do not belong at the initial stages of witness to a Muslim. They often create antagonisms, which are never resolved. The Early Fathers suggest some advice, which is appropriate to the situation.

Irenaeus for instance, calls attention to the large accessions to the Christian faith from the Goths who had no Scriptures in their own language. They were won by the oral preached word of the Christians. They were won in the same way that individuals became Christians before the New Testament was written. God gives power to the proclamation of His message, even if it is not written. This fact of history mentioned by Irenaeus should comfort and encourage those who are face to face with the rejection of the Scriptures.

Another bit of counsel can be seen in the writings of Athanasius. For Athanasius the Word of God is not primarily the written Word but the Person of Christ. In long paragraphs he consistently refers to Christ as the Word of God; this emphasis of Athanasius is indeed Scriptural and is an emphasis to which we would do well to take heed. Though the Muslim may object to the phrase "Son of God," he will not object to the phrase "Word of God." Jesus is even called the Word of God in the Qur'ān. Though Muslims regard this Word as a created Word, like Arius, it is still an expression, which they will tolerate and through which many of God's truths can be made known. The Christian who attempts to equate Word with Book will find that Muslims usually equate Word with Book. Such an approach usually ends up as a battle between the authority of the Bible and the Qur'ān. Since it is historically easier to prove the word-for-word accuracy of the Qur'ān with the original message of Muḥammad than to prove the word-for-word accuracy of the Bible with the message of the original prophets and writers, the Christian who uses this approach is on shaky ground. The writer knows of no Muslim who has been convinced of the truth of the Bible by this method. But when the Christian places in the Living Word, the Christ, and unfolds the message and work of Christ before Muslims, they will find this Word to be an attractive force as it was to the Goths and many others. The truth of Jesus, "If I be lifted up, I will draw all men unto myself," is experience. The Letters of the Qur'ān are no match for the Living Word.

Finally, some advice of Tertullian on the use of Scripture is worthy of attention. Most Muslims have no acquaintance with the Christian Scriptures. But, there is one sect, mentioned previously, the Aḥmadiyyas, who use Scriptures to prove the truth of their contentions against Christianity and to advance their own claims. They tear isolated texts out of context and use the Bible as a proof-text in one moment, and attack the Bible as unreliable in the next moment. Their method is very similar to that used by some of the Gnostics and other heretics at the time of Tertullian. Tertullian's advice on this subject is sound:

> Now this heresy of yours does not receive certain Scriptures; and whichever of them it does receive, it perverts by means of additions and diminutions, for the accomplishment of its own purpose; and such as it does receive, it receives not in their entirety; but even when it does receive any up to a certain point as entire, it nevertheless perverts even these by contrivance of diverse interpretations. Truth is just as much opposed by an adulteration of their meaning as it is by a corruption of its text. Their vain presumptions must refuse to acknowledge the writings whereby they are refuted. They rely on those which they have falsely put together, and which they have selected, because of their ambiguity. Though most skilled in the Scriptures, you will make no progress when everything which you maintain denied on the other side, and whatever you deny is by them maintained. As for yourself, indeed, you will lose nothing but your breath, and gain nothing but vexation from their blasphemy.[23]
>
> A controversy over the Scriptures can, clearly produce no other effect than help to upset either the stomach or the brain.[24]

The fact is that a Christian cannot convince such people or the basis of Scripture. Though they use Scripture they use it in a different way; there is no common basis. Furthermore, such arguments are also confusing to those who are not so versed in their faith. Their faith is shaken when they see that their leader cannot conclusively answer the objections and observations of the Aḥmadiyyas. As Tertullian observes, the doubter or people of weak faith "will go away confirmed in his uncertainty by the discussion, not knowing which side to adjudge heretical."[25]

Problems Posed by the Grace of God

There are many similarities between Muslims and Pelagians. Like the Pelagians, the Muslims have a place for Christ in their system, but He is really not so vital. The corruption of humankind through the fall of Adam is denied and the capability of human to choose and to do, that which is right, is affirmed. Sin is not regarded as a rebellion against God stemming from something vitally awry in the nature of human, but as a "mistake," a transgression against the specific commands of the moment, a deed whose consequences can be wiped out by a later good act. Sins are isolated acts of disobedience, which have no relation to the inner rotten core of natural human. This shallow view of sin produces an indifference to the redemptive work of Christ when a Christian presents it to a Muslim. We have already seen that the Muslim thinks that a mere decree would have been sufficient, and is sufficient. When the grace of God is emphasized, a grace, which is prevenient to any work of "man", the Muslim is quick to charge the Christian with antinomianism and for advocating free sin because "grace abounds." Therefore the treatise of St. Augustine on *Grace and Free Will* is especially helpful when speaking to Muslims.

The Muslims not only have grave reservations about grace; they also have a great interest in the question of free will. The first doctrinal controversies in Islām arose because of the commands of God in the Qur'ān, which seemed to imply free will and the verses, which tend to make God the Sole Actor in all events. Orthodox Islām finally accepted a doctrine called *Kasb*, namely, that God creates all of human's, both good and evil, and that human being exercises responsibility to the extent that he/she appropriates these acts to themself. But even the power to appropriate is the work of God. Thus the Muslim actually has a form of double predestination, which even Calvinists never affirmed. There have been various rational and mystical reactions to this doctrine in Islām through the centuries, but by and large it is still the doctrine, which is taught in the schools and lived by the people. One could wish that every Muslim could read and grasp the thoughts found in Augustine's writings *On Nature and Grace*, *On the Grace* of *Christ*, and *on Original*

Sin, as well as *On Grace and Free-will.* Perhaps Augustine has summed up the problem of both Pelagians and Muslims when he states that they over-emphasized God the Creator:

> Beyond this, however, although he flatters himself that he (Pelagius) vindicates the cause of God by defending nature, he forgets that by predicating soundness of the said nature, he rejects the Physician's mercy. He, however, who created him, is also his saviour. We ought not, therefore, so to magnify the Creator as to be compelled to say, nay, rather as to be convicted of saying, that the Saviour is superfluous. Man's nature we may indeed honor with worthy praise, and attribute praise to the Creator's glory; but at the same time, while we show our gratitude to Him for having created us, let us not be ungrateful to Him for healing us.[26]

Although it is expecting too much for Muslims in their present state of mind to become acquainted with these works, it is to be recommended that all Christians who carry on a theological dialogue with Muslims fill themselves with some of Augustine's thoughts. In these works, they will find that Augustine steers a sharp course between the sovereignty of God and the responsibility of human. They will discover answers to questions posed by Muslims as well as insights for fruitful witness.

Conclusion

In the foregoing we have attempted to see how the Early Church Fathers can be of help in the Christian-Muslim dialogue. Actually, only the surface has been skimmed; but perhaps enough has been presented to show that "their works do follow them."

Endnotes

[1] Erich Bethmann, *Bridge* to *Islam* (Nashville: Southern Publishing Association, 1950), 238.

[2] Cyril of Jerusalem, *Catechetical Lectures: The Nicene and Post-Nicene Fathers*, Second Series, Vol. XI (Grand Rapids: Eerdmanns, n.d.), 7.

[3] *Athanasius Against the Arians* (VIII).

[4] Muḥammad Zafrullāh Khān, *Islam: Its Meaning for Modern Man* (New York & Evanston: Harper and Row Publishers, 1962), 91.

[5] Khan, *Islam: Its Meaning for Modern Man*, 93.

[6] H. A. R. Gibb and J. H. Kramers, *Shorter Encyclopedia of Islam* (New York: Cornell University Press, 1961), 35.

[7] Athanasius, *The Incarnation of the Word of God* (New York: The MacMillan Co., 1946), 31-32.

[8] Against *Arians*, II, 58-70.

[9] Irenaeus, *Against the Heresies: Ante-Nicene Fathers*, Book V, Ch. 1-3 (Buffalo: The Christian Literature Publishing Co., 1885).

[10] Athanasius, *The Incarnation of the Word of God*, 46.

[11] Athanasius, *The Incarnation of the Word of God*, 76.

[12] Athanasius, *The Incarnation of the Word of God*, 78.

[13] Athanasius, *The Incarnation of the Word of God*, 78.

[14] Irenaeus, *Against the Heresies: Ante-Nicene Fathers*, Book IV, Ch. 38:1 (Buffalo: The Christian Literature Publishing Co., 1885).

[15] Athanasius, *The Incarnation of the Word of God*, 44-45.

[16] Kenneth Cragg, *The Call of the Minaret* (New York: Oxford University Press, 1956), 297.

[17] Athanasius, *The Incarnation of the Word of God*, 54.

[18] Athanasius, *The Incarnation of the Word of God*, 52.

[19] Athanasius, *The Incarnation of the Word of God*, 52.

[20] Athanasius, *The Incarnation of the Word of God*, 57.

[21] Cragg, *The Call of the Minaret*, 298-299.

[22] Cragg, *The Call of the Minaret*, 298.

[23] Tertullian, *Prescription Against Heretics: Ante-Nicene Fathers*, Vol. III (Grand Rapids: Eerdmans, 1957), 251.

[24] Tertullian, *Prescription Against Heretics: Ante-Nicene Fathers*, Vol. III, 251.

[25] Tertullian, *Prescription Against Heretics: Ante-Nicene Fathers*, Vol. III, 251.

[26] Augustine, *On Nature and Grace*, Ch, 39, 134.

The Gospel and the Mission Task of the Church

Roland E. Miller

Here we seem to be on safe ground. If the gospel and the mission task of the church do not belong together, what does? The gospel reveals a God whose very nature is missionary, and it constitutes the people of God whose very *esse* is *missio*. The gospel's good news, absolutely good and absolutely news, creates the mission and determines its nature, extent, and urgency. The gospel and mission go hand in hand. What could be more obvious than this?

For some the implication of this truth is quite plain. There is really nothing to talk about, except possibly for some discussion on methods. Both the nature of the gospel and our proper response to it are simply stated, and all else is secondary. So the matter, for some, is closed. Let us now get on with the job!

There is no debate about the fact that we must get on with the job. Not everyone, however, will agree that there is really nothing further to discuss about the gospel and the mission task. On the contrary, the issue is raised in full force when we restate our concern as: "The relation of the gospel and the mission to contemporary humankind." Again and again events take place in the mission of the church that raises the most serious questions. An example is the monumental decision taken in India in 1950. B. Ambedker, one of the architects of Indian freedom and the leader of India's outcaste community, had lost faith in the capacity of Hinduism to reform itself. He and his followers turned to Christianity, examining it hopefully. Failing to discover there what to his satisfaction seemed to be an effective principle of human dignity and equality, Ambedkar turned to Buddhism. Declaring himself a Buddhist at the World Congress of Buddhism, he stated as his reason: "Buddha has made equality the fundament of his doctrine."[1] In the following decade the Buddhist population in India grew a remarkable 1,670 % (from 181,000 to 3,250,000), largely as the result of the movement from the outcaste community.[2] This rejection is something to talk about.

The Problem

The problem may be this, that the gospel seems unrelated to contemporary humankind, their hopes, problems, and dreams, so far as can be judged from his/her reactions. The many glorious exceptions only underline the general pattern of response. We live, if we are alive at all, in complex situations. We know that the gospel is disregarded in those situations, and we have experienced the feeling that this leaves with those who live by the gospel and for the gospel and who see the gospel as the hope of humankind. It is perilous to avoid this primary datum of the current mission context, for this is God's gospel and God's world. These two, meant for each other, in whose union is humankind's hope, stand apart in drastic measure in the world today.

Mission "is not a calculus of success, but an obligation in love."[3] If we are to consider realistically the relation of the gospel and the mission task of the church today, we must begin with the agreement to describe things as they are. "Hold tight, hold tight, we must insist that the world is what we have always taken it to be."[4] This sentiment is one kind of reaction to the challenge of the present. This reaction, fortunately, does not typically describe the church today. The church in mission is now able to assess and face this new situation because it is no longer bewitched by the mirage of "Christendom." While the "younger churches" were being established in Asia and Africa, the erosion and partial disintegration of the base churches were taking place under the impact of modern forces. The awareness that unbelief and the ignoring or rejections of the gospel are universal marks of contemporary humankind, that therefore all lands are mission lands, and that the frontiers of mission now include the boundaries of every Christian's personal environment, has struck with existential force.

The church in mission is therefore involved in a process that combines both external opposition, internal decay, and its rapidly increasing minority status. In 1907 the Christian population was 34.3% of the world's population; in 1963 it was 29.2%.[5] The figure may be reduced to 15% by C.E. 2000. The true gravity of the situation is underestimated by linking the retrogression primarily to the population explosion. The critical problem is "civilized human." In the areas of hope for the growth of the church, the inverse relationship between the attraction of the gospel and the relentless forces of modern life is clearly demonstrated.[6] The mission cannot depend on new "Christendoms."

In seeking the causes of the present situation we reckon with both the fearfulness of human pride and the power of demonic forces. But as far as the mission task of the church is concerned, either the gospel is not being proclaimed, or the proclaimed gospel is not being accepted. Without ignoring the former, we suggest that it is the latter that is the particular mark of our time. If this is so, we face a rigorous theological task. Theological work "stands on the field where the gospel meets the spirit of our time."[7] To learn why the world is ignoring or rejecting the gospel, the church must let the world speak about itself and the church must listen. This necessity thrusts the church into a living and profound encounter with the world.

We must pause here to look at two red flags that may have been dropped. The first alarm is the necessity to recognize the offense of the gospel. By its very nature the gospel is "a stumbling-block to Jews and folly to the Gentiles." Its burden is to be alien to the "carnal mind" and, therefore, its inevitable cross is scorn and rejection. This is the true constant in the history of the church's mission, which must always await the *kairos* of the Spirit. The second objection questions the epistemology involved in listening to the world. The world is precisely not the source to which we look for understanding about either the gospel or our mission task. The gospel is the changeless declaration of God's objectively saving action for humankind in Jesus Christ, who is the same yesterday, today, and forever, and it is witnessed to be a changeless Scripture.

The first contention, the offense of the gospel, is amply testified to in both Scripture and experience. What must be brought together with this is the actual history of the church in mission. It is normal experience in church life that similar situations in different hands produce differing results. Personality, character, zeal, sensitivity—all may be factors involved. Though we do not understand all the implications, we see from our daily experience in mission that God in a real sense has bound the gospel to its bearers. We may extend this thought to the corporate church in mission. The ignoring or rejection of the gospel does not always happen because of its inherent offense, but sometimes because the church itself is insensitive, irrelevant, unloving, or even offensive as it offers God's gospel to humankind. Therefore the church must listen not reluctantly but eagerly to the world, which as God's strange agent speaks to it about its bearing of the gospel.

When Ambedkar's Buddhists, Islām, communism, and the U.S. Supreme Court—each in their own way declare that caste and racism is wrong at a time when churches themselves are either amazingly sightless or powerless, to rectify anomalous situations even within their own circles, not to speak of rendering is not the offence of the gospel but the offense of the church that is involved. When for that very reason the world withdraws from Christ the church is involved in that rejection.

The second contention, the epistemological concern, suggests that the world informs us not only about its own nature and about the character of the church but also about the character of the gospel. This is not a sudden and inadmissible departure from the givenness of the gospel as it comes to us with all the authority of the saving and sending God. The world informs the church's understanding of the gospel. It does this in a negative way by exercising what Tillich called "the judging function of the secular," by judging Christian failure to apply the inherent meaning of the gospel. It also does this in a positive way, however, not directly, to be sure, because it does not know the gospel, but indirectly. It unconsciously speaks to that inherent meaning of the gospel itself, saying to the church, "There is more in your gospel than you dreamed of, dimensions of meaning that you have either forgotten or never known."

Is this possible? We are ordinarily ready to admit that the Lord of the gospel is greater than our capacity to apprehend Him. We are also certain that this great Christ is an endless source of new goodness as His Spirit leads the church into all truth. When He encounters the thought world of the great religions or animistic cultures new and unexpected things take place."[8] But that experience of the church at the seemingly distant frontier is not unique. Church history's most remarkable testimony is the Reformation discovery and emphasis on justification by faith as the key to the understanding of the gospel. This is a parable of the Spirit's work on the church in the world, for this emphasis is not noticeably present in the writings of the anti-Nicene fathers, nor does it appear to fall naturally on modern ears.[9] The entire thought world of the Reformation era, it seems, focused on the great scriptural theme of justification by faith. Under the Spirit this dimension of the gospel was discovered then; it is ours now, not to be lost. That Holy Spirit has power to uncover to us that which enlarges our understanding of the gospel. That discovery will come primarily from fresh experience with God's surprising Word.

But if it should be that the world also helps us in that discovery as we try to put gospel-mission-world together, let us neither be doubtful nor defensive.

> To say that the world is in no way to be part of the subject matter and substance of theology is to deny the meaning of *logos* or word and meaning, to deny one side of historic Christian theology, and to join in the prophecy and assertion that God is dead, eclipsed, abolished, or at least in no way involved with the world.[10]

Whatever does come to us from the world, if it is good, is from God, who alone is good. God's speech and action in the world (Romans 1 and 2) are not contradictory to the gospel, and therefore (since there is no alternative) are supportive of it when understood by redeemed men "interpreting spiritual truths to those who possess the Spirit" (1 Cor. 2:13). We may therefore boldly and hopefully ask: What is the world saying to us?

Factors Significant For Missions

What are some of the dominant factors in the world that are held to be significant for the mission task of the church today? Opinions in answer are many and varied, reflecting the actual complexity of the situation.

Some suggest that the really significant factor is the technological revolution, born in the West but now a universal phenomenon. The dramatic new context for mission is well summarized by Kenneth Cragg:

> Aside from human nature itself, it is the supreme common denominator of our existence. For the first time in recorded history we have a pattern of civilization which is effectively universal, not in degree or completeness but in quality and essence.[11]

Others see the critical factor in the development of a mood of triumphant secularism that follows upon the scientific explosion. Humankind in general has assumed the stance of self-sufficiency.

> Humanism is a confidence of this kind, an enthusiasm for human possibilities, and a fine quality of living, nourished by knowing how. Increasing mastery of logistics makes possible a strategy not only for the advancement of learning but also for the advance of humankind. Humanity is seen to be a social creation, a product of culture, something in the making; with a creative present, a boundless future, and not without achievements in the past.[12]

"I am an eagle," the cry of the Russian astronaut Titov in orbit, is the cry of secular human.[13] To face this conviction is to engage in what A. van Leeuwen calls "the true confrontation with our time."[14]

As opposed to this strong mood of secularism is the confidently programmed secularism of the communist movement, widely regarded as the critical problem for the church in the 20th century. Not since Islām gulped down half of the Christian church in the seventh and eighth centuries has the Christian church suffered such a numerical and geographical defeat as it has in its encounter with the militant materialism of the proletarian revolution. This "worship of collective human power on a world-wide scale"[15] challenges the spiritual assumptions by which humankind has understood the universe. It offers a message of hope, hope for this life. To that message humankind assents often by the free exercise of personal choice.[16] Where persuasion does not avail, the challenge is made through a combination of fanaticism, the application of technological means, and the use of force. The fact of communism presses hard on the church's thinking on gospel-mission.

There are those who see the key factor in none of these; but rather in the current demand, which is the mark of all societies, for justice, earthly justice of all kinds, but especially economic justice. This visceral demand for basic human satisfaction is screamed out, as hunger, poverty, unemployment, and disease continue to accompany a large portion of the human race as its ever-present and ever-willing companions. On the 20th anniversary of the Declaration of Human Rights the Secretary-General of the United Nations, U Thant, said:

> There are still too many areas where unemployment under mines the right to work, where illiteracy inhibits the right to education, where poverty and squalor make mockery of the right to health, where conflict and violence negate the enjoyment of human rights and fundamental freedoms.[17]

Different from these is the negative mood of secularism that follows upon the alleged defeat of science. Some hold that science has been tried and found wanting. One reaction this conviction brings is disgust with humankind as he/she is and disgust with what he/she produces. Flowing from this feeling and combined with it is despair. Humankind lives, but because he/she lives without hope, he/she is, in effect, dead. J. C. Hoekendijk concludes: "We are given the impression that the actual theme of tomorrow is already fixed—namely, 'Man is dead.'"[18] Human beings, as a result, may live in a kind of perpetual angst.

> What ambush lives beyond the heather...
> And beyond the sinking moon?
> And what is being done to us?
> And what are we and what are we doing?
> To each and all of the questions

> There is no conceivable answer.
> We have lost our way in the dark.[19]

On the other hand, one may lash out against the despair with a revolutionary fervour, seeking release in either the exotic or the violent. Or one may coolly accept the fact and go on, because that only is what is left to do.

Others detect the key factor for mission in the political realm, namely, in the spirit of nationalism that is so obviously and so contradictorily the sign of our age. These movements, which are externally political, usually secular, and at least nominally democratic, derive their real strength from their internal cultural and religious aspects. "We are living at present through a world situation of which it cannot be said too often that it is unprecedented."[20] The separations that have been produced are bedrock in nature. On the whole they have effectively slowed the expansion of the church in the world by traditional mission methods, and in some areas have stopped it entirely. Christopher Dawson in 1959 asserted that the fact of the different world of nations

> is the fundamental problem that Christianity has to face. ... It has hitherto proved an insurmountable obstacle to the ecumenical development of the Christian faith and has confined Christianity to one very limited portion of the human race.[21]

Developments of the last decade forcefully accentuate this judgment.

Related to this is the massive renaissance of the major non-Christian religions. This recovery of meaning and resurgence of elan has far-reaching implications.

> One must be aware of their new spirit in order to understand what is going on in the world. There is a change which has overwhelmed us Christians in our introverted and surfeited existence.[22]

The general effect has been to reduce Christianity from its "ready-made" position to the status of an equal among the religions. In the natural homelands of the religions where it has been combined with nationalistic views the renaissance has put Christianity under attack and at times has endangered its representatives.[23] Missionary zeal has accompanied it. Even more important, however, is the non-formalized spread of the religious philosophies involved. Coming into "the existential crisis and religious vacuum of contemporary western societies,[24] they have had major impact. Not only has this forced a rethinking of the geographical orientation of mission, it has confronted with strange and challenging theological contexts a gospel that has been largely formulated and proclaimed in terms familiar to the hearing of semi-Christianized Western man.[25] This encounter, previously restricted to the mission fields, faces the whole church.

The thrust toward the unity of humankind is regarded by some as the significant factor for the church in mission. This developing movement toward togetherness is expressed through a vast variety of social, political, and economic agencies. One of the characteristics of the movement is the increasing pressure toward a common world religion. In this search for a new harmony the mission of the church with its call to radical discipleship strikes a seemingly discordant note. It is suggested that the view of God as love requires a reinterpretation of the traditional understanding of the gospel. We ought to

> try to purge our Christianity of the traditional Christian belief that Christianity is unique. ... In the past this arrogant view in Christianity has in fact led ... to the rejection of Christianity. … The same Christian arrogance if Christians fail to purge it out now, will lead to the rejection of Christianity in the future.[26]

The demand that religion play a constructive role in the drive toward the unity of humankind places a heavy obligation on those concerned with gospel mission to reflect and speak.

This sketch of the factors confronting the church in mission as it considers its task in the world today is intended to be suggestive rather than exhaustive. We have not discussed the uplift in educational standards, the spirit of revolt, the breakdown in morality, and others that might be cited in this connection. We cannot fail, however, to point to the bare fact of the present rate of population growth which suggests a total population of three billion before the century closes. What, it is argued, could be more significant for mission than the very fact of these burgeoning multitudes, who pass through life un-confronted by the Lord of all? *Veni Creator Spiritus*! For even to think of what lies ahead is to crush the bruised reed and the smouldering flax of the church's tired will.

The Prime Factor

As we attempt to consider the gospel and the church's mission task against this background, we are overcome by its very complexity. Within these bewildering circumstances is there no focal point to which the gospel can relate? Is it not possible to detect an underlying theme that binds the whole together?

We suggest that the theme is there. *It is the discovery of humankind.* Since the evidence for this is all about us, we risk stating the obvious. Yet nothing is so much needed as the formal recognition that this is what the world is saying to the church in mission. Here, then, is the basic grist for the mill of Christian thought and action in today's world.

It may be objected that the judgment is centuries late. From the Middle Ages and the Renaissance through the period of the Enlightenment to the anthropocentrism of the 19th century, humankind's developing preoccupation with human is evident.[27] While this is true, we may nevertheless affirm that never before has "everyman" discovered humankind as he/she has done today. This concern for humankind as he/she moves into the last third of the 20th century is both ecumenical and revolutionary in quality. His/her rights, needs, and hopes are no longer only debated in the *schola* but are demanded in the *agora*. The psalmist's address to God, "What is man that Thou art mindful of him?" has changed to a cry to humankind, "Man, you had better be mindful of us." Jerald Brauer says of those involved in the student revolution: "They are fighting for what they feel is their essential humanity.[28] This phrase likewise describes the vital, aggressive discovery of humankind by every person in our age.

This theme, the discovery of humankind, expresses the underlying unity in the factors indicated above. Technocracy at its best is a construct by human for human. The secular mood is a concentration on the subject of human. In communism the emphasis is on man in society. The cry for freedom, justice, and human rights represents both the demand of human and a program for human. The 20th century nationalisms are expressions of human's desire for self-identification and self-realization. The thrust for the unity of humankind as human's noblest quest is a principal 20th century expression of the discovery of humankind.

Nowhere does this theme so strikingly assert itself as among the major non-Christian religions. Nothing is more startling than the developing concern for humankind in life philosophies which have not previously been noted for this. The humanist trends of Western philosophy and the ethics of Christianity have streamed in to the major religions to be consciously adopted or unconsciously assimilated. In this process the Christian view of humankind is fill in the theological systems of Islām, Hinduism, providing both a new respect for the dignity of and an acocial massage.

Humankind has never allowed themselves to be discounted or subdued completely in any religious system. His need for recognition, for meaning, for a present and a future have always provided an inner pressure on religious systems. The radically changed response to that pressure is typified by Islām. With its emphasis on overpowering sovereign will, Islām saw God but not human. Human's relation to God as *'abd* (slave) and the subjection to God's *qadar* (His absolute predestination power) yielded no room a meaningful doctrine of humankind. Abul Mughīth al-Ḥallāj (d.922) was an example of a Muslim's attempt to bypass the theological impasse by mystical experience aimed at the reunion of God and humankind. In the end, utilizing Jesus as his example, he affirmed that it is in the human who has attained to this experience that one can best see God.

> If ye do not recognize God, at least recognize His signs I am that sign. I am the Creative Truth, because through that I am a truth truth eternally.[29]

Al-Ḥallāj seemed poised on the double edge of a great truth and a great blasphemy. But for his daring statement "I and the Creative Truth," he was executed for blasphemy.

In this century, however, Sir Muḥammad Iqbāl (d.1938), the revered poet-philosopher of Islām and hero of Pakistan, speaks of the same al-Ḥallāj as "martyr-saint." He further builds a new Islāmic understanding of the relation between God and human about the concept of the ego. He speaks of Allah as the "infinite creative ego" and of human as the "finite creative ego." Humankind is therefore no longer locked up in a predetermined situation. Rather, his/her is a free personal causality who shares in the life and freedom of the Ultimate Ego. The latter has permitted the emergence of a finite ego, capable of private initiative, and has thereby limited the freedom of one's own will.[30]

> When attracted by the forces around him, man has the power to shape and direct them; when thwarted by them, he has the capacity to build a much vaster world in the depths of his own inner being, wherein he discovers sources of infinite joy and inspiration. Hard is his lot and frail his being, like a rose-leaf, yet no form of reality is so powerful, so inspiring, and so beautiful as the spirit of man! Thus in his inmost being man, as conceived by the Qur'ān, is a creative activity, an ascending spirit who, in his onward march, rises from one stage of being to another.[31]

This affirmation of human is a radical intrusion in a traditionally God-dominated faith. While extreme in its form, it is not exceptional in its emphasis. In his commentary on the first sūra of the Qur'ān, the famed orthodox theologian of Indian Islām, Maulānā Abul Kalām Azād says of a true worshiper of the one God:

> He will not belong to this or that race, community of group but to mankind; he will be a man, and his allegiance will be to humanity. This is the call of the Qur'ān, the real spirit of its message.[32]

Al-Ḥallāj's journey from execution to exaltation is a parable, then, of the uneven but definite advance of the doctrine of human in the major religions of the world.[33]

From all about us, therefore, comes the call to the church in mission to discover human. There is sharp suspicion in the air that the church does not know what to do with this call, that human is a stranger to the church. A baby-loving doctor summarizes such opinion as he explains the proposed title "A Belief in Man" for a statement of personal philosophy. "If we have gotten away from religion, we must replace it with something else."[34] So organized religion and belief in humankind are regarded as antithetical. A Christian politician recited this impromptu poem to an assembly of bishops: "Look through your less dark glasses daring as much for man as for God."[35]

It is not correct to say that Christianity has failed completely to reckon with the discovery of human. Easiest to document is its theology, which is extensively engaged in reflection upon the doctrine of human, especially in the areas of creation, Christology and ethics.[36] That reflection is empirically oriented. "Man as he encounters us concretely in his life relationships and in the total structure of society is the centre of our configuration."[37] As a result theology is undertaking a determined dialogue with the world. On the one hand, it wants first to discover just who modern human is.

> Such theology must ask, who is the modern man to which it hopes to speak. But perhaps instead we should speak of modern men rather than modern man. Never has there been a time when it was more difficult to put one's fingers, on the essence of the age.[38]

Second, it wants to address itself to the questions modern human asks, and to speak in terms that actually communicate.

On the other hand, theology is listening for new unfolding understandings of the meaning of human. That leads to new understanding of the nature of the Good which the gospel intends. As human's creative powers and ebullient spirit cast off shackles, cast out demons, and cast up noble works and structures for human's good, new images of the ultimate purpose of God in Christ stand revealed. Revealed with it is the torment of human unable to cast out the ultimate demons. The process of listening therefore also produces a new realization of the depths of need to which the gospel speaks. So, for example, to "the desperate search for human community today" comes the response that is "the universal theme of the theological renaissance today," namely, that the true human community can come into existence, not through human effort alone, but through a discovery that God through His own forgiving love does bring human into a sane, humble, and personally creative relationship.[39]

The Church's Response

Less easy to calculate is the church's pragmatic response to the theme of the new age. In general, the church in mission has answered the discovery of human by a new appreciation of its own call to servant hood, by the attempt to understand contemporary human, by a fresh spirit of identification with the hopes of human, by more intimate involvement in the structures of society, and by tangible efforts to meet human need. It has affirmed that the church's mission is to the whole humankind and that its ministry of peace and healing is all-inclusive. The selfless ministry of Jesus Christ, fully "the man for others" representing in concrete action His self-understanding of the nature of His own presence in the world ("I am among you as one who serves"), is seen as the pattern of the church's presence in the world. The church admits that its following of Christ into the world of humankind's needs and hopes is marked by serious inadequacy, misdirection, inconsistency, and hypocrisy. But to its confession of sin is added a strong and growing determination to "bear fruit that befits repentance."

Basic to this response is the church's self-discovery that it cannot stand apart from the meaning of the gospel. There is everywhere sudden, overwhelming realization that the world will not believe what it cannot see, and will not believe when what it sees contradicts what it hears. It is no longer possible to avoid the conclusion that "the Church, as it stands is itself, in most places, the stumbling-block for the spread of the Gospel."[40] The churches are therefore engaging in call to repentance, revival, and renewal. The church has become aware of the need for radical discipleship and obedience to Christ in today's world. Daniel T. Niles declares that the evangelistic thing is a boomerang. The Church which would call the world to order is suddenly called to order itself. The question mark which it would throw into the world: "Do you not know that you belong to Christ?" comes back as an echo. The Church discovers that it cannot truly evangelize, that its message is unconvincing, unless it lets itself be transformed and renewed, unless it becomes what it believes it is. Thus, evangelism, if taken seriously, will force the churches to pray and work for that radical renewal which will make them into letters from

Christ, written not with ink but with the Spirit of the Living God.[41]

But what has the gospel to do with the discovery of human that marks our common life, sets the theme for our secular and religious world, and reflects itself action? It is the gospel, understood as the good news of God's burden-bearing in Jesus Christ that defines the mission. But it is this news which speaks of God's grace that seems to be the square peg in the round hole of the present pattern of felt need and response. For human's attention is elsewhere. They are concerned with his/her own being and doing. The problem, therefore, is that the very content of the gospel comes to him/her in categories that seem to have little or nothing to do with the discovery of human. The gospel in today's world seems to be singing a song: "I am but a stranger here, Heaven is my home." But the world is not singing along.

Perhaps we have not been very effective in answering the questions, "What shall we do with the gospel?" At one end of the spectrum of response is dogged avowal of past patterns. We shall go on proclaiming the gospel as we have, in obedience and in trust, confident that inherent in it is sufficient power for the present as there has been for the past. The operative words for this view are "as we have." At the other end is a response typified by the words of a great convert from Islām to the Christian faith, whom the present situation moves to say; "I commend a period of reticence for the church."[42] This view is reflected in those of the apostolate who see the unqualified service to human needs as that which represents the true response of the Christian conscience to the contemporary world, that this is a time for the lived gospel and the *shalom* of God made present in the life of the Christian community.

The instinct of the concerned Christian is that the answer to the question, "What has the gospel to do with the discovery of human?" does not lie in the restricted views of either the "logists" or the "ergists," but in a fresh encounter with Christ Himself. He is the Man among humankind, the "speaking and doing in the world" human. He and He alone can provide the final meaning, the ultimate dimension that liberates human from the slavery of his/her discovery and fulfils it. But to say that the final solution is in Him is to say that it is in the gospel, where He makes Himself known to us. He, the Lord of the gospel, from within the gospel itself tells us what the gospel has to do with this and sends us to the doing. The gospel of Jesus Christ is good news for a world that has discovered human. It says to the world: There is more in your discovery than you dreamed of. It both declares the glory of human and makes them glorious.

The gospel does not do this without carrying out its "strange work." It cries "No" to human's "Glory be to me! I am the Lord! Behold your God!" The church in mission at this point has no choice and wants no choice. Its task is not to enthrone human but to prepare the way of the Lord in the wilderness of human self-esteem and self-acclaim. Therefore the voice cries first that "all flesh is as grass" which withers (Is. 40:6). The gospel's "No" is to all forms of self-worship, gross or subtle. Its "No" is therefore also directed against any glorification of Jesus Christ as authentic human which ignores His testimony that human's authenticity depends on His relation with One who is Father. The attempt to appropriate Jesus Christ on terms other than His own is characteristic of both secular and religious humanism. But Jesus Himself castigates man-worship, especially based on ethical calculation. "Why do you call Me good? No one is good but God alone" (Mark 10: 18). "The Father is greater than I" (John 14: 28). "I have come down from heaven, not to do My own will but the will of Him that sent Me." (John 6:38)

But this righteous Nay to human pretension yields quickly to the gospel's message, God's accepting and transforming Yea to human. The gospel is the glad tidings of the grace of God in Christ Jesus for humankind. In the gospel God reveals Himself as "the Incorrigible Humanist."[43] In His self-giving concern for human God testifies not only to human's tragic rebelliousness and lostness but also to human's greatness. Twice God knelt down in the dust for human, once to shape and then to reshape him/her in His image. To look biblical testimony squarely in the face with respect to human is to gasp in wonder and astonishment. Who is this human who is God's special creation and His vice-regent over nature? Who is he/she to be the friend, son/daughter co-worker and co-ruler of the Almighty? Who is this human whose life God shares, cleanses and ennobles forever? Who is this who is "a little less than God and crowned with glory and honour" (Ps. 8:5)? Who is human? The world's discovery of humankind demands of the church in mission that it takes another look at the Word that affirms human so powerfully, and that it search out the full implications of that affirmation—and all this for the sake of human.

The church will do this in the light of the glory reflected in the face of Jesus Christ. The mystery of human, the final glory and greatness, is both veiled and revealed in the person of Jesus Christ, whom the church therefore proclaims as humankind's good news. The profundity of that good news is both captured and opened up by the fact that Jesus called Himself the Son of Man. His personalized use of this name is the true "divine surprise." Though the title is recorded 81 times in the gospels, it is not applied to Jesus by others. The significance of this all-embracing title is therefore indubitable, but "the problems raised by this phrase are among the most complex and difficult in New Testament study."[44] There is a hidden quality in the Son of Man. Yet may we not hope that the Holy Spirit will provide new resources from this very concept for the understanding of the gospel and our mission task in a world full of thoughts about human? Its links with other concepts significant to modern human, such as creation, incarnation, second Adam, Suffering Servant, and the eschaton, hold promise of reward to match the effort involved in seeking out its meaning.[45] In the Son of Man the church in mission has a message for a world that looks for the well-being and glory of humankind.

Some understand the meaning of Son of Man as descriptive of Jesus' actual or ideal humanity; some stress its eschatological implications. The usage in the gospels is summarized by Vincent Taylor:

> Contrary to Christian usage at the time when the Gospels were completed, all the evangelists use the name Son of Man freely. They do so in terms of suffering and rejection, but with an eschatological emphasis, which is most pronounced in Matthew and Mark. In John the name describes the Divine Son in the circumstances of His earthly lot and as prophetic of His predestined glory.[46]

Jesus emphatically takes up the eschatological idea and applies it to Himself. The Son of Man will come in glory with His angels at the end of time. But Jesus adds to this that the Son of Man who comes in glory come first as a humble servant among humankind, and for their redemption. St. Paul advances the theme by building around the idea of the second Heavenly Man a total Christology.

It is not possible in this essay to develop the fruitful lines of thought that stem from this great theme. They are there in abundance. It is important, however, to point up the pre-existence of the Son of Man. The Son of Man is not only with God at the end-time. He comes to the Ancient of Days at the end, and is given dominion, glory, and the kingdom (Dan. 7: 13). But that is possible only because it is His rightful place, because He is with God from the beginning. He who is at the same time Son of God and Son of Man[47] is ever with God. "What if you were to see the Son of Man ascending where He was before" (John 6:62) "The second man is from heaven." (1 Cor. 15:47)

Because Christ is the Son of Man, he is the pre-existent Heavenly Man, the pre-existent pure image of God, the God-Man already in his pre-existence.[48]

As such the Son of Man is the perfect image of God who bears the very stamp of His nature and reflects His glory.

When God, in whom is eternally existent the Son of Man, creates humankind. He must therefore create them in His own image. Humankind as created by God is the self-expression of His own nature in spontaneous love, the pattern of divinity. Human is not God; they are the creation of God. They are not worthy of receiving worship. The Son of Man is not incarnate as the first man, Adam, but as the second Man, Jesus. But the image that Adam bears is the image of true manhood and thereby he is the bearer of the glory of God. So also when human losses that relation with God, they lose their human hood. The moment human seeks to be God rather than to reflect God, they ceases to be human. But when this happened, "the Son of Man came to seek and to save that which was lost" (Luke 19: 10). The Son of Man's mission is to redeem humankind by freeing them from the self-idolatry that destroys their true glory, and to restore it by re-creating human to be the image of God. The role of the Heavenly Man is to redeem human by making them what He Himself is, the image of God. That is his mission. But human are sinful; the first human, Adam, the representative of all humankind sinned, and redemption from sin requires atonement. The Heavenly Man, the divine prototype of humanity, must therefore himself enter sinful humanity in order to free it from its sins.[49]

In His dying to the old human and rising to the new life, the Son of Man incorporates in His human hood, and in Him human is once again crowned with glory and honour (Heb. 2:9). To put on Christ is to put on the new human. To put on the new human is to be restored in the image of God. To bear the image of God is to know the glory of human, even to their final glory, which is to be in God and God in them.

It has been suggested that "salvation is indeed nothing but humanization," *Missio Dei* is *Missio Dei* and has to be revealed to us. It is not our work; it is not the work of rigid perpetuation of institutionalism. It is the work of God, manifested in human history. It is indeed human history itself. The history of humankind is the history of salvation, of liberation from dehumanizing slavery; salvation is indeed nothing but humanization that is the concrete form of belief in the incarnation.[50]

But the greatness of God and His grace and the meaning of human are not understood unless we see as His startling discovery to us in Jesus Christ that humanization is, in a sense, deification. Not until the sons of Adam become the sons of God do they become the sons of human. It is the *Missio Dei* that they so become. So Saint Athanasius wrote:

> For men had not been deified if joined to a creature...Nor had man been brought into the Father's presence, unless He had been His natural and true Word who had put on the body that He might unite what is man by nature to Him who is in the nature of the Godhead, and his salvation and deification might be sure.[51]

The ultimate Christian answer to human's discovery of the greatness of human is a truth so subject to misunderstanding and corruption that it is uttered with trepidation. The moment the psalmist says, "You are gods, sons of the Most High, all of you," he leaps to add, "Nevertheless, you shall die like men" (Ps. 82:6). Yet at the same time the truth must be proclaimed—that human shares in Christ the greatness of God.

His divine power has granted to us all things that pertain to life and godliness, through the knowledge of Him who called *us to His own glory and excellence*, by which He has granted us His precious and very great promises, that through these you may escape from the corruption that is in the world because of passion, and become *partakers of the divine nature.* (2 Peter 1:3-4)

So God gives humanhood back to human through the Son of Man. The good news is that the Son of Man both reveals the glory of humanhood lived in God, and then grants its possibility as a gift. In this gift is incorporated validation of all that is gloriously human. The honourable, the just, the pure, the lovely, the gracious "if there is any excellence, if there is anything worthy of praise, think about these things" (Phil. 1:8). Creation is restored to humankind with the gift of humanhood. Even more, human is restored to themself. God's continuing mission through His Spirit is that every personal human existence bear the mark of the divine life, so that it might be "changed into His likeness from one degree of glory to another" (1 Cor. 3,T8). His continuing mission, too, is that the mystery of giving and receiving as expressed in the life of God the Father, Son, and Holy Spirit be experienced as human possibility. To that end He not only validates the goal but also creates and brings into the new order of life, whose principle is divine love, a people for His possession. He sends this possessed people into the world of human as His gift to humankind. They are His gift to human because they are the bearers of the great words that make sense to today's world and by which He calls men to Himself and to their true destiny—to re-create, reconcile, live, overcome. And they are His gift to human because they are the first fruits of the Son of Man's vision of a new humanity. In that gift of true humanhood which is hid with Him in God the Son of Man declares His final Amen to humanity until He comes.

That Amen of Jesus Christ is so buoyantly liberating and powerfully creative for truly human living because the Son of Man who declares it is the Suffering Servant. In Him we see not Only that to be human is to be divine, but that to be divine is to be among human and to be the suffering servant of human. In the New Testament the concepts of Son of Man and Servant of Cod are indissolubly linked. "The vocation of *ebed* becomes, so to speak, the main content of the Son of Man's earthly work."[52] It is the mission of the Son of Man to be a "man of sorrows and acquainted with grief" so that human who thankfully respond, "Surely, He has borne our grief and carried our sorrows," may in turn become the willing and joyful burden-bearers of the world.

As we see that great apocalyptic figure, the Triumphant One, the Son of Man, not grasping at His equality with God but humbled among human in the Servant and obedient to the death of the cross, the glory of human stands revealed. It is the glory of suffering and victorious love. Because it is the very nature of humanhood to do so, God's people take up the cross of humanity. As human's high destiny is revealed in the Son of Man who came to the Ancient of Days, so his true nature is revealed in the Son of Man "who came not to be ministered unto, but to minister and to give His life a ransom for many" (Mark 10:45; Matt 20:28). What destroys the temptation to corrupt the discovery of human is the figure of the Man on the cross. There, in the moment when the capacity for human's self-destruction is divulged, the Son of Man reveals what true human is like and what one does. The quality of life that brings the Son of Man to human in this way takes those who are in Him, and who testify to Him crucified, along that same seeking and finding way.

Thereby the church in mission discovers its own life in self-giving love and becomes God's sign to the world, the sign of true humanity possible and realized through union with God in Jesus Christ. "The blind receive their sight and the lame walk, lepers are cleansed and the deaf hear, the dead are raised up and the poor have good news preached to them" (Matt. 11:5). World, you need not wait for another. So also God's humanity treads the oath of His glory. "Because of the suffering of death, so that by the grace of God He might taste death for every one" we see Jesus crowned with glory and honour (Heb. 2:9). As God highly exalted Him who was crucified and gave Him the name that is above every other name, so human shall be lifted up to become the partakers of Christ's glory.

The gospel of Jesus Christ is good news for a world that has discovered humankind. The mission task of the church is to proclaim it.

Endnotes

[1] Ernst Benz, *Buddhism or Communism* (New York: Doubleday & Co. 1965), 48.

[2] "Census of India", Paper No. 1 of 1963 (Delhi: Manager of Publications, 1963), ii.

[3] Kenneth Cragg, *The Call of the Minaret* (New York: Oxford University Press, 1956), 334.

[4] T. S. Eliot, *The Family Reunion* (New York: Harcourt, Brace & World Inc., 1939), 43.

[5] *Map of the World's Religions and Missions*, 4th ed. (Berne: Geographical Publishers Kummerly & Frey, 1966).

[6] Nothing so spectacularly illustrates this point as the development of the "cargo cults" in the South Pacific islands, especially in New Guinea. A paganized worship of the white man's secret power over money and things—these cults are an extreme expression of the power of materialism.

[7] Daniel Day Williams, *What Present-Day Theologians Are Thinking* (New York: Harper & Brothers, Publishers, 1959), 20.

[8] The necessity to re-examine and deepen our understanding of the concept "Son of God" as a result of our encounter with Islām is an apt example of this process. In the area of ethics we may cite the rethinking forced upon the church by the Hindu concept of ahimsa as expressed through Mahatma Gandhi's principle of nonviolence.

[9] Cf. the comment of the Rev. Marc A. Splingart, Executive Secretary of the French Lutheran Hour, quoted in "The Lutheran Layman" (St. Louis: The Lutheran Layman's League, September 1968), 3: "In reality the Frenchmen of this century appear strangely perplexed when face to face with justification by faith. They are much more pre-occupied with the organization and future of this world than with their eternal salvation ... Far be it from us to deny the Scriptural character of this doctrine. Nevertheless, it is a fact, first of all, that the notion of a juridical relation between God and us no longer 'speaks' to human of today; and secondly, it is also a fact that this juridical notion by no means exhausts the Biblical revelations about our redemption."

[10] Martin Marty, "Religion in General," in *Operation Theology*, edited by Andrew J. Buehner (St. Louis: The Lutheran Academy for Scholarship, 1967), 40-41.

[11] "Encounter with Non-Christian Faiths," reprinted from the Union Seminary Quarterly Review in *Religion and Society* XIV (March 1967), 38.

[12] H. J. Blackham, "Modern Humanism," in *Religions and the Promise of the Twentieth Century*, edited by G. S. Metraux and F. Crouzet (New York: New American Library, 1965), 157.

[13] As this is written, headlines cry, "Man Circles Moon" The feeling aroused is summarized by the comment of K. Gatland, Vice-President of the British Interplanetary Society, quoted in *The Indian Express* (Dec. 25, 1968), 1; "The human spirit this day has begun to soar to new dimensions of experience, exploration and discovery." Despite the humble Christian witness of the first astronauts to circle the moon, nothing is more calculated to further exhilarate secular human than this victory.

[14] "Reply to Critics: A Defense of Christianity in World History," in *Religion and Society*, 56.

[15] Arnold Toynbee, *Christianity Among the Religions of the World* (New York: Charles Scribner's Sons, 1957), 79.

[16] The state of Kerala, India, is now passing through its second extended period of communist rule, freely chosen by an intelligent and religiously minded electorate.

[17] Quoted in *The Indian Express*, Dec. 11, 1968, 6.

[18] I. C. Rettenberg, trans., *The Church Inside Out* (Philadelphia; The Westminster Press, 1966), 172-73.

[19] Eliot, *The Family Renuion*, 128.

[20] Hendrik Kraemer, *World Cultures and World Religions* (London; Lutterworth Press, 1960), 272.

[21] *The Movement of World Revolution* (New York: Sheed & Ward, 1959), 158.

[22] Georg F. Vicedom, *The Challenge of the World Religions* (Philadelphia: Fortress Press, 1963), 7.

[23] There is a great company of the prosecuted among the members of the church in mission to the word today. It is composed of those who are actually suffering deeply for Christ's sake. On the one hand, their number will never be fully known; on the other hand, it is frequently indiscreet to publicly point to the known cases. It is sufficient that the church be aware that it is so.

[24] Mircea Eliade, "Paul Tillich and the History of Religions," in *The Future of Religions*, edited by Paul Tillich (New York: Harper & Row, 1966), 31.

[25] Eliade, "Paul Tillich and the History of Religions," in *The Future of Religions*, 31. Eliade reports how Tillich in his last days felt that a new systematic theology was needed, one "taking into consideration not only the existential crisis and the religious vacuum of contemporary western societies, but also the religious traditions of Asia and the primitive world together with their recent crises and traumatic transformations." Tillich himself stated in his last lecture concerning such a "period of interpenetration," of systematic theological study and religious historical studies: "This is my hope for the future of theology."

Significantly Hendrik Kraemer, the doyen of the church's mission in the 20th century and Tillich's theological opposite, takes a similar position, maintaining that the theologians have not yet taken these issues into their perspective. There "arises for the Church and the theologians the imperious demand to leave all parochialism and regionalism aside and ascend to a yet unknown dimension of world-embracing, mundial thinking." Kraemer, *World Cultures and World Religions*, 23.

[26] Toynbee, *Christianity Among the Religions of the World*, 97-98.

[27] See August Comte's (1798-1857) proposal for a final religion, "The Religion of Humanity."

[28] Andrew J. Buehner, ed., "The Student Revolution," in *The New American Revolution* (St. Louis; The Lutheran Academy for Scholarship, 1968), 52.

[29] Quoted from his *Kitab-al-Ta-wasin* in A. J. Arberry, *Sufism* (London: George Allen & Unwin Ltd., 1950), 60.

[30] Mu%ammad Iqbāl, *The Reconstruction of Religious Thought in Islām* (Lahore: Mu%ammad Ashraf, n.d., rept. 1962), 108.

[31] Iqbāl, *The Reconstruction of Religious Thought in Islām*, 12

[32] Ashfaque Husain, *The Quintessence of Islām, A Summary of the Commentary of Maulānā Abul Kalām Azād on Al-Fāti%a* (Bombay: Asia Publishing House, 1960), 92.

[33] The end of the tale is not yet told. There is every indication that the next stage in this chain reaction will be an inverse effect resulting in definite change in the doctrines of God in the religions. When we now find signs of such change in the doctrine of God in response to the discovery of human, we see how these two doctrines tightly interact. In fact, they stand and fall together.

[34] Quoted in *Newsweek*, Sept. 23, 1968, 29.

[35] Quoted in *Newsweek*, Nov. 25, 1968, 54.

[36] See, for example, the Lutheran World Federation sponsored study of the theme, "The Quest for True Humanity," which has been going on since 1964.

[37] Hoekendijk, 85.

[38] Wm. Hordern, *New Directions in Theology*, I (London; Lutterworth, 1968), 151.

[39] Williams, *What Present-Day Theologians are Thinking*, 25.

[40] H. D. L. Abraham, "Church and Evangelism," in *International Review of Missions* XLV (1956), 171.

[41] "Editorial," *Ecumenical Review* II (1949), 2, quoted in Hans J. Margull, *Hope in Action*, translated by E. Peters (Philadelphia: Muhlenberg Press, 1962), 135.

[42] Daud Rahbar is an address to the student body at Concordia Seminary, St. Louis, Mo., 1968.

[43] Hoekendijk, 189.

[44] T. W. Manson, *The Teaching of Jesus* (Cambridge: University Press, 1963), 211. See his entire section on Son of Man, pages 211 to 36. For an older but exemplary introduction to the subject see S. R. Driver, "Son of Man," *Dictionary of the Bible*,

edited by James Hastings (Edinburgh; T & T Clark, 1902) 579-88. A brief summary of modern views is found in J. Campbell, "Son of Man," *A Theological Workbook of the Bible*, edited by Alan Richardsod (New York: The Macmillan Co., 1959), 330 to 31. In terms of our present study the most stimulating treatment is to be found in Oscar Cullmann, *The Christology of the New Testament* (London: SCM Press, 1959), 137 to 92. Cullmann states (152): The question whether and in what sense Jesus designated himself the Son of Man is one of the most discussed and contested problems of the New Testament

scholarship.

[45] The church in mission is heavily dependent on the efforts of the church's exegetes to quarry new insights from the mine of Scripture that will help it to be the church of the living Word. "Son of Man" illustrates both the need and the challenge. Appropriate is Jaroslav Pelikan's call and warning: "The Protestant theology of the United States needs a period of fresh new exegesis, not merely of crypto-systematic 'biblical theology,' if it is to learn to speak Christologically again." See "Bonhoeffer's Christologie of 1933," in *The Place of Bonhoeffer*, edited by Martin Marry (London: SCM Press, 1963), 164.

[46] *The Person of Christ* (London; Macmillan & Co. Ltd., 1959), 22.

[47] Wm. Sanday, "Jesus Christ," *Dictionary of the Bible*, II, 623, states; "As Son of God Jesus looked upwards to the Father: as Son of Man He looked outwards upon His brethren."

[48] Cullmann, *The Christology of the New Testament*, 127.

[49] Cullmann, *The Christology of the New Testament*, 172.

[50] T. Veerkamp, "Looking Forward in Hope," in *Religion and Society*, XV (March, 1968), 31.

[51] Orationes II, 69, in *The Nicene and Post-Nicene Fathers of the Christian Church*, Vol. IV, Athanasius, edited by A. Robertson (New York: Charles Scribner's Sons, 1903).

[52] Cullmann, *The Christology of the New Testament*, 161.

Muḥarram in Hyderabad

David T. Lindell

After discovering the description of "The Chief Shīʿa 'Alams of Hyderabad" by Miss Greenfield in a copy of "News and Notes" from 1935, I thought it might be of interest to see what the picture of Muḥarram is like in the city after nearly forty years. Therefore, with her article as reference and a Muslim friend as guide I set out on the fifth night of Muḥarram to visit some of the places which she mentions. In the following piece a report of this visit is incorporated together with other material on Mu¢arram in general and its observance in Hyderabad.

Muḥarram

All of the Muslim festivals are fixed according to the lunar calendar and therefore move backwards through the seasons of the solar year, completing one cycle in about *three and half* years. Thus, the Muslim New Year may fall in the winter at one time and gradually shift until fifteen years later it falls in the summer season, Furthermore, the actual timing of the festival is not determined simply by astronomical calculations but in reference to the actual sighting of the new moon by two witnesses.

This always generates a certain air of anticipation and suspense which is not altogether contrived. This year, for example, all of the calendars indicated that the Tenth Day of Muḥarram was scheduled to fall on the third of February. However, the moon watch to determine the beginning of the month did not sight the crescent as expected and the New Year got off to a late start. There was confusion for a couple of days until the Government could take official action to postpone the holiday by one day.

Muḥarram, the first month of the Muslim year, provides one of the more prominent festivals of Islām. 'Āshūrā', the tenth day of Muḥarram, coinciding with the Jewish "Day of Atonement," was earlier observed as a major fast by Muḥammad and his followers. Later, as the month of Ramaḍān was designated as the time for fasting, 'Āshūrā' was given less importance. Nevertheless, it is marked by Sunnī Muslims as the day when the first rain fell; when Adam and Eve were created; when the ninth heaven was created and the divine mission was granted to many prophets.

But the month of Muḥarram has special meaning for Shī'a Muslims as a season of mourning for the martyrdom of 'Alī and his sons—Ḥasan and Ḥusain. After several days of suffering, Ḥusain the grandson of Muḥammad, together with his family and a small band of faithful followers, met their death on the tenth day of Muḥarram at Karbalā' in Iraq, and around this date is gathered the memory of all the members of the Prophet s family who came to a tragic end at the hands of rival contenders for the Caliphate.

Although the full period of mourning extends for forty days, the first ten days of the month receive special emphasis leading to a climax on 'Āshūrā'. While the theme of this festival is common, the details of the ceremony vary considerably from place to place in India. The commemoration of Muḥarram has become a significant event in Hyderabad as a result of the traditional patronage of the Nizāms and a number of Sunnī Muslims as well as Hindus join with the Shi'a community in various public activities.

Common symbols used during Muḥarram include the *Tā'ziyah* and the *'Alam.* In India the word *Tā'ziyah* is used to designate a replica of the tomb of Ḥusain, commonly made of bamboo and paper, which is the characteristic especially of the observance held in places like Lucknow and Bidar.

In Hyderabad *'Alams* are the predominant symbols in use. These "standards" or "ensigns" are the banners of the various martyrs and take a number of traditional forms. The *panja* is in the shape of a hand with the five fingers representing Muḥammad, Fāṭimah, 'Alī, Ḥasan and Ḥusain. These five names are mingled together in an Arabic calligraphic pattern to form another common design. Some represent the sword and bow of 'Alī or the shoe from his horse.

It is customary to erect these *'Alams* at the beginning of Muḥarram and to keep them in place for ten days. In many Shi'a homes a sheltered corner of the courtyard or a small room is set aside for this purpose. Many of the important *'Alams* are placed in special buildings known as 'ā*shūr-khānās*. These are visited by the pious who garland the *'Alams* with jasmine flowers as they seek the intercession of the martyrs or affirm their loyalty to the family of the Prophet. On specific days, certain *'Alams* are carried in procession through the city.

A central feature of Muḥarram is the *majlis* or gathering to remember the tragedy of Karbalā'. This may be a gathering of the family and a few friends in the home or a large assembly of people in some 'āshūr-khānās. The mosque is reserved for prayer and is never used for these Muḥarram observances. Such *majālis* are held in one place or another during the first ten days of Muḥarram, with a special theme assigned to each day. On these occasions poetic lamentations are read recounting in sad detail the sufferings of the martyred Imams.

The response to such somber remembrance takes the form of *mātam* or mourning. Generally this is expressed by a gentle beating of the breast and shedding tears of grief. However, in the public *maj'alīs* more formal rituals develop as the people join in antiphonal chanting, "Yā 'Alī! Yā Ḥusain!" and specialized groups of young men take turns in violent and rhythmic beating of breasts, sometimes cutting themselves until they are bathed in blood. The profound sorrow of these events is a moving experience for anyone who witnesses them.

The Chief *'Alams* Revisited

The following observations have specific reference to the article written by Miss Greenfield and should be read in that context. The discrepancies which appear, both in the descriptions and in the historical data, should not be taken seriously. The local informants in this kind of situation are not always very well informed nor do they always try hard to distinguish between fact and fancy. Also the whole experience for the visitor is extremely impressionistic and even though I consciously tried to observe things and to make notes with this report in mind, I find that there are still many questions and uncertainties about just what I did see. I have noticed also that in subsequent visits I was sometimes given different information than the first time. But then this confusion and mixture of the mythical and the factual is in itself a very real part of the total experience.

a) The *Bādshāhī 'Āshūr Khānā* is south of the Musi river not far from the Naya Pul or New Bridge. This 'Āshūr *Khānā* was built by Sultān Muḥammad Qulī Quṭb Shāh sometime between 1595 and 1597 (depending on which book one reads), which makes it one of the earliest structures in Hyderabad City which was founded in 1591 by the Shah.

The walls are covered with colorful tiles of Persian enamel decorated with ornate inscriptions and arabesque designs. When the Golconda kingdom fell to the Mughals, Aurangzeb turned the building into a stable for horses and it was not restored to its present use until the time of the second Nizām (1763-1803) who also provided the *'Alams* currently on display there. There is a small shuttered window in the left hand corner above the *'Alams* where the Nizam is said to have sat and observed the proceedings. The flood of 1908 damaged the lower part of the walls which have been only partially restored by painting.

The five major *'Alams* are indeed splendid and could well be gold or more probably gold plated, and their *dhattīs* are of a golden fabric. In addition, along the walls on each side there must be a hundred or more smaller *'Alams* set in ranks two or three deep. Some are draped in red and others in black *dhattīs*. They include almost every style and design and several have calligraphy which has been worked into the quaintly grotesque face of an animal—some almost human in aspect.

b) The "heaviest *'Alam*" is still in place but it is difficult to believe that it weighs anywhere near 2-3 tons. It is about four to five feet in diameter and appears to be made from a heavy gauge brass sheeting.

The *'alāwah* or fire pit is not really a pit but a stone or cement brazier standing about 3-4 feet high and about as wide, with iron spikes around the rim. Apparently this is no longer used as it was in the past.

c) It is not clear whether the *nāl ṣāḥib* mentioned by Miss Greenfield was a particular *'Alam* of significance in Hyderabad or just one style of *'Alam* of special interest. Actually the largest one with the thickest accumulation of sandalwood paste was at the shrine of the *qadam-i rasūl* but I saw this symbol of the horse shoe in other places as well, although it was less common than most other types.

d) The *qadam-i rasūl* proved to be one of the more interesting stops along the way. This purports to be the foot print of the Prophet Muḥammad impressed into stone. This relic is housed in a casket like structure under a canopy of wood which is said to be a model of the tomb of Muḥammad. The whole thing is overlaid with silver sheeting (or silver paint where the sheeting has been torn away) and is draped with rather ancient and dusty ornate fabrics.

The foot print was brought from Arabia many years ago and the present custodian of the shrine is 94 years old and represents the fourteenth generation of the Arab family that came to Hyderabad with the sacred stone The old gentleman was most hospitable and talkative but significant information was hard to come by and the main thrust of conversation illuminated the indifference of the present world, especially to the financial needs of his particular establishment.

When asked to see the *qadam-i rasūl* we were informed that it was now locked up. The day before Muḥarram a padlock is put on the small door in the side of the casket or cabinet. On the tenth day as the huge Muḥarram procession passes by, it pauses while the *bībī-kā-'Alam* is brought into the shrine and held up against the door. Then a miracle happens —the lock pops open of itself and again gives access to the holy relic. So we could not see the foot print, but I was invited to return to witness and photograph the events on the afternoon of the miracle.

The *jhūla* or cradle was under wraps over to one side and would have passed unnoticed except that I asked about it. It was then uncovered and lights were turned on to show not only a small swinging cradle about a foot long, but also another model bed, both housed in a circular mini-pavilion about three feet high with pillars all around and a dome on top.

We shall return to the *qadam-i rasūl* to describe what happened when I accepted the invitation to come back and see the miracle.

e) *Panja Shāh*, the "Royal Hand" is housed in an 'Āshūr *Khānā* just across the street from the *qadam-i rasūl.* The central object of veneration here was a stone slab which preserves the hand print of 'Alī. Permission to view this relic was readily granted although a photograph was not allowed. (This was the only time when I encountered any restriction on taking pictures and even here I was free to photograph anything else I wanted—except the hand print itself).

In the dark stone is a stylized impression of a right hand of giant proportion—nearly twelve inches long. We were told that it was brought from Iraq by Haji Mir Devish 'Alī Najafi some 350 years ago and the shrine is still tended by his descendants.

There were three central *'Alam* on display in front of the case containing the hand print. Two of these were designed by combining twelve ensigns as described but they were of the sword motif rather than the hand. In addition there were the relics of the *pīr*, Mīr Maḥmūd, who lies buried on a hill south of the city. He is reported to have woven the chain by hand from heavy wire and it is a substantial thing, about three quarters of an inch thick and nearly twenty feet long. Water washed over the inscriptions hung on this chain is said to cure the sick and there are stone trays on the floor to receive the thank offerings of those so benefited. The black stone slab or bar is perhaps six feet long and Maḥmūd used to carry it across his shoulders as an exercise in asceticism or something.

It is interesting to note the tendency to attribute uniqueness or rarity to many of these objects as though to enhance their sacred quality. This "rare stone not found in the Deccan" appears to be dolerite, as does the shoulder bar, the offering trays and indeed the stone with the print of 'Alī's hand. So also is a huge stone bowl, six feet in diameter, which is carved out of a single chunk and is set in the court yard to hold water or sherbet during Muḥarram. This too "is the only one in India." (The "black marble" benches in the Mecca Mosque are of the same material.) This kind of rock, far from being rare, is available in the many black dolerite dikes that crisscross the granite bed rock of the Deccan plateau.

Miss Greenfield's informant further indicated that only two such imprints of the hand of 'Alī are known in the world, the second being in Arabia. Yet the entire guide books of Hyderabad tell of another one which appeared on a hillock north of the city at a place called Maulā 'Alī. It seems that during the reign of Ibrāhīm Quṭb Shāh (1550-1580) a eunuch by the name of Yāqūt was resting at Lalaguda when a man clad in green Arab garb appeared in a dream and led him to this hill where he saw Ḥazrat 'Alī seated on the summit. In the morning when he again visited the spot he discovered a hand print in the stone. He erected an arch on the hill and subsequent additions to the shrine have been made through the years. But for some reason this relic is not open to view. A neighboring hill is called "qadam-i rasūl" and sacred relics of the Prophet have been assembled there by Muḥammad Shukrullāh Khān during the eighteenth century.

f) *Bībī-kā-'Alam.* The 'Āshūr *Khānā* which houses this symbol of Fāṭima is reached by a series of narrow twisting streets and I am sure I would need a guide to find it again. The golden *'Alam* is flanked by three on each side wrought in the sword motif out of burnished steel. It seems there was an attempt to steal the bags of diamonds a few years ago so a police guard was on duty which carefully controlled the approach of those who came to venerate the *'Alam.* Another relic associated with this *'Alam* is a stool alleged to have been used by the daughter of the Prophet.

The Salar Jung Palace

Early in the morning of the ninth day we set out to join the *majlis* which gathered in a court yard of the Sālār Jung Palace. We arrived around 4 a.m. and found a young boy at the microphone reciting Muḥarram narratives while the final touches were being made on the *'Alams*. The preparation of the *'Alams* is a highly intricate process with a complex symbolism developed over the years. Each 'Āshūr *Khānā* is administered by a trust which is usually hereditary. This particular one had been patronized by Salar Jung and one of his relatives was now involved both in the *'Alams* ritual and in the reading of the tragic story during the *majlis*. The main *'Alam* was centered between three others on each side, all of them fashioned from what appeared to be sandalwood paste and loaded with garlands of jasmine.

The theme of this observance focused on the episode in which 'Abbās met a martyr's death. 'Abbās was the son of 'Alī by another wife after Fāṭima had died and was thus a half-brother to Ḥusain. During the siege at Karbalā' when Ḥusain's party was cut off from any access to water, Ḥusain's baby daughter began to cry from thirst. 'Abbās took a leather water bottle and rode his horse to the river in an attempt to get a drink for the little girl. The enemy intercepted him on his return and cut off his right arm. He grabbed the water bag with his left band but that arm too was severed. Catching the bag in his mouth he tried valiantly to reach the camp when a spear was thrust through his body. As he fell mortally wounded an arrow pierced the leather bag and the precious water spilled out onto the sands.

When we arrived the crowd in the courtyard was still fairly thin and I moved up front to get some pictures of the *'Alams*. I had barely made one or two exposures when the first group of mourners came in with a rush and in moments the square was filled with people, tightly packed together. I was caught standing to one side right next to the *mimbar* or pulpit and for the next two hours it was virtually impossible to move from the spot. In fact it was an effort in that press of humanity simply to turn around or to lift the camera up to take a picture.

In spite of the intense emotional quality of the gathering and the large number of individuals and special groups that participated at various times, the program proceeded in a remarkably controlled and orderly fashion. The large crowd of both men and women wept softly as they listened to the cadenced recitation of traditional poetry that elaborated the tragic theme of Karbalā' and preserved the memory of those melancholy events in agonizing detail.

At times the leader would launch into a kind of litany in which the whole gathering would beat their breasts and respond in unison with shouts of "Yā 'Alī, Yā Ḥusain." Or again one group or another of young men, stripped to the waist, would beat their breasts in rapid rhythm with all their might until their skin was raw and red with blood.

The high point was reached when the *'Alams* were carried out to the gate of the palace and back again. The entourage was led by an *'Alam* in the shape of a tiger or lion head which is the traditional precursor in all such processions. (There were pictures of tigers on the courtyard wall both here and in many other places which seemed to be symbolic of 'Alī who has been called "the tiger or lion of Allāh.") Two other *'Alams* were then taken from their stands and carried through the crowd.

The *'Alam* of 'Abbās was shaped like an armless torso and when it was lifted from its place it was "staggered and then let fall to the shouts and wails of the people as a re-enactment of the mortal wounding of 'Abbās. While the *'Alams* were on their way, there was extensive *matam* or mourning among those in the courtyard awaiting their return.

Toward the end of the service there were two or three times when the entire gathering paused to repeat selected sūrahs from the Qur'ān silently together. As a hush fell upon the group one could watch their lips moving in rapid recitation. After announcements were made of coming events the *majlis* came to an end and the people began to move off. Only then was I able to rejoin my friend and guide and as we found our way out to the street the first signs of dawn began to lift the darkness from the eastern sky.

The 'Āshūrā' Procession

The Tenth Day is the big day. The *Bībī-kā -'Alam* is mounted on a huge and venerable elephant and borne in ponderous procession through the crowded streets of the old city. The viewing is best if one can gain admission to an upstairs window or a roof top overlooking the street below.

The procession itself is not a large one and does not take more than ten or fifteen minutes to pass a given point, although it takes all afternoon to cover the full route of fourteen kilometers. In the vanguard are a few incense burners, earthen pots of charcoal either mounted on a cart or carried on a man's head. Into these small packets of incense powder are thrown by devotees along the way. Then two or three camels loaded with people ride by and a brass tiger's head mounted on a staff comes to indicate the approach of the *'Alams*.

A large sandalwood *'Alams* (the *nal sahib* or horse shoe perhaps?) is carried under an ancient and dilapidated red silk umbrella and is followed by an elephant load of people. Then the resplendent white-faced pachyderm with the *Bībī-kā -'Alam* trods along in stately fashion. The steel martial *'Alams* come next and are carried six abreast. Behind these are a few carts with cakes of ice and tubs of water which recall the terrible thirst of the martyrs. From these drinks are poured out for the pious along the way.

Finally there are associations of young men, each group identified by its own banner, who perform a special kind of *matam*. Every so often the procession stops and about a dozen of these men spread out in the street and begin to beat their bare backs with whips made of five chains, each with a sharp steel blade on the end. One member stands by with a bottle, or even a bucket, of disinfectant to wash the wounds. When someone gets carried away in their zeal and excessively lacerates himself, others step in to restrain him. I am not sure just how this *matam* is organized but I would imagine that the members of the associations take turns during the course of the afternoon.

As the procession moves along its course it pauses at appointed places to permit dignitaries from the traditional feudal families or from the municipal or state governments to view the *'Alam* and to offer a garland or a *dhatti*. By evening the *'Alams* reach Chaderghat where they are immersed in the waters of the Musi river.

One of the major halts along the way is at the *qadam-i-rasul*. It was here that I came this year to observe the miracle that was scheduled at around 3 p.m. I came early at one o'clock to avoid the crowds and to give myself plenty of time to find a vantage point for taking pictures. There was a five foot wooden railing that ran across the front of the portico which housed the shrine and in the center a gale swung back against the railing to create a ledge on top, six or eight inches wide. It was suggested that I could perch on this ledge next to a pillar during the proceedings and take my pictures. Since this would put me right in the center of things and allow me to look down on the activity in all directions I readily agreed.

I joined a small group of men seated on a low platform to one side to observe the preliminaries and to await the arrival of the *'Alam*. Some of these men must have been up much of the night in some *majlis* for they kept nodding off to sleep and a few had bandages on their heads covering the wounds of *matam*.

All the time people kept coming to pay their respects or to express their petitions. Some brought a small packet of flowers or a garland, others special strips of cloth and these were placed upon the shrine. More commonly the offering was a small coin. Each visitor carried away some ash from the censer and perhaps a few flower petals. This ritual was administered by children, including some very cute young girls, who presumably were members of the custodian's family. Some received the bit of ash in their hand and others upon their forehead. I got the impression that this might have differentiated the Muslims from the Hindus, for there were obviously a large number of Hindus among those who came.

After an hour water buckets were brought in to wash off the verandahs and the general public was confined to the outer courtyard. Now men, all dressed in black shirts or shirvanis, began to gather and I retreated to my perch up on the fence. Most of the *'Alams* that had been displayed for 10 days were now put away, but a few remained and these together with the *jhula* were now taken in procession around the court, out to the gate and back, and then were set aside. A loud speaker was installed and there was some recitation of traditional poetry while the ranks of the mourners continued to grow.

A stir in the crowd outside indicated that the hour had come and a police escort cleared a path for the *Bībī-kā-'Alam* as it was paraded through the courtyard and up to the shrine. Right next to me on a wooden stand some seven feet high one of the officiants was waiting to receive it. As it was brought before him he unloaded all the rose garlands and other items that had been added along the way. The *'Alam* was then carried back and forth the length of the verandah a few times before it stopped in front of the shrine where it was lowered and brought in under the draperies up against the locked door of the cabinet. Silence fell as the people waited—perhaps a full minute passed—and then the signal was given that the lock was open.

The *Bībī-kā-'Alam* was lifted up erect once more and held before the shrine while the old patriarch, in a hoarse quavering voice, recited lamentations and verses from the Qur'ān accompanied by the keening of the crowd. By this time the air was blue with incense and the people were covered with sawdust that had been sprinkled liberally over all.

In fifteen minutes it was all over, the *'Alam* went on its way and the men dispersed. Now the women came in to gather up whatever might be left of the religious aura of the occasion.

As for the miracle, whatever happened or did not happen was kept under wraps. I never once saw the door or the lock either before, during, or after the event. The antique coverings of the shrine shrouded the whole thing. And even if some wonder did occur it is difficult to imagine what the point of it would be. On our first visit we were told that the footprint could not be seen until after this Muḥarram observance was complete. Sometime later when I visited again I was told that it was open to view only at Muḥarram. So the footprint of the Prophet also remains hidden in a mystery, or at least in a box.

I did not leave at once for I had seen two pictures that I wanted to photograph. One was mounted under the canopy just above the shrine and depicted the holy family seated together. Muḥammad was holding Ḥasan and Ḥusain, one on each knee, and had ʿAlī and Fāṭima on each side. Behind them the archangel hovered protectively in classic Byzantine style. The other picture hung on a side wall and was even more unusual. I had been promised that it would be taken down afterwards so that I could read the inscriptions more carefully and photograph it in better light. After several reminders this was finally done.

In the center was a portrait of Muḥammad holding the Qur'ān being flooded with rays or light from a shining cloud. Around this was a circle of smaller pictures of other prophets. From the top right and moving clock-wise there were the following:

- Noah on the ark releasing the dove
- Moses standing atop Mt. Sinai
- Jesus praying in Gethsemane
- Jacob blessing his grandsons (crossing his hands so his right hand would fall on Ephraim, the younger and his left on Manasseh, the older. Gen. 48:14 ff.)
- Solomon standing upon a royal staircase passing judgment
- Joseph with his father and his coat of many colors
- ʿAlī seated with a drawn sword in his hand
- Joshua leading the people of Israel through the Jordan into the promised land
- David as a shepherd with his flock
- John the Baptist preaching to the people

- Daniel in the lions' den
- Abraham with the Ka'bah in the background
- Adam and Eve being driven from the garden by an angel with a flaming sword.

The thing that struck me when I first saw the picture was the ease with which I could identify most of the figures without even looking at the captions. Most of them were of the Sunday School genre familiar to me as a child. Notable among these was the picture of Jesus which was the famous painting by Hofmann showing Jesus at prayer in the Garden of Gethsemane. Should you visit the *qadam-i-rasūl* it is possible you might not find this picture. The last time I was there it had not been replaced on the wall and I saw no evidence of it around.

The Muḥarram Fire Walk

There are at least two places in Hyderabad where the *'Alam* procession is associated with fire walking. Both of these take place later on near the end of the month of Muḥarram. One of these in Habeebnagar is a small affair which is quickly done about one or two in the morning.

The other function held each year in Musheerabad is far more impressive. It seems that many years ago a Hindu weaver from Bombay discovered an old *'Alam* in a well. In a dream he saw himself sitting in the middle of a fire holding this *'Alam.* Accepting this as guidance he began the next year in Muḥarram to carry the *'Alam* through a bed of red hot coals and it is reported that he would even sit in the fire as long as half an hour without ill effects. His grandson carries on the tradition today but not quite in this fashion.

Matam is observed through the night in an 'Āshūr *Khānās* while a huge bonfire burns in a street nearby. As morning nears the hot coals are spread out to form a blanket about ten by twenty feet and six to nine inches deep. When all is ready two or three men come with *'Alams* and walk with steady pace through the fire. Perhaps ten or fifteen others, mostly young lads, then run across after them. The *'Alams* are carried back and forth this way about five times during the course of fifteen minutes or so. There were a few men who would stand in the fire for five seconds while they beat their backs with bladed whips.

It is interesting to note that a similar ritual has been introduced in Lucknow as the following report indicates. " … On the sixth night *mātam* on fire is performed at Imāmbard-e- Aṣāf-ud-daulā. A long ditch is dug in the center of the outer courtyard and it is filled with firewood. When the big flames have turned to burning coals, about a hundred devotees in several groups, walk on the fire, shouting, 'Ḥusain, Ya Ḥusain' to the beating of breasts. This ceremony was introduced to Lucknow during the Second World War by the Burmese Shī'as who migrated to the city."[1]

The Significance of Muḥarram

It is difficult to evaluate just what the Muḥarram experience means for the Shī'a Muslim. Obviously it will mean different things to different people, or perhaps on different levels to the same person. Still the significance of Muḥarram would seem to include some of the following elements

The observance of Muḥarram has a powerful educational function in terms of religious and cultural identity for the Shī'a Muslim. Even many who have become largely secularized in many ways will still observe Muḥarram for this reason and will be deeply moved by the occasion.

This is a time in which the Shī'a Muslim can strongly affirm his loyalty and commitment to 'Alī and Ḥusain and the family of the Prophet as the true successors to the leadership of Islām. This concept has at least two consequences. In the first place there is a stress on the religious or spiritual quality of the Imam rather than on the political dimension. This playing down of the political element in Islām together with a distrust of Sunnī rule leads many Shī'as to prefer a good non-Muslim government over an orthodox Muslim rule which has little sympathy with the cause of 'Alī and his family.

Further, there is a widespread acceptance of the belief that the martyrs exercise an intercessory role or even a savior role on behalf of those who enter into the spirit of the Muḥarram observance. Many would consider the faithful performance of *matam* to be far more efficacious than strict and rigid attendance to the prayers and other duties of Islām.

Still the moral power of suffering has not yet been greatly developed either philosophically or theologically. The suffering of the martyrs is still recalled mainly in terms of denouncing the evil of Yazīd and the Sunnīs rather than as a force that gives any kind of positive and creative meaning to the experience of human suffering.

Certainly there would seem to be depths of meaning here that go far beyond the superficial superstition that is such an obvious part of the Muḥarram ceremonies that we have witnessed and described.

Endnotes

1 "Lucknow", Lucknow Publishing House, 1968, 54.

The Henry Martyn Institute of Islāmic Studies

David T. Lindell

The roots of the Henry Martyn Institute reach as far back as 1906 when the "First Conference of workers in the Muslim world" was convened under the leadership of Dr. Samuel Zwemer in Cairo, Egypt. Here it became clear that if there was to be any meaningful and effective witness to the Gospel among Muslim people, it was necessary to give Christian workers an understanding of Islām and to prepare literature that was responsive to the special needs of the Muslims. Again at the World Missionary Conference of Edinburgh in Edinburgh in 1910, Dr. Zwemer gave a passionate appeal on behalf of the Christian apostolate to the "house of Islām" that did much to awaken the Churches to the unique character of Christian-Muslim relationships.

A "Second Missionary Conference on behalf of the Mohammedan World" was organized in 1911 in Lucknow, India. Once more Dr. Zwemer was the leading spirit and attention was focused on the need for special literature and worker training. This led to the formation of an informal prayer fellowship the following year, known as the "Missionaries to Muslim League". They published a monthly circular called "News and Notes", which eventually became the "Bulletin" of the HMI. They even organized summer lectures and reading courses on Islām and arranged examinations as early as 1914.

The Edinburgh Conference of 1910 set in motion a number of other developments that ultimately were to converge in the formation of the Henry Martyn School of Islāmic Studies. One was the inauguration of the International Missionary Council in 1921. One of their first actions led to a series of meetings in Muslim countries, which culminated in a General Conference in Jerusalem in 1924. Here, for the first time we find a specific proposal that a center for Islāmic Studies should be established in India.

Another result of Edinburgh Conference was the formation in 1912 of what was later to become the National Christian Council of India. This Council had a Committee and a Secretary for work among Muslims which also began to function as the Christian Literature for Muslims Committee that was established in 1923.

In 1925, the Theological School at Bareilly opened a department of Islāmic Studies with John Subhan in charge. At the same time several British Missionary Societies began to give serious support to the idea of a study center in India and at their request the NCCI in 1926 developed a scheme for "The Christian School of Islāmic Studies" to be established in Lahore. Even as efforts were undertaken to secure the buildings, budget and, faculty for the new school many of the future staff were already engaged in conducting short courses in Islāmic studies at various centers around the country under the sponsorship of Regional Christian Councils.

On 27 January, 1930, the Henry Martyn School of Islāmic studies finally became a reality with L. Bevan Jones (BMS) as Principal and L. E. Browne (SPG) and John Subhan (MEMS) as other full time staff members. M. T. Titus who was Secretary of Muslim Work under the NCCI remained closely associated with the School as well.

Henry Martyn 1781-1812 has been called "the first modern missionary to Muslims". Although he came to India as a chaplain of the East India Company, his real love was for the Muslims of the sub-continent. Within a year of his arrival in 1806, he undertook the translation of the New Testament into Urdu, Arabic, and Persian. Ill health forced him to leave for home but on the way he stayed for a year in Persia to revise his translation into that language. Finally in 1812 he began the difficult journey overland to Europe but death overtook him on the way. His name was given to the School for it signifies a standard of scholarship, a commitment to the Gospel and a burning love for Muslim people which still ought to move and inspire us all today.

It is significant that the first resident students at the School in Lahore were three women from South India, indicating not only the all-India character of the School but the all-India character of the mission among Muslims. Many people do not realize that the 75 million Muslims in India today are probably the third largest Muslim population in any country of the world. And they are to be found widely spread with significant numbers in nearly every State of India. This was one important factor that led to the decision for the School to remain in India after the partition that came with independence in 1947.

The NCCI report which drew up the design for the HMSIS indicated three basic functions:

a. Staff study and research of Islām with special reference to the Indian context.

b. The preparation of Christian literature that was sensitive and understanding of Muslim feelings and positive in Christian witness.

c. Teaching and training of those who would be sent for Christian work among Muslims.

The years that followed saw many changes. The Study Center shifted from Lahore (1930-1938) to Landour (1938-1940) to Aligarh (1940-1962), to Jabalpur (1962-1966), to Lucknow (1966-1971) and finally to Hyderabad where at last the Institute is at home in its own property. The nation has moved through the suffering of partition to the freedom of independence. Christian responsibility has shifted from foreign missions to indigenous churches. The Henry Martyn School has become the

Henry Martyn Institute. Yet through it all the basic pattern of concern set forth fifty years ago remains essentially unchanged.

Today the purpose of the HMI is officially stated, "To assist the Church and other institutions to realize and fulfill their evangelistic obligation to Muslims by fostering an adequate and sympathetic understanding of Islām." Often it is necessary to underscore the words, "To assist the Church" since suggestions are often made that would in effect have the HMI doing the job for them.

Research has always been essential in the containing religious encounter. One can break through the stereotypes to gain genuine understanding and insight only by the patient study of Islām and by sustained friendship with Muslim people. Along the way staff members and extension work associates have made significant contributions in this respect. Bevan Jones' *The People of the Mosque* (1932) has served as a standard text through the years and is currently about to appear once more in a revised edition. John Subhan has written with personal insight about *Ṣūfism: Its Saints and Shrine* (1938 with subsequent revisions). The first volumes of Sweetman's study of Islām and Christian Theology began to appear in 1945. Several more could be mentioned but these are perhaps among the more familiar.

There have been fewer publications of this kind in latter years. Rather the emphasis has been on providing booklets in various languages that would be available at low cost as practical aids to pastors, evangelists and lay persons. These include an *Introduction to Islām*, *The Integrity of the Bible according to the Qur'ān and the Ḥadīth*, *Jesus in Islām: A Christian View* and *Christian Witness among Muslims*. A Hindi *Introduction to Islām* by D. S. V. Bhajjan and Dr. B. Khan won a literary prize from the Government of U.P.

A basic tool for research is a library and the HMI has developed a library specialized in Islāmic Studies that would be difficult to equal in India. Not only is this available to the staff but local Muslim scholars often have recourse to it and university students find it a great help in their studies. On occasion individuals will visit our center for some days or weeks to consult our resources in their private research.

"The Bulletin" is a quarterly publication to which both Christians and Muslims are encouraged to contribute articles. Often papers presented at various seminars sponsored by the HMI are published. "Huma", an Urdu quarterly, is also intended as an organ for Christian-Muslim conversation.

Literature for Muslims takes many forms and the role of the HMI in this whole area has often been indirect. When the Christian Literature for Muslims Committee was established in 1932 the Executive of the NCCI Committee for Work among Muslims was asked to function as the Committee. Some place along the way the governing Board of the Henry Martyn School became ex-officio of the Christian Literature for Muslims Committee and having adjourned their own meetings would take up the business of literature. For a long time NCCI funds were available through this Committee to subsidize up to half the cost of publishing Christian literature for use among Muslims. Churches and missions were encouraged to undertake various projects under this scheme and a large number of tracts, booklets, Bible correspondence courses and the like were produced in many languages in this way. For the most part therefore the HMI was not directly involved in the neither financing nor distribution of this literature but served to encourage and coordinate the enterprise.

After the NCCI phased out both its committee and its subsidy, the whole literature programme began to flounder and was maintained on an ad hoc basis with help from the HMI. In 1973 the situation was finally resolved when the Board of the HMI set up a sub-committee to deal with literature and began to provide regular budgetary provisions for its work. Thus in the end the HMI has become more directly involved with literature, at least in an official capacity, than it ever was before.

Almost from the very beginning, it became clear that the concept of a School to provide long term, in-depth training to a body of residential students did not quite fit the practical needs of the missions and churches.

There were very few who had time or the interest to pursue the study of Islām on this scale.

In contrast, the short summer courses for language students in the hill stations and extension courses in different centers on the plains during the winter were reaching a large and responsive number of people. Still, the vision persisted and in 1944 Dr. Donaldson, as principal, proposed a $ 100,000 plan that called for a small campus in Delhi with additional staff residences in Lahore, Landour and Bangalore where staff members could be associated with other institutions. Needless to say, this dream could not survive the post war changes that came to the sub-continent. However, it was not until the Nagpur Consultation on the future of the Henry Martyn School in December of 1958 that the idea of a residential school was laid to rest and the notion of a flexible extension service, which in effect had dominated the teaching programme of the HMS for years, was recognized as the constitutive character of the Institution. This new self-consciousness was formally expressed when the Board resolved to change the name from the Henry Martyn School to the Henry Martyn Institute.

Today the most common form of training is given through institutes, designed to meet the particular needs of the local situation. They may be sponsored by a group of local churches, a regional Council of Churches of some other kind of institution. Sometimes they are for special groups such as pastors, students, evangelists, school teachers, nurses, or Christian lay persons. Often they are a mixture of all kinds of people who are interested. These institutes vary in length from a few days to a week but generally include from 10 to 15 periods for lectures and discussions. The material covered is of a simple, introductory nature and touches on the faith and practice of Muslims, the history and development of Islām and the common problems of misunderstanding that always seem to haunt any kind of Christian-Muslim relationships.

One fruitful effort of long standing has been the annual summer training institute which reaches mainly for seminary students and is held for a week to ten days just after the school year ends. With such a group of 25-30 people it is possible to go into the subject with somewhat greater depth than in the shorter programmes. Traditionally these have been held in the South, although students have come from all over India and instruction has been in English. In recent years a parallel programme has been developed in Hindi for north India. Out of these annual institutes there have come a few individuals who have gone on for specialized study and even graduates work in Islāmic Studies.

The concern to keep in touch with the theological institutions of the church has enabled the HMI to assist several seminaries with special lectures on Islām to supplement their regular curriculum in the study of religions. At times staff members have been called upon to assist with the Serampore exam papers on Islām. Also, in an attempt to focus on the oft forgotten Islāmic dimension of the Indian context in which Christian theology must be done, seminars were organized on two occasions for representative professors from each of the major seminaries in the country. For a week they were able to listen to a wide range of Muslim scholars and to discuss with them the issues that are important to Islām. In addition, the HMI has been able to sponsor visits from leading Islāmic scholars from the west from time to time and to bring them into contact with significant elements of both the Christian and Muslim communities.

From the very beginning, one of the prominent characteristics of the whole movement of interest and concern for Muslim people has been the ecumenical spirit in which it was undertaken. This has been especially true of the Henry Martyn School which was started as a cooperative venture by several mission societies who were then joined by others as time went on. In fact, at the time of partition, one of the reasons given for remaining in India was to preserve this ecumenical dimension in the life and service of the school since some of the missions that were involved with the HMS did not have work in Pakistan. Today the HMI seeks to remain as widely and as deeply ecumenical as possible. For a number of years Roman Catholics as well as Protestants of all persuasions have been regular participants in the various programmes of the HMI.

During the last decade or two the word "dialogue" has become widely used, and perhaps misused, to describe an activity which has become increasingly important in our pluralistic world. The concept is not a new one for the HMI for the records from the very beginning speak of mutual relationships, both on a personal and an institutional level, which today would be called dialogue. Yet it is true, perhaps, that there is a wider recognition among Christians that "dialogue" expresses a more appropriate attitude toward other people than was often the case in the past. It represents a shift from confrontation to conversation. It accents the need to listen and learn rather than to declare and dominate. It recognizes the worth and integrity of other people who find their identity and values in cultural terms and patterns that differ from our own. And it reminds us that the gospel is not our possession but the gift of God which calls us to reconciliation with God and with our neighbors in love, trust, openness and freedom.

A Historical Analysis of Success and Failure in Our Approach to Muslims

David T. Lindell

History has a way of repeating itself—and although one could mention numerous individuals that stand large in story of Christian-Muslim relationships down through the years and identify various Conferences that mark important stages in missionary effort still there is a remarkable similarity in the recurring patterns of Christian witness through the centuries. Consequently our historical references will be brief although hopefully typical and illustrative.

No attempt is made here to report or analyze the many attempts in recent years to break out of the historical rut and find more creative and positive ways in approaching and relating to Muslims. In a sense these belong to current events and are not yet a part of history. Although many of them are exciting and show promise it is still a bit early to be talking about success or failure.

Historical Note

a) John of Damascus—b. circa 700 C.E.—served in a responsible position in the Caliph's Court and later became a leading theologian in the Greek Church. He was the first outstanding figure to address the Muslim world as a Christian. He had thorough knowledge of Arabic, Islām, the Qur'ān and Ḥadīth as well as Christian theology. The topics he selected and the arguments he used in his dogmatic and polemic works "have been so constantly repeated by similar champions from the eighth century to the twentieth that a brief summary of their content will be useful."

> Like many of his medieval successors, John regarded Muḥammad as essentially a heretic rather than the founder of a new religion. He was a false prophet who probably derived his knowledge of the Scriptures from an Arian monk. The final point to be made, therefore, is that Muḥammad has no credentials as a prophet sent by God, He is never fore told in the Old or New Testaments and he can offer no compelling witness to the authority of his revelation. Denying the Muslim accusation that the Jewish Scriptures have been corrupted, John turns to them for proof of the divinity of Christ. Even the Qur'ān calls Christ 'the Word of God,' and since God's Word can hardly be outside of God, we must believe that Christ was in God and of God. In conclusion, the author rebuts the charge that Christians practice idolatry and counters with an attack upon Muḥammad for permitting polygamy, concubinage and lax divorce. Typical of much later controversy is this combination of assault upon the Prophet's personal authority, confidence in metaphysical argument, and emphasis upon the low character of Muslim morality.[1]

Christian apologists who lived among Muslims tended to be relatively moderate and fair in their comments moved by an awareness of their minority status as well as a more authentic knowledge of Islām. Those who wrote from within the shelter of Christendom tended to be less restrained. Typical is *Nicetas,* a philosopher of Byzantium (9th century). Not only was Muḥammad a false prophet, but "he was utterly ignorant, shameless liar and the son of Satan." The Qur'ān is "an unintelligible tissue of lies and fables, with no claim to divine origin" and the denial of the Cross etc. is evidence of "the devilish wickedness of Muḥammad himself." This kind of language and the assessment of Islām it represents continued to be typical of the Christian approach to the Muslims until relatively recent times. Even today there are not a few who share this perspective although their language is far more chastened and polite.

b) The 13th Century begins with attempts by St. Francis of Assisi to meet with Muslims in Egypt and Morocco (1219). Both Franciscans and Dominicans were active for nearly 70 years without much success. It is notable; however, that in this period of closer relationships with Muslims there was a more accurate knowledge and a less harsh judgment of Islām.

Ricoldus de Monte Crucis, a Dominican who finally settled in Baghdad in 1290, is best known for his "Confutatio Alcorani" a polemic piece that exerted a strong influence for several centuries. It rehearses the traditional arguments for Christianity and against Islām but is notable for his generous treatment of the Muslims, praising their hospitality, zeal for study, charity to the poor, respect for Jesus and the prophets, devotion to prayer and reverence for God.

c) Raymon Lull (1232-1316) was a Courtier in the court of both James I & II, kings of Argon. Converted at 31 years he devoted the rest of his long life to the conversion of the infidels. His approach provided some innovative variations on the basic theme. First he devoted 9 years to concentrated study of Latin, philosophy, theology and Arabic to prepare himself. Next he wanted to write Christian books that would win by irrefutable logic the minds and hearts of the Muslims and to set up colleges to train missionaries for the task. He did compose several massive tomes but was never able to persuade popes or kings to support his college scheme with much more than promises. In 1292 he finally ventured forth alone to try out his compelling arguments on the Muslims of Tunis. Banished for his efforts he now began to push for a crusade so that he could appeal to the unbelievers under Christian protection. Fortunately this effort also failed. After an abortive visit in 1307, he once again returned to North Africa in 1314 and lived out his final days in preaching and disputation until he fell under the stones of an angry mob in Bugia.

d) Henry Martyn (1781-1812) was true to his type and time in his utter contempt for Islām. He loathed it as a form of sin. Keen polemic was a contest between the powers of light and the powers of darkness; in his own words, it was "aiming a stab at the vitals of Mohammad." The teachings of "the imposter of Mecca" were for him merely "all this Muḥammadan stuff." Later in India he was to gain a new respect for his Muslim adversaries. "A new impression was left on my mind, namely that these men are not fools, and that all ingenuity and clearness of reasoning are not confined to England and Europe." Month after month there would be many hours spent in argument about the authority of the Scriptures and of the Qur'ān, the miracles of Muhammad, God's power and human's free will, the Trinity and the Incarnation.

Yet all along there were signs of doubt in this method. "Frigid reasoning with men of perverse minds seldom brings men to Christ. However, as they require it, I reason." "I have now lost all hope of ever convincing Muḥammadans by argument ... I know not what to do but pray for them" ... "I am preparing for the assault of this great Muḥammadan Imām. I have read the Qur'ān and notes twice for this purpose, and even filled whole sheets with objections, remarks, questions, etc.; but alas! What little hopes have I of doing him or any of them good in this way?"[2]

e) Karl Pfänder (India 1837-58) chiefly known for his book *Mizān al-Ḥaqq* (*The Balance of Truth*) written in Persia and still in limited circulation. The major premise is that satisfying knowledge of God can only come by revelation and since the Christian and Muslim claim to revelation differ only one of them can be true. He then proceeds to define the criteria of True Revelation by describing his conception of Christian revelation and comes to the obvious conclusion that Islām fails the test.

Still when he joined a colleague, Thomas French, in a two day debate with two maulvīs, he did so reluctantly "well aware that generally very little good is done."

f) Cairo Conference 1906: Grave doubts began to emerge about the effectiveness of the controversial method. From India Dr. Weitbrecht notes that nearly all missionaries are opposed to the use of disputation. In Lucknow Conference (1911) Dr. Bowman insists that though a Muslim can sometimes be convinced by pure argument, he will become a merely intellectual Christian, whose devotional and spiritual life has been neglected.

Each succeeding decade has produced an increasing volume of testimony to the same effect; avoid argument, controversy and disparaging references to Mohammad, the Qur'ān and Islām. In place of frontal attack launched on the intellectual level, the best of modem missionaries to Islām pursue a mode of approach which was seldom neglected by their predecessors but which was never quite trusted to bear full fruit—the method of intimate personal fellowship, of loving service, of sympathetic testimony, and of united prayer. Believing that the essence of conversion is direct experience of the saving power of Christ, they seek to lead the Muslim to that experience by helping him to sense his deepest needs, by appealing to what he has already known of God in his inner life, and by sharing with him what Christ has done for them, counting upon Christ Himself, and not theories about Him, to exert a drawing power.[3]

g) A Postscript: In addition to evangelism or proclamation two other kinds of missionary activity may be noted.

In the 19th century patterns of educational and medical work began to develop and in many areas the Christian presence was limited to these efforts by the concerned governments.

In recent years the concept of 'dialogue' has gained some prominence in context of Christian approaches or relationships with people of other faiths.

Observations - Questions - Propositions

i) Success and Failure: Any attempt to assess this question is futile unless one first defines the intention or goal of our effort. Two common formulations come to mind. a) Conversion and/or baptism: The aim is to persuade or help a person to make the decision to stop being a Muslim and to become a Christian. b) Witness: The aim is to witness to the Gospel in terms that a Muslim can understand as Gospel, or to make the love of God real in the life of a Muslim by what we say or do. I suggest there is a valid, important and not so subtle distinction between these two. I would suggest further that by either category our level of success has been rather low.

ii) Addison observes two characteristics of the Church in the 7th century, which sapped its spiritual vitality and left it ignorant, impotent and vulnerable before the advent of Islām. These were the Church's alliance with state politics and power and its preoccupation with doctrinal disputes and heresy-hunting.[4]

The question remains – in the context of our current attempts to evangelize Muslims – to what extent is the Church identified with and involved with Western powers and Western culture? And to what extent are Christians exclusive, sectarian and non-cooperative because of assumed dogmatic superiority?

I think we must learn to live with the fact that we will not all agree on matters of doctrine nor on methods of approach to Muslims. This means among other things that we need to remain in serious and thoughtful dialogue among ourselves as we reach out in our relationships with Muslims.

iii) If our logical arguments and syllogistic dogmas are unconvincing and futile - why do we still preach and peddle them?

a) In spite of the almost unanimous verdict of history to the barrenness of this approach evangelists have an almost irresistible urge to prove the truth of controversial Christian doctrines and we are constantly being flooded with literature in the same vein.

b) In most of these efforts the reasoning is full of fallacies and is generally convincing only to a person who is committed to the truth of the particular proposition for reasons other than reason.

c) Often our zeal to win leads us to conclusion we may not intend. Examples:

Attempts to prove the sonship or divinity of Jesus on the basis of the Virgin Birth lead to implications of Divine paternity, which is rightly rejected, by both the Qur'ān and Christian doctrine.

Attempts to prove the authority of the Scripture can lead to trying to match a verbally inspired Qur'ān with a verbally inspired Bible and thus descend to the Muslim idea of divine revelation.

iv) A serious study of Islām is important: This seems to have been a strong element all through the history of Christian efforts to approach Muslims. The intention and nature of such a study has not always been the same.

Study it to refute it: To expose its weakness and to demonstrate falsity. It is a question whether a person can ever really know or understand Islām from this perspective no matter how skilled he may be in the language and literature of Islām.

Study it to understand what it means to people as a source of faith and meaning, of spiritual and moral power in their lives. If we care about Muslims as people it follows that we ought to care about those things which they hold to be important and holy.

v) The traditional points of controversy in the history of Christian-Muslim encounter are of relatively minor importance in the immediate context of our approach of Muslim. Their importance lies elsewhere.

The initial objections to the Trinity, the 'Son of God' and the corrupted Scriptures can usually be dealt with by agreeing that God is one and did not have a wife, suggesting that we are speaking in metaphors and inviting them to read the only bible we have—and see for themselves. Elaboration on these issues can usually be reserved until a much later time.

The importance of these issues is for us as Christians. They ought to stimulate us to rethink our assumptions to see what we really mean by them and how we can express this meaning in terms that communicate more effectively in the Muslim context. Unless we do we may not have much that is helpful to say at a much later time.

This process is neither easy nor comfortable, but is good for us. Perhaps it will enable us to:

a) Distinguish between our doctrinal formulations and the Biblical record.

b) Attend to the history of doctrine so as to understand the theological intentions and non-theological factors involved in their development.

c) Recognize the need for and the possibility for fresh theological reflection and expression in the light of current issues that did not seem to be pressing in the minds of the Church Fathers.

d) As a minimum clean up the sloppy God talk which characterizes so much preaching today—(Examples can be provided in profusion free of charge.)

vi) "The Christ of theology was vindicated by a process which derided every virtue for which the Christ of history stood."

Thus Addison speaks of the triumphs of orthodoxy by means of church politics personal rivalry and bitter vindictive theological strife. (Orthodoxy is the position of those who won). This could also be said of the goal and the methodology of so much that has passed for evangelism among Muslims.

There is far too much preaching of dogmatic conclusions about Christ rather than the Gospel of Christ. The Gospel is essentially a story—the story of a man called Jesus who went about doing good, healing the sick, speaking a word of reconciliation to sinners, of hope and comfort to the poor, of judgment to the self-righteous and preaching the coming of the Kingdom of God. He was crucified and buried and God raised him from the dead. People listened to him and felt his claim on their lives and as they began to follow him they begin to sense that in this man they encountered none other than God in a unique way. In order to understand this mystery and speak about it they began to draw on a number of names and ideas and concepts both from the Jewish traditions and the Gentile world. So began the theologizing process that was to formulate certain classical creedal formulations after some centuries and was to continue as long as human heed his call to discipleship. It would seem logical—if we are still enamoured of logic—to begin at the things rather than at the end.

There are further implications as well which we can only note in brief form.

a) Religious truth in its deepest sense is existential rather than abstract or prepositional. The Bible speaks of 'doing' the truth.

b) Most of our theological arguments in the Muslim context have been cast in ontological categories of scholasticism. In contrast in Biblical language the stress is on function, what God does rather than what he is in his essential being. The former tends toward metaphysical speculation. The latter seems more suited to the dynamic and relational character of living faith.

vii) Diakonia and dialogue are legitimate and authentically Christian ways in relating to Muslims and do not depend on evangelism to validate them.

a) They should not be regarded as methods of evangelism. To do so can endanger both the integrity of diakonia or dialogue on the one hand and evangelism on the other.

b) Some stress the need for great care to keep them separate to avoid even the appearance of manipulating persons toward conversion.

viii) Abandon all forms of triumphalism, which so often characterize our attitudes and relationships with Muslims.

a) We should cleanse our minds and our mouths of all military metaphors and concepts of controversy. Don't even mention 'crusading', 'proving', 'winning', 'strategies' etc. (When the Bible uses language of this sort the 'enemy' is usually, Satan or evil powers or sin, not people).

b) We are not called to defend the Bible or Christ or the Truth, but rather to take up a cross and follow Jesus. The appropriate Christian stance is one of weakness, humility, patience, willingness to lose an argument, to say we don't have all the answers. ('Martyr' is a word that is misused more often than not. They are an inspiring company but not all of them bear close scrutiny. The line between being a 'fool for Christ' and being a 'fool in your own right' is rather fine and not always evident to a stone throwing mob).

c) The Cross is the very real risk that ultimate success for God is not what we think it is going to be.

ix) Our whole enterprise is conditioned by historical, cultural, sociological and even economic factors to a far greater degree than we may like to admit and we must give close attention to those matters.

a) Muslims rejection is often a psychologically conditioned negative reaction to a slogan we preach on them rather than a conscious turning away from a Gospel, which they come to understand.

b) The dynamics of identity and community usually have much more to do with operative meaning of conversion and baptism in an inter-faith situation than all of our sophisticated theology on the subject.

c) The Islāmic law of apostasy, which is in tension with if not counter to the Qur'ānic injunction against compulsion in religion, is an expression of the kind of sociological barrier, which makes it difficult to respond to anything other than Islām. Religious freedom is part of human freedom, and is not exclusively a Christian concern. Is it perhaps best to deal with the issue on a secular basis?

x) Success in any real sense seems to be associated with Christians who take the time to really care about Muslims in terms of genuine friendship that is sensitive to their needs, their values, and their identity as people. There are no short-cuts or substitutes for this kind of love.

Endnotes

[1] Addison, 26-27.

[2] Addison, 178-179, 211-212.

[3] Addison, Chap. XVI.

[4] Addison, 17.

The Problem of Evil in Islām

Henry J. Otten

In the Christian faith the problem of evil involves accounting for evil in the light of God's power and goodness or love. The discussion in Islām also relates to God's power, but tends to stress his unity and his justice rather than his goodness or love; it is usually only the mystics of Islām who give central place to his love. Perhaps it will be helpful to treat the subject historically.

Pre-Islāmic Arabia

In Arabia before Muḥammad the spirit of fatalism was very strong. The concept of time of an impersonal Destiny was regarded as the cause of all earthly happiness and misery. Since there was no belief in the life after death, time was also regarded as the great destroyer. Although Omar Khayyām lived long after this period, the prevailing sentiment is expressed in one of his poems about life:

> Tis all a chequer-board of nights and days
> Where destiny with men for pieces plays;
> Hither and thither moves and mates and slays
> And one by one back in the closet lays.

Muḥammadand the Qur'ān

In this milieu Muḥammad (570-632) began to preach about one sovereign and majestic God who was also compassionate and merciful. He introduced ideas of the judgment, life after death, along with vivid descriptions of heaven and hell. It was not an impersonal time or destiny that controlled people's lives, but a living, powerful, knowing, and willing Lord. Muḥammad addressed his hearers as those who were responsible for their faith and life and solicited their positive response in the form of submission, to the one God, the Compassionate, the Merciful, the Lord of the worlds, and the Master of the Day of Judgment. After, Muhammad's death his revelatory messages were collected into a book called the Qur'ān. Like the Bible the Qur'ān contains material which seems to predicate evil to God as in the passage, "Jacob I loved, but Esau I hated." (Rom. 9: 13) A number of passages in the Qur'ān speak about God "guiding aright whom he will," and "leading astray whom he will," and also picture him as "filling hell with jinn and man" At the same time there are verses which describe God's wonderful provisions for daily life and appeal to a sense of gratitude for mercies received.

The Early Followers of Muḥammad

The early followers of Muḥammad regarded him as a prophet/apostle and the Qur'ān as the Word of God. They looked for guidance and direction in the Qur'ān, and tended to accept it very literally. But they soon ran into problems and issues which were not directly mentioned or answered in the Qur'ān. Their first reaction was to look for parallels in the life of Muhammad, and to appeal to his example or customary way of doing things as an authority. The reports of Muhammad's words and actions became a separate body of literature from the Qur'ān called Ḥadīth or Traditions. In the course of time, spurious or apocryphal Traditions arose just as in the case of the Gospels. Many "thoughts were attributed to Muḥammad which really came from other sources.

The significant factor to note in the context of our topic is that some of the fatalism which characterized the pre-Islāmic Arabs began to enter the thought-patterns of Islām via the Traditions, and even affected the interpretation of the Qur'ān. The God of Islām was pictured as the unfeeling time or Destiny exemplified in the poem of Omar Khayyām. One of the more horrendous 'Traditions' describes God as bringing some offspring from Adam predestined to the Garden and others to the Fire, and, himself not caring either way. The fatalism is further seen in one of the earliest Muslim creeds which Says" "What reaches you could not possibly have missed you; and what misses you could not possibly have reached, you."[1] The allusion seems to be to the flight of an arrow towards its target. Another Tradition illustrates the point: King Solomon discovered that the Angel of Death was about to take away two of his scribes. When he heard about it, Solomon sent the two scribes into another country to escape. The next day he saw the Angel of Death smiling. When he asked the Angel why he was smiling, the angel replied, "Because you sent the two scribes to the exact place from which I was ordered to fetch them.

So in this type of early Islām the sovereignty of God becomes combined with a sense of destiny or fate which works both good and evil in an inexorable process with practical ramifications in the direction of irresponsibility or blind resignation among people. The author remembers hearing a young Muslim in Kerala suffering from a creeping paralysis arising from venereal disease saying of the act which brought on the disease, "I couldn't help it; God made me that ,way." Health authorities in Egypt trying to enlist the help of the public in fighting disease by exterminating flies were met with the response, "The flies are here by God's will; if he wants, he will remove them."

In the early period of Islām people who looked upon God as a fateful Predestinator were called *Jabriyyah* which comes from an Arabic designation for God as *Al-Jabbār*—the Compeller. Since the strands of divine sovereignty in the Qur'ān and harsh predestination of the Traditions were closely intertwined in early Islām every reformer in later Islām who appealed to the fundamentals of the Qur'ān and the early Traditions ended up with the same conception of God as the Force.

The Period of Interaction with Philosophy (from about 750)

The early Muslims did not concern themselves with systematic thinking about the problem of evil, but this changed when the Abbasid dynasty took over the leadership of Muslims in 750 with administrative headquarters at Baghdad. The Muslim conquests had brought them into contact with other religions and cultures, including the Manichaeans and people acquainted with Greek philosophy. These contacts also forced the Muslims to defend their faith against critics. Several of the Abbasid caliphs encouraged new learning and promoted the translation of Greek thought into Arabic. This thought gave an impetus to rationalism in Islām and helped add another authority for Islāmic faith and life along with the Qur'ān and the Traditions namely analogical reasoning (*qiyās*).

A new group of thinkers arose called the Mu'tazila (from an Arabic word meaning to "withdraw"). They regarded themselves as the champions of the unity and justice of God. Against the Manichaeans they upheld the Qur'ānic doctrine of the unity of God, and proclaimed that it was idolatry (*shirk*), the unforgiveable sin in Islām, to posit another creator in the universe to explain the origin of evil. Their own explanations for the presence of evil fall into the category of the Free-will Defence. They reacted strongly against the Jabriyyah— those who attributed everything to the direct action of God, and explained evil as the interaction between the justice of God and the free-will of humankind. Under the influence of Greek thought the Mu'tazila introduced new categories such as "what is best" and "what is fitting" to be applied to God and his actions. This was in contrast to the Jabriyyah who were content to accept God literally as he was described in the Qur'ān and traditions. In order to absolve God from evil the Mu'tazila emphasized human responsibility and claimed that people have power (*qadr*) over their own acts. They taught that God is the Creator of people, and that people are the creators of their own acts. Since they attributed power to people, they were called the Qadariyyah. One of the Mu'tazila Abbād ibn Sulaimān (d. 972 ca.), compared the divine/human roles in human action to conception. Just as a man has power over his wife's conception, although he does not have power to conceive, so God may have power over evil, but not the power to do evil. That only resides in human.

Al-Ash'arī (873-935)

Al-Ash'arī was one of the most influential theologians in Islām. He grew up as one of Mu'tazilah but became disillusioned with the movement when he discovered that rationalism did not have all the answers. Thereafter he promoted a more conservative Qur'ānic based type of theology which still holds sway in large areas of the Muslim world today. But he did not abandon reason altogether. Although he ruled out reason as an authority in religion, he used rational arguments to defend the faith and silence his opponents. His main interest was to up Al-Ash'arī uphold the unity and the power of God, to "let God be God." He accused the Mu'tazilah of polytheism. *Shirk*, because they set up ethical standards outside of God, such as the philosophical concepts of "good" and "fitting." They tended to judge God and his word (Qur'ān) by those outside standards rather than to let the Word and God decide what is good and fitting to him. Al-Ash'arī also charged them with the *shirk* of setting up other creators beside God by speaking of people as the creators of their own actions. In one of his creedal statements, in the *Maqalāt*, Al-Ash'arī writes:

> They (Muslims) confess that there is no creator at all, save God; and that the evil actions of creatures are created by God; and that the good actions of creatures are created by God, and that creatures are unable to create anything.

However, Al-Ash'arī did not revert back completely to the old Jabriyyah concept of God, who was exalted to such a degree as to be almost indifferent to good and evil. He seemed to have a "gut reaction" against ascribing moral evil to God. He distinguished between the evil actions of human and the evil thereof. The actions were empowered by God, but he was not responsible for the evil tone of those actions. He illustrated his point by the Biblical/Qur'ānic stories of Abel and Cain and Joseph and his master's wife. The goodness of Abel set up a situation in which murder resulted. Even though Abel was involved in the situation he did not become evil thereby. In the same way Joseph's faithfulness resulted in an injustice—his imprisonment. But Joseph was not tainted with that injustice. Later followers of Al-Ash'arī maintained this distinction in a creed called *Fiqh-i Akbar II*:

> All acts of obedience are obligatory on account of God's command, wish, good pleasure, knowledge, will, decision and decree. All acts of disobedience happen through His knowledge, decision, decree, will; not according to His wish, good pleasure, or command.

Interestingly enough, Al-Ash'arī and his followers, held that people are intuitively conscious of the difference between a good action and an evil action. This seems to presage Ricouer's emphasis on the phenomenon of conscience.[2]

Islāmic Mysticism (Ṣūfīsm) and Emanation Philosophy

These two topics may be treated together because they run somewhat concurrently and both tend to monism.

a) There are elements of mysticism in the Qur'ān itself. For example there is one verse which describes God as being nearer to a person than his jugular vein (50:15). From the very beginning of Islām there were pious ascetics who were interested in being near to God and were also repelled by the worldliness of some of the Muslim rulers. Later these same types of people felt dissatisfied with the sterile discussions of some of the theologians and philosophers about God. They began to emphasize experience rather than reason as the way of access to God. Since they sometimes wore a special garment of wool (Ṣūf), they became known as Ṣūfīs. The Ṣūfīs were more interested in the immanence than the transcendence of God and had contacts with Persian and Indian mystics also.

While some mystics were content to pursue a pious life motivated by the love of God (e.g. Rābia', the Mystic d. 801), others became involved in esoteric and even antinomian practices in which they hoped to experience oneness with God or to be "annihilated in his unity." On the basis of Qur'ānic verses which speak of God as the First and the Last, some of them believed that the created world will finally be annihilated and absorbed back into God just as it was created. Some extremists such as al-Bisṭāmī and al-Ḥallāj (858-922) became virtual pantheists and identified God with themselves. However, the positive elements of Ṣūfīsm were finally incorporated into Islāmic orthodoxy and made respectable through the efforts of Al-Ghazālī (1058-1111), who ranks with Al-Ash'arī as one of the formative theologians of Islām.

Al-Ghazālī started life as an Ash'arīte, but by that time Muslim theology had degenerated into a form of dry scholasticism. Al-Ghazālī could not find spiritual peace in that atmosphere and turned to the Ṣūfīs, giving up his security as a respected professor in his search for real life. Like Rābia', Al-Ghazālī immersed himself in the concept of love, and found at least some amelioration from the pain of evil in that process.[3]

Eventually, the mystics produced their own philosopher Ibn 'Arabī (1165-1240), who formulated a philosophy of unitary mysticism in which the distinction between good and evil become blurred or absorbed into the unity of God and all phenomena, good and bad. This is illustrated in the poem of one of Ibn 'Arabī's contemporaries, Jalāl-al-Dīn Rūmī (d. 1273):

> I am the Gospel, the Psalter, the Qur'ān;
> I am Uzza and Lat—Bel and the Dragon.
> Into three and seventy sects is the world divided,
> Yet only one God; the faithful who believed in him am I.
> Lies and truth, good, bad, hard and soft,
> Knowledge, solitude, virtue, faith
> The deepest ground of hell, the highest torment of the flames,
> The highest paradise,
> The earth and what is therein,
> The angels and the devils,
> Spirit and man, am I.

b) Emanation Philosophy: The first Muslims who became interested in Greek philosophy did not distinguish between the historic Plato and Aristotle and Neo-Platonism. Two philosophical works which greatly influenced the philosophers of Islām were the *Theologia Aristotelis* by an unknown Greek author and Proclus' *Elements of Theology*, known in the Middle Ages as *Liber de causis.* Both of these works reflect the Neo-Platonism of Plotinus more than the actual teachings of Plato and Aristotle, but they were a great influence on men such as Avicenna (Ibn Sīnā) (979-1037), one of the greatest Muslim philosophers. In one of his works on Predestination he comes close to the Principle of Plentitude in showing the place of evil in the world:

> There is nothing whatsoever in the entire world, and in all its high and lower parts, which is excluded from the statement that God is the cause of its being and its origination in time, that God has knowledge of it and disposes it, and that God wills it to exist ... For if this world were not

> compounded of the effects of good and evil forces and of the produce of both righteousness and corruption in its inhabitants, the world order would never have been fulfilled completely.

The Modern Period

In the modern period Muslims have been forced to defend their faith and way of life against the critics of a vigorous West. Muslims have been charged with having an un- progressive and lethargic society. Often the brute predestination concept of God in much of popular Islām has been pointed out as the reason for this static condition. So reformers and apologists of Islām, usually try to amend the grim deterministic tendencies of orthodox Islām by a reinterpretation of the Qur'ān, a critical selection of the Traditions, and an emphasis on human responsibility.

a) Daūd Raḥbar, a contemporary from Pakistan, is a good example. In his book, God of Justice, he laments that Muslim theologians and philosophers have obscured the real character of God revealed in the Qur'ān. Raḥbar believes that God's justice is the dominant theme of the Qur'ān, and that God's actions are not based on past Divine Decrees, but on the present response of human beings to him.

> We have found no statement among all the contexts examined ... which may be quoted to prove that all human action is by an arbitrary decree of God. The very basic sense of *qādir* and *taqdīr* is arranging things by due measure, and excludes the idea of arbitrariness.[4]

Just as Christians might say that God hardens those who have already hardened themselves, Raḥbar claims that the Qur'ānic God does not lead people astray "from eternity," but only leads those astray who have already gone astray themselves. The Qur'ānic references to God's knowledge and foreknowledge are not the determination of events beforehand, but only a reminder to believers and unbelievers that God knows everything which is happening to each individual. The verses which speak of God's records and decrees are not prescribing the history of people before they are born, but merely a noting of events as they happen for the purpose of divine justice.

In Raḥbar's theodicy the world exists to demonstrate the justice of God. He recognizes that Christians give the highest place to God's love but holds that the Islāmic thrust is on God's justice. The full display of justice requires both good and evil, the former for reward and the latter for punishment.

> Had God willed, He would have made the world a single nation of guided men, but He has created a world of vice and virtue that He may judge and reward on the final day ... Allah is, before anything else, a Judge. The universe exists so that God may reward men the wicked will surely be thrown into hell; hell is not made to be kept vacant. He created a world in which men could be wicked and good, men who would be responsible for their deeds.[5]

When some other Muslims criticized Raḥbar for limiting God's power by making room for human responsibility in evil, he countered, "God Himself exercises self-restraint from evil, and thus limits His own power. To know Him as a moral Being in Qur'ānic terms we must know him as such, and not as a Force 'let loose.'"[6]

Raḥbar feels that the Qur'ānic phrase, "God is mighty over all," which occurs some 30 times in the Qur'ān, is not a metaphysical phrase implying absolute Omnipotence, including the power to do evil. "It does not mean that God can create another God, or that He can annihilate Himself permanently or temporarily, or that He can say that two and two make five and yet feel happy."[7]

b) The Aḥmadiyya movement. Another example of modern teaching on the subject is the Aḥmadiyya Movement in Islām which takes its name from its founder, Mirzā Ghulām Aḥmad (1835-1908) in India. In stark contrast to Daūd Raḥbar, one of the exponents of the Movement, B. Maḥmūd Aḥmad (d. 1965), denies that justice is one of the attributes of God at all, terming it an "ill-devised" attribute which Christians ascribe to God. Instead B. Maḥmūd Aḥmad emphasizes the mercy of God, together with His authority as Master, and works out a theodicy where God finally overcomes all human evil by temporary remedial punishment, resulting in the eventual salvation of all.

The same author also makes an attempt to rescue God from the charge of creating evil by categorizing different kinds of evils. First of all, he takes up physical evils such as "wild and savage animals, worms and reptiles, pains, troubles, ailments, and pestilences."[8] He explains that these are not evils in themselves; they only seem evil to people who do not know enough about their true nature and God's purpose.

> If their true nature is considered, they add to the praise and glory of God and do not in any way detract from it ... they have all been created for a useful purpose man ought to praise God for their creation.[9]

Secondly, the same author takes up moral evils and describes them as a departure from the laws of nature. God did not create the transgressions of the laws of nature, but he created the consequences of failing to observe the laws. If someone gets hurt jumping from a high place, he cannot blame God for his jump and his injury. God created the laws of gravity, but not the transgressions of those laws. The evils which result from failure to abide by the laws of nature help people to understand the principles of those laws better and avoid transgressions in the future. Thus the evil consequences which follow transgression serve a beneficial purpose. Human advances. Disease or sin which may follow from ignorance or an infringement of the laws of nature "does not in any way detract from the perfection of God's Beneficence."[10]

Thus we see that Islām in the course of its history has taken up the problem of evil in its own ways. Some of these ways parallel similar efforts among Christians.

Appendix to the Problem on Evil in Islām

1. A Qur'ānic verse alluding to God's power

To Allah belongs the sovereignty of the heavens and earth. He createth what he pleaseth, giving to whom He pleaseth females and to whom He pleaseth males. Or conjoining them males and females, and He maketh whom he pleaseth barren; verily He hath knowledge and power (42:48ff).

2. A Qur'ānic verse indicating human responsibility

And say, "The Truth is from your lord; so who wills let him believe and who wills let him disbelieve," verily We have prepared for the wrong-doers a Fire ... but those who have believed and done worlds of righteousness—verily We do not allow to go lost the reward of any who do well in deed. For these are Gardens of Eden … (18:28-30).

3. A Qur'ānic verse suggesting Pre-destination

As for those who have disbelieved, it is all one whether thou hast warned them or not; they will not believe. Allah hath set a seal upon their hearts and over their hearing and their sight is a covering; for them is (in store) a punishment mighty (2:5-6).

4. A Qur'ānic verse suggesting that God only punishes those who have sinned themselves:

We wronged them not (i.e. those who were punished but they wronged themselves (11:103).

5. Traditions which point to a fatalistic type of predestination

Adam and Moses were once disputing before their Lord and Moses said, 'Thou art Adam who God created with His hand and breath into thee His Spirit and angels worshipped thee and He made thee dwell in Paradise and then thou didst make men to fall down by thy sin to the earth.' Adam replied, 'Thou art Moses who God distinguished by sending with thee His message and His book and He gave thee the tables on which all things are recorded. Now tell me how many years before I was created did God write the Torāt (Pentateuch)?' Moses replied, 'Forty years' said Adam, 'and did you find written there, Adam transgressed against his Lord?' 'Yes' said Moses. Said Adam, 'Then, why do you blame me for doing something which God decreed before He created me by forth years?'[11]

(The Prophet said) 'It may be that one of you performs the works of the people of Paradise, so that between him and Paradise there is only the distance of an arm's length. But then his book overtakes him and he begins to perform the works of the people of Hell, which he will enter. Likewise, one of you may perform the works of the people of Hell, so that between him and Hell there is only the distance of an arm's length. Then his book will overtake him and he will begin to perform the works of the people of Paradise, which he will enter.'[12]

6. Statement on God and evil from Muslim creeds

We confess that the decision concerning good and evil wholly depends upon Allāh. For whoever should say that the decision regarding good and evil depends upon another than Allah would thereby be guilty of unbelief regarding Allah, and his confession of the unity of Allah would become invalid.

We confess that works are of three kinds, obligatory, supererogatory and sinful. The first category is in accordance with Allāh's will, desire, good pleasure, decision, decree, creation, judgment, knowledge, guidance and writing on the preserved tablet. The second category is not in accordance with Allah's commandment, yet according to His will, desire, good pleasure, decision, decree, judgment, knowledge, guidance, creation and writing on the preserved tablet. The third category is not in accordance with Allah's commandment yet in accordance with His will; not in accordance with His desire, yet in accordance with His decision; not in accordance with His good pleasure, yet in accordance with His creation; not in accordance with His guidance; in accordance with His abandoning and His knowledge, yet not in accordance with His intimate awareness or with His writing on the preserved tablet.[13]

Allah created the creatures free from unbelief and firm belief. Then He addressed them and gave them commandments and prohibitions. Thereupon some turned to unbelief. And their denial and disavowal of the truth was caused by Allah's abandoning them. And some of them believed—as appeared in their acting, consenting and declaring—through the guidance and help of Allah.

Allah did not compel any of His creatures to be infidels or faithful. And He did not create them as faithful or infidels, but He created them as individuals, and faith and unbelief are the acts of human ... All the acts of human—their moving as well as resting are truly their own acquisition but Allah creates them and they are caused by His will, His knowledge, His decision, and His decree.[14]

Allah is the creator of all the actions of His creatures whether of unbelief or of belief, of obedience or of disobedience. And they are all of them by His will and Desire, by His judgment and His ruling, and by His decreeing. His creatures have actions of choice for which they are rewarded or punished. And the good of these is by the good pleasure of Allah and the vile in them is not by His good pleasure.[15]

All that happens, happens through the will of Allah.... Allah was free to create the world as well as not to create it. Allah has not created the world either with a view to what is salutary to human, or on any other ground; but He knew from eternity that He would create. Allah is free to make the whole world vanish and to make it return. It would be absurd to suppose that Allah should wrong anyone. He is free to impose suffering on innocent children and animals, without indemnifying them.[16]

7. Statements from Muslim theologians and philosophers

a. Wāṣil ibn 'Atā' (d. 748)

The Creator being wise and just, it is forbidden to establish a relation between Him and evil or wrong. So it cannot be conceived that His will regarding His servants should be different from His commands; likewise He would not punish them on account of His own decision. So human is the author of good, evil, faith, unbelief, obedience, and transgression, and is rewarded for his acts; but the Lord gives him power for all this.[17]

b. Regarding Abul Huzail, one of the early Mu'tazila (d. 841?)

Abul Hudhail, with many others, held that God had power to do evil, but that He did not actually do it because of His wisdom and compassion. Alternatively he argued that evil only proceeds from deficiency, that there is no deficiency in God, and that therefore it is impossible to suppose Him doing evil.[18]

c. Regarding Bishr B. Al-Mu'tamir (d. 825), another early Mu'tazila

The omnipotence of God was taken more seriously by Bishr than by most of the Mu'tazila. He even seems to have used it in a curious way to deal with the problem of evil, arguing that because God is omnipotent there must always be something better that He can do. Since His goodness is infinite and without limit, it is absurd to expect that any actual manifestation of it is the best; all that human may fairly expect of God is that He will do what is best for them in their religion.... In general God is not obliged to do what is best for human.[19]

d) Al-Ashʿarī (873-935)

They (Muslims) confess that there is no creator at all, save God; and that the evil actions of creatures are created by God; and that the good actions of creatures are created by God; and that the creatures are unable to create anything ...

They confess that God helps believers to obey Him and abandons unbelievers; and that He favours believers and has compassion on them and makes them righteous and guides them, but does not favour unbelievers or make them righteous or guide them; and that, if He were to guide them, they would be guided. But God can make unbelievers righteous and favour them so that they will be believers. However, He has not willed to mike them (unbelievers) righteous, and not to favour them so that they will be believers, and has rather willed that they be unbelievers, as He foreknew, and He abandons them and leads them astray and sets a seal on their hearts.

They confess that good and evil are by God's decision and determination; and they believe in God's decision and determination, its good and its evil, its sweet and its bitter.[20]

e) Majid Fakhry on Al-Ashʿarī

The concept of co-creator with God (view of Muʿtazila), according to Al-Ashʿarī, amounts to polytheism and involves a radical curtailing of God's absolute power. Despite these strictures he does not concur with the Traditionists in their claim that human does not play any part whatsoever in the drama of moral activity. In his doctrine of *Al-Kasb*, or acquisition of the merit or demerit for the deed done, Al-Ashʿarī seeks a way out of the moral dilemma of responsibility without sacrificing the omnipotence of God. Voluntary actions, in his view, are created by God, but acquired by the human agent or imputed to him. Creation differs from acquisition in that the former is the outcome of "eternal power" whereas the latter is the outcome of the "created power" of the agent, so that the same action is said to be created by the one and acquired by the other. Stated differently, human acquires the credit or discredit for the deed created by God, since it is impossible that God should acquire it in time, while He is its author eternally. In this subtle verbal distinction between what is acquired in time and what is created or pre-destined eternally, lies, according, Al-Ash'arī, the distinction between voluntary and involuntary action, and also that between the merit or demerit which attaches to the latter. Human, as the locus or bearer of "acquired action," becomes responsible for such action, whereas for involuntary action, such as trembling or falling, etc., one is totally irresponsible.[21]

For, whereas the latter (Mu'tazila) held that human can determine rationally what is good and evil, prior to revelation, the Ash'arites adhered to a strict voluntarist ethics. Good is what God has prescribed, evil is what He has prohibited.... God's power and majesty are such that the very meaning of justice and injustice is bound up with His arbitrary decrees. Apart from those decrees, justice and injustice, good and evil, have no meaning whatsoever. Thus God is not compelled, as the Mu'tazila had argued, to take note of what is "fitting" in regard to His creatures and to safeguard their moral or religious interest, so to speak, but is entirely free to punish the innocent and remit the sins of the wicked.[22]

e) Abbād B. Sulaimān (d. 972)

His insistence that God did no evil went to such lengths that he is alleged to have denied that God made the unbeliever, since "unbeliever" is a combination of "man" and "unbelief", and God did not create the "unbelief." Further, contrary to the rest of the Mu'tazila, he maintained that illness and disease, and even punishment in hell, were not really evil. Those who said they were ought to call God an evildoer.[23]

f) Ibn Ḥazm of Cordova (994-1064)

Having repudiated all forms of analogy or deduction in juridical matters, Ibn Ḥazm next dismisses all forms of scholastic theology as vain and pernicious. The speculation of the theologians, whether Mu'tazilites, Ash'arites, or others, on such questions as the essence of God, the composition of substance, the nature of moral responsibility, etc., is entirely futile.

Human must resign themself to the impossibility of plumbing such mysteries, and in particular, the mystery of God's essence and the rationality of His ways only what lies within the grasp of our senses or is an object of direct intellectual apprehension, on the one hand, or is laid down explicitly in Scripture, on the other, is a genuine object of knowledge. We must affirm justice and goodness of God and deny injustice and wickedness of Him, not on the rational ground (proposed for instance by the Mu'tazila) that this is what His perfection logically requires, but simply on the ground that justness and goodness are predicated of God, and unjustness and wickedness not predicated of Him in the Qur'ān.[24]

g) Al-Ghazālī (1058-1111)

The most important of all the qualities which are necessary consequences of the mystical virtue of the love of God is satisfaction with His decree (*qazā*). Anyone who has strong love for God necessarily remains satisfied with all that his Beloved does. Satisfaction with those works of God which are against his passions and natural desires, especially with the affliction which occasionally befalls human, is also easy for those who have practised love of Him. There are two ways in which this is shown to be easy. One of them is that a lover's mind is so much engrossed in the love of his Beloved that he does not feel the pain of affliction befalling him.... The other way is that the lover does indeed feel the pain of affliction, but is not only satisfied with it but also desirous of it, since he knows with certainty that the reward to be given for this satisfaction is far more than the pain of suffering it.[25]

h) Ibn Rushd (Averroes) (1 126-1198)

So they (the masses) must recognize that He is the creator of both things together (good and evil) and since misguidance is evil and there is no Creator beside Him, it is necessary that evil should be attributed to Him just as there is attributed the creation of good. But it is not fitting that this should be understood absolutely, but only as He is the Creator of good for its own sake and the creator of evil for the sake of the good i.e for the sake of the good associated with it- It is on this account that His creation of evil is justice on His part.[26]

i) Aḥmed B. Taymiyah of Syria (1262-1327)

"I have examined all the theological and philosophical methods," he writes, "and found them incapable of curing any ills or of quenching any thirst. For me the best method is that of the Qur'ān. In the affirmative I read 'The Merciful sat upon the throne (Qur'ān 7:54) … in the negative, 'Nothing is like unto Him' (Qur'ān 42:11)." Indeed, he claims, no one who has partaken of his experience will doubt the futility of these methods.

The philosophers and the theologians have been unable to prove conclusively the justice or the wisdom, the mercy or even the truthfulness of God. And although some of them might be closer to the truth than others, none is free from error altogether. In fact, the only safeguard against error is the unconditional submission to the authority of the ancients.[27]

j) Muḥammad 'Abduh of Egypt (1849-1905)

Other controversies which set the Muslim sects against one another have centred around the questions of responsibility and reward, free will and predestination, etc. With regard to the latter question, some (the Mu'tazila) have argued that God must take account of the welfare of his servants in whatever He does, whereas others (the Ash'arites and Ḥanbalītes) have declared His actions entirely free from any determination. The former err in reducing God to the status of a servant who is subject to the dictates of his master. The latter have reduced Him to a capricious despot who acts arbitrarily and irresponsibly. Both sects agree, however, that His actions must manifest His wisdom and that irresponsibility or falsehood cannot be predicated of His because of the perfection of His knowledge and His will. The differences between them are often purely semantic. In applying the categories of necessity to God, the former are guilty of impertinence. In applying caprice to Him, the latter are guilty of folly. The problem of free will has generated the same endless disputes. The whole difficulty turns on the relation of the providence of the Almighty to free choice as a predicate of rational agent. Its solution is part of that mystery of free will and predestination of which we have admonished not to delve into.[28]

Note: In regard to the last sentence of the above compare the answer of Avicenna when asked to explain the meaning of the Sūfi saying, "To make known the secret of predestination is an act of heresy":

This is an extremely recondite problem, and one which cannot be put on paper save in the language of cypher, a matter which may not be made known except as a hidden mystery: to disclose it in full would work much mischief to the people at large. The fundamental text in this connection is the saying of the prophet: "Predestination is the secret of God; do ye not disclose God's secret." It is related that a man asked the Caliph 'Alī about predestination, and he answered, "Predestination is a deep sea; do not embark upon it." Asked a second time, he replied, "It is a hard road; do not tread it." A third time asked, he retorted, "It is an arduous ascent; do not undertake it."[29]

Endnotes

1 Art. 3, *Fiqh Akbar I* ca. 750.

2 See, Paul Ricouer, *The Symbolism of Evil.*

3 See Appendix, point 5.

4 Daud Rahbar, *God of Justice: A Study in the Ethical Doctrine of the Qur'ān* (Leiden: E.J. Brill, 1960), 119.

5 Rahbar, *God of Justice: A Study in the Ethical Doctrine of the Qur'ān*, 79, 80, 81.

6 Rahbar, *God of Justice: A Study in the Ethical Doctrine of the Qur'ān*, xx.

7 Rahbar, *God of Justice: A Study in the Ethical Doctrine of the Qur'ān*, 47.

8 Bashiruddin Mahmud Ahmad, *Aḥmadiyyat: or the True Islām*, translated by Muḥammad Zafrulla Khan, 3rd edition (Washington: American Fazl Mosque, 1951), 35.

9 Ahmad, *Aḥmadiyyat: or the True Islām*, 35.

10 Ahmad, *Aḥmadiyyat: or the True Islām*, 36.

11 Zwemer, *The Muslim Doctrine of God*, 96.

12 Watt, *Free Will and Predestination in Early Islām*, 18-19.

[13] Quoted in A.J. Wensinck, *The Muslim Creed: Its Genesis and Historical Development* (New York Barnes & Noble Inc., 1965), 126-127.

[14] From *Fiqh Akbar II*, quoted in Wensinck, *The Muslim Creed: Its Genesis and Historical Development*, 190-191.

[15] From a creed formulated by al-Nasafi (d 1159) quoted in Al-Taftazani Sad al-Din (Masud ibn Umar al-Taftazani), *A Commentary On the Creed of Islām*, translated with introduction and notes by Earl Edgar Elder (New York: Columbia University ress, 1950), 80.

[16] From *Fiqh Akbar III* (11th century) quoted in Wensinck, *The Muslim Creed: Its Genesis and Historical Development*, 266-267.

[17] Quoted in Wensinck, *The Muslim Creed: Its Genesis and Historical Development*, 80-81.

[18] Watt, *Free Will and Predestination in Early Islām*, 72.

[19] Watt, *Free Will and Predestination in Early Islām*, 75.

[20] From *Maqalat* quoted in McCarthy, *The Theology of Al-Ashari*, 239-241.

[21] Majid Fakhry, *A History of Islāmic Philosophy* (New York and London: Columbia University Press, 1970), 234.

[22] Fakhry, *A History of Islāmic Philosophy*, 238.

[23] Watt, *Free Will and Predestination in Early Islām*, 82.

[24] Fakhry, *A History of Islāmic Philosophy*, 349-350.

[25] Quoted in Abul Quasem, *The Ethics of Al-Ghazālī* (Selengor: Central Printing Sendirian Berhag Petaling Jaya, Selengor, 1975), 188-1 89.

[26] Quoted in J. Windrow Sweetman, *Islām and Christian Theology*, part I and II (London: Lutterworth Press, 1945), 172.

[27] Fakhry, *A History of Islāmic Philosophy*, 351-352.

[28] Fakhry, *A History of Islāmic Philosophy*, 380-381.

[29] Arthur J. Arberry, *Avicenna on Theology* (London: John Murray, 1951), 38.

The Church and Mission among Muslims[1]

David T. Lindell

It is intended in this short paper to present a few impressions and observations about the way the Church has been involved in mission among Muslims in India. The history of the relationships between Christians and Muslims has not been a story to be proud of on either side. Yet there has been interest and concern for a Christian witness among Muslims almost from the beginning of Islām. In this connection we could name St. John of Damascus, St. Francis of Assisi, and Ramon Lull, as examples. But as far as India is concerned, this interest has been a part of the so-called "Modern Missionary Movement." Ziegenbalg and Plutschau took special note of the Muslims in the South when they came in 1706. And of course, Henry Martyn was considered the first Protestant missionary among the Muslims when he came in 1806. And it was the Cairo meeting in 1906 when Samuel Zwemer brought the "household of Islām" into sharp focus as a special area of mission.

Thus the mission among Muslims was a part of the initiative and commitment that came from the churches and missionary societies from the West. However, even during this time, the attention given to the Muslims was comparatively minor. My own sense of vocation in this respect was shaped to a large extent by a presentation made by a Rev. Westmo at a Student Missionary Conference back in 1943. He told us that out of the 400 million people in India, every fifth person, or 80 million, were Muslims. But out of the five thousand missionaries working in India, you could count on the fingers of one hand the number of missionaries working full time among the Muslims. These are figures for India under the British Raj, of course, but the point is quite clear.

This was still pretty much the situation when I came to India. Out of three hundred or more new missionaries at language school in Landour, hardly a dozen were studying Urdu. The proportion of missionaries who are engaged primarily in Muslim work is probably much higher today, since there are still a handful of fingers around, while most of the other missionaries are gone.

During the last forty years, as far as I am aware, about the only mission/churches that had developed some kind of "Muslim work Department" or set aside personnel especially for this work, were the United Lutheran Church in America (U.L.C.A.) in Andhra Pradesh, the Wesley Methodists in Hyderabad, the Missouri Lutherans in Kerala and Tamil Nadu, and the Swedish Hindustani Mission in Maharashtra. There were other missions and churches that were supportive of H.M.I. in terms of staff and finances, but did not give special emphasis to any work among Muslims. The American Baptists, for example, seconded Ian Douglas to the staff and contributed most generously to the Institute while he was Director, but as soon as he left, their support ended.

By reason of missionary policy and government restraints, there have been drastic changes in the life of the Church in India. Responsibility for mission in India has devolved from foreign missions to the Indian Church in terms of congregational life and growth, evangelism and service institutions such as schools, hospitals etc. Financial support from overseas agencies is still substantial, but it is targeted for particular short-term projects rather than a general subsidy for church budgets and running expenses.

Naturally this has resulted in major adjustments in the life and work of churches. Our concern here is to observe how this has affected the work among Muslims. In general it can be said that with the departure of foreign missionaries and the phasing out of budget subsidies, the churches have discontinued what little specialized work they may have had. The experience of my own church may be typical. When I arrived in Guntur, the India mission of the United Lutheran Church in America (and the Augustana Lutheran Church), together with the Andhra Evangelical Lutheran Church (A.E.L.C.), had a well-developed "Muslim Work Department" of long standing. There were already four missionaries on the field, one about to retire. There were three Urdu elementary schools for Muslim girls, about eight evangelists and fifteen or so Bible women trained in Urdu working among the Muslims in the villages. Today there is nothing of this left. When approached to support the H.M.I. the A.E.L.C. expresses a passing interest, but nothing ever happens.

Very much the same thing has happened to the initiative started by the Missouri Lutherans and the Wesley Methodists. The one exception is the Hindustani Covenant Church which, from the beginning, grew out of a missionary effort that was almost exclusively committed to reaching Muslims.

In addition to this rather "institutional" or specialized mission to Muslims, the churches have been touching the lives of Muslims in various ways through their general witness and service in the community. Through schools, hospitals and general public witness, Christians have been in mission among Muslims. And this still continues as a significant part of the present picture. I think we need to be aware of this and encourage the churches to be aware of the possibilities of this situation.

Within this context there have been individuals who have sensed a special interest or commitment to relate to Muslims. In some cases they have become interested through a course or programme of H.M.I. A few of them have gone on for further study, either sponsored by their churches or on their own. However, it is rare that a church will recognize or encourage their special interest and place them in situations where they can use their training to good advantage.

Perhaps it would be well at this point to say a word about Muslim converts. There had been converts in the past and continue to be some, but their numbers are small. In general it has been difficult for the churches to integrate Muslim converts into the life of the Christian community. One can suggest a number of reasons for this, but the point I would like to make here is that the idea that Muslim converts are automatically good candidates for doing Christian work among Muslims is as dangerous as it is common. During my first term I spent more time trying to talk Muslim inquirers out of taking baptism than I did trying to persuade them to become Christians. With only one exception, every candidate was ready to be baptized and sent off to Bible school to be trained for a job as an evangelist. The exception was a young lad in love with a Christian girl who disappeared when she was married off to someone else.

There are notable exceptions, of course, but in most cases this is not the answer to integrating the convert into the church. Often when there has been a convert who has been effective in mission, they have not always had the support of their churches or for other reasons they have become associated with other overseas agencies that are eager to provide financial support. In which case the result is a small community or congregation that is independent of the Indian Church and dependent on foreign subsidy. This trend is common generally in what we might call "free enterprises mission" where individuals establish direct connections with individuals or congregations in the west and start up orphanages, schools or evangelism as a family business to draw on the resources thus available.

It is important to take note of the apostolate among Muslims that has developed in the Catholic Church. Twenty five years ago they had virtually nothing going along this line. It was the policy of H.M.I. to try and include the Catholics in our programmes as much as possible. Some of their seminary students began to attend our summer courses, and we were invited to give lectures in their colleges. Fr. Wijngaards from the St. John's Regional Seminary was especially interested in getting the Church to begin to work with Muslims and was influential in securing official recognition for this in the hierarchy. As a result, there are a number of clergy people who have completed doctoral work in Islāmics and are committed to this apostolate. They have formed a fellowship called "Islāmic Studies Association" (I.S.A.) which serves to coordinate their concerns for mission to Muslims.

Just a few days ago we had a visit from Dr. Borge Schantz, who is the Director of the Seventh-Day Adventists' Global Centre for Islāmic Studies, based in the U.K. They have become involved with developing centers in strategic places for contact with Muslims and Hindu and he indicated the possibility of something here in India.

In summary, there has been little change since the beginning of "modern missions in India": Christian mission has been preoccupied with the Hindu majority and has largely neglected the significant Muslim population. The potential for the Church to become involved in a mission to Muslims is great—if only we can succeed in bringing this ministry into focus.

Our planning process here at H.M.I. has resulted in a commitment to try and challenge the churches of India to assume the regular support of the Institute for at least a core programme which would currently require about two lakh rupees. A look at the last audited statement shows how far we must go. Out of a total income of just over four lakhs, approximately fifty-four percent comes from overseas grants, forty-three percent from interest on investments, and the remaining three percent split between funding from Indian churches and donations from institutions we have served or miscellaneous gifts.

Within the churches there are pastors, church workers and lay persons who could be encouraged to become active in one way or another in the Church's mission to Muslims. Right now, however, the infrastructure is limited. For example, although the Serampore syllabus provides for special courses in the study of Islām few seminaries have professors qualified to teach the students who might like to take these courses. United Theological College in Bangalore has had an M.Th. course in Islām, but this has had to be held in abeyance for lack of qualified staff. Thus our biggest challenge is simply to draw this ministry within the life of the Church in India.

Endnotes

[1] This article was presented as a background paper at the November 1990 "Consultation on the Church and Islām in India."

The Exploitation of Islām[1]

Rājib al-Banā
Translated by Steven Benson

Why has Islām become a tool for anyone with ambitious or deceitful designs? And why do some work to undermine the Islāmic awakening by presenting Islām in a distorted image as if it were a religion that had no calling except to backwardness and a primitive life-view? As if it had no message except to consecrate despotism; had no goal other than using force and suppressing opinion by killing and oppression. As if it had no cause other than to support the oppressor over the oppressed; no calling except to abort the humanity of women? As if it were the law of the mob, and not a lofty, ideal religion linked to the will of God who is Truth and Justice.

Is this really Islām? The matter is deeply sensitive and profoundly important, but it is not new. There are black pages in Islāmic history that could be gathered together under the title "The Abuse of Islām" or "The Exploitation of Islām." Sometimes this has been done to serve the goals of Islām's enemies, at other times to serve the ambitions of those in power; but at all times and in all ages there have been groups of Islāmic people who are ready to use the weapon of jurisprudence (*fiqh*) to make rulings: "God Most High said ..." or "Our leader the Messenger of God ..." They do not fear God's accounting on the Resurrection Day of the pretentious crimes they perpetrate and of their offenses against the law (*Sharīʿah*) of God. They ridicule it by interpreting (*tafsīr*) God's judgments contrary to God's will, and by using the principles of *Sharīʿah* contrary to their situation; attempting to seduce the Muslim public by exploiting their innocent emotions and sentiments.

The last chapter in this book "The Abuse of Islām" is being written these days. We are living its lines in blood and tears beginning with the assault by the Muslim President of Iraq on the Muslim country of Kuwait and ending with the destruction of Muslim cities and their wealth; a fire destroying their oil and the waste of riches in the land of Islām to the advantage of Satan. All this (rape of a Muslim country, the violation of Muslim dignity, the plunder of wealth in the Islāmic world and its burning and destruction, and the killing of Muslim civilians) takes place under the banner of Islāmic slogans covering everything. Indeed, it is done almost as if it is for God the most High, for His satisfaction and in obedience to His commands. It shocks us, this strange, suspicious theatre which has appeared beating the drums and announcing that President Saddām Ḥussein does what he does only from the greatest heights of Islām!

President Saddam Ḥussein has a long history of political activity based on completely secular concepts. It is known and publicized that for years he has wanted to ride the wave of Islāmic awakening and to exploit it for his own benefit. Now he is using Islāmic vocabulary for the first time in his entire reign. The last of his announcements a few days ago began with an appeal calling Muslims to a holy struggle (*jihād*) with him! He preceded this with a decision to write the slogan "God is the Greatest" (*Allāh ʾAkbar*) on the Iraqi flag in an obvious play for Islāmic sentiments.

Is it possible that Islām really would permit a believer who is powerful to murder a believer who is weak and steal his property? Is it possible that Islām would forbid oppressed Muslims to request help from whomever they choose to recover their stolen right if Muslims were unable to? Did not the Prophet (Peace be upon him) make a treaty with the Jews for the defence of Madīnah? Did not the Prophet turn to one of the polytheists to be his guide to a secret place during the most dangerous action in the life of the Prophet and of Islām, i.e.: the *hijrah* from Makkah to Madīnah?

Is not the Lord of Peace the one who forbids tyranny as is said in the *ḥadīth qudsī:*

> O My servants, indeed I have forsworn tyranny for Myself, and have forbidden it among you, so do not tyrannize.

Then who is it who announced a jihād: the brutal abductor or the victim of brutality whose land has been abducted? Is not your Prophet (P.B.U.H.) the one who legislated for you that:

> Whoever dies defending his land, whoever dies defending his wealth, whoever dies defending his property: that person martyr.

Or do any of you have a different *sharī'ah*?

Ibn Khaldūn in his renowned "Introduction" (*muqaddamah)* discusses aggression as if he were sending to us—in our age—a letter to wake up careless minds and to expose devious minds. He says:

> Violent aggression does not occur except among barbaric nations – those living in wastelands – because they make their living by the points of their lances. Their livelihood comes from what is in other people's hands. Whoever therefore defends their property even if by war – and whether they themselves or others whom they appoint – those people are only seizing what is theirs. As for what this is called in the *shariah* of *jihād*, this is a just war.

Jihād is a just war, and Muslims do not make war except for the sake of a cause. Moreover, did not the Prophet (P.B.U.H.) order the leadership of his armies:

> Attack ... but do not attack by surprise ... and do not deceive... nor make an example of someone by mutilation ... and do not kill babies.

Apply that to what was done by "the leader (*Imām*) of the Muslims" or "the *Imām* of the righteous warriors (mujahidin)" Saddam Hussein.

Does not Islām forbid treachery (*ghadr*) and legally require that warning (*inzār*) is a required condition before fighting (today this is called "a declaration of war") even with unbelievers?

> So if you fear a breach of treaty from a people, renounce it likewise to them. (8:57)

These words of God Almighty can only mean that it is necessary to announce specific violations of agreed treaties before the first arrow flies. In the same way, the experts in religious matters (*fuqahā'*) have said:

> Indeed, Muslims certainly know regarding a nation which has not received news (intention of war); it would be commendable (*mustaḥibb*) for you [the Muslims] not to change [your stance] toward them until you inform them, otherwise this would have the appearance of deception.

Abū Dāwūd and al-Tirmīzī among others write that there was a treaty between Mu'āwiyah and Byzantium (*al-Rūm*). He went toward their lands to attack them, and a man came on a horse saying, "*Allāh 'Akbar Allāh 'Akbar!* Honesty, not deception, so be alert!" This was 'Amr bin 'Īsā al-Salmī. So Mu'āwiyah went to him and asked him, [and he replied] saying: "I heard the Prophet of God (P.B.U.H.) say that if there was a treaty between himself and a people, let him witness his contract, and he will not dissolve it until one of them breaks it or violates it in some way." So Mu'āwiyah returned with his people. (*al-Sir al-Kabīr*, section 3).

If that was with unbelievers and with non-Muslims, what has the "Imām of Muslims" and the "*Imām* of the *Mujāhidīn*" President Ḥussein done with Kuwait and its people? Did not the *Caliph* of our Prophet (Abū Bakr aṣ-Ṣiddīq) command Usāmah bin Zayd, his envoy heading military forces warring against the unbelievers:

> Do not act treacherously ... do not deceive ... do not mutilate ... do not kill children, the aged, or women ... and do not strip or burn date palms ... do not cut down fruit-bearing bushes ... do not kill sheep, cattle or camels except for food. You will pass by peoples who have fled to solitary cells - leave them alone as well as what they have left behind....

Look what it says: "Do not cut down bushes!" So what do you think of someone who sets fire to oil wells and destroys a country? That is not *jihād*—it is treachery. But lustful people or unaware people do not differentiate (or they do not want to differentiate) between the two.

God knows whether this crime of theirs is one of the forgivable sins, or if the souls which have been annihilated and the blood which has been spilled and the riches which have been squandered will remain on the necks of everyone who perpetrated this crime and attempt to justify it until the Day of Resurrection when they will meet their just reward.

Endnotes

[1] This article was originally published in Arabic in the 27 January 1991 issue of al-Ahram (Cairo).

Forgiveness from God as Expressed in the Qur'ān and as Interpreted by Muslims and Christians

Steven Benson

> Oh, that those who do evil had but known, (on the day) when they behold the doom, that power belongeth wholly to Allāh, and that Allāh is severe in punishment – *al-baqarah* (2:165).[1]
>
> Despair not of the mercy of Allāh, Who forgiveth all sins. Lo! He is the Forgiving, the Merciful – *al-zumar* (39:53).

In the minds of many Christians, Islām is a "religion of the law" in which God exercises coldly calculated retribution based on what human beings earn by their behaviour. It is often said in Christian circles that Muslims do not know the grace and forgiveness in the God/human relationship and highlight what they perceive as the lack of this dimension in Islām as one of its greatest weaknesses. It is rare for our Institute to hold a series of lectures for Christians on Islām without once hearing the question, "Do Muslims know anything about forgiveness?" One Christian observer of Islām has attempted to draw a connection between his perception of Muslims' lack of pre-occupation with forgiveness with what he considered to be their inadequate sense of human sin and God's righteousness.[2]

Yet Muslims know God primarily as the Most Merciful, the Mercy-giving. This contrast with the strong accusations mentioned above speaks clearly of the need for Christians to understand better the place that concern, or indeed, accusations may not be based on mistaken impressions. Firstly, I will look forgiveness plays in a Muslim believer's relationship with God, so that expressions of con at some of the declarations in the Qur'ān which relate directly and indirectly to God's forgiveness as extended to believers. Secondly, I will draw on the work of both Christian and Muslim commentators on the Qur'ān to build a framework for our discussion. Thirdly, I will look at some selected Muslim writers to see how they have described the place of forgiveness in the God/human relationship. Lastly, I will attempt to draw conclusions from this study as they seem appropriate. A short appendix of some *Ḥadīth Qudsī* relating to God's forgiveness will serve to re-enforce these conclusions.

The two quotations at the beginning of this article illustrate that the Qur'ān speaks vividly about God's justice and God's punishment of wrongdoers, but it also speaks strongly about God's mercy and forgiveness. As I already indicated, the first side of this balance sheet forms a major part of many Christians' image of Islām, while the second side is not recognized nearly so well. Even a casual reading of the Qur'ān reveals numerous references to God's forgiveness, pardon, mercy, or relentment towards humans who have sinned. According to the concordance, words based on the root *ghfr* (forgive) occur 235 times in the Qur'ān. If this count is augmented by words which carry a related meaning, we find 37 occurrences of the root *fw* (pardon) and 93 occurrences of the root *twb* (relentment).[3] Certainly, the number of occurrences alone attests to the importance of forgiveness as a Qur'ānic concept.

However, the fact remains, that Muslim literature, even *tafāsīr*, seldom deals extensively with the subject of forgiveness. This leads Christians, for whom forgiveness is frequently a topic of theological discussion, to conclude that the Muslim concept of God has little to do with forgiveness. Let us begin with sūrah *al-baqarah* (2), which is the longest in the Qur'ān and therefore has a special right to the commonly held claim that each chapter is complete in itself with regard to the essential teachings of Islām. Ma¢mūd Ayūb has given us a useful tool to understanding the Qur'ān by compiling some of the important commentators.[4] Sūrah *al-baqarah* (2) is full of references to God's forgiveness. The following three are examples:

> And when We did appoint for Moses forty nights (of solitude), and then ye chose the calf, when he had gone from you, and were wrong-doers. Then, even after that, We pardoned you in order that ye might give thanks. (*al-baqarah* 51-52)

> ...These [idolaters] invite unto the Fire, and Allāh inviteth unto the Garden, and unto forgiveness by his grace, and expoundeth thus his revelations to mankind that haply they may remember. (*al-baqarah* 221)

> The devil promiseth you destitution and enjoineth on you lewdness. But Allāh promiseth you forgiveness from Himself with bounty. Allāh is All Embracing, All-Knowing. (*al-baqarah* 268)

The commentators whom Ayūb chooses seem to show little interest in the topic of forgiveness itself. Two verses are exceptions to this and they do give insight on how some Muslims have seen forgiveness in the Qur'an. In 2:58 Ayūb points out that most commentators explain the unusual word *ḥittah* as meaning, "to take a burden off something"; speaking of sin as a burden to people which need to be lifted. The act of pronouncing, "there is no god but God", is an act along with other acts, which takes away the burden of sin. In Shia commentaries the Imāms are the 'gate' of *ḥittah,* the source of divine mercy and forgiveness.[5] Qur'ān2:285-6 is an important revelation concerning an earlier revealed verse which the people considered too difficult to bear. According to commentators, God's response to human incapacity to fulfil divine will is based at least in part, on the attitude of the believer who attempts to do that which is commanded, even if the attempt meets with failure. A humble willingness to obey the command by asking forgiveness for shortcomings precedes the revelation which abrogates the command in question along with an assūrance that, "God shall not charge a soul except to its capacity."[6] We can assume that human defiance which insists that God's commands be more reasonable would not be met with the same response from God, if indeed *response* is a word which can appropriately apply to a word or action from God.

Meagre as these two verses and their commentary might seem, they do give us a starting point for understanding Qur'ānic teaching about God's forgiveness. Under which circumstances may sin be forgiven? Confession of faith in the oneness of God and submission to divine will are both acts which prepare the way for God to forgive the sinner. With those observations in mind let us survey other Qur'ānic verses in which the roots *ghfr, jw,* or *twb* occur.

One of the most striking things about Qur'ānic verses which speak of God's forgiveness is that they are most often closely connected with faith and or repentance. When forgiveness is promised, it is promised to those who believe in God or to those who fear God. Forgiveness is never offered to unbelievers except on the condition that they desist from their unbelief and turn to God. Sūrah *al-Anfāl* (8:38) is an example, "Tell those who disbelieve that if they cease that which is past will be forgiven them; ..." Again and again it becomes clear that the one the one sin which can never be forgiven is the sin of *shirk* (ascribing partners to God).[7] (Sūrah *al-Nisā'* 4:48):

> Lo, Allāh forgiveth not that a partner should be ascribed to Him. He forgiveth [all] save that to whom He will. Whoever ascribeth partners to Allāh, he hath indeed invented a tremendous sin.

Many times repentance is also tied to forgiveness. Sometimes this repentance is spoken of as 'remembering' God, as in sūrah *al-'Imrān (*3:135-6):

> And those who, when they do an evil thing or wrong themselves, remember Allāh and implore forgiveness for their sins ... The reward of such will be forgiveness from their Lord ...

This might seem to imply that the sin would not have been committed in the first place, if God had not been "forgotten". True repentance then, involves: a) remembering the primacy that God has over everything in life, thus causing an awareness of sin; b) asking forgiveness from God; and c) genuinely making the intention to refrain from this sin in the future.

Beyond those very general impressions there are some apparently peripheral observations which should also be noted. Firstly, while faith is clearly paramount, there is no doubt that good deeds are evidence of a person's belief, while sins are clear evidence of unbelief. Secondly, there are a few passages in which strong and graphic statements about the severity of God's judgement/punishment are dramatically juxtaposed with equally strong statements about the generosity of God's forgiveness. Sūrah *al-Ḥijr* (15:49-50), "Announce unto My slaves that verily I am the forgiving, the Merciful, and that My doom is a dolorous doom." Sūrah *al-Burūj* (85:12-14), "Lo! the punishment of thy Lord is stem. Lo! He it is Who produceth, then reproduceth, and He is the Forgiving, the Loving." Thirdly, forgiveness is offered to believers for "smaller" or "lesser" sins, if one avoids the "greater" or "more serious" sins. Fourthly, forgiveness is readily available to believers for sins which were either unintentional or unavoidable because of circumstances, or into which one was forced unwillingly by another. Fifthly, in all matters there are no circumstances in which God is bound to forgive or to punish. God always remains free to punish whom He wills and to pardon whom He wills. Finally, verses which speak of God's relenting *(twb)* do not mention God overlooking the sins which are "lesser" or "unavoidable", but only mention a change in heart on the part of the sinner as evidenced by repentance, a request for pardon, or a turning to the path of righteousness. Also mentioned along with two (relentment) is God's free will to elect or to pardon whom God chooses.

How do others interpret the Qur'ān's statements on forgiveness? Dāwūd Raḥbar's well-known study of Qur'ānic ethical doctrine strongly refutes the view of many other Christian students of Islām, who held that God in the Bible is portrayed as the God of grace and love, while God in the Qur'ān is portrayed as the God of wrath. Dāwūd Raḥbar makes the case well that God in the Qur'ān is not the God of wrath, but rather the God of merciful justice. He gives an early hint as to what he sees as the controlling concern. He states that while early Muslims tended to make divine justice an aspect of divine mercy, he understands the Qur'ān to make divine love and mercy subservient to divine justice.[8] Regarding divine *maghfirah* (forgiveness), Dr. Ra¢bar says: "... faith in

God is ... the most essential condition of God's forgiveness. God does not pardon unbelief and a person's belief can win them pardon for what is bygone."[9]

Forgiveness is only granted when asked for,[10] but the request must be accompanied by actions which show that there is true repentance. To follow God's guidance is to earn forgiveness, while to pursue the path of error is to earn torment. In short, "Be good and God will forgive you."[11] Statements to the effect that "God forgives whom He wills" do not mean that God acts impulsively, but that no one else has the power to prevent God from forgiving whom He wills.[12] Raḥbar summarizes the Qur'ān's teaching about *maghfirah* in the statement. "I shall pardon you if you repent and act aright, and I shall punish you if you don't.[13]

On the subject of divine *afw* (forgiveness) Dāwūd Raḥbar sees many of the same themes, but the place of repentance as a necessary precondition for God's forgiveness becomes clearer and pardon is seen as God's acceptance of repentance.[14] There is some mention of conditions for forgiveness of some "lesser" or "unavoidable" sins, but we also see the caution that although God forgives, this does not mean that persistent sinners will escape punishment.[15] Again, the same themes recur in the discussion of divine *tawbah* (relentment). The emphasis is even stronger on genuine repentance with the reminder that the decision ultimately rests with God to relent towards whom He will.[16]

Close to the centre of Raḥbar's understanding of Qur'ānic ethics is his treatment of divine *raḥmah* (mercy). Its importance for our understanding of God's forgiveness can be seen in the fact that, as a divine epithet, *ar-raḥīm* and *al-ghafūr* almost invariably accompany each other.[17] We can understand how Ra*ḥ*bar sees mercy as being subservient to justice in his emphasis on the Qur'ānic cautions that while God is merciful, this does not mean that the transgressors will not be boiled in the fire (Cf.: 4:33-34). Although God is merciful, this does not mean that the defiant ones will have any share of His Mercy, rather it means that the door to corrective repentance is not closed.[18] Raḥbar summarizes the discussion of divine *raḥmah* in a manner almost identical to his summary of divine *maghfirah,* "Believe and act aright and God will have mercy on you. And if you don't, God will punish you.[19]

Dr. M. Mahdī Allam is a modem Muslim scholar of the Qur'ān who writes on the subject of forgiveness. The basic premise underlying his work is somewhat different from Dāwūd Raḥbar's. He concludes, from his examination of the Qur'ān's teaching about forgiveness and how it says it, that the ultimate aim of punishment in the Qur'ān is reform.[20] This is significantly different from saying that divine mercy is subservient to divine justice. In fact, it is almost the opposite. Dr. Allam's typically Muslim treatment of the subject deals almost exclusively with matters of a human being forgiving another human for a wrong done, rather than with divine forgiveness. Still, some of his observations prove instructive for our purposes. Allam points out that the Qur'ānic ideal is put forth in three degrees: namely, that of God, that of the Prophet, and that of the best type of human being, the most pious.[21] Therefore, while there is allowance for the individual's inability to meet the highest ideal, an ideal is nonetheless held out as often being the best means for repelling evil, even if it is a method which does not come naturally to humankind.[22]

Another useful introduction by a non-Muslim to an Islāmic understanding of sins and their forgiveness has been offered by E.E. Elder.[23] Elder focuses his attention on four points which he sees as central to the discussion: the kinds of sins; the intention of the sinner; the sinner's repentance for sins; and the intercession of someone on the sinner's behalf.[24] Elder points out that much discussion among early Muslims centred on the division of sins into great and small sins which was alluded to above. While many Muslims concentrated on classifying or listing specific sins into one category or another, at least some have tried a more "psychological" approach by defining a great sin as one which corrupts the one who commits it. Of course, the greatest sin is unbelief with nothing else comparable to it.[25] Another subject of much discussion has been how strictly sin should be identified as a sign of unbelief with nearly everyone agreeing that righteous deeds are an essential part of belief. In spite of this close connection of deeds with belief, the most commonly accepted position which evolved has been a most lenient view that even the sinning believer is still reckoned as a believer. Nothing can remove even a sinning believer from the rights and hopes of the faithful, except denial of the unity of God or other things which signify unbelief.[26] Since al- Ash'arī's day, however, it has been assumed by most that some provision would be made for believers to be punished by God for certain sins before eventually receiving their reward for belief, thus giving them both punishment and forgiveness.[27]

Repentance is described in Elder's study as something which is encouraged with the caution that no human activity, even repentance, can oblige God to forgive whom he will not. In theory, God even has the freedom to forgive one who does not repent.[28] The same kinds of things are true of intercession for sinners, which may only be carried out by a messenger. While the intercession of Muḥammad on behalf of believers on the Last Day is assumed by most Muslims, it is completely overshadowed by the absolute freedom of God to forgive whom He will.[29]

Thus far our examination of God's forgiveness in the Qur'ān has been dominated by the interpretation of non-Muslims. This is partly because, as noted above, Muslim writers seldom view the matter with as much importance as Christians do. This point will be interpreted later. At this stage it is helpful to see how some of the themes discussed above are reflected in the commentaries of two Muslim *mufassirūn,* Baidāwī and Zamakhsharī, on sūrah *al-zilzāl* (99: 6-3) which mentions the "atom's weight of good or evil", which is made known to each person on the Last Day:

> Perhaps the good deed of the unbeliever and the evil deed of him who keeps away from major sins will bring about some lessening of punishment and reward. However, others say that the verse is to be interpreted with the understanding that there will be no cancellation (of good deeds) and no forgiveness (of evil deeds). (Baidāwī)

> One may now say: The good deeds of the unbeliever are devalued through his unbelief, while the evil deeds of the believer are forgiven if he has kept away from the major sins ... Whoever has done an atom's weight of good refers to the group of the blessed, and whoever has done an atom's weight of evil refers to the group of the damned. (Zamakhsharī)[30]

In both of these comments we can see a concern for maintaining a difference of treatment between believers and unbelievers, even though this distinction is not mentioned in sūrah *al-zilzāl* itself. Because the difference is clear in other *sūrat* of the Qur'ān, it is a valid consideration for the interpretation here. The interpretation by Baidāwī that there will be no cancellation or forgiveness reflects the assumption mentioned above that it might be possible for a believer to be held accountable for one's sins while still eventually receiving the reward of faith. Zamakhsharī's interpretation shows the influence of one's belief or unbelief in much stronger terms, while including the criterion of keeping away from "major sins."

These two commentators also give us an example of the debate on the "greater" and "lesser" sins. Zamakhsharī reflects much of the classical discussion when he comments on sūrah *al-dukhān* (44:2-6) in this way:

> Forgiveness occurs in that night (the blessed night). The Prophet has said: 'In this night God forgives all Muslims with the exception of the soothsayer, the sorcerer, the one who is disobedient to his parents, and the one who is unchaste.'[31]

This is an example of the tendency to make a distinction on the basis of "lists" of sins which are either "major" or "lesser." But Baidāwī takes a somewhat different approach when he comments on sūrah *al-nisā* (4:31) by first informing us that the gravest sin is that of "associating", and the lightest is the soul which harbours sinful thoughts. He goes on to say that in a circumstance where one is drawn toward two sins and avoids the graver, then one is forgiven for the sin actually committed as a reward for not committing the graver.[32] The differences and similarities between these two Qur'ānic commentators on these points give us a glimpse into the diversity of Muslim interpretation concerning some of the latitude inherent in the Qur'ān when it speaks of forgiveness.

In order to explore these themes farther we must move beyond the bounds of Qur'ānic commentary to the direct or indirect treatment of God's forgiveness in the more general writings of Muslim thinkers. Perhaps the most auspicious beginning for this is that seminal and pivotal person in Muslim intellectual history, Al-Ghazālī (d. 1111), and the most obvious place to begin is his *al-maqṣad al-asnā*.[33] Of the "ninety-nine names", there are six which shed light on our topic.

Al-Raḥmān (the Merciful)

The most instructive parts of al-Ghazālī's description which reflect his understanding of God's forgiveness are where he talks of "man's portion of *al-Raḥmān*", which is to look upon the sinners with eyes of mercy, not eyes of censure. Of the mercifulness in punishment he says that "a little pain is a blessing rather than an evil when it ultimately serves the cause of great joy". Al-Ghazālī interprets, "My mercy precedes My anger", as telling us that "God wills good for the good itself, but wills evil not for itself, but rather for the good that is within it."[34]

Al-Ghaffār (the very forgiving One)

It is interesting that Al-Ghazālī chooses to describe the forgiveness of God by saying that God "veils what is disgraceful." He says that the sins (of human being) are among the most disgraceful things which He veils by placing a veil upon them in this world and disregarding their punishment in the hereafter.

Here Al-Ghazālī is playing off two meanings from the same root: *al-ghaffār,* which means "the forgiving"; and *al-ghafr,* which refers to "veiling." Al-Ghazālī describes three veils. The first is that God has formed the human body in such a way that its ugly parts are hidden. The second veil is that God has hidden our most reprehensible thoughts in the depths of our hearts. The third veil is:

> forgiveness of sins for which he (the sinner) deserved to be disgraced in the sight of mankind. God has promised that He will exchange good deeds for man's misdeeds so that He might cover the repulsive qualities of his with the reward of his good deeds when he has proved his faith.[35]

This places forgiveness not in the realm of removing sin from the sinner, but instead making it unnoticeable or by counteracting its effects with good deeds which have been performed by the same person.

Al-Ghafūr (the One who forgives much)

Al-Ghazālī notes that the difference between this and *al-ghaffār* is in the emphasis on the completeness of forgiveness rather than the abundance of forgiveness. "[God] forgives perfectly and completely and thereby reaches the ultimate degree of forgiveness."Although Al-Ghazālī is not more specific than this, it would seem that this indicates that God's forgiveness can go beyond mere "veiling."[36]

Al-Ḥalīm (fee Forbearing One)

... the One who witnesses the disobedience of the disobedient, the One who sees the violation of the command *('amr)*. But anger does not rouse Him and rage does not seize Him, he is not one who is prompted by haste and recklessness to take swift vengeance, even though He has unlimited power to do so ...[37]

Al-Tawwāb (the One who constantly turns people to repentance)

... the One who keeps on facilitating the cause of repentance for His creatures time and time again by showing them some of His signs, by conveying to them some of His warnings, and by revealing to them some of His deterrent and cautions with the intent that they, having been apprised of the danger of their sins, might be filled with fear by His frightening them and subsequently turn to repentance. Through [His] accepting (the evidence of their penitence) the favour of God Most High [once again] reverts to them.[38]

Again, we see God's mercy even in His harshness, making forgiveness possible for the sinner by facilitating the sinner's repentance.

Al-Afuw (the One who erases sin)

> ... the One who erases sin and disregards acts of disobedience. This concept approximates the sense of *al-ghafūr,* though the former is more far reaching than the latter. For *al-ghafūr* indicates a veiling [of the sin] whereas *al-afuw* indicates an erasing, and the erasing [of sin] is more far-reaching [than the simple veiling of it].[39]

Here Al-Ghazālī clearly states that God's action in dealing with human sin is much broader and more far-reaching than merely "forgiving" sin, and perhaps gives us a hint as to why discussions of forgiveness are rare among Muslim writers.

In al-Ghazālī's discussion of the divine names many of the Qur'ānic themes on forgiveness come together in a more integrated way. He treats God's mercy and His wrath in a unified manner, making justice and forgiveness part of the same movement. God's mercy is shown as much by His threats for punishment as by His promises of forgiveness, since both of them turn the sinner to repentance and thus bring the sinner back to God.

Margaret Smith shows us even more depth in Al-Ghazālī understanding of repentance and forgiveness in her treatment of his mysticism: "Praise be to God ... Who turns men's hearts to repentance and forgives their transgressions, who casts a veil over their sins and comforts them in their sorrows - to Him be praise." *(Iḥyā III,* p. 2)[40]

This repentance can be brought about by cultivating in the sinner the emotions of fear or hope, or a combination of the two. Knowing God's mercy toward the sinner and God's wrath toward sin can cause one to look toward the sin, which produces suffering and fear, or cause one to look toward the mercy of God, which produces joy and hope. The sign of fear is flight and the sign of hope is search.[41]

It is in this way that the pain or threat of punishment can actually be manifestations of God's mercy.

> Repentance is the realization of the separation from God caused by sin, and it involves spiritual suffering greater than the physical suffering inflicted on the body ... Those possessed of spiritual insight ... feel this separation from God most keenly ...[42]

Repentance can then be seen as a movement of faith to faith: "Repentance is the beginning of the Way and the key of happiness ... for it means the return from alienation to proximity, and it is based on faith, the conviction that there is no god but God."[43]

Thus while the sinner may indeed seek out God's forgiveness because God's punishment is feared: " ... yet the highest form of Fear is not the Fear of chastisement, nor even of sin, but only the servant's fear lest he should be debarred forever from the contemplation of the Eternal Beauty."[44]

Al-Ghazālī's unified view of God's manifold activity undoubtedly has its roots in early Muslim mysticism. Indeed, seeds for this kind of unified approach to two apparently different actions of God can be seen in the hermeneutics of the Sūfi Sahl al-Tustarī (d.253/896) as interpreted by Gehard Bowering:

> When man performs an activity in conformity to the divine Command and Interdiction, he is granted the divine succour of God's help *(ma'ūnah)* and assistance (*taufīq*) and is bound to an act of thanksgiving (*shukr*). Should he commit an action in opposition to the divine Command and Interdiction, man places himself outside the divine custody and thus is deserted by God who withdraws His protection (*imāh*) and forsakes man (*khidlan*). The way by which man must return to God's custody is that of repentance (*taubah*) when he commits and evil deed (*sayyiah*).[45]

Here we clearly see unity of action in both divine and human action. God's action will always be consistent with the maintenance of harmony in relationships, while it is incumbent on the human servant of God to consistently turn to God either in praise or in repentance. Whether one sins or whether one performs good deeds, the important thing is always to turn to God. In other words, the primary consideration is that of faith.

As a contemporary interpreter, Āyātollāh Murtazā Mutaḥḥarī uses language that is more suited to contemporary ears, but one can still detect in his call to faith themes which are consistent with the above interpretations of the Divine/human relationship. As with the vast majority of Muslim writers, he doesn't use the term forgiveness at all, but his comments on the need for humanity to fit into the divine plan and order give greater breadth to our understanding of the balance between accountability or punishment and forgiveness with respect to human sin. One of the underlying principles in Mutaḥḥarī's understanding of Islām is the high priority which it places on the way human beings treat each other. Putting it quite strongly, he says, "Islām, in being a religion ... exists to institute social justice."[46] The model and the means for accomplishing this goal is the divine Unity which extends into and undergirds all that we know as life:

> ... What has the possibility to exist is a determinate, universal and immutable system. Therefore the phenomenon of the universe has the possibilities of existing with this determinate system and of not existing at all therefore, either the universe exists with a determinate system or nothing exists. Lastly, the whole universe as an independent unity, not one part in the absence of another, has the possibility to exit. Therefore, what can be contemplated by wisdom is the existence or nonexistence of the whole, not the existence of one part and the nonexistence of another part.[47]

What is most instructive in the vision of reality which Mutaḥḥarī sees in Islām is that as we consider the consequences of actions undertaken in harmony with the divine plan (good works) or actions which go counter to the divine plan (sins), what is at stake is not merely obedience/ disobedience or even reward/ punishment. What is ultimately at stake is existence itself. This would mean that God's promise of reward and God's threat of punishment are both proffered with the same goal in mind of offering the human individual and the human community the possibility to exist. By inviting the things which make for life and warning against that which destroys life, God is offering humanity life itself.

A well-known contemporary interpreter of Islām who is not given to Sūfism, Fazlur Raḥmān, also says virtually nothing about forgiveness, choosing instead to emphasize that, "every man and woman individually and every people collectively are alone responsible for what they do."[48] In addition to stressing human responsibility however, Fazlur Raḥmān makes it clear that the Qur'ān is an, "invitation for man to come to the right Path.[49] The threat of punishment from God is aimed at far more than mere retribution, since, "all human acts which are apparently perpetrated on another person, in a more ultimate sense recoil upon the agent himself", so that "all injustice is basically reflexive".[50] Therefore, one must be saved, not so much from the wrath of God, but rather one must be saved from oneself. Given this understanding, we might again assume that the real goal is not simply justice, but to turn human hearts back to God so that their true nature and purpose might be realized.

With that purpose in mind whatever method would achieve that goal, whether threat of punishment or promise of forgiveness, would be acceptable, if the desired result were achieved. This purpose is clearly present in such passages as the above mentioned *al-baqarah* (2:51-52) in which God forgives the calf-worshipping Israelites in order that they might be thankful, implying that their thankfulness would signify faith in God, which would in turn lead to a forsaking of calf-worship. Indeed, it is striking how throughout the Qur'an thankfulness or giving thanks is almost a synonym for belief or faith.

> ... [Solomon] said: This is of the bounty of my Lord, that He may try me whether I give thanks (*ashkuru*) or am ungrateful (*akfuru*). Whosoever giveth thanks (*shakara*) he only giveth thanks for the good of his own soul: and whosoever is ungrateful (*kafara*) (is ungrateful only to his own soul's hurt), *al-naml* (27:40)

> ... My Lord! Arouse me that I may give thanks *(ashkura)* for the favour wherewith Thou has favoured me and my parents, and that I may do right (*'amala ṣāliḥan*) acceptable unto Thee... Lo! I have turned unto Thee repentant *(tubtu),* and lo! I am of those who surrender (*al-muslimīn). al-aḥqāf* (46:15).

The link is clear between being thankful to God and believing in God. This thankfulness is the basis for righteous living *('amala ṣāliḥan),* while to be ungrateful (*kafara*) is the attitude of the unbeliever (*kāfir*). Both of these attitudes and their resultant actions are reflexive. The reward or punishment which comes is only fruits of the seed which were sown by the person who is responsible for his/her own choices in life.

What can we say then, by way of conclusion for this brief study? If God's forgiveness is mentioned so prominently in the Qur'ān, why does it not figure more prominently among Muslim writers? What is the proper role of the hope of forgiveness in a life which is lived in Islāmic faith? Perhaps one thing which must be said is that Islām is a goal-oriented faith, and Islām is a religion of unity. If human sin has caused a breach in this unity, then sin must be eliminated. Both the justice/wrath of God and the forgiveness/mercy of God are tools to that end. While the Qur'ān speaks often and eloquently of God's forgiveness, it also speaks graphically of God's judgement. Muslim thinkers through the centuries have thought it either unnecessary or unwise to speak too much about forgiveness for the sinner. Unwise since too much talk about easily available or guaranteed forgiveness would be less likely to engender reform and more likely to undermine a sense of human responsibility before God. Unnecessary, because Muslims primarily know God as the Mercy-Giving, the Most-Merciful, and what is the Most-Merciful God, if not Much-Forgiving?[51] Despite Dāwūd Raḥbar's painstaking efforts to prove the contrary, the vast weight of Muslim interpretation remains with the earliest interpreters that God's justice is indeed subservient to God's mercy. In other words, a summary statement of Qur'ānic teaching on the subject is not so much, "Believe and act aright and God will forgive you; if not, God will punish you" (see note 19), as,

> Those who trust in God, respect God, fear God, are thankful toward God without associating partners *(shirk)* to God in this reverence to such people the door of forgiveness is open (to those who may be recognized by their honest efforts to live righteously). Those who do not have faith in God, to them the door of forgiveness is closed (those who may be recognized by their pride (*takabbur*) or injustice (*zulm*).

Why is it that Christians and Muslims so often, seem to misunderstand each other on issues such as this? What is the source of this tendency for Christians to see and to understand something very different from Muslims when reading Muslim Scripture or other literature? (It must be remembered that the same misunderstandings are equally evident when a Muslim interprets Christian Scripture or tradition). I would suggest two sources for these difficulties: 1) the frame of reference; and 2) the envisioned goal. Because we share so many things in common and often use very similar language, it is too easy for us to forget that we often approach these issues from very different perspectives. Because most Christian discussion has been from a theological perspective, that is what a Christian looks for and sees when reading Muslim writings. Even after realizing that the Muslim concern has usually been more with *sharī'ah* or with ethics, the Christian finds it difficult to read or to hear with other than a theological frame of mind.

But the priorities which form any discussion always play a big role in shaping the choice of words, the phrasing, and of the emphasis in that discussion. The same person expressing the same viewpoint will do so in quite different ways according to the context of the discussion: e.g. the particular audience listening to a presentation; the environmental setting of that presentation; and the experiential context of the previous week's/month's events before the presentation, etc. Unless we can be flexible enough to receive within the framework in which something is offered, we will never fully understand.

There is also the difference of ultimate goal. I do not want to make too much of this difference, since it is not really an absolute difference between the two traditions, but is more a difference in dominant strands or aspects of each tradition. Whether or not it is an accurate reflection of biblical teaching, much Christian theology especially that influenced by European pietism, has been more ultimately concerned with what happens to the individual believer's soul after death than what happens among the community of believers in this earthly life. That concern has not been absent from Muslim thought and writing either. Because of the background which a Christian brings to a reading of Muslim texts, however, the preponderance of Qur'ānic references to eternal reward or punishment are understood by the Christian in a manner not completely consistent with their intention. Those promises and warnings are a means to an end which is as much concerned with this temporal life as it is with the hereafter. They are intended to convince the human soul of its ultimate dependence on God, with the assumption that such a realization will necessarily effect a change in behaviour. As Dāwūd Raḥbar says, the goal of either threat or promise is corrective repentance. For the Qur'ān, the issue is not merely a matter of the individual soul's escape from punishment. The issue is in fact a much more holistic vision of salvation which intends the reform of human life in community with the basis for that reform being respect for and faith in God alone.

The point could be raised that these lofty principles are only an ideal. Is it not true that the "average" Muslim understands things in a much simpler way, characterized more by a basic fear of God's punishment? Quite likely. Even as it is true that opinion polls demonstrate that most

Christians believe that they will go to heaven only if they lead a "good life", but will go to hell if they are "bad" in spite of the Christian doctrine of "salvation by grace". It is clear from the above discussion that Muslim and Christian "ideals" are not so diametrically opposed as many have previously thought. It is quite possible that both Muslims and Christians could benefit greatly from a mutually respectful sharing of perspectives on these matters, which might enrich both sides.

From the viewpoint of this study, a believer's proper attitude toward God's forgiveness should include at least four points. Firstly, the promise of God's mercy and forgiveness should be a powerful motivation for one to return to God and to strengthen one's faith, leading to a more righteous life. This promise is preferred as a motivator over the threat of punishment. Secondly, the promise of forgiveness in no way diminishes human responsibility for living in conformity to God's will. Thirdly, the prime determining human factor with regard to forgiveness is belief, which includes trust, respect, fear, thankfulness, repentance toward God which may be evidenced by an honest attempt at righteous living. Lastly, no human action of any kind, not even faith or the act of repentance can be seen as obliging God to act in a way that God does not see fit to act. Yet God can be trusted to be merciful and forgiving, for He has prescribed for Himself that His mercy shall precede his wrath. Perhaps no one to this point has said it better than al-Ghazālī :

> The servant's hope of forgiveness should be like the hope of the sower, who seeks for good ground and sows therein good seed ... and then sits down, expecting that God, by His grace, will keep away thunderbolts and all sources of injury until the seed has grown and the crop is ripe. Such expectation is called Hope. Though God's mercy is due to His grace, not to human merit, yet the servant must at any rate strive to be worthy of it.[52]

Addendum

Selected Ḥadīth Qudsī[53] on God's Forgiveness

> Your Lord delights at a shepherd who, on the peak of a mountain crag, gives the call to prayer and prays. Then Allāh [glorified and exalted be He] says: Look at this servant of Mine, he gives the call to prayer and performs the prayers; he is in awe of Me. I have forgiven My servant [his sins] and have admitted him to Paradise. *(Ḥadīth qudsī)*

O My servants, you sin by night and by day, and I forgive all sins, so seek forgiveness of Me and I shall forgive you. *(Ḥadīth qudsī)*

The gates of Paradise will be opened on Mondays and on Thursdays, and every servant [of Allāh] who associates nothing with Allāh will be forgiven, except for the man who has a grudge against his brother. [About them] it will be said: Delay these two until they are reconciled; delay these two until they are reconciled. *(Ḥadīth qudsī)*

A man said: By Allāh, Allāh will not forgive So-and-so. At this Allāh the Almightly said: Who is he who swears by Me that I will not forgive So-and-so? Verily I have forgiven So-and-so and have nullified your [own good] deeds (or as he said [it]). *(Ḥadīth qudsī)*

A man sinned greatly against himself, and when death came to him he charged his sons, saying: when I have died, burn me, then crush me and scatter [my ashes] into the sea, for, by Allāh, if my Lord takes possession of me, He will punish me in a manner in which He has punished no one [else]. So they did that to him. Then He said to the earth: Produce what you have taken and there he was! And He said to him: What induced you to do what you did? He said: Being afraid of You, O my Lord (or he said: Being frightened of You) and because of that He forgave him. *(Ḥadīth qudsī)*

A servant [of Allāh's] committed a sin and said: O Allāh, forgive me my sin. And He (glorified and exalted be He) said: My servant has committed a sin and has known that he has a Lord who forgives sins and punishes for them. Then he sinned again and said: O Lord, forgive me my sin. And He (glorified and exalted be He) said: My servant has committed a sin and has known that he has a Lord who forgives sins and punishes for them. Then he sinned again and said: O Lord, forgive me my sin. And He (glorified and exalted be He) said: My servant has committed a sin and has known that he has a Lord who forgives sins and punishes for sins. Do what you wish, for I have forgiven you. *(Ḥadīth qudsī)*

O son of Adam, so long as you call upon Me and ask of Me, I shall forgive you for what you have done, and I shall not mind. O son of Adam, were your sins to reach the clouds of the sky and were you then to ask forgiveness of Me, I would forgive you. O son of Adam, were you to come to Me with sins nearly as great as the earth and were you then to face Me, ascribing no partner to Me, I would bring you forgiveness nearly as great as it. *(Ḥadīth qudsī)*

Our Lord (glorified and exalted be He) descends each night to the earth's sky when there remains the final third of the night, and He says: Who is saying a prayer to Me that I may answer it? Who is asking something of Me that I may give it him? Who is asking forgiveness of Me that I may forgive him? And thus He continues till [the light of] dawn shines. (*Ḥadīth qudsī*)

Endnotes

[1] For the sake of consistency, all English renderings of Qur'ānic passages are taken from the 1977 edition of the Muslim World League, Rabita Mecca, Al-Mukarramah, Saudi Arabia, with explanatory translation by Muḥammad M. Pickthall.

[2] R.A. Blasdell, "The Muslim Attitude Toward Sin" in *The Moslem World* 31 (1041), 145-148.

[3] Muammad Fu'ad Abdul-Baqi, *al-mujam al-mifahrus li alfa al-Qur'ān al-Karim* (Cairo: Darwa Matabi al-Shab).

[4] Mahmoud Ayoub, *The Qur'ān and Its Interpreters*, Vol. 1 (Albany: State University of New York Press, 1984).

[5] Ayoub, *The Qur'ān and Its Interpreters*, 107.

[6] Ayoub, *The Qur'an and Its Interpreters*, 277.

[7] Note, however, al-baqarah (2:51-52) mentioned above, where it appears as though God forgave the banī-Isrā'īl even for the sin of *shirk* in the hope that they might be thankful (*lā alakurm tashkrarūna*). It is indeed surprising that this issue would be ignored by Ayoub's commentators.

[8] Dāwūd Raḥbar, *God of Justice—A Study in the Ethical Doctrine of the Qur'ān* (Leiden; E.J. Brill, 1960), xv. It is always dangerous for anyone to interpret the Scripture of another religious community than one's own, and especially to go against the current of that community's interpretation. Dāwūd Raḥbar takes great care to build his case. The reader must judge how well he has succeeded.

[9] Raḥbar, *God of Justice—A Study in the Ethical Doctrine of the Qur'ān*, 141.

[10] Even his prerequisite of asking for forgiveness might be challenged. The reader is referred to the selections of *Ḥadīth qudsī* toward the end of this article.

[11] Raḥbar, *God of Justice—A Study in the Ethical Doctrine of the Qur'ān*, 142.

[12] Raḥbar, *God of Justice—A Study in the Ethical Doctrine of the Qur'ān*, 143-144. Cf. M.M. Bravmann, "Allāh's Liberty to Punish or to Forgive" in *Der Islām*, 47 (1971), 236-237

[13] Raḥbar, *God of Justice—A Study in the Ethical Doctrine of the Qur'ān*, 149.

[14] Raḥbar, *God of Justice—A Study in the Ethical Doctrine of the Qur'ān*, 152.

[15] Raḥbar, *God of Justice—A Study in the Ethical Doctrine of the Qur'ān*, 154.

[16] Raḥbar, *God of Justice—A Study in the Ethical Doctrine of the Qur'ān*, 157.

[17] Raḥbar, *God of Justice—A Study in the Ethical Doctrine of the Qur'ān*, 163-164.

[18] Raḥbar, *God of Justice—A Study in the Ethical Doctrine of the Qur'ān*, 165.

[19] Raḥbar, *God of Justice—A Study in the Ethical Doctrine of the Qur'ān*, 166.

[20] M. Mahdī Allam, "The Concept of Forgiveness in the Qur'ān," in *Islāmic Culture*, 7 (July 1967), 139.

[21] Allam, "The Concept of Forgiveness in the Qur'ān," in *Islāmic Culture*, 142.

[22] Allam, "The Concept of Forgiveness in the Qur'ān," in *Islāmic Culture*, 142

[23] E.E. Elder, "The Development of the Muslim Doctrine of Sins and their Forgiveness" in *The Moslem World*, 29 (1939), 178.

[24] Elder, "The Development of the Muslim Doctrine of Sins and their Forgiveness" in *The Moslem World*, 179.

[25] Elder, "The Development of the Muslim Doctrine of Sins and their Forgiveness" in *The Moslem World*, 182.

[26] Elder, "The Development of the Muslim Doctrine of Sins and their Forgiveness" in *The Moslem World*, 185.

[27] Elder, "The Development of the Muslim Doctrine of Sins and their Forgiveness" in *The Moslem World*, 185.

[28] Elder, "The Development of the Muslim Doctrine of Sins and their Forgiveness" in *The Moslem World*, 184.

[29] Elder, "The Development of the Muslim Doctrine of Sins and their Forgiveness" in *The Moslem World*, 187.

[30] Helmut Gatje, *The Qur'ān and Its Exegesis*, translated by Alford T. Welch (Berkeley/ Los Angeles: University of California Press, 1976), 178.

[31] Gatje, *The Qur'ān and Its Exegesis*, 50.

[32] Gatje, *The Qur'ānand Its Exegesis*, 188.

[33] Raḥbar, *God of Justice—A Study in the Ethical Doctrine of the Qur'ān*, 8-18. Ra%bar's caution about the dangers of relying too heavily on lists of the "Ninety-nine Names" for an adequate understanding of the Muslim concept of God is well taken. In the context of analyzing the Qur'ān and the $adīth, however, such discussions can be a very helpful source for understanding how Muslims understand the Qur'ān.

[34] Al-Ghazālī, *Al Maqsad Al-Asna*, translated by Robert Charles Stade as *Ninety-nine Names of God* (Ibadan: Daystar Press, 1970), 15-17.

[35] Al-Ghazālī, *Al Maqsad Al-Asna*, 36-37.

[36] Al-Ghazālī, *Al Maqsad Al-Asna*, 70.

[37] Al-Ghazālī, *Al Maqsad Al-Asna*, 68.

[38] Al-Ghazālī, *Al Maqsad Al-Asna*, 114.

[39] Al-Ghazālī, *Al Maqsad Al-Asna*, 115.

[40] Margaret Smith, *Al-Ghazālī, the Mystic* (London; Luzac & Co., 1944), 102.

[41] Smith, *Al-Ghazālī, the Mystic*, 164-65.

[42] Smith, *Al-Ghazālī, the Mystic*, 154.

[43] Smith, *Al-Ghazālī, the Mystic*, 152.

[44] Smith, *Al-Ghazālī, the Mystic*, 41.

[45] Gerhard Bowering, *The Mystical Vision of Existence in Classical Islām—The Qur'ānic Hermeneutics of the Sufi Sahl al-Tustari* (Berlin/NewYork: Walter de Gruyter, 1980), 179.

[46] Āyātollāh Murtazā Mutaḥḥarī, *Fundamentals of Islāmic Thought—God, Man and the Universe*, translated by R. Campbell (Berkeley: Mizan Press, 1985), 53.

[47] Mutaḥḥarī, *Fundamentals of Islāmic Thought*, 125.

[48] Fazlur Raḥmān, *Major Themes of the Qur'ān* (Chicago/Minneapolis: Bibliotheca Islāmica, 1980), 19.

[49] Raḥmān, *Major Themes of the Qur'ān*, 20.

[50] Raḥmān, *Major Themes of the Qur'ān*, 25.

[51] Yusuf Ali, *Holy Qur'ān, with English translation*, 4th edition (Delhi: Kutub Khana Ishayat-ul-Islām, 1975), 14, note 18. In support of this theory, see Yusuf Ali's commentary on *al-fātiḥah* (1:1) "... Mercy may imply pity, long suffering, patience, and forgiveness, all of which the sinner needs and God Most Merciful bestows in abundant measure. But there is a Mercy that goes before even the need arises, the Grace which is ever watchful, and flows from God Most Gracious to all His creatures, protecting them, preserving them, guiding them, and leading them to clearer light and higher life. For this reason the attribute Raḥman (Most Gracious) is not applied to any but God ... To make us contemplate these boundless gifts of God, the formula: 'In the name of God Most Gracious, Most Merciful': is placed before every Sūra of the Qur'ān(except the ninth), and repeated at the beginning of every act by the Muslim who dedicates his life to God, and whose hope is in His Mercy."

[52] Smith, *Al-Ghazālī, the Mystic*, 165.

[53] Ḥadīth Qudsī (divine saying) is a statement from a unique body of statements which are considered to be direct words of God, although they are not part of the Qur'ān. They are revered in popular Muslim piety at a level above the prophetic Ḥadīth (Ḥadīth nabawi), and are often quoted without an isnād (chain or transmission). The selections given here are taken from a collection of forty such Ḥadīth qudsi which is part of a database of Islāmic resources compiled by Shahīd N. Shāh titled "The Alim" (ed. 2.01, Washington: 1993). The compiler does not list his source, but one of the very few available in English is "Forty Ḥadīth Qudsī" compiled by Ezzeddin Ibrahim and Denys Johnson-Davies, (Beirut/Damascus: Dar al-Horan al Kareem, 1980). For a seminal treatment of this body of literature the reader is referred to William Graham's, *Divine Word and Prophetic Word in Early Islām* (The Netherlands: Mouton Pub., 1977).

Feminist Critique of Religion under Neo-Liberal Globalisation

Gabriele Dietrich

Preamble: The Struggle for Life and Livelihood

It is difficult for me to talk on this topic in the present situation, because of the civil war which is going on in the North of Sri Lanka and it appears to be a war to the finish. There is a strong resonance in Tamil Nadu to this situation and some people and organizations have felt that this was genocide, because it is a situation where three lakhs people are trapped in a shrinking territory, trapped from both sides. I was therefore very pleased when one of our friends here gave me a little card, which some of you may have seen. What is written on it in English reads as follows:

a) Could we not Care instead of Warring
b) Could we not Save Lives, instead of Taking them
c) Could there not be a Victory that we could all share?

The astonishing thing is that while it is very carefully formulated in English, the Tamil rendering is more affirmative and determined, so it comes out shorter than the English, while normally the Tamil version will be longer. It says:

yuththathai thavirththu
uyirhalai kaththu
vettriyai namethaakkuvom

This is a very strong statement which says: We will make the victory ours by stopping the war and protecting life; no to war and yes to life. It means that even in the face of total adversity these women want to protect life.

I am saying this also in memory of Rajani Rajasingham, whose death anniversary of twenty years will be this year in September and whom I have known since 1977, when I held bible studies for the WSCF World Assembly in Bandaranaike Hall.[1] She was one of those women who very bravely critiqued religion and society and was striving for a radical transformation of society and religious institutions. She did this courageously and consistently till the end. She exposed all human rights violations, be it of the government, the IPKF or the militants.[2]

I believe even in the present situation this is what women's organizations must try to do: saying no to War yes to Life. The lives of three lakhs of people in the war zone are at stake. They cannot be sacrificed on the altar of ethnicity, religion, identity politics or War on Terror. War cannot solve this predicament. A democratic political process is needed. But to get into such a process, the war must be stopped from both sides.

I come from India, where "War on terror" is also a central concern which erodes democracy and leads to civil wars, especially in adivasi areas like Chhattisgarh. This has clearly to do with the neo-liberal attempt to appropriate natural resources, to do mining, to produce and appropriate energy resources. So I am not only talking of feminist critique of religion, but also on feminist critique of neo-liberal globalization. Religion has become much more communalist, fundamentalist, charismatic, driven and appropriated by political processes over the past two decades. It is this fanatical use of religion which has very distorting influence in the political process and on civil society and people's life worlds. This contributes to a type of identity politics which distracts from the economic situation and instead of achieving social justice becomes divisive.[3] The question has been raised in this seminar whether the present crisis of capitalism is temporary or whether it is something deeper. Wesley Aryaraja was maintaining that the crisis is only temporary. In India we believe that this is something deeper. Ninan Koshy agrees with me on this.

So the question arises whether there is Hope in the face of the deepening crisis, which is not only a crisis of capital and of international finance institutions, but also an ecological crisis defined by energy crunch, global warming and possible war over water.

The crisis is aggravated by the fact that nuclear energy is today propagated as a remedy to global warming, which is based on disastrous misconceptions. Nuclear technology is incomplete, as there is no solution to waste management. It is also so expensive that it is uneconomic. Besides it is intrinsically linked with nuclear bombs, which in this region are conceptualized as Muslim bombs vs. Hindu bombs. The nuclear reactor in Kudankulam, which is extremely close to Sri Lanka, was started in order to acquire technology for nuclear submarines which are crucial to protect nuclear arsenals. The basic needs of ordinary people are in the meantime of no concern.

It is a situation where poor local communities are up against corporates in competition for land, sustenance of agriculture, artisanal fisheries and Right to Work.

In the women's movement we have said for a long time that we want a mode of production centred on the Production of Life and Livelihood instead of Production for Profit. Today, even this terminology becomes problematic, because production processes get appropriated by corporates and bio-technology becomes a way of manipulating all life forms. So one has to add that we are talking of resources in people's hands, democratic processes of decision making, inclusiveness regarding women, third sex, ethnic and religious minorities, differently abled and dignity and respect for people and nature, "loving relationships" as someone called it in the recent deliberations.

What is happening to religion under neo-liberal globalization?

As quite a few of us in this audience have been politicized during the sixties, let me commemorate that this was also a period of liberation theologies in different continents. As far as my own background goes I have no denomination and have not been socialized into any church culture. The city of Berlin where I grew up was the place which inspired Harvey Cox to write his famous book: *The Secular City*. Nevertheless, there was a ferment of protestant culture in the Students Movement in Berlin which had to do with the history of resistance of the Confessing Church against fascism. One of the important factors was Latin American Liberation Theology, which was encouraged by the Second Vatican Council, but in Vietnam we saw Buddhist Monks supporting the uprising against American sponsored dictatorship. In Thailand the students' revolt had resonance with some Buddhist clergy. Yohan Devananda explored Buddhist protest potential in Ibbagamuva. Neo Buddhism started to explore Marxist inspirations in Maharashtra in the seventies. The student movements during this period were in many places Marxist inspired and strongly secular.

Likewise, the women's movements which arose in the seventies were strongly secular and many of the women were leftist inspired. In India, the Emergency was declared in summer 1975 and this led to repression of resistance and suspension of constitutional rights. But Women's movements were seen as innocuous. The period also coincided with International Women's Year. So women were encouraged to organize. I remember a big women's conference organized by the journal *Social Scientist* in December 1975 in Trivandrum.[4] Though the organizers were close to the CPI-M, there was a very wide democratic participation by "autonomous" women. I remember spirited presentations by Kumari Jayawardena, Gail Omwedt, Chhaya Dattar and many others. Many women were with working class organizations, peasant organizations, Adivasis. They were focused on labour questions and survival issues, but faced difficulties in raising domestic violence and male domination in their own organizations.

It was only during the eighties that the question of religion came up in a major way. One of the major reasons was the rise of the Khalisthan movement in Punjab and the anti-Sikh riots after the assassination of Indira Gandhi in the wake of these events.[5] These were commented by Rajiv Gandhi with the laconic remark: when a great tree falls, the earth shakes.

There had been an assumption during the sixties, the so-called international development decade that development was leading to secularism. This was also the phase when the contradictions between rich and poor widened dramatically, which in turn led to new class struggles and rise of Naxalism in India. The Emergency with its Twenty Point Programme was an attempt of streamlining capitalism and freeing it from some of the Feudal hangovers. However, *garibi hatao* (eradicate poverty) soon turned into *garib hatao* (eradicate the poor) with slum evictions and forced sterilizations.

It was the Emergency, which led to strange alliances in the jail, where Leftists, Socialists and RSS cadres faced a common repression. Jaya Prakash Narayan's "Total Revolution", which galvanised rural masses and students cadres, was not free from such pitfalls. This paved the way for alliances of socialists with communal forces in the nineties and in the new century. Ever since the anti-Sikh riots, the secular credentials of the Congress in India have been in question. It was the women's movement which was on the roads to pick up the pieces after the riots. It was the women's movement which canvassed for a gender just civil code during the eighties, but had to retreat into reform of separate religious family laws after the BJP had appropriated the issue of a "uniform civil code" after the Shāh Bān*ū* judgement, which upheld the right of a Muslim Woman under Cr P Code Art. 125 to receive maintenance. It was Rajiv Gandhi who appeased the "Muslim community" (the men, that is) by pushing the Muslim Women's Protective Act, exempting Muslim women from the secular right to maintenance. When this raised an outcry from the Hindu Right, he decreed to break the locks of the Babrī Masjid to allow worshipping of the Ram Lalla idol for Hindus. This victory of the Hindu Right has sown the seeds for the destruction of Babrī Masjid in the early nineties.

As I said above, all these events also coincided with the demise of socialism in Eastern Europe by the fall of the Berlin Wall in August 1989 and the disintegration of the Soviet Union and also with the suppression of the students' uprisings on Tiananmen Square in May 1989, which prevented the democratic reform of Socialism in China. I mentioned already that it became visible during that period that the new enemy of the capitalist World was going to be Islam.[6]

This has led to debates whether it is a situation where there is "more religion" under globalisation or whether religious identities are increasingly used for political purposes. It is obvious that international events like 9/11 in 2001 have led to worldwide polarizations, which in turn lead to "War on Terror" as a major tenet of politics. This is of course the major pre-occupation in Sri Lanka; where Buddhism is very close to being a state religion. This reminds us also of the Buddhist military regimes in Myanmar and Thailand. India, in contrast to her more non-aligned past, is today hand in glove with Sri Lanka and Myanmar for obvious geo-political reasons regarding energy policies, control over oil and gas and military control over the Indian Ocean. While it is true that religion is used more for political purposes, it is also true that the poor and the middle classes are facing increasing economic insecurity. Thus, religion as a safety mechanism and expression of aspiration and Hope is also on the increase. This in turn is used by ruling powers as well as non-State agencies, to divide people along the lines of identity politics. In Western countries this has led to new debates on Secularism and the curtailing of religious symbols in public life (France, Germany), while in some places it has led to polarizations, which have strengthened communal and fundamentalist forces (the UK and the Netherlands).[7] It is in the latter context that Amartya Sen raised his voice for the exploration of multiple identities.[8]

Feminist Critique of Religion

It is in this larger context of struggle for Life and Livelihood and the sharpening of religious identity politics that the feminist critique of religion evolved. It can roughly be summarised as follows:

a) During the sixties and seventies, when the feminist movement arose as a new wave of women's uprisings, there was an identifiably Leftist ferment in India and Sri Lanka, which gave women a critical frame of reference regarding religion. In Christian circles, this opened up avenues of liberation theology and feminist theology, but on the whole, this was a phase of secularist perceptions.

b) The early eighties were a phase of rising ethnic and communal contradictions. This led to strong interest of women's movements in peace keeping and intervention in situations of communal carnage. In India interventions during the anti-Sikh riots in India by progressive forces like Delhi University teachers and Swamy Agnivesh also galvanised the women's movement for minority rights. This also raised interest in the more peaceful contents of Sikh religion.[9]

c) This led to a debate on whether religion could be "private", which was a widely held view among the middle class. However, it is obvious that privacy is not really a concept among the mass of Indian population, where life from birth to death is public. Obviously, religion is a public affair and the question is how inclusive or exclusive, harmonious or conflictual such public manifestations are. Many places of worship, like e.g. the shrine of Mary in Velanganni or the Mosque in Nagoor and innumerable Hindu shrines are visited by people of different religions. However, it became increasingly clear that caste and untouchability were a crucial factor. In India, conflictual debates took place during the Indian Association for Women's Studies (IAWS) conference in Jadavpur University in Kolkata in 1989 where I myself presented a paper on "Women's Movements and Dalit Movements," and Flavia Agnes, a battered woman of Roman Catholic background, who later became a famous Women's Rights lawyer[10] chastised the women's movement for having unrecognized majority communalist tendencies.

d) This question of latent majority communalism also arose during the controversies over the Shāh Bānū case. Shāh Bānū was a divorcee in Indore, who had won a suit for maintenance under Cr P Art 126 against her wealthy lawyer ex-husband. The Indian women's movement rallied behind her[11] and connected this with the wider demand for a gender just secular civil code. This led to severe protest from the men in the Muslim community. The Hindu Right appropriated the issue to lobby for the generalisation of the Hindu Law as a common civil code. This forced the women's movement to backtrack on the campaign. The energies got divided between the effort to reform existing religious family laws (which up to a point succeeded) and the effort to devise a secular gender just civil law for all, which would afford women a general secular registration of marriage, and leave open possible religions sanctification of marriage irrespective of the secular law. In fact, a secular law is available in the form of the special Marriages Act, which is for the purpose of inter-religious marriage, but can be accessed by everyone. However, practically using it is cumbersome and often meets with obstruction.

e) There was also a debate going on, whether the women's movement could be a force against communalism.[12] This was based on the assumption that women were united by their sufferings under patriarchy and could transcend divisions of religious community and caste more easily. However, it turned out that this was not fully holding true. While even the privileged women in the women's movement were often basically progressive, it became clear that special vigilance was needed to counteract the efforts of Hindu communalists and Muslim fundamentalists to recuperate women into their identity politics. This became particularly visible during the riots which tore society apart after the destruction of Babrī Masjid.[13]

f) This polarizing trend became extreme after the fire in Godhra in which a large number of Ayodhya Yatris were killed, most likely by accident, but which was used by the State to trigger off the communal riots against Muslims in Gujarat, which were in fact State organized pogroms against the Muslim community, which led to thousands of deaths and 1.5 lakhs internal refugees. The scale of violence against Muslim women during those weeks was of extreme cruelty and the shocking fact was that Dalits, Adivasis and women of the majority community got actively involved in this violence.[14] Hindutva groups are now having courses for women as self-defence to ward off the rape of Mother India by Muslim vandals.

As usual, the women's movement got into the picture and involved in the healing of communal riots. However, SEWA, the biggest women's union in the country, with lakhs of members and headquarters in Ahmedabad, kept silent, obviously under the Narendra Modi and the BJP Government of the centre at the time.

Genuine Religions Reform and Interreligious Dialogue

There is a fall-out on genuine religious reform and on inter-religious dialogue in this constellation. To the extent that ordinary women get more subsumed under communal and fundamentalist forces, the women's movement in India is less inclined to entertain reform and dialogue at all. There is deep mistrust against existing religious leadership co-opting women into the fold and stream lining their hold by adopting emancipatory rhetoric. Women becoming spokespersons of fundamentalist and communalist trends are not uncommon today.[15]

While there has been a strong trend of feminist theology in Christian circles, which incorporated historical critical method, but carried it forward towards creative development of the hermeneutical cycle, there was also a critique of the process of canonization.[16] This has led also to rediscovery of materials left out of the canon and to enrichment of theological perceptions.[17] However, while this has happened at academic levels, this has not in any way reached the churches in South Asia. The reaction against the novel by Dan Brown, *The Da Vinci Code* has shown high levels of animosity and lack of information.[18]

There is clearly a wide gap between feminist critique of religion and the need for genuine religious reform and for inter-religious dialogue outside conference halls, related to the survival struggles for the Right to Life and Livelihood, which is in jeopardy under globalization. There have been attempts from Muslim feminists to rethink on Quran and Hadith in a feminist perspective. Fatima Mernissi in Morocco has powerfully written on feminist re-interpretation of scripture and tradition.[19] However, there is no opening for historical criticism of scripture and the field of doctrine remains heavily male dominated. There are new attempts in Indonesia by feminists to reform Islam.[20]

It is striking that there is no strong voice of women regarding a critique of militarized Buddhism, despite the protracted detention of Burmese fighter for democracy Aung San Suu Kyi in Myanmar. This seems to have to do with the fact that in many of the Buddhist countries women are quite side-lined within the Sangham. In Thailand it required a protracted struggle by Chatsumam Kabilsingh to re-establish the right of nuns to be part of the Sangham.[21] It has been pointed out by Uma Chakravarthi, that Buddhism in India has had the advantage of having been ousted from power positions in the historical process.[22] This has led to a powerful re-casting of Buddhism in the re-interpretations of Dr. Babasahib Ambedkar, the father of the Indian constitution,[23] who initiated mass conversion of Dalits to neo-Buddhism towards the end of his life.[24] This emancipatory movement of Dalits in Maharashtra is of wider significance and also led to massive participation of women.[25] However, Dalit neo-Buddhism has been ignored or looked down upon by the established Buddhist nations.

It has been pointed out that inter-religious dialogue has come to a dead end over the years, as it was dominated by male religious leaders who are concerned with doctrines and hierarchies. On the other hand, dialogues which were organized among women dealt with perspectives from the margins and were thus informed by real life issues, taking on board "the messiness of life."[26] The real dialogues which happen on the road side and happen in women's struggles for life and livelihood, often go unrecorded and undocumented.

In the meantime, appropriation of popular culture by chauvinistic and communal forces is systematically carried out. On my way to Colombo, I travelled via Thiruvanandapuram and to my astonishment found the streets occupied by an act of mass-cooking called *Pongala*. This was originally a festival of the Aattukal temple, which was not very significant and only attended by people in a particular area. Now it is made a general festival by the RSS, which appropriates food security as a religious issue and re-enforces women's role as cooks by making them to squat on the road to cook for the festival. There were about 2.5 lakhs of women participating in this all over the city in communist ruled Kerala. Clearly, religion is not private, it is very public. It matters how we approach it. There is an on-going challenge to the feminist critique of culture and religion, which requires a creative response. We have to dare to take unorthodox positions on the ground of real life experiences. We have to venture into re-interpretations without being co-opted by the "experts", within the churches and within academia. This we can achieve only on the road, in people's struggles for Life and Livelihood. We have to fight these struggles with our bodies, hearts and minds.

Endnotes

[1] Gabriele Dietrich: *Would That All the Lord's People Were Prophets* (Hongkong: WSCF Asia Books, 1977).

[2] Rajan Hoole, Daya Somasundaram, Rajini Thiranagama, K. Sritharan, *The Broken Palmyra* (The Sri Lanka Studies Institute, Cleremont USA/July 1988).

[3] The divisiveness of identity politics as it gets exploited by corporations has very clearly been exposed by Susan George, *The Lugano Report: On Preserving Capitalism in the Twenty First Century* (Pluto Press, 1988).

[4] See the Special Number on Women. Social Scientist No. 40-41, Dec.1975 (Trivandrum).

[5] A detailed analysis of the anti-Sikh riots and their aftermath tool place in the Delhi based journal *Manushi*. I have recapitulated part of the events and their analysis in the Sardar Amarjit Singh Endowment Lecture on Guru Gobind Singh Studies, Madurai Kamaraj University on 28th August published as "Religious Identities and Cultural Processes in India," *AJTR* XV (Jan-June 2002): 10-29.

[6] See my article "Religious Conflicts and changes in Indian Political Culture," in *Social Action* 44/2 (Oct-Dec.1994): 65-82.

[7] A very sensitive analysis on the "modernity" of ethnic and religious identity politics and its onslaught on enlightenment values can be found in Chetan Bhatt, *Liberation and Purity: Race, New Religious Movements and the Ethics of Post Modernity* (London: UCL Press, 1997).

[8] Amartya Sen, *Identity and Violence: The Illusion of Destiny* (Penguin Books 2006). Amartya Sen's position is more helpful in the UK with its post-colonial cosmopolitan outlook than in South Asia, where kinship systems are still a major support structure.

[9] See Madhu Kishvar's interview with Sant Longowal before his assassination. *Manushi* 30/5 (Sept-Oct.1985)

[10] Flavia Agnes, *My story: Our Story of the Re-Building Broken Lives*. See also the monumental research, *Women and Law in India*, with an introduction by Flavia Agnes comprising Flavia Agnes, *Law and Gender Inequality*; Sudhir Chandra, *Enslaved Daughters and Monmayee Bami Hindu Women and Marriage Law* .

[11] See e.g. Nandita Haksar and Anju Singh, *Demystification of Law for Women* (Lancer Press, 1986), which has a grand finale in support of Shah Bano. See also Asghar Ali Engineer, ed., *The Shah Bano Controversy* (Hyderabad: Orient Longman 1987).

[12] Gabriele Dietrich, "Can the Women's Movement be a Force Against Communalism"? in *Women's Movement in India: Conceptual and Religion Reflections* (Bangalore: Breakthrough Publications 1988). This article has been printed in many different places and some feminist friends in Bombay pulled it out of their handbags when they met me in a train. However, a lot of the aspirations did not come to be fulfilled.

[13] See my article "Women and Religious Identities India after Ayodhya" in Kamla Bhasin and Nighat Said Khan and Ritu Menon, eds., *Against All Odds: Essays on Women, Religion and Development from India and Pakistan*, 35-50. See also Paola Bachetta's article, "All Our Goddesses Are Armed: Religion, Resistance and Revenge in the Life of a Militant Hindu Nationalist Woman," 133-156 in the same book.

[14] See e.g. *Communalism Combat* Year 8, No.77-78 (March-April 2002), Genocide Gujarat 2002. People's Union for Civil Liberties (PUCL) Vadodara, and Vadodara Shanti Abhiyan: "Violence in Vadodara: A Report" (May 2002) also, PUCL and VSA: "At the Receiving End -Women's Experiences of Violence in Vadodara" (May 31, 2002).

[15] This happened during the investigation of communal attacks on young women who had visited pubs in Mangalore in 2009. The views of the communal forces were even re-enforced by one of the members of the NCW who went to investigate the matter.

[16] The most path breaking work remains Elisabeth Schuessler Fiorenza's, *In Memory of Her: A Feminist Theological Reconstruction of Christian Origins* (SCM Press 1983).

[17] Karen L. King, *The Gospel of Mary of Magdala: Jesus and the First Woman Apostle* (Polebridge Press, 2003).

[18] Dan Brown, *The Da Vinci Code* (New York: Doubleday 2003).

[19] Fatima Mernissi, *Women and Islam: An Historical and Theological Enquiry* (1993).

[20] See e.g. *In God's Image* 28/1 (March 2009), Women and Religions especially the article by Hindun Anisah and Nehik Sri Hidayati on "Women and Islam."

[21] Chatsurman Kabilingh, "The Future of the Bhikkuni Sangha in Thailand," in *Speaking of Faith: Cross-cultural Perspectives on Women, Religion and Social Change*, edited by Diana L. Eck and Devaki Jain (1986). She is now venerable Dhammananda Bikkhuni

[22] Uma Chakravarthi, *The Social Dimension of Early Buddhism* (1987). Uma Chakravarthi points out that Buddhism emerged in a phase of expansion of production

and tackled social justice concerns in contrast to stagnant Brahmanical Hinduism. In discussions she points out that Buddhism in India is lucky not to have been in political power and therefore to have preserved some of its progressive fulcrum. See *AJTR* XVIII/2 (July-Dec.2005): 49-57.

[23] Babasahib Ambedkar, *The Buddha and his Dhamma* (Bombay: People's Education Society, 1951)

[24] Gail Omvedt, *Towards Enlightened India* (New Delhi: Penguin/Viking, 2004), the chapter on Ambedkar's conversion

[25] Sharmila Rege, *Writing Caste, Writing Gender: Narrating Dalit Women's Testimonios* (New Delhi: Zubaan, 2007).

[26] See the very instructive Dissertation by Helene Egnell, *Other Voices: A Study of Christian Feminist Approaches to Religious Plurality East and West* (Uppsala 2006)..

HMI Publications

Islam
A Historical Survey (Indian Edition, 1979)
H.A.R. Gibb

Evangelism, Dialogue, Reconciliation: The Transformative Journey of the Henry Martyn Institute (1998)
Diane D' Souza

Approaches, Foundations, Issues and Models of Interfaith Relations (2001)
David Emmanuel Singh and Robert Edwin Schick

Jesus the Messiah in Muslim Thought (2002)
Olaf Schumann

From Converting the Pagan to Dialogue with Our Partners: HMI's Fifty Years Work of Evangelism and Interfaith Relations (2009)
Andreas D' Souza

The Jesus Verses of the Qur'ān (2011)
Karel Steenbrink

The Sufi Movement
East and West (2014)
Jan Slomp

Mysticism, Spirituality and Secularism
An In-depth Search for Meaning and Authenticity in a Pluralistic World (2015)
Varghese Manimala

My Father is a Farmer
Biblical Reflection on Sustainable Agriculture (2016)
Daniel Prem Kumar

Seeking Communion
A Collection of Conversations (2018)
Joseph Victor Edwin SJ

Letter to an Unknown Friend
Children Promote Peace between India and Pakistan (2018)
Joseph Kalathil SJ

Understanding Hinduism (2018)
Mahesh Badhe

www.ingramcontent.com/pod-product-compliance
Lightning Source LLC
Chambersburg PA
CBHW030929020726
47498CB00001B/170
* 9 7 8 9 3 8 8 9 4 5 1 0 3 *